VIA Folios 76

THE FIRE IN THE FLESH

THE FIRE IN THE FLESH

by Garibaldi M. Lapolla

Edited with an introduction by
Steven J. Belluscio

Bordighera Press

Library of Congress Control Number: 2012935824

Cover: "Brownstones in Winter — NARA — 559149," Painter unknown
http://commons.wikimedia.org/w/index.php?title=File:Brownstones_in_Winter_-_NARA_-_559149.tif&page=1

Printed in the United States.

Published by
BORDIGHERA PRESS
John D. Calandra Italian American Institute
25 W. 43rd Street, 17th Floor
New York, NY 10036

VIA Folios 76
ISBN 978–1–59954–038–2

ACKNOWLEDGEMENTS

I would like to thank the Research Foundation of the City University of New York for its support in the completion of this reprint. I would also like to thank Carmine Pizzirusso and Dean Anthony J. Tamburri of the John D. Calandra Italian American Institute for invaluable assistance with the preparation of the manuscript. Many thanks are extended to Paul M. Lapolla for his permission to reprint *The Fire and the Flesh* and for the hours he has spent talking to me about his father. I would like to show appreciation for the support of my colleagues at Borough of Manhattan Community College/CUNY, especially Professors Maria Enrico, Frank Elmi, and Joyce Harte. Also, I would like to thank Bordighera Press for its interest in this project and for all it does for Italian American studies. Finally, I would like to thank my parents John and Marilyn; my brother Chris; my wife Vanessa; and my children Sophia, Annalina, and Julian.

Contents

Chronology

1888 .... Garibaldi Mario Lapolla is born April 5 in Rapolla, Basilicata, province of Potenza, Italy, to Biagio Oreste Lapolla and Marie Nicola Buonvicino. In honor of his grandfather's Italian nationalism, he is named after Giuseppe Garibaldi (1807–1882), the George Washington of the modern Italian nation.

1890 .... Immigrates to New York City with his parents. Over the next decade, over 650,000 of his fellow Italians would follow suit.

1891 .... Eleven Italians are lynched in New Orleans in connection with the unsolved murder of Police Chief David Hennessy.

1898 .... Spanish-American War.

1910 .... Earns A.B. at Columbia University. Begins his public school career teaching English at DeWitt Clinton High School, Manhattan, New York, where he remains for more than a decade, with an interruption for World War I military service.

1912 .... Earns A.M. at Columbia University after writing a thesis on British romanticist Percy Bysshe Shelley (1792–1822) entitled "Shelley and the Political Parties of His Day."

1914–1918 ...... World War I. Italian immigration stopped.

1917–1918 ...... Enlists in the U.S. Army and is stationed at Fort Ontario, Oswego, New York. Mess sergeant for the hospital. Meets Nurse Margaret McCormick, whom he marries soon after. Signs a letter published in the New Republic on May 26, 1917, arguing that conscientious objectors be allowed to serve non-combat roles in the military. Is transferred to Washington, D.C. Promoted to sergeant first class.

1919 .... Son Paul McCormick is born February 11.

1921 .... Emergency Quota Act severely limits immigration from southern and eastern European countries.

1922 .... Summoned by the Advisory Council on the Qualification of Teachers, formed by Frank Graves, state commissioner of education, to determine the patriotism of teachers in New York State. Lapolla is questioned about the 1917 New Republic letter he signed. Son Mark Orestes is born February 17.

1924 .... Immigration Act of 1924 enacted, an even harsher version of the 1921 law. It prohibits Asian immigration entirely.

1925 .... Publication of F. Scott Fitzgerald novel, *The Great Gatsby.*

1926–1930 ..... Chairman of Thomas Jefferson High School English Department.

1927 .... On August 23, Ferdinando Nicola Sacco (b. 1891) and Bartolomeo Vanzetti (b. 1888), two Italian anarchists, are executed for the 1920 murder of two pay clerks in South Braintree, Massachusetts. Given the antiradical sentiment of the court, many argue they did not receive a fair trial.

1927–1932 ..... Principal of Thomas Jefferson Summer High School.

1928 .... Serves as judge in a Brooklyn Borough high school finals for the National Oratorical Contest on the Constitution.

1929 .... Publishes *Better High School English through Tests and Drills* with Kenneth W. Wright at Noble & Noble. Edits with poet and literary critic Mark Van Doren *A Junior Anthology of World Poetry,* published by Albert & Charles Boni, and praised highly in the *New York Times.* Divorces Margaret McCormick.

1930–1934 ..... Principal of New York Public School 112.

1930 .... Exchanges letters with famed teacher and educational theorist Leonard Covello, refusing to allow the latter to use the as yet unpublished *The Fire and the Flesh* (then with the working title "La Dantone") as a sociological document for a study of Italian Americans because "it ain't no such beast."

1931 .... Publishes *The Fire in the Flesh* at the Vanguard Press to generally positive reviews in *Books* and the *New York Times.*

1932 .... Publishes *Miss Rollins in Love* at the Vanguard Press. Receives lukewarm review from the *New York Times.*

1934 .... Marries Priscilla Sherman. Is featured (with other Italian American authors) in *Gazzetta del Popolo.*

1935–1953 ..... Principal of New York Public School 174.

1935 .... Publishes *The Grand Gennaro* at the Vanguard Press to acclaim in the *New Republic,* the *New York Times, Books,* the *Boston Transcript, Review of Reviews,* and the *Saturday Review of Literature.*

1937 .... Publishes *Required Grammar in the New York City Public School* at Noble & Noble. Interviewed on WEVD New York for a radio program about overcrowding in city schools.

1938 .... Speaks on June 29 at the conference of the National Council of Teachers of English and criticizes tendency to insist upon a "puritanical type of speech" no one actually uses and to reinforce it through teaching of grammar and usage.

1939 .... Publication of Pietro di Donato novel *Christ in Concrete.*

1939–1945 ..... World War II. Over one million Italian Americans serve in the armed forces. About 250 Italian Americans, 11,000 German Americans, and 100,000 Japanese Americans are interned for reasons of "national security."

1945 .... In February, son Mark Orestes, trained as an Army Air Corps flight officer reported missing in action over Brod, Yugoslavia, after completing eighteen missions and receiving the Air Medal. His death was confirmed eleven months later.

1946 .... Serves on a Teacher-Author Committee of New York City school and college instructors to protest Board of Education bylaw requiring textbook authors to turn over royalties.

1950 .... Unsuccessfully brings action against the New York City Board of Education in favor of uniform pay for principals of all city schools, elementary, junior, and senior.

1953 .... Publishes and illustrates *Italian Cooking for the American Kitchen* and *The Mushroom Cookbook* at W. Funk. The former is praised and widely publicized by reviews and interviews in publications such as the *New York Times,* the *San Francisco News, Il Progresso Italo-Americano,* the *Chicago American,* and the *Sunday Herald.*

1954 .... Dies in his sixty-fifth year on January 13 at Mount Sinai Hospital after a massive stroke. His death is mourned and career celebrated by colleagues, administrators, students, and parents. The Parent Teacher Association donates to Public School 174 a plaque lauding Lapolla as "Educator, Leader, and Friend."

1965 .... Immigration Act of 1965 overturns Immigration Act of 1924.

Introduction

When Thomas J. Ferraro declared Italian-American writing "one of the better kept literary secrets of [the twentieth] century," he had in mind Garibaldi M. Lapolla, among other authors.[1] In their detailed and sensitive treatment of everyday life in turn-of-the-century Italian Harlem, Lapolla's three published novels — *The Fire in the Flesh* (1931), *Miss Rollins in Love* (1932), and *The Grand Gennaro* (1935) — form a cornerstone of early Italian-American fiction for readers familiar with the likes of Silvio Villa, Giuseppe Cautela, Louis Forgione, Frances Winwar, John Fante, Mari Tomasi, Pietro di Donato, Guido d'Agostino, and Jerre Mangione. However, Garibaldi M. Lapolla's writing has not garnered nearly the attention it deserves despite his renown among scholars of Italian-American literature, the similarity of his fiction to that of canonical ethnic writers such as Abraham Cahan and Anzia Yezierska, and the recent entry into the canon of other Italian-American fiction writers (such as Pietro di Donato and John Fante). To be sure, one obvious reason is unavailability. While Lapolla's novels were generally well reviewed — especially *The Grand Gennaro,* considered to be his best work — they soon went out of print. And despite an Arno Press resurrection of his first and last novels in 1975, Garibaldi M. Lapolla's name continues to remain in underserved obscurity; he could very well be the best kept secret of Italian-American literature.

Teacher, Soldier, Writer

Born April 5, 1888, in Rapolla, Basilicata, Province of Potenza, Italy, to Biagio Oreste Lapolla and Marie Nicola Lapolla (née Buonvicino), Garibaldi Mario Lapolla (his given name reflecting the Italian patriotism of his paternal grandfather) left Italy and immigrated to New York City with his parents in 1890 before age two. He would lose his mother at age nine.[2] An exceptional

[1]Thomas J. Ferraro, "Ethnicity in the Marketplace," 398.
[2]Maria Luisa, "Conversazioni del Giovedì," 1; Olga Peragallo, *Italian-American Authors and Their Contribution to American Literature,* 138; Martino Marazzi, "King of Harlem: Garibaldi Lapolla and Gennaro Accuci 'Il Grande,'" 190, 207.

student in public school as a child, Lapolla attended Columbia University, earning a B.A. in 1910 and an M.A. in 1912, after completing a thesis on British romantic poet Percy Bysshe Shelley.[3] In 1910, Lapolla began teaching English at DeWitt Clinton High School, then located in Manhattan, where he left a great impression on his students, including Mortimer Adler, who would become one of America's most celebrated philosophers and public intellectuals of the twentieth century.[4] Thus began Lapolla's rich, productive, and lifelong career as an educator and educational theorist — a career interrupted only by military service during World War I in which he "held every position from buck private to cook to lecturer on personal prophylaxis to sergeant to lieutenant of artillery."[5]

From 1917 to 1918, Lapolla was stationed at Fort Ontario, Oswego, New York, where, after an "early [. . .] career [. . .] underscored by black marks" in which "he seemed temperamentally incapable of complying with regulations," "he disciplined himself to become a good soldier."[6] As mess sergeant, he nurtured what would become a lifelong passion and what had been a family tradition of sorts: his father had owned restaurants in Montreal, Quebec, and New York, and was known to claim descent from "a long line of cooks" dating back to Ancient Rome.[7] While a soldier in Flower Unit N, Post Hospital No. 5, Fort Ontario, Lapolla met his future wife, Nurse Margaret McCormick, with whom he conceived two sons: Paul McCormick (born February 11, 1919) and Mark Oreste (born Feburary 17, 1922).[8] Lapolla also served on the Associate Board of the *Ontario Post* newspaper and wrote for it, taught in the fort's school, played guard and tackle for its football team, and worked as a chap-

---

[3]Lawrence J. Oliver, "'Beyond Ethnicity': Portraits of the Italian-American Artist in Garibaldi Lapolla's Novels," 6; Robert Hornsby, e-mail message to Belluscio, 2 Oct. 2007. Lapolla's degrees were granted by Columbia College, not Columbia Teachers College, as has been erroneously assumed.

[4]Mortimer J. Adler, *Philosopher at Large: An Intellectual Biography,* 29.

[5]From the book jacket of the Vanguard Press edition of *The Fire in the Flesh* (1931), Oversized Folder 1, MSS 64, Garibaldi M. Lapolla Papers, Historical Society of Pennsylvania, Philadelphia (these papers are hereafter cited as GMLP).

[6]"Editor's Notebook," *Sunday Herald* 21 June 1953, newspaper clipping, box 4, folder 12, GMLP.

[7]Garibaldi M. Lapolla, *Italian Food for the American Kitchen,* ix.

[8]Paul Lear, e-mail message to Belluscio, October 1, 2007; Paul Lapolla, telephone interview by Belluscio, June 25, 2007.

lain's assistant before he was transferred to Washington and eventually promoted to Sergeant First Class.[9]

After his successful tenure at DeWitt Clinton High School, where he taught on the faculty alongside famed educational theorist and Italian-American activist Leonard Covello, Lapolla served as chairman of the Thomas Jefferson High School English Department from 1926 to 1930 and principal of the Thomas Jefferson Summer High School from 1927 to 1932. In 1929, Lapolla's first marriage ended in divorce; in 1934, he married Priscilla Sherman, a fellow faculty member. From 1930 to 1934, Lapolla was principal of Public School 112, and from 1934 to his death in 1954, principal of Public School 174.[10]

Lapolla fought for social justice throughout his life, even running "for every office from Alderman to Congressman on the Socialist ticket" before World War I.[11] Unwilling to sell short immigrant students, he campaigned endlessly for more intelligent, student-centered pedagogical practices in the tradition of John Dewey and a more pragmatic approach to teaching English grammar, rankling school administrators but advocating what would eventually become educational orthodoxy. In keeping with his democratic educational vision, Lapolla also challenged Board of Education by-laws requiring textbook authors to turn over royalties to the school district and fought for uniform pay for principals of all city schools.[12] This fighting spirit often got him into trouble. For example, in 1922, he was interrogated by the Advisory Council on the Qualification of Teachers — a by-product of the 1919 Joint Legislative Committee to Investigate Seditious Activities (also known as the Lusk Committee) — about his co-signed letter printed in the May 26, 1917, issue of the *New Republic,* which argued that conscientious objectors ought to be allowed to serve non-combat roles in the military during World War I and, more broadly, that there ought to be "a social setting within America

---

[9]*Ontario Post* 22 Sept. 1917; 29 Sept. 1917; 8 Dec. 1917; 20 Apr. 1918; 25 May 1918; 1 June 1918.

[10]Marc K. Blackburn, "Register of the Garibaldi M. Lapolla Papers," GMLP, 1–2; *New York Times* 14 Jan. 1954, 29.

[11]This quotation, taken from the book jacket of *The Fire in the Flesh* (1931), is qtd. in Blackburn, "Register," 2.

[12]"Teachers Oppose Loss of Royalties," *New York Times* 17 Sept. 1946, 7; "Principals Lose Pay Case," *New York Times* 2 June 1950, 12.

sufficiently hospitable to all conscientious objectors."[13] Upton Sinclair would later relish the irony of Lapolla, "an artillery officer" during the war, "now . . . sitting on the bench, humbly waiting his turn to be browbeaten."[14] While Lapolla escaped the investigation unscathed, he would be unable to avoid similar controversy in the future. As principal of Public School 174 in Brooklyn in the early 1950s, Lapolla vigorously defended teachers persecuted by the House Un-American Activities Committee, arguing that they should be judged not for their beliefs but, rather, their ability in the classroom. "Aren't we, in fact," Lapolla wrote, "chasing a phantom that, in a more reasonable period, we would recognize and admit as such?"[15] Throughout his educational career, Lapolla remained aggressively committed to winning justice for students, teachers, and administrators and maintaining quality in education.

As an English specialist, Lapolla taught "grammar, American literature, English literature, poetry, Shakespeare, and remedial English."[16] Frequently dissatisfied with the status quo of English pedagogy, Lapolla published textbooks designed to teach English grammar more practically and to deliver an appreciation of literature to young students. During his career, he penned *Better High School English* (1929) and *Required Grammar in the New York Public Schools* (1937) to serve the former purpose and co-edited with Mark Van Doren *The Junior Anthology of World Poetry* (1929) to serve the latter. Lapolla was also interested in educating the general public about the delights of the Italian cuisine he had grown up enjoying and masterfully learning to prepare. In 1953, he published *Italian Cooking for the American Kitchen,* designed to help Americans learn the variety of Italian cooking; that same year, he also published *The Mushroom Cookbook.* Lapolla also left behind a wealth of unpublished writings — essays, poems, plays, short stories, a novel titled "Jerry," and other unfinished manuscripts.

---

[13]"Teachers Secretly Quizzed on Loyalty," *New York Times* 17 May 1922, 18; Norman Thomas, et al., "The Religion of Free Men," letter to the editor, *New Republic* 26 May 1917, 109.

[14]Upton Sinclair, *The Goslings: A Study of the American Schools,* 84.

[15]Garibaldi M. Lapolla, "Letter in Answer to Dr. Lefkowitz about So-Called Communist Teachers," GMLP, Box 1, Folder 2, 3–5.

[16]Marc K. Blackburn, "Register," 2.

The unifying thread of most of Lapolla's written work — his textbooks, his cookbooks, and his novels — is the continuous negotiation between Italian and American cultures. His textbooks were designed with the Italian immigrant student in mind and the concern of how best to serve them in the American public school system. His cookbooks attempted to teach an American audience about Italian food and thereby provide an entrée into Italian history, culture, and geography: as Americans learned to prepare and appreciate Italian cuisine, these so-called foreigners in their midst would come to seem less foreign. Finally, his novels used turn-of-the-century East Harlem as a fictional staging ground for the oft-troubled coexistence of Italian ancestry and American dreams. All the while, *Professore* Lapolla is the patient and compassionate pedagogue, challenging his student — the reader — to grow beyond the limitations of prior experience.

Lapolla traveled widely during his lifetime throughout North America, South America, and Europe, including his native Italy. Lapolla was an avid artist; many of his pencil sketches, pen and ink drawings, and water colors — mostly urban scenes, rural pastorals, portraits, and still lifes — serve as a record of the people and places he encountered at home and abroad. Lapolla even supplied the pen and ink drawings of various foods for *Italian Cooking for the American Kitchen.* An expert letter writer, Lapolla infused his correspondence with wry humor and keen wit, both high- and lowbrow. He would regale his reader with evocative accounts of his New York surroundings before matter-of-factly addressing the main subject matter of the letter. His letters to younger son Mark Oreste Lapolla while the latter served in Foggia, Italy, as an Army Air Forces flight officer during World War II are ample evidence of this. In these letters to "Oreste," Lapolla discourses about Italian language, geography, and culture; the progress of the war; and the mood of Americans back on the homefront. Of themselves, these letters are little gems of geopolitics, cultural criticism, and homespun wisdom.[17] Some of the best of these letters were returned, for Mark Lapolla went missing in action over Brod, Yugoslavia, while flying a mission during February 1945. On January 5, 1946, he

[17]Garibaldi Lapolla to Mark O. Lapolla, returned letters, December 25, 1944; January 7, 1945; January 15, 1945; January 31, 1945; February 6, 1945, box 1, folder 3, GMLP.

was reported to have been killed there.[18] An emotional man, Lapolla took his son's death very hard, and during his 1953 trip to Italy, he visited Oreste's gravesite with his wife Priscilla, writing in his trip diary, "I couldn't have come here and not done it."[19]

When Garibaldi M. Lapolla died of a massive stroke on January 13, 1954, at the age of sixty-five, Priscilla received an outpouring of condolences for "Gari," as he was affectionately known, from colleagues and friends throughout his life and career praising his qualities as an educator, intellectual, artist, and fellow human. The Parent Teacher Association donated a plaque to New York Public School 174 lauding Lapolla as an "Educator, Leader, and Friend." Although he died much too young, he had the great fortune of being remembered, and celebrated, by friends and acquaintances for all the many things he had accomplished.

"Method Realistic, But Intent Romantic"

Garibaldi M. Lapolla's reputation as a novelist, however, would be neglected until the 1980s, when scholarship began to recognize his talent and importance as "East Harlem's novelist" — or, at least, Italian Harlem's novelist.[20] Critics have rightly attributed Lapolla's obscurity in part to his refusal to accede to the aesthetic trends of the 1930s: high modernism and proletarian literature.[21] In course lecture notes, it is clear that while Lapolla was by no means opposed to the literary experimentation of the early twentieth century, he disliked the use of "pyrotechnical coloring and devices" for their own sake; and while Lapolla was himself a socialist, he dismissively refers to proletarian literature as "propaganda" "mainly concerned with revealing the life of

---

[18]"Missing Flight Officer Now Is Reported Killed," *New York Times* 6 Jan. 1946, 30.

[19]Paul Lapolla, telephone interview by Belluscio, 11 Nov. 2007. Lapolla, European trip diary, 1953, Box 1, Folder 9, GMLP.

[20]Robert Anthony Orsi, *The Madonna of 115th Street: Faith and Community in Italian Harlem, 1880–1950,* 22. Richard A. Meckel considers Lapolla to be "as good as many of the better known ethnic/immigrant social realists of the 1930s and 1940s" ("A Reconsideration: The Not So Fundamental Ideology of Garibaldi Marto Lapolla," 127); and Lawrence J. Oliver claims, "outside of Puzo and Pietro di Donato, no writer has so skillfully portrayed the marble beneath the mud, to use Nathaniel Hawthorne's expression, of the Italian-American immigrant experience ("'Great Equalizer' or 'Cruel Stepmother'?," 116).

[21]Martino Marazzi, "King of Harlem," 191; Richard A. Meckel, "A Reconsideration," 128.

worker-classes as they are allegedly developing a historic class-consciousness."[22] Furthermore, Lapolla celebrated what he called the "newer romanticis[m]" of contemporary authors who

> have held to the notion that the novel was made to please, that factual scenes immediate to the readers' experience are not the inevitable material of the novel, that readers are still interested in the carefully organized plot, in remote peoples and times, in themes that have no bearing on modern conditions save in a large way, that propaganda for any cause is not the purpose of fiction.

Lapolla admired Pearl Buck's writing for providing "pictures which please by their combination of the familiar in human nature against a background of the unfamiliar," her "method realistic, but intent romantic."[23]

This description goes a long way toward explaining Lapolla's own aesthetic approach. While his fictions are rich with the realistic specifics of place and people — East Harlem and the Italians who once lived there — the pastness of these very specifics lends them, even from the perspective of the 1930s, the luster of historical romance. Furthermore, Lapolla frequently imbues his settings with firelight, moonlight, shadowplay, and religious iconography, elements more typical of Nathaniel Hawthorne or Edgar Allan Poe than William Dean Howells or Henry James. The traditional Southern Italian folk beliefs fictionalized by Lapolla — with their fascinating interplay of Christian providence, saint worship, Marianism, and occult mysticism — further add to the otherworldly romanticism of the novels. Finally, Lapolla's novels feature characters who attempt to rise above their sordid urban surroundings toward a transcendental plane of spiritual and — given the recurrence of the artist figure in all three of his works — artistic fulfillment.[24]

---

[22]Garibaldi Lapolla, "The American Novel," box 2, folder 3, GMLP.

[23]*Ibid.*

[24]As Lawrence J. Oliver writes, "Lapolla's novels display the ethical idealism — the belief that the people can rise above corrupting and degrading influences to a higher moral plane — that marks [. . .] romantic literature in general. Indeed, if a label must be applied to Lapolla's novels, the most appropriate would be that coined by Frank Norris, 'romances of the commonplace'" ("Beyond Ethnicity," 18–19).

Miss Rollins in Love *and* The Grand Gennaro

In Lapolla's second published novel, the Italian Harlem-set *Miss Rollins in Love,* the orphaned and intellectually gifted protagonist Donato Contini and the thirty-year-old classics teacher Amy Rollins are at the center of both the business and love plots. In the former, Donato and Amy must cope with a cold, rigid, and often hostile school system ill-equipped to nurture the talents of Donato. In the latter, Donato and Amy engage in a torrid sexual affair that, while in some ways symbolic of the proper loving relationship between student and teacher, is both flawed and short lived. Still, Donato is able to rise above the hurtful circumstances of his life: his gangster brother is executed; his mother dies of a broken heart; and his father, an accomplished but financially unsuccessful puppeteer, dies soon after his wife. Donato's success in his father's profession blossoms into a lifelong passion for sculpture, which provides him with transcendental, and then, when he encounters fame and fortune, physical, escape from his harsh surroundings.

Its first chapters set during the late-nineteenth-century flood of Italian immigration to the United States, Lapolla's third and final published novel, *The Grand Gennaro,* tells the story of Gennaro Accuci, a Calabrian immigrant to Italian Harlem who rises from a small-time laborer to owner of a junk business, and then "minor dictator" of the local Italian-American community.[25] By pluck, luck, and unscrupulous business practices, Gennaro is able to "make America" and become "The Grand Gennaro," in effect an Italian-American "Great Gatsby." Modeling himself after the worst of the actual robber barons, Gennaro, who at the beginning of the narrative is a penniless laborer, violently wrests control of his friend Rocco Pagliamini's junk business. Gennaro's assimilative program of hyper-masculine greed and brute force is ironically underscored by the series of women he beds (consensually or not), molests, or otherwise abuses — before and after he finally sends for his wife Rosaria and his children Domenico, Emilio, and Elena.

Toward the end of the narrative, however, Gennaro grows increasingly uneasy with his aggressive Americanism. He humanizes his business practices and, remorseful for having robbed Rocco Pagliamini of a livelihood, makes

[25]Rose Basile Green, *The Italian-American Novel: A Document of the Interaction of Two Cultures,* 74.

his old friend the manager of his rag business. Gennaro also sees the fruition of a long-term project: the construction of Saint Elena the Blessed, a Catholic church for local Italian Americans. Initially a monument of self-serving hubris, the church, in Gennaro's state of moral reformation, becomes a kind of penance. Rocco, however, has never forgiven Gennaro and even stirs up discontent among Gennaro's workers, who threaten to strike for better wages. When Gennaro manages to settle the labor dispute peacefully and beneficially for the workers, Rocco, enraged by another defeat by his former friend, murders Gennaro. Like so many other European immigrant protagonists — Abraham Cahan's Yekl and David Levinsky, Guido d'Agostino's Emilio Gardella, and Samuel Ornitz's Meyer Hirsch, to name just a few — Gennaro is made to pay for his hyper-assimilative indiscretion.

The Fire in the Flesh: *Desire and Italian-American Art*

In 1931, Garibaldi M. Lapolla published *The Fire in the Flesh,* the first of three Vanguard Press novels dealing with the adjustment of an immigrant family — in this case, the Dantones — to life in turn-of-the-century Italian Harlem.[26] While early critical reception to the novel was mixed, more recent critics, starting in the 1970s, have attempted to rehabilitate the novel's reputation. However, Lapolla's debut has yet to be considered from the perspective of desire, which is unequivocally the novel's leitmotif, signaled by the evocative and suggestive title and artfully figured throughout the text. This brief introduction will map the function of desire in *The Fire in the Flesh* and determine its moral, aesthetic, and artistic significance for Lapolla.

The narrative economy of *The Fire in the Flesh* is not simply enriched by the depiction of desire, which it undoubtedly is; additionally, desire gives fuel to the narrative's very motion. Furthermore, Lapolla's rendering of desire has clear aesthetic and generic consequences that provide insight into his own motivations as a novelist. In the novel, Lapolla describes desire as an unavoidable, unquenchable, and biological fact of life: indeed, the "fire in the flesh" that motivates every human. The characters of the novel are motivated by six basic desires: familial love, erotic love, violence, socioeconomic mobility,

---

[26]The remainder of the introduction is adapted from a longer article entitled "Garibaldi M. Lapolla's *The Fire in the Flesh*: Desire and Italian-American Art," forthcoming in *VIA: Voices in Italian Americana.*

power, and the transcendent. When characters do not attempt to satisfy these desires — an endeavor that, by the logic of desire, is destined for failure — they attempt to sublimate them through work and moneymaking, which simply produces yet another desire for more moneymaking. If desire is, as Lapolla would have it, unavoidable — if, in other words, we are always located in the middle ground between desire and fulfillment — it is best to use this in-between state productively as we seek to achieve the beautiful and transcendent in our work, even if absolute fulfillment is ultimately impossible to achieve. Lapolla represents this ideal through the figure of the artist, in this case Giovanni Dantone, the illegitimate second-generation son of Agnese Filoppina and Padre Gelsomino, who finds himself caught between the desire of daily life in Italian Harlem and the fulfillment of an artistic dream he cannot quite name. This condition reiterates itself through a number of analogous binaries Giovanni negotiates through his art, which is productively located in the middle-ground between the mundane and the sublime, the bodily and the transcendent, the real and the romantic, and ultimately, between Italian and American. Neither side of these binaries is wholly achievable, and, in Lapolla's creative vision, this is for the best, for the artist operates best within the give and take of these polar opposites, using the everyday world as a starting point for art that ideally transcends any locality or temporality. Thus, for Lapolla, the Italian-American artist ideally would desire to create Italian-American art that uses *italianità* ("Italianness") as a starting point for a conversation with a broader national, even international, community. As we shall see, Giovanni's artistic journey is a representation of Lapolla's own middle-ground between realism and romanticism and between his Italian past and his American future, as he used Italian subject matter as a starting point for fiction that ultimately resists easy ethnic or generic categorization.

The novel begins in late-nineteenth-century Villetto, Italy, where the well-liked Padre Gelsomino is performing the ceremony of Annunciation, only to be interrupted by a proud and defiant Agnese Filoppina, who rushes into the church clutching their illegitimate son Giovanni and accusing the beloved priest in no uncertain terms: "Unholy villain, this is your child."[27] In the wake of the ensuing public scandal, Agnese, after refusing nearly every

---

[27]Lapolla, *The Fire in the Flesh,* 5. Hereafter referred to in the text as "FITF."

other eligible bachelor in the town, lovelessly marries Michele Dantone, the dim-witted barber's apprentice, and departs with him, her father Gesualdo, and her brother Luigi, for America. Gifted with aggressive, if not always ethical, business acumen, Agnese arranges while still on the "Conte Bertoldi" for *padrone* Francesco Crino to help open a barbershop for Michele, which touches off the business plot of the novel. Once in Italian Harlem, the Dantones become upwardly mobile due almost entirely to Agnese's shrewdness and acquistiveness, and they are able to move from a comparatively humble abode to a brownstone (*FITF* 98). While Luigi becomes a successful contractor, Agnese, never satisfied with what the Dantones already have, buys a share of the city dump and takes control of a number of junk shops, only later to enter into an agreement with Luigi and rival contractor Antonio Farinella to purchase property and build a row of houses (*FITF* 125). Simultaneous with the business plot is a complex love plot in which Agnese mutually desires not Michele, whom she does not love, but Padre Gelsomino (who left his parish and the priesthood for America in disgrace and in the hope of reuniting with Giovanni and Agnese) and Antonio Farinella, her erstwhile business rival. Additionally, Lapolla crafts a family plot centered around Giovanni, a sensitive, young, artist and intellectual who does well in school but receives no encouragement, much less love, from his parents, who at best view him as impractical and idealistic and at worst view him as a painful and unwanted reminder of Padre Gelsomino and Agnese's adultery. Meanwhile, after her mother dies, Agnese exercises an iron grip on the family's affairs, and Lapolla takes great pains to underscore her unapologetic reversal of traditional gender expectations. Luigi and the generally emasculated Gesualdo and Michele are powerless to stop Agnese, as her acquisitive desires dictate every major decision the family makes. Indeed, desire lies at the heart of every major event in *The Fire in the Flesh* and thereby is the prime mover of the plot.

For example, the desire for familial love is a motivator for many of Giovanni's and Padre Gelsomino's actions. Giovanni longs for attention and affection from his mother and stepfather, who cannot understand his scholastic and artistic aspirations. Then, when Padre Gelsomino talks with his estranged son, the two experience a mutual longing that Lapolla uses the language of desire — insatiable desire — to describe. As the two walk by the East River: "Giovanni flushed perceptibly, he felt himself overwhelmed with a soft warmth that became a sweet pain in his heart" (*FITF* 265–66). Lapolla also lends violence — often retributive — great narrative power in *The Fire in the Flesh.* Giovanni's frustrated desire for familial love manifests itself in Oedipal rage toward his father, who detests him: "There were times when the boy quivered with a savage desire to strike back, to kick, to bite," which he eventually does (*FITF* 36). The desire for violence is also given ethnic specificity by Lapolla, who attributes it in many cases to men desiring to preserve female honor. Of course, the love plot of the novel is driven entirely by the erotic desires of Agnese, Padre Gelsomino, Antonio, and Michele. While all three desire the beautiful Agnese, she desires only Gelsomino and Antonio, leaving her husband perennially frustrated. Predictably, the business plot of the novel is driven by the desire for moneymaking and social mobility, especially on the part of Agnese and Antonio, who are continually on a quest to "make America," a motif that repeats several times and that carries social, economic, and sexual significance. In the novel, characters also struggle with their desire for power. Agnese begins by taking power over her family, a decided reversal of traditional Southern Italian family structure that bewilders Michele, who himself craves what he takes to be his due respect from his wife and Italian Harlemites. Finally, characters desire the transcendent in *The Fire in the Flesh,* in absolution for having sinned and in the creation of art. Both Agnese and Gelsomino repeatedly pray for forgiveness for their adultery. However, this passive request for the intervention of the divine is given only limited power by Lapolla, and he depicts it as being somewhat disingenuous. It would seem that Lapolla prefers a more active approach to achieving the transcendent, and he represents this through the artist, Giovanni, who moves closer to the transcendent through his creative work. In fact, when Giovanni sees local artist Gino Birrichino paint, Lapolla has Padre Gelsomino tell him "It's like God to be a painter" (*FITF* 110).

As Lapolla suggests in *The Fire in the Flesh,* desire is an unquenchable, biological constant that allows characters to self-preserve, but that also allows them the capability to destroy themselves. The power and ubiquity of desire is symbolized by recurring fire imagery that appears during scenes in which desire is foregrounded. The fire comes mostly from the gashouses of East Harlem, an eerie and imposing emblem of American enterprise, and from cressets in religious shrines encountered in homes and churches, which are linked directly to the religious desire of characters in the novel. The importance of fire imagery in representing the persistence of desire is, of course, first announced by the title of the novel, which has not received the critical attention it deserves. When Lapolla figures desire as "the fire in the flesh," he establishes the stubborn persistence of desire and, by placing desire within "the flesh," roots it firmly within our biological natures. No one, whether they are as powerful as Agnese or as holy as Padre Gelsomino, is able to rid him or herself of desire. As we might expect, the title and variations upon the title reassert themselves in scenes of desire, such as when Antonio Farinella tells Agnese, "you are a fire in me" (*FITF* 148).

Characters attempt to ward off desire by sublimating it through their work. For example, Antonio and Agnese both employ this strategy — and unsuccessfully, for the consequent moneymaking simply produces a desire for still more moneymaking. Indeed, moneymaking, while certainly necessary for survival, is quickly proven to be an empty endeavor when it becomes the sole reason for a character's existence.

Desire is not only a narrative element, though; it also manifests itself aesthetically in a peculiar syntax revealing characters' inability to describe, even give name to, exactly what they want. For example, when Antonio attempts to tell his wife Catarina about his feelings for Agnese, he is barely coherent:

> But my heart burned all these years . . . it burned to possess another . . . to hold her body till it should crack in my strength. . . . I bore an insult for her . . . deep in my heart there's the scar of it . . . men know about it and I have said nothing . . . stuck to my trade . . . built up the business . . . reared a family . . . been a good husband . . . but the fire in me was hot . . . it kept up and up . . . and now . . . and now . . . Catarina. . . . You understand . . . you understand . . . you will say nothing . . . you will do nothing . . . you will not get on your knees before that saint . . . *Porca Maria del Carmine* . . . you do . . . you do it once . . . understand . . . *santissima*. . . . (*FITF* 167)[28]

[28]The overall aesthetic effect is akin to Lee Clark Mitchell's description of literary naturalist style, in which characters' inability to possess a will of their own — or in this case an inability to satisfy desires forever burning away at them — results in a "stuttering syntax" often filled with repetitions that "depriv[e] both characters and readers of an otherwise comforting sense of autonomy; Mitchell, *Determined Fictions,* xii, 20–21.

Here, Antonio attempts to describe his desire — using the fire metaphor yet again — and his attempt to sublimate it through his work and family. However, Lapolla's repeated use of ellipses represents both the blinding heat of desire and Antonio's inability to adequately verbalize its nature. Still, he manages to reference desire for sex, money, and religion before dissolving into blasphemy ("*porca Maria*") and then violence as he shakes his wife roughly.

Predictably, desire strikes a fatal blow to those characters who struggle most unsuccessfully to manage it, and, in one climactic scene, desire reaches a logical, destructive conclusion. Later in the novel, when Padre Gelsomino hears of local organized criminals' intent to burn down Agnese's massive building project, he rushes to warn Agnese and arrives at the brownstone at the very same time Michele does, clutching a rabbit knife in a murderous daze. As the houses burn across the street, Michele fatally stabs Gelsomino, and Agnese grabs the knife from Michele and stabs him in return. Just then, "everything about [Agnese] achieved a sudden illumination as if a light blazed and roared close at hand," and this fire casts a decidedly Gothic light upon the entire scene as nearly each of the novel's desires reappears (*FITF* 339). In addition to violence, the desire for power appears in Michele's inability — once again — to perform his masculine duty and avenge Agnese's loss of honor. The desire for sex appears in Agnese's and Gelsomino's final affectionate words to each other. Finally, the desire for money appears at the end of the scene when Antonio rushes in crying, "The houses, Agnese," and Agnese now realizes that the fire in the flesh has the capability of destroying everything it had helped to build (*FITF* 341). If we accept that Lapolla uses the house as a symbol of the immigrant's standing, then it would seem that he is sounding a warning that desire has the additional capability of compromising Italians' New World status. As we discover in the final chapter entitled "Christmas Day," Michele is not killed but, rather, is reduced to a "simpering" "half-wit child" (*FITF* 344). Reduced to this state, desire is no longer even a cognitive matter anymore: Michele has no memory of the murder but still feels an uncontrollable urge to murder his wife, who now cares for him as a still unsatisfying penance for her sins and desires. Luigi aptly sums up the animalistic persistence of desire: "They're like animals in a trap . . . like animals in a trap, gnawing at each other, and they can't move, can't get their teeth out" (*FITF* 346). On Christmas morning, Agnese views the row of buildings, now nearly rebuilt after the fire: "'Ashes — ashes!' she said to herself, addressing them. 'You're built up almost, and who knows there was a fire in you? Like me. Who knows the fire in my flesh — burnt up, all burnt up" (*FITF* 346). This, of course, is a lie because in the novel's final scene — at Gelsomino's grave — Agnese admits that she continues to love Gelsomino (*FITF* 348-49). She tells Gelsomino of Michele's continual desire: "but it's all hate — all hate" (*FITF* 348). However, she also tells Gelsomino of Giovanni's desire: "He is very sad. A fire burns in him too. He is always painting. Do you know why? Because he loves, and you are with him when he paints . . . ." (*FITF* 347). This is significant because despite Giovanni's sadness, he is still the most redeemable character in the novel and is arguably its hero.

Through Giovanni, Lapolla seems to be saying that given desire's biological inevitability, it is best to direct it toward good by finding the transcendent in one's lifework, and Giovanni does this through his art. Unlike the novel's penitent sinners who passively expect God to come to them, Giovanni's art serves as a way of moving him closer to God. To be sure, Giovanni is like everybody else in that he is permanently suspended between desire and fulfillment. By the novel's end, he is still "sad" and can never find complete satisfaction. However, unlike everybody else, he uses the tension between the polar opposites of this in-between condition as an impetus for creative genius. In Giovanni's thoughts and deeds, the reader finds him permanently and productively located between the mundane and the sublime, the bodily and the transcendent, the real and the romantic, and the Italian and the American. In this regard, Giovanni is Lapolla's characterization of the ideal artist, for, like Lapolla, he uses the raw material of everyday life and uses it to transcend the everyday.

Indeed, Giovanni comes to represent the epitome of Lapolla's Italian-American aesthetic. In Giovanni's most closely described work in the novel, he paints a monk walking in Harlem backgrounded by the ever-present gas tanks and the East River. In this painting, Giovanni fuses each of the novel's artistic polar opposites: the earthiness of East Harlem with the otherworldliness of the monk; the realism of the background with the romanticism of the subject, who, "eyes absorbed, wide-open, gaze[s] into a nothingness that he explore[s] futilely for meaning"; and the Americanness of the background with the Italianness of the Catholic monk, who may very well be a thinly veiled rendering of Padre Gelsomino (*FITF* 262). Furthermore, the painting serves as a moving depiction of the "in-betweenness" of desire. Never able to find the meaning he is looking for, "the monk presented a picture of intense hope and moving despair, affirmation and negation, bewilderment and understanding" (*FITF* 263). Gelsomino at first does not understand the painting's unique fusion of opposites, and when Giovanni attempts to explain it, he can only resort to the stilted language of frustrated desire: "He's a poor monk . . . I don't know . . . I can do them . . . but see, behind them I have the river, too, and dome see . . . ." (*FITF* 264). The desire to create art is yet another fire in the flesh that is never to be extinguished; however, Lapolla privileges this desire above all others in the novel. Even Agnese, of all people, comes to see the value of it by the end of the work.

The painting of the monk can be viewed as metafictional, for its aesthetics neatly mirror Lapolla's own. Like Giovanni, Lapolla embraces the fusion of the real and the romantic. Realism places great value in the miscellany and the activities of the everyday world, and *The Fire in the Flesh* is filled with painstakingly close descriptions specific to the everyday world of Italian Harlem. In a description of the East Harlem waterfront viewed from the perspective of Giovanni, Lapolla does more than merely list items encountered during a typical day at the East Harlem waterfront. Additionally, he personifies many of these items, pairing them with action verbs and thereby conferring value upon them: lumber, blocks, and bricks *formed* natural sheltering places; "tugs *puffed* with confident strength"; "green-banked islands *held aloft*"; "a white slow steamer *moved by silently.*" However, unlike the realist, Lapolla does not view the everyday world as the sole means and ends of art. Immediately after this description, we are told "Giovanni's look was more than a survey of the scene" — the gaze of the realist — additionally, "It was a singing in his heart" — the perception of the romantic, who sees beyond the "immediate" to a transcendental "delight that was, and could not be" (*FITF* 63). Lapolla's fiction exists in this fertile middle ground between the real and the romantic. He sets the novel in the familiar Howellsian homes and streets of Italian Harlem, but his continual use of firelight casts an eerie, Hawthornian glow upon everything that is more consonant with the romancer's aesthetic and sensibility.[29]

---

[29]For a discussion of Lapolla's fiction as Frank Norris's ideal "romances of the commonplace," see Lawrence J. Oliver, "'Beyond Ethnicity': Portraits of the Italian-American Artist in Garibaldi Lapolla's Novels."

Given the textual and intertextual evidence, it is very difficult to place Lapolla squarely within any generic category, and this is precisely the author's intent, for Lapolla believes the author exists best in the middle-ground between the very same opposites Giovanni is situated between. It bears mentioning that Lapolla is also situated in the middle-ground between "Italian" and "American." An Italian who wrote and taught in America, Lapolla never discarded Italian subject matter in his decidedly American novels. Although he would never fulfill his own desire to become a successful writer, his work is living proof of his first novel's thesis — that the Italian-American artist's supreme desire ought to be to create art that is, and isn't, Italian American.

Bibliography

Note: GMLP= MSS 64, Garibaldi M. Lapolla Papers, Historical Society of Pennsylvania, Philadelphia

Adler, Mortimer J. *Philosopher at Large: An Intellectual Autobiography.* New York: Macmillan, 1977.

Blackburn, Marc K. "Register of the Garibaldi Mario Lapolla Papers, 1930–1976, MSS. Group 64." GMLP.

"Editor's Notebook." *Sunday Herald* 21 June 1953.

Ferraro, Thomas. "Ethnicity and the Marketplace." *The Columbia History of the American Novel.* Ed. Emory Elliott. New York: Columbia UP, 1991. 380–406

Green, Rose Basile. *The Italian-American Novel: A Document of the Interaction of Two Cultures.* Rutherford, NJ: Fairleigh Dickinson UP, 1974.

Hornsby, Robert. E-mail to the author. 2 Oct. 2007.

Lapolla, Garibaldi M. "The American Novel." Box 2, folder 3, GMLP.

___. European Trip Diary. 1953. GMLP, Box 1, Folder 9.

___. *The Fire in the Flesh.* New York: Vanguard, 1931; rprt., New York: Arno, 1975.

___. *Italian Food for the American Kitchen.* New York: Funk, 1953.

___. "Letter in Answer to Dr. Lefkowitz about So-Called Communist Teachers." GMLP, Box 1, Folder 2, 3-5.

___. Returned letter. New York, to Mark O. Lapolla. 25 Dec. 1944. GMLP, box 1, folder 3.

___. Returned letter. New York, to Mark O. Lapolla. 27 Jan. 1945. GMLP, box 1, folder 3.

___. Returned letter. New York, to Mark O. Lapolla. 15 Jan. 1945. GMLP, box 1, folder 3.

___. Returned letter. New York, to Mark O. Lapolla. 31 Jan. 1945. GMLP, box 1, folder 3.

___. Returned letter. New York, to Mark O. Lapolla. 6 Feb. 1945. GMLP, box 1, folder 3.

Lapolla, Paul. Telephone interview. 25 June 2007.

___. Telephone interview. 11 Nov. 2007.

Lear, Paul. E-mail to the author. 1 Oct. 2007.

Luisa, Maria. "Le Conversazioni del Giovedì." *Il Progresso Italo-Americano* 2 Apr. 1953: 1.

Marazzi, Martino. "King of Harlem: Garibaldi Lapolla and Gennaro Accuci 'Il Grande.'" *'Merica: A Conference on the Culture and Literature of Italians in North America.* Ed. Aldo Bove and Giuseppe Massara. Jan. 2003. Rome and Cassino, Italy. Stony Brook, NY: Forum Italicum, 2005. 190–210.

Meckel, Richard A. "A Reconsideration: The Not So Fundamental Sociology of Garibaldi Marto Lapolla." *MELUS* 3.4 (1987): 127–39.

"Missing Flight Officer Now Is Reported Killed." *New York Times* 6 Jan. 1946: 30.

Mitchell, Lee Clark. *Determined Fictions: American Literary Naturalism.* New York: Columbia UP, 1989.

New York Times January 1954: 29.

Oliver, Lawrence J. "'Beyond Ethnicity': Portraits of the Italian-American Artist in Garibaldi Lapolla's Novels." *American Studies* 28.2 (1987): 5–21.

___. "'Great Equalizer' or 'Cruel Stepmother'?: Image of the School in Italian-American Literature." *The Journal of Ethnic Studies* 15.2 (1987): 113–30.
Ontario Post 22 Sept. 1917.
___. 29 Sept. 1917.
___. 8 Dec. 1917.
___. 20 Apr. 1918.
___. 25 May 1918.
___. 1 June 1918.
Orsi, Robert Anthony. *The Madonna of 115th Street: Faith and Community in Italian Harlem, 1880–1950*. New Haven, CT: Yale UP, 1985.
Peragallo, Olga. *Italian-American Authors and Their Contribution to American Literature.* Ed. Anita Peragallo. New York: Vanni, 1949.
"Principals Lose Pay Case." *New York Times* 2 June 1950: 12.
Sinclair, Upton. *The Goslings: A Study of the American Schools.* Pasadena, CA: Upton Sinclair, 1924.
"Teachers Oppose Loss of Royalties." *New York Times* 17 Sept. 1946: 7.
"Teachers Secretly Quizzed on Loyalty." *New York Times* 17 May 1922: 18.
Thomas, Norman, et al. Letter to the editor. *The New Republic* 26 May 1917, 109–11.

The Fire in the Flesh

Table of Contents

THE FIRE IN THE FLESH

To P.S.

I. VILLETTO

– 1 –

Noonday had penetrated the old provincial cathedral of Villetto. The light showering through the colored panes danced off the marble floors and touched the images in obscure niches. On Padre Gelsomino it cast a glare which transformed his surplice into the rigid folds of a carven image. He stood on the altar motionless and silent as the St. Chrysostom and the St. Paul to either side of him. He had stood thus for many minutes.

His eyes had not moved from the far-off door through which he expected to see the procession enter. For he had heard the band approaching and was ready to confer upon the many worshippers the holy benediction of God and the Church. As a rule, by way of direction, he would have snapped his fingers at his chief altar boy to hurry with the lighting of the candles. But a shadow in one of the aisles had so suddenly disappeared behind the image of the Holy Virgin at the foot of the stairs that he seemed transfixed either by its novelty or by something too disturbingly familiar about it. The boy, too, had seen the hastening figure and had run to catch a more detailed impression.

"Nothing, padre," he whispered. "Only a woman . . . a woman with a child. . . ."

But the padre did not stir. A pallor had come upon his face and fright into his eyes. The boy hurried off, not without a sidelong look back and a mock sign of the cross. He had heard the lusty sounds of the band and knew that the procession was upon them. Seizing his censer he faced the doors as the noisy worshippers of Our Lady of Mid-August streamed in.

The huge image of the Virgin almost toppled from the shoulders of its bearers as they shoved their way to the front.

The procession was a motley queue — a fantastically uniformed band with a sprinkling of musicians in homespun. Women in heavy shawls sweating under the burden of candles, often too huge even for their peasant robustness. Hard-handed shambling men, their backs bent. Priests in full vestments dragging their cassocks in the hot dust. Little girls and boys swaying censers. The enormous clay image of the Madonna oscillated in her palanquin, beaded and befringed and heavy with silks, bestudded with medals, laden with money offerings pinned in great profusion over its sides. It was the portrait of a frightened girl with her infant held much too lightly in the crook of her arm. The tired men who carried it made no attempt to hide their relief as they bore the revered image down the long aisle of the cathedral, while the rest of the procession filed behind, the band silenced, the whispers hushed, the tread of feet softened in the mild gloom.

Padre Gelsomino waited with hands outspread in benediction.

"Let us pray."

It was all he said, for the whole church broke into confused cries. From behind an image near the altar, where she had hidden, there rushed to the side of the young priest Agnese Filoppina, holding an infant in the crook of her arm even as the Holy Virgin.

"The witch. . . ," yelled a shrill woman.

"The devil's daughter. . . ," another cried.

Vile epithet followed vile epithet. Nothing was too lurid, too coarse, too filthy to be uttered even within the sacred precincts of the blessed cathedral itself. The ceremony had come to an intense termination, a strong, pulsing excitement, a hubbub that rose to the turbulent pitch of riot.

Agnese Filoppina ignored it all. With a brusque gesture of her free hand, she grasped the hand of Padre Gelsomino, turned him to her savagely, and shouted, "Unholy villain, this is your child."

"She devil . . . whore . . . wildcat. . . ."

The crowd was not disposed to accept an accusation thrown so madly on this holiest of days against a priest whom they all loved and revered.

Several men attempted to seize her. With incredible swiftness, she ran up to the steps of the altar and took her stand immediately below the sanctuary. She turned like an animal. Her small thin body, worn by recent privations, quivered with anger. The baby in her arms cried with fright.

"What do you know? Why do you attack me? Have you no daughters? I was an innocent girl. When he had his way, he threw me aside. From shame I ran to the grottoes, lived like an animal until my baby came. I had him like an animal. But he . . . he. . . ," pointing to the priest who stood limp, head down, arms hanging loosely, "he celebrates mass, prays to God unashamed, gets your love, your adoration. Strip his cassock from him. Don't lay hands on me."

The consternation produced by her shrieks was like a stinging sensation of whips. The people looked at each other and then at the priest. Taking advantage of the momentary quiet, he waved his hands weakly to the men at the altar, and said, "Let her remain there."

Then he raised his hands in the benediction which had been so wildly interrupted, and said softly, "Oremus . . . Deo Sancto. . . ."

He allowed no pause to intervene between the Latin prayer he uttered and the words he had prepared to speak in the vivid dialect of the people. He spoke rapidly as if he feared to stop, looking now and then as if a hope were crossing his heart that the words he said would fall like a solemn interdiction on the mind of the enraged woman. His voice rose into a sing-song pitch as he told of the solemn ecstasy of the Virgin receiving the message of Gabriel. It was a rich bass voice, sonorous with thoughts that he had never fully uttered, a voice of one who had not altogether accepted the implications of the intense career of the priesthood. The hollow of the cathedral took up the voice and carried it into every recess, but not into the hearts of the congregation. They heard it, but their thoughts did not receive it. Agnese's thin figure, pathetically leaning against the white altar with the crying baby she was trying to still clutched to her, was too poignant to allow the soothing rhythms of the priest's intonations to fall upon them like soft hands quietingly and solacingly. The situation was too dramatic to permit of an undisturbed transition from the wild language of the woman to the gentle language of the priest. Padre Gelsomino continued with redoubled energy as his fear grew that Agnese would again step forward and once more tell the horrifying story. He seemed like one fleeing from a pursuer, too afraid to turn, too afraid to stop, and too weak to proceed.

Another entrance brought the scene to a climax. Agnese's fifteen-year-old brother, true to the local tradition that required him to be his sister's avenger, had just returned with a sickle that glittered in the cathedral dimness as he held it high above his head. The people made way for him, too frightened to halt his progress.

Padre Gelsomino stopped talking with impotent suddenness. He turned surprised, saddened eyes upon the boy and, with a gesture, the first intense one he had made, restrained several men who had rushed forward to seize the boy.

"What is it you want, Luigi? To kill your padre?" he asked. "Why? Do you know the truth? Do any of us know the truth? Take your sister home. Give her food. Be kind. . . ."

"Kind, kind," shrilled Agnese. "How does a beast like you know how to be kind?"

It was fortunate that some men kept their heads. Some made a human wall around the priest, while others seized the boy from behind and gradually wrested the gleaming weapon from his grasp. Agnese and her brother were taken home, and the ceremony and the celebration of the Annunciation concluded with as much solemnity as was now possible.

– 2 –

In so small a town as Villetto the disappearance of anyone at all would not only be immediately known, but would become a dramatic event in itself. When a person so vivid, so sharp-willed, so boldly beautiful, independent and assertive as Agnese was seen one evening but not the next day nor the days following, the whole town was completely shaken. No one knew exactly when she had left. Some talk there had been of a secret love affair, or a lover in another town or even in America who had sent for her. The brusque determined taps of her knobbed heels rang no more on the village cobbles. But for each tap there was loosened a voice, and no voice in praise or even pity. Conjecture varied from accidental death to a life of shame. When Matteo Saltone returned from the army he established beyond peradventure of a doubt what she had become. He had had good silver pieces in his pocket, he had been in a very large town indeed, he had drunk, he had seen, he had paid. He shrugged his shoulders in his infinite pride and his infinite pity.

For a long time all the eligible young men of the village and of nearby hamlets had paid their respects to the father and mother of Agnese, and each had asserted his superior ability to marry her. As long as her mother was alive, Agnese had now and then consented to have one or another of the young men present himself formally, and in the stiff aloof manner of village courtship would sit in complete silence for a whole evening in a corner of the only room which made up the whole of their one-story stone house. Her mother's death, however, had left her in control of the situation. She dictated the family life, and her father and brother were glad to follow. She ruled unerringly and decisively. And so, before long, it was only the priest who called — the priest, and Michele Dantone, the barber's apprentice.

Padre Gelsomino was still under thirty, and retained the roving brightness of his jet-black eyes. He made a practice of looking fixedly at one who spoke to him and allowing a noticeable pause to intervene between the last words of the speaker and his own reply; and his hearer carried away with him a feeling of exaltation, of heightened spirits, of a new wisdom. Better than his replies was the soft cadences of his voice, a sibilant liquid song of whispers and only an occasional rise to emphasis. He had been a peasant lad who had worked hard on the family farm, made a mark for himself at school, and then decided, out of respect for the wishes of his mother, to enter the priesthood. He had rarely mingled with the other young men of the town before going to the seminary, and was noted there for reticence and a marked interest in his studies. The more surprising was it, then, that he had become so popular a priest in the locality in which he was born and reared, and still more surprising that his popularity embraced the whole population — men, women, and children. The children ran after him to hold his hand, and the men as they plodded home from their labors in the fields thought nothing of postponing their heavy evening meal that they might pass the time of the day and a few words about this and that with the ever-patient, ever-listening young padre.

His constant callings at the home of Agnese Filoppina occasioned no surprise. Not a shadow of doubt or suspicion could ever have fallen on his good name. The father and the brother often left the girl working about the household chores when all the other lamps and candles in the village had been put out, and thought nothing of Padre Gelsomino staying on to finish the last glass of wine that had been poured out for him.

Agnese herself, although suspected by the villagers of possessing an inordinate pride and a determined temper, bore herself with such modesty and quietness in the general life of the town as to be taken for a model young woman. Her repeated refusal to consider the numerous marriage proposals, which for a year or more attested with enviable frequency to her beauty and desirability, was interpreted as a mark of her great pride. Besides, it was known with what unrelenting jealousy her young brother regarded her, and how careful a watch he kept over her movements. On one occasion he had driven away a group of too insolent serenaders, still under the influence of the new wine they had drunk, and so menacing was his manner that they had made no attempt to return.

The inevitable had occurred. The marriage proposals had stopped. Agnese was indefinitely postponing her marriage to what distant date no one knew. And though her aunts and their women friends kept persistently forecasting a dire barren future to one so self-willed, Agnese would have no one. Michele Dantone alone, because he was the least handsome, the least talkative, the least spirited of the available young men, seemed willing to accept her repeated rebuffs. For over two years now he had sent his grandmother, the only relative still alive in a family never large, to renew his pledges of interest in Agnese and his desire to marry her. He had supplemented the visits of his aged go-between with a practice that had won him the ridicule of the whole neighborhood, and complete ostracism from the society of the young blades of the town. On pleasant evenings, after he had closed the barbershop in which he worked, he invariably sought the small green-doored stone house of the Filoppinas, knocked, and waited a reply. And after several months of this he might have waited all through the night had he not exercised the only stupendous bit of courage he possessed. He had formed the habit of knocking twice and then, answer or no answer, he opened the door and entered.

"I have come to inquire after the health of your father, Agnese. Is he well?"

"Yes, you pig-snouted poltroon, he is well," Agnese shot back, or just merely laughed, or said, "Go away, the priest is coming and he will have none of you."

"But I am glad to hear he is doing well. And you?"

"Well, fool."

"You are very beautiful. . . ."

And Michele sat down without being invited, and kept his seat whether anyone else came in or not. Generally he said nothing, but merely followed Agnese with quiet, dog-like eyes as she moved about the big stone-flagged floor. Occasionally her father suggested that he would teach the devoted lout a lesson and drive him off, and Luigi went so far as to take Michele aside one day in the barbershop and tell him in no uncertain terms that he was making a fool of himself and the whole Filoppina family and would have to answer for it very shortly.

Agnese had put a stop to this, however. She had no intention of having the patient, quiet young fellow come to any harm. In fact, out of some queer perversity of spirit, she had grown to expect his coming. It had become a symbol to her of the devotion of all the young men who had ever sought her hand in marriage. She had a great contempt for them all, but she would have enjoyed having them all come like Michele and sit in painful humble devotion at her feet. And so Michele kept making his evening visits, and with equal frequency the soft-voiced sensitive priest sat down on another chair.

Evening after evening he waited until Michele had gone. He sipped his second glass of wine, and nibbled at the *tarrallino* Agnese had saved for him. Although the town was amused, nothing was thought of it for more than three years. And then one day nothing more was seen of Agnese.

Agnese's disappearance had loosened all the tongues in the village. Villetto had never experienced such a thing before. The padre averred he knew nothing; Michele became stolid, morose, and even turned angrily upon his questioners. No one knew just what to do about it. The military were finally informed about it, but they, too, discovered no trace of her. The episode eclipsed the memory of the disastrous earthquake of several generations before, of the only snowstorm that had fallen in the town, of the murdered man found in one of the ancient Roman grottoes malodorous with the refuse of years.

The solitary ways of Agnese suggested, by the very starkness of her history, the possession of impulses and desires intense and vivid, and dark and evil. There was ascribed to her, now that her sharp answers need not be feared, traits of character of the most degraded women.

Luigi attempted in frantic wild ways to combat the evil rumors that gradually wound about his sister a mesh of ugly suspicion. The distracted father went to his work with his head lowered, his face pale, his eyes red from the sleepless vigils he kept. But one who had been self-willed could expect no sympathy. Her heartlessness, her self-keeping ways, her haughty chin-lifted demeanor had made the people angry with her, and they avenged themselves on her now — on her, and on her old father, and on her proud brother.

Michele kept to himself. Padre Gelsomino said nothing. For the two months she was gone, he had mentioned her only twice in his prayers. He still continued to greet everyone with his fixed, steady look, listened to the talk of all those who cared to come to him, and left upon them the gentle impress of his love.

– 3 –

Agnese's return broke up the procession earlier than usual. The energy that was to have gone into religious fervor and the merrymaking that filled the night of a feast day was deflected into gossip, malicious accusations, ribald reconstructions of the whole story of priest and girl and loutish barber. The leaders of the town realized the possibilities of catastrophe inherent in the situation. What Luigi and his father would do, what even the timid Michele might attempt, they understood only too well. It was decided to keep a guard over the Filoppina home until the next morning when, it was thought, some formal legal action might be taken. That Padre Gelsomino was the father of the child very few doubted although very few were willing to assert it openly. But even those who spoke openly about it in no instance held him to blame.

The women in particular made it quite clear that such a bold girl as Agnese, with her slip of a figure, her caressing eyes, her self-willed, independent, haughty ways, had been the prime instigator. Why had she refused so many men? Why had she encouraged the priest's visits? They shook their heads and shrugged their shoulders. Formal pity for her plight came to their lips. But in their hearts "she-devil" echoed and re-echoed. Even the conventional pity they pretended to show was soon changed to undisguised anger and contempt when they were turned away from her door, whither they had gone, out of curiosity as well as sympathy, to look upon the child and offer assistance.

The aloofness which distinguished Agnese she maintained throughout the weeks that followed the open avowal of her illegitimate motherhood. To it she added insolence and a silence that was even worse. One might have thought that she would have kept to her house, and not gone out into the streets, to the market-place, to the public washing fountains in the middle of the piazza. Not a word she spoke to anyone, not a word did she pretend to hear.

Padre Gelsomino went about his duties as if nothing had happened. The smile that played about his tight, thin lips, the bright attention he always vouchsafed to those who talked to him, the soft, austere kindness he invariably displayed still marked him as the incomparable Padre. For a time the townspeople, in their turn, showed no less respect for him than before the startling disclosure. Whatever of change came about was to be seen only in the increased number of women who went to him for confession the Saturday following the feast of the Annunciation.

No one opened the subject in his presence and he had no reason for doing anything quite so rash. Once, only, they realized that he had been deeply affected by the situation. Michele Dantone had been seen entering the priest's house. Sharp voices had been heard, the lights in the parish house had gone out, an ominous quiet prevailed. But Michele opened the shop at his accustomed time, and everyone heaved a sigh of relief. And then Padre Gelsomino entered the barbershop to be shaved and have his hair cut. Everyone crossed himself, and general ease again prevailed.

Nevertheless, the situation was a painful one. It was understood that the affair had been brought to the attention of the bishop. An unexpected announcement created even greater consternation and more open talk. On the second Sunday following the fateful feast, Padre Gelsomino in a firm, unbroken voice proclaimed the banns of Agnese Filoppina and Michele Dantone.

They were to be married the following week. If Agnese's actions for the year past had produced astonishment, her betrothal to Michele, the town stupid, the barber's apprentice, the laughing stock of the young men, broke like a storm upon the town. The ribaldry that had been only a furtive, half-expressed accompaniment of the affair between the Padre and Agnese now became open, insistent, even raucous. The obscene suggestions, the coarse implications, the prurient items of the whole event were discussed amid laughter that was far more cruel than the original absence of sympathy. But Agnese walked about with her chin still high, none of the bold light dimmed in her eyes. Michele Dantone seemed to have become possessed of new springiness in his gait, and on his features was a light not seen before. Padre Gelsomino still talked benignly and intently with all who approached him; and there was no diminution of the gentle smile that made his features so eminently priestlike.

A further and even more astounding announcement closed the incident. After the marriage of Michele and Agnese, the whole Filoppina family with the baby and the new husband left the town and everyone knew that they were bound for America.

II. ON THE "CONTE BERTODLI"

– 1 –

The presence of Agnese with a three-months infant on board the *Conte Bertoldi* was not a rare phenomenon. In the dark, congested hold were other newly-born immigrants, barely capable of distinguishing the gray of the inner ship from the open blaze of the crowded decks. They raised scared voices of discomfort, or maintained a steady wailing of protest against an unrhythmic rocking which tossed them from one side to the other of the narrow wooden troughs supplied by the steamship companies for beds.

Rarely did Agnese throughout the nineteen days of the trip take the child on deck, and sit with the other women among the rigging and ropes, leaning against rough boxes that should have been stored below. That omission more than the child itself was the extraordinary feature of the Agnese group, and made her a person apart — that and the evident control she exercised over them all. Her imperturbable aloofness, her unbroken silence, her quick shrug of the shoulders punctuated forcefully by a brisk, wry laugh, and the manner in which the rough, coarse-spoken men followed her about the deck with their eyes, further raised her above the common plane. Few enough the women were, and fewer still women who retained the sparkling in the eye, the fresh texture of youthful skin, the clear tones of adolescent laughter that called to the marrow in the bone. Despite an obvious weight of thought, a suggestion of persistent brooding that was almost moroseness, Agnese moved about the decks, or sat in a corner, or leaned on her folded arms over a salt-sprayed gunwale, a still, appealing figure, a symbol of warm human response to warm human feelings — the luscious grape crushed and bubbling in the vats for men dancing in naked feet to drink.

"*È civetta* . . . a shameless creature!"

When she was out of hearing, the other women found an outlet in vigorous epithets — the more energetic, because in reality undeserved. Agnese made no effort to interest the men, only infrequently entered into the general gossip, and raised her voice in the common lamentations and the protests of abused resignation to fate which characterized the talk of the women. And as far as they could observe, she never spoke to a man unless her husband or her brother or father were present. It was the remarks of the men, blown to them on chance winds, or made frankly in their hearing, that aroused their anger.

Her superiority they realized, not knowing the exact cause of her unbroken silence. Frequently enough the men's comments were of such unrelieved coarseness, frank expressions of franker desire, as to disgust them, and often enough they were so humorously ribald as to provoke their laughter. Occasionally, and then the reactions of the women were of marked resentment, some bit of rustic poetry on the lips of a younger man portrayed Agnese in terms of crimson passion and stinging beauty.

"And what made her marry that awful stick?"

"It's unnatural. She treats the baby worse than an animal's cub."

"Have you seen her slap it when it bites her nipple?"

"She never rocks it, never sings to it, never talks to it! Bah! "

"The husband's scared of her. . . ."

"But he worships her. . . ."

"He's like a dog, slinks after her, licks his chops. . . ."

So it went. Agnese was aware of it, and ignored it all. That is, for the most part. She minded strictly her own affairs, simple as these were, and kept to her own men folk. The impetuous Luigi would have jumped cheerfully at the throats of both men and women but that his sister held him back. Once, when one of the gayer striplings had inquired of him rather knowingly, but unaware of the relationship Luigi bore to Agnese, what might be done to achieve a further romance, Luigi seized the youngster by the wrist with savage fingers, and glared like a beast into his eyes.

"Keep your ugly snout shut. . . ."

Her husband overheard and said nothing. The extent of his reaction was to suggest to Agnese that he ought to make an example of one of the men.

"Mind he doesn't feed you to the fish," was all she said. He merely smiled wanly after that, and resumed his walk around the deck, carrying his head manifestly at an elevation.

– 2 –

Gesualdo, her father, had aged many years from the day of Agnese's disappearance, and faster since the day of her dramatic return in the church. But he, too, said nothing. Like his daughter, he was small and lacking in the stockiness that distinguishes the southern Italian. His face had become prematurely wrinkled and dry, his small hands unduly gnarled, and his expression bore the stamp of one who had walked in the way of duty without rebelling. It had pained him when he learned of the birth of the child and who the father was. His first intention had been to go quietly to the house of Padre Gelsomino and cut his throat. Agnese had taken him by the shoulders, and looked silently into his eyes, and something in her manner made him draw back, and say nothing. He had gone off into a corner and wept, his whole body racked with his sorrow.

"None of that, none of that!" Agnese whispered, coming close to him, and pulling at his gnarled fingers with her own. "It's my cross, not yours. I'll bear it. You keep quiet, no talk, no tears. It is shame you want me to feel? Why? Quiet, I say, quiet."

She had bent and kissed him savagely and there had been no more affection after that. A fear, a nameless dread of what she was capable, entered his heart that day. From that time he seemed to understand nothing of what was going on, looked blankly at everyone and everything, talked in low whispers as if anything he said might be overheard by a punishing phantom always hovering by, and no matter what he was saying, came to a sudden silence immediately upon Agnese's approach.

He was all the more convinced of this feeling when he saw how Agnese silenced the jealous Luigi, more like her in character than he himself was. The lad had brought her home, his unused sickle hanging impotently from his belt, a sick-dog terror in his eyes, and his lips bleeding from his biting of them to restrain his cries. Placing the infant on the corn-husk mattress, she at once took the sickle out of Luigi's belt, wiped the boy's lips and, without warning of any kind, pressed him madly to her breast, saying all the while, "Weep it out now, weep it out now, brother mine, brother mine!"

She stroked his back and held him closer, kept stroking his back as the convulsive sobs came and went, and as she did so crooned to him, rhythmically, "Weep, little brother, weep, and say no more, no more."

And from that moment on, Luigi had said no more; he went around with his head as high as ever, but took no action. It was Agnese who had announced to them that she intended to marry Michele, and soon after go to America.

"I'll make that sanctimonious dog lay out the money!"

The quickness with which she went about the task, the precision of each movement, the perfect assurance she displayed had finished the ruin of Gesualdo's authority over her, and implanted in him that dread of her words and actions which completely dominated him. And so, the actions of all of them were dictated by the unconscious submission to Agnese's imperious will which she contrived to exact from them by a pride and a self-confidence beyond their everyday experience to match.

Toward the infant their attitude in similar fashion was determined by Agnese. She left nothing undone to feed and keep him clean and quiet. Other than that, she controlled with iron persistence whatever weakling gesture or soft feeling her mother nature might have inspired. They were aware of no other motive in her relation to the child, and they took her cue from it. The puny Giovanni Dantone, as they had christened him in due fashion on the eighth day of his birth, from his first days was learning to expect no unusual show of sentiment, no special interest, and no affection beyond what was required to maintain his body and soul as an entity.

– 3 –

For days the *Conte Bertoldi* rocked and heaved across the Atlantic. Crowded miserably in the hatches, the ruddy-faced peasants had already begun to lose their open-air color, but none of their animal spirits. They sat around improvised tables — boxes and boards, or an upturned trunk — played at *tocco* for drinks, gambled over cards, or hummed or sang to the whine of accordions. Mandolin players on clear nights filled the salt air with soulful strumming of old folk tunes. Little or no presentiment of hardship or exile, little or no trace of regret marred the spontaneity of their gatherings. The voyage had already taken so long that they had come to know each other by their first names, and many groups had joined to form still larger ones on the basis of an alleged community of feeling because of deriving from a similar province.

To one of these clans, almost in spite of their willfully segregating themselves, the Dantones and the Filoppinas became unconsciously attached. At their head was Francesco Crino, short, fat, and muscular, with chubby creased hands like a baby and black full mustache that dominated an otherwise creaseless face.

He had been in America before and appointed himself official advance cicerone, promising to find work for everyone, and a place to live. He boasted of inexhaustible knowledge as to where this or that family was to be found, and where most of the folks of this town or the other town had set up their colonies in New York or other cities. Trust to him, and America would yield its richest rewards. Who would want to return to the old country and dig in muck that never paid you back, when, like him, one could fill one's pockets with bills? One could tell one's betters a thing or two in America! There were people who lorded it over one in Italy, and made one take off one's hat to them, and call them signori, and send them gifts at Christmas time. These begged from you in America, and you rented rooms to them, or went before the magistrates to intercede for their wayward children. But you had to know how to do it. You set up a business if it was nothing else than assorting the refuse that came to the dumps on the rivers.

"I made my pile!" His fat fingers caressed the overbearing mustache with appropriate vigor. "And I didn't break my back working either, the way my father did on his mortgaged farm. Look at me now," and unashamedly, proudly he laced his chubby baby-like hands over his rotund abdomen. "Plenty to eat I have, and rings to my fingers, and wine when I want it, and I can tell Mastro Gaspare and Mastro Giuseppe and Signorone this and Signorone that to look at what I do with my fingers."

Agnese listened with the intentness of a child.

"What did I do to make my pile? Ha, ha, ha," he laughed. "I wasn't ashamed to work, picking rags, turning over the garbage on the dumps." This last in a whisper to Agnese as if, deep in his heart, he were ashamed of it.

"And now," he cried one day after a particularly glowing account of his exploits and the money he had amassed, "and now, who wants a job as soon as he lands? Let me see."

Men crowded around by the score.

"I see you mean to make America. Good! What's your name?"

In a short time he had contracted to supply upwards of three hundred men with work, some on the railways, some on construction jobs, some on garbage dumps. And as he inscribed each one in his notebook, he said, "Of course, there is a little charge for this. When they give you your first pay, they will take out a dollar for me. Just one little dollar in a land of many dollars."

Agnese listened with attention.

"Except my brother, I have two corncobs for men," she said to her pounding heart. "But I'll give them guts. . . . This good-for-nothing thief is piling it up fast. I'll do the same."

"You're the smart chap," she told him, and with her eyes made him believe a great deal more.

Michele had made a display of jealousy one afternoon when she emerged from behind a mass of cordage with Francesco in grinning, humble tow.

"Poltroon, mind your business," she said. "What do you know of America? He has just promised me to start a barbershop for you. . . ."

– 4 –

One night it had been too uncomfortable below decks. Men, women, and children had come up, foregoing sleep. In all corners was the strumming of mandolins, the sibilance of many voices, the laughter of young men.

Over two weeks had gone by since the sailing from Naples. The voyage had begun to wear on all of them. Crowded too close and with no outlet for their feelings available, complaining of the coarse unpalatable food and the foul conditions of their sleeping quarters, and yet receiving no satisfaction anywhere, they had begun to droop, to show instant irritability at all things. Quarrels had become more and more frequent, and at least on one occasion the ship's officers were compelled to interfere. Tonight there was laughter and gayety, and song rose high above the unceasing slapping of the water against the ship's side. Even Agnese had left her father below in charge of the infant, and was sitting with Michele where their group had made a clearing and were prepared to dance to the music of combined accordion, mandolin, and guitar.

Francesco Crino hopped about, talking volubly to everyone, inviting the young men and the women to form a figure for the tarantella.

"Let's be merry. Work's ahead of us soon, and life's too short."

"Eh, there, Agnese Dantone, bring out that husband of yours, and start the dance."

They all looked quickly in her direction, wondering whether she would venture and realizing all too ludicrously what a grotesque contrast she would make with Michele.

Agnese had noticed as she took her seat on the deck floor near her husband the eyes of Antonio Farinella fixed with undisguised admiration upon her. He still affected the colored waistband at his trouser's belt, and now in the fitful light of the ship's lamps the red of it emphasized ominously the story that his eyes told. His was a lithe figure with the suppleness of one just home from the army, a figure made to leap with unrestrained abandon in the passionate gyrations of the tarantella. The contempt she had shown all the men of Villetto had been too genuine for her to evince now even the slightest feeling of interest or indifference at the unabashed scrutiny of Antonio or the frank jovial good-fellowship of Francesco Crino.

"Oh, come, oh, *bella,* oh, *bella,* and dance!" sang out Francesco.

Michele's eyes were riveted in a strong eager appeal upon her. Some desire to cut a dashing figure mingled with his usual sense of being inadequate. Whether it was this, or the strong animal appeal in the eyes of Antonio, and a hope that in some way he would displace Michele as the dance developed, or whether it was the infectious joviality of Crino, she rose with suggestive flowing agility and took her place next to the other couples. Antonio turned and stretched his body out, supporting himself on one elbow, and followed Agnese with an intentness that made Michele wince uncomfortably. Crino clapped his hands as he shouted "Brava, brava" and caused the whole assemblage to burst into applause.

Already on the decks above had gathered the cabin passengers and several ship's officers to watch the impromptu revelry. Guitars and mandolins broke quickly into the fast movement of the tarantella. The slap of the waters and the moan of the retreating waves made a steady noise as of distant hamlets rumorous with the sound of procession and the merrymaking on the piazza on a holiday. The sky was still, without stars, or clouds, or moon, a taut immovable curtain drawn about the ship. From below decks came the wail of a child, fitfully lost in the strumming of the guitars and the subdued infinite murmur of the ocean.

Back and forth and around, swinging to and fro with stamping of feet and clapping of hands, the four couples moved first slowly, easily, languorously until the music quickened its tempo, the mandolins lifted their cicada-like utterances into a frantic sibilance. Something of the innately barbaric in people close to the soil, joined with impulses too long cabined in bodies used to activity, gave a savage elasticity to the steps of the dancers. Their hands raised above them, they snapped their fingers in rhythm to the accelerating music, a tambourine joined the other instruments, cries of "Bravo" came from the onlookers. It was at the point when the intricate figure simplifies into groups of dancing couples who never once lose the fast tempo thus far attained.

At first no one knew exactly what had happened. Agnese was without question the sprightliest and most animated of the dancers. Her face glowed poppy-red in the night. Crino had noticed that Antonio never once removed his gaze from her as if he could pull her to him like a magnet and have his will of her. And once, at least, in the dance he observed a flash from the eyes of Agnese seek the eyes of Antonio, red leap to her cheeks and to those of her inarticulate lover.

Michele and Agnese were close by Antonio when there was a cry, the fall of a body to the deck, a movement as of a herd rushing into a furious stampede. All the dancers had stopped, all but Agnese, and she held close in the arms of Antonio, was making the final wild gyration of the dance. The crowd held its breath. It was a trespass of the most insulting kind, equivalent to entering the bridal chamber on the nuptial night.

It had all occurred too swiftly for immediate reprisal. From the decks above came the clapping of hands as the lithe, able dancers swayed and whirled, elbows interlocked for a breath, hands on each other's shoulders for the next, and a sudden rush into each other's embrace for the last maddening gyration.

Michele lay stunned not only from his fall but also from his previous exertions. He had risen to his knees, when Luigi from his sitting position leaped upon Antonio and brought him in a frantic clinch to the floor. Michele lunged forward and they all saw the mad flash of teeth as he dug his face into Antonio's neck.

The cry that escaped from Antonio was like that of a wounded animal. The officers were already down when Crino had pushed forward and was attempting to pull off the enraged Michele from where he clung to the prostrate form of Antonio. Motionless, Agnese stood speechlessly by, biting the side of her hand. The cries of the wounded man rose into the darkness, a lone sound in the vast silence of the night.

"Off, you dog, off!" shrieked Agnese suddenly.

Michele rose, looked at her with half-wit helplessness, and without warning flung himself into her arms, weeping convulsively, while she patted him softly, and spoke to him crooningly as if no one else had been hurt but he, as if she had just come upon the scene to protect a child that had strayed from home.

"The witch. . . ."

"The devil's whore. . . ."

"She deserves the puling whelp. . . ."

She heard but ignored it all, and while the officers restrained Antonio she led the weeping Michele to their berth in the overcrowded hold.

Up betimes the next morning, Agnese sought out Antonio where he stood near the hatchway leading to her part of the sleeping quarters. His tall, agile figure seemed straighter because of the bandage about his neck, which he was trying to hide from pitying or contemptuous eyes by a gaudy green and red shawl muffled about him.

His muscles moved across his face as if they were slipping over the bones and catching themselves quickly into their fixed contours. As he knitted his jaws together upon her approach, the whole expression became a sinister conflict between contempt and admiration — contempt for her conduct, admiration for the bold elastic beauty of her motion and her body. He smiled wryly, and stripped her swinging skirts from her with an audacious, unashamed sweep of the eyes.

"Forget last night," spoke Agnese in a determined staccato. "Not one more word!" And as she said this, she seized his hand and pulled down his arm stiffly, brusquely to the side of his body, and gazed steadily into his eyes, already dancing with unabashed desire.

He made a movement to draw her to him, but she let go his hand as suddenly as she had seized it, and walked forbiddingly away. She saw him once again stooping over to her husband where he sat cutting a cigar to share with her father. But she did not overhear nor did Michele tell her what Antonio whispered: "I'll see you in America!"

III. THE DANTONES

– 1 –

Report card day in school brought a tense silence as of eager anticipation not altogether cherished. Students who had reason to fear the consequences attempted to work off in laughter and excessive noisiness much of their concern. The few who might display with pride whole series of eighties and nineties sat uneasily in their seats more than desirous of manifest approval. Giovanni Dantone, alone, best speaker of the upper grades, president of the literary society, and superior scholar, showed little if any outward desire for his monthly ratings, which, without doubt, would be the finest in the class. He sat morose and silent, his only movements an occasional scratching with a pencil in a book already filled with queer fantasies of lighthouses, huge dogs, and weird mustachioed *banditti.* On other days he was a lithe, quivering animal, all action, all excitement, reciting volubly, leading in all the games in the playground, first in all class meetings.

No one knew the cause of the perturbation which settled on his spirits the first day of each month. Miss Skinner, in whom he had learned to repose all his confidences, was not aware of it. As she gave him his card she knew that he took it without looking at it, put it rapidly into his pocket, and returned it the next day, signed in a large, groping scrawl "Michele Dantone."

"Did you like your report?" she asked.

"Yes."

"What's the matter with it, Giovanni?"

Giovanni said nothing. His large restless black eyes looked at her evenly.

"Father like it?"

"He signed it."

"Mother?"

"She doesn't care. She doesn't want to see it. She says it's all stupid. She says school is not for people like us. She hates it. . . . She wants me to get through right away. . . ."

The school authorities, however, had other plans for Giovanni. He had been the first of the growing number of Italian children to display unusual qualities. The school was situated in one of those sections of Manhattan which in the early years of the century had changed steadily from quiet, reserved stone stoops, like a row of hushed girls in church pews, to cheap brick tenements thick with fire-escapes and noisy children. A German population now Americanized had given way to a pushing group of Irish. The wastrels among both groups, who had had no luck and were compelled to keep working at menial jobs and trades, had remained as their more fortunate compatriots moved away to make room for the swarthy hordes of laborers and peasants, streaming in from Southern Italy. Their push carts and junk carts, their dingy dirty cafés and pasticerie, their even more ill-smelling saloons, their bread stalls covered with loaves of numerous and incomparable shapes and sizes crowded the basements of what once had been sedate, aristocratic brownstone residences. Their children swarmed barefooted, at times almost naked, in all the streets. The empty lots knew their cave-making habits, the East River docks were covered with their restless, excited gangs. The police had often to be called out to stop their stone battles carried occasionally to extremes of violence and even bloodshed. Mission societies had rented empty stores to hold services and bring the heathen hordes to God and cleanliness, and on more than one occasion discovered that they had better first supply a scuttle of coal, and bread and beans. Small wonder that the youngsters at school were like dirty barbarians, bewildered by the order and overcome by the cleanliness.

– 2 –

Giovanni Dantone was a conspicuous exception. He had learned English rapidly, spoke it fluently and correctly, wrote with sensitiveness and understanding, his unusual juxtapositions of words achieving at times a fantastic poetry. Information he amassed with astounding ease. He was in great demand as reciter and actor in the school dramatics. It was in days when rigid conventions in art prevailed; otherwise his drawings, with their juvenile inaccuracy of outline and their juvenile accuracy of essential mood and character, would have stood out.

The teachers made much of him, and he made much of them. Whatever time he could, he spent in school. With him was always a group of boys attached to him with a personal loyalty accorded by others to leaders of rougher gangs. And at times he could and did join with the rowdy hordes to invade the adjacent "English" territory or wage relentless stone fights against the boys of the older immigrant groups. Or they assisted at the erection of the huge bonfires which to them seemed an essential feature of election days, and they were the most vociferous and the most explosive of all Fourth of July celebrants. Where mischief brewed, he was as active as where his talents were called for.

He spent most of his real life in activities decidedly outside of the family round. It was the result of impulses instinctively awakened and directed. His mother and father belonged to that set of peasants whom their fellow immigrants dubbed as American made. They had "made America" and were wearing swallow tails who had only pushed the plow and tended sows. Their betters were working in sweatshops and glad enough to keep a hard loaf ahead on the pantry shelves. Bitter were the comments they inspired and the attitudes they provoked. But ignoring their less fortunate countrymen, they proceeded to amass fortunes. Ragpickers had become little nabobs and strutted abroad like village grandees. Foremen of railway gangs came back from mysterious regions called the track with double eagles in their pockets, lent out money at fancy rates and purchased the ramshackle tenements that served the ever-swelling number of arrivals.

Agnese and Michele Dantone belonged to the small group that enjoyed the most malignant comment, as they had without doubt succeeded in making the biggest pile. Their barbershop stood on the busiest corner and had become the rendezvous for all newcomers, a bureau of information and a gathering place for those out of work and ready to let themselves out at the most pitiable wages. Michele, in his quiet, stupid way, saw nothing particularly fortunate in the circumstance. It was Agnese who sensed the potentials of wealth and exploited them mercilessly.

She herself was, in fact, a chief factor in the prestige of Dantone's barbershop. She had brought with her a reputation from the other side which suggested to the homeless men who poured into the country ahead of their wives and families a fling at the flagons of life. Her quick eyes and sharp repartee, her pulse-stirring figure, her laughter with its low, suggestive tones brought back to the men moonlit nights on the piazza with the wine flowing, the heavy walk home, and the drugging passion that followed. She was not slow to add the suggestive word and a more than meaningful twinkle.

"So you like the American ladies best, Miguccio. What will Catarina say to that?"

The crowd of men laughed. "Why, they wouldn't give such a pock face a look-in."

"Never you mind. He can get good Italian stuff, hey, Miguccio?"

Michele said nothing. He was being made, without his will, and certainly without his efforts, to occupy a commanding position in the community. The local politicians were turning to him for advice, and depending upon him to get the new voters. He rarely spoke, but plied his trade diligently. His silence was taken to be mere canniness, and what he might tell, the men felt, would be the making of many of them.

This his wife shrewdly capitalized. In her own way, she said little or nothing of substantial import, and answered none of the questions about the chances of work, places to be had for a family just come, where to get free medical attention. Invariably she disclaimed all knowledge, and asked her questioner to wait until she could consult her husband. The consequence was that when Michele spoke at all his words seemed unusually valuable. All he had to say was, "Well, anybody who had the vote ought to vote for Peetro Doolan," and Peter Doolan got the votes.

In the same manner, he dropped the hint that a hundred men were wanted on a big job upstate, good wages, and cheap quarters with overtime. They flocked to the barbershop, and he collected a dollar apiece for the name and address and a card that would insure a job. In the meantime he had already contracted, Agnese at the forefront of the negotiations, to receive a dollar for every man he sent.

The Dantones had prospered, had prospered considerably, but still retained the barren simplicity of their peasant customs, made no departure from the parsimonious habits of their first few years in New York. Beans cooked with *pasta,* the inevitable macaroni, an occasional meat dish, and fish on Fridays, black coffee and fruit, and only now and then a splurge into fresh vegetables, and the Dantone appetite was satisfied. Wine they had, and cheese, but little or nothing else save on the big holidays.

The four rooms of the dingy railroad flat, one only lighted for several morning hours, they had never carpeted or laid with linoleum. The boards, always spotlessly scrubbed, showed huge seams and hollows where the feet of many occupants had rested for many evenings, many years. The painted walls glared green or blue or brown, as at varying times they were newly painted and, with the light of two or three cressets below the image of the Virgin and Saint Joseph and Saint Biagio, darkened and brightened with fitful shadows.

"*Che cafoni!* What peasant louts! What boors!"

Agnese was aware of the talk. It made no difference to her. She knew no better. All she understood was that it was better to have money than spend it and not have it. All she thought of was to devise means to gather more.

Giovanni sensed keenly how helpless the school was to aid him. His fight with his mother and his father was his own. Giovanni realized too well that the conception of America and American ways his mother had formed and had forced upon his father, she would force upon him. Evidence on every hand bore out his mother's reiterated statement:

"What do you want with school! Stay while the law says you must. Put the jingle in your pockets! That's the way!"

He had talked it over with some of the other boys. Peppino Totillo, tall, growing to be a giant, with fair hair, and a smile that was a substitute for everything he did not know and would not learn, already leader of a gang, holding up the boys on enemy streets and rifling their pockets — Peppino Totillo averred that his mother was right.

"I am going to become a lawyer, make money, get into politics!"

Something vaguer than making money, something with rose in it and a mist that filigreed away from it in tantalizing spirals, a gleam of water with sunlight on it, impossible pictures that came out of a mysterious fund of memories without name and outline — these were in Giovanni's mind. Their full power never came upon him except at night as he lay in his windowless room, coaxing sleep, or when he sat back in his seat while the teacher droned and catechized. They became then a stinging sensation, an experience of being dead — dead to the world of barbershop and school and street warfare. But he knew a sweet relief. It was to be alone — drawing crude hills and water, houses and fleeing rails. He picked at the mandolin strings on a quiet evening in the darkness of the kitchen, with its stove still showing fire. The teachers, he knew, could be no help. And so Giovanni groped through a world that was in reality darkness.

– 3 –

On the day he received the report card his feelings pulled like strings stretched too tight. He wanted to be praised, and to be questioned, his father and mother to sit quite quietly while he told them of it all. But he would have to listen to his mother's contempt of all things schoolish, let her snatch the report card out of his hand, throw it to Michele, with a curt "Sign the damn thing!" He was afraid he might burst into tears, or scream harsh, brutal words at his parents. Some such possibility was always on the point of happening, and he knew that once it happened his mother would stop at nothing to make the chastisement thorough.

It was the time of the afternoon when his father went upstairs for his late dinner. The warm, murky June day with its suggestion of rain had filled the large-floored room with ghosts of insufferably hot days in southern Italy. His father, he knew, liked the room just that way. It made him delightedly torpid like an amphibian baking by a muddy river. By bringing the old-fashioned shutters only partly to Agnese added to the memory. In shirt sleeves, tightly rolled up above the elbow, eyes blinking eagerly at the dish of peas and onions in a light tomato sauce, he sat silent, contented, looking at his wife with an up and down all-enveloping gaze that made Giovanni uncomfortable and questioning. The sense of being exalted had never passed out of Michele's eyes from the first days the banns were announced over twelve years before. It had become an established outlook which determined his gait, his manner of talk, even his attitude toward the customers.

He gave the impression of being secure in the shadow of unquestioned power, and the little stammer that often made him keep his mouth shut, suggested that he deliberately mocked all those outside the region of grace.

Giovanni, not knowing the exact circumstances of his birth or the actual relationship between him and Dantone, had nevertheless been acute enough to realize that this air of over-grand homunculus at the head of an empire which characterized Dantone, assumed toward Giovanni himself a further quality of hostility, even of meanness. When his mother was by, Giovanni felt fairly safe against unwarranted rebukes or an occasional quick backhand slap with loose fingers.

There were times when the boy quivered with a savage desire to strike back, to kick, to bite. That something, not in the nature of the relationship between father and child, existed between them, again and again flashed across his mind like a wave of heat.

He could not observe the other boys walking down the street their hands in their father's hands, their faces up-turned with a trusting assurance of reply, their little steps quickening as their fathers stepped along. It made him turn too quick an eye upon himself and wonder that such experiences had never been his.

He entered slowly that hot afternoon, his report card in his pocket. Neither his father nor his mother would care to see it. He would not open the subject of going to high school as the teachers suggested. He knew the sharp, quick fire of rebuke that would greet him. Michele bent over his dinner, bulked like a huge figure of satisfaction in the miraculous goods of the world. He caught the frightened manner in Giovanni's hasty plunge into the middle darkness of their railroad flat where his room was, and a mean smile illumined his almost beardless face.

Agnese sat with folded arms several feet from the table, her straight back making a hard parallel to the chair. Her voluminous skirts hung in decided pleats and a white frilled apron sat efficiently on her lap. She watched Michele through eyes half closed, her lips touched with the slight glow of a smile that could never be translated into words. To Michele it was as a soft sun on calm waters, like dawn in pools of early spring freshets at the foot of Villetto. He never fully permitted himself to suspect its genuineness, to doubt its warmth and satisfaction in him.

On this day, the tight lips moved with too persistent a wryness and the smile slid over them like water over rocks. He never realized the unexpressed contempt for him that Agnese showed only too occasionally or he would have trembled with fear that this perfectly ordained existence might end for him. Giovanni sensed a difficult time ahead for him, his report card, and his ambition. Agnese saw the exchange of glances and remained imperturbable. She had long wearied of the contest between putative father and son but had never revealed her complete indifference to them both. Giovanni, more sensitive, alone inferred it, and often withdrew from it in a quiver of agony and fright.

"What's keeping you?" shouted Michele. "Come and have your dinner."

The silence caused Michele to draw his napkin folded to ribbon narrowness over his lips before holding up a glass of red wine, faintly sparkling in the shadows.

"That boy's insolence!" he blurted timidly in his slightest stammer, and bent angrily over his dish again.

"That boy's insolence," he repeated on an intake.

"What's keeping you, Giovanni?" called Agnese, ignoring her husband.

Giovanni came out brusquely, marked out in shadow, a glint not to his mother's liking giving his eyes an unusual mobility. "I don't want to eat. I want to talk. I want to know. . . ."

"Quiet and sit down. Eat and no more chatter-chatter."

"Well," added Michele, drawing the napkin once more across his lips and chin. "That boy's insolence."

"I don't want to eat. Will you sign. . . ?"

"Sign what?"

"My report card."

"*Ancora o' billillo, hè!* Still teacher's darling, what?" sang Michele.

"Sign my report, mam-ma!"

"*Che* sign and sign!" Something in Giovanni's eyes and the clenched fist at his side stopped the full flow of her contempt. "Well, this is the last month for a while. All right, Michele, sign the damn thing!"

"But I want you to look at it. I want you to know that I am a good scholar, best in the class. I'm going to skip — understand I'm going to skip — very few boys do. Oh, mam-ma, mamma. . . ."

He was bending forward, every movement a plea to be seized in her arms and rocked and made much of. Agnese got up precipitously and with a swish of her skirts moved to the window, pulled aside the curtain and looked coldly out on boxed-in yards and cluttered fire-escapes and clothes motionless in the gray murk.

"Bring the thing here," said Michele with a complete peremptory move of his hand.

"What do you know? Who wants you to sign? I want my mother to sign. Mam-ma, I say, mam-ma. . . ."

"You talk that way to me!"

Michele rose, noisily shoved back his chair, and made his way with great care between the stove and the table to where Giovanni had advanced.

"You talk to me that way . . . to me . . . your father . . . you. . . ."

Giovanni glared in a sort of fascination as he saw Dantone step toward him, something furtively cruel for once in open display touching his every movement with life and purpose. Over Giovanni's face came a slow, uncertain smile as when one is aware of a massive inevitable danger closing in on one. Agnese seemed to have heard nothing and continued looking out, as quiet as the curtain she was crumpling in her hand.

Michele struck the boy a savage blow across the face with his knuckles.

Not a sound came from Giovanni, too shocked for a reflex, and Michele struck again with the other hand in a similar way.

Long-standing impulses catapulted forward in the lad. He jumped for the stove-handle, threw it full at Michele. Hearing it strike against his father's face, he grew nauseous and blanched. Then, without premeditation, unaware of his mother or anything else, he leaped toward the door and hurtled out and down the steps. The clatter of his shoes on the hollow wooden stairs echoed back into the room, and only then did Agnese turn about and notice blood flowing from Michele's cheek as he lay huddled on the floor.

"*Dio santo!* What's happened?"

She was not one to waste superfluous motion. She raised her husband's head to her lap.

"Just what happened? How did it happen? Where's Giovanni? "

"That priest's brat it was! That priest's. . . ."

"Shut your mouth, imbecile. This blood ought to be enough for you. . . ."

Fear contorted his face into a brusque silence, the blood spurting with the effort from the small hole-like wound right over his cheek bone. It flowed down into his neck and globbed over on Agnese's white frilled apron.

"Not much of a hurt," she said. "Be quiet. Sit up on the chair. Let me bathe it. We'll call the doctor!"

"Gio-Giov-vanni! The stove-handle. . . ."

"Let him come home! Let him come home . . . *o' malandrino. . . .*"

After she had bathed his face, she ordered him to hold a matted cloth over it while she went downstairs to tell the employed barber not to expect Michele back and to send her father to fetch the doctor.

– 4 –

The old man learned on his return the cause of Michele's wound, but, as was his wont, merely shook his head feebly, and said nothing. He watched Agnese as the doctor took a stitch in the cut and marveled in his silent way at the absence of any feeling on her face, the escape of no word from her lips. Agnese had become accustomed to calling in an American physician, clean-shaven, middle-aged, lanky and long-limbed, with just the slightest stoop to his shoulders, and Agnese had always had, what seemed to her father, an undue interest in him. To Gesualdo the doctor appeared to be as conscious of the unremitting gaze of Agnese upon him as he was aware of his work, and once stopped to look up. Gesualdo understood the sidelong glance, the dancing pupils, the slight flush, and unobserved made the sign of the cross. Her hold over men puzzled him, and he had come to believe in the popular epithets he had heard applied to her from the time she was barely sixteen and had had her child by Padre Gelsomino.

"You finish quick," she said, as Doctor Grace turned to her. "You don't think it take long?"

"Oh, he'll be all right. Coupla days," and he stroked her familiarly the whole length of her hand.

Her laughter was rich and low, and slightly trembling.

"You come again tomorrow?"

It was his turn to laugh low as he addressed himself to Michele, his mind all the while on something in the expression of her olive-tinted face that made him restless and uneasy.

"Go to sleep soon, and don't worry. In a week you'll never know you had anything."

Michele was too shocked by the blow he had received to realize how long a while the doctor and Agnese were in taking their farewells on the landing outside. When Agnese returned she lost no time in getting her husband to bed, and then told her father the whole story of the affair.

"Where do you think the scoundrel is now?"

Gesualdo looked squarely at her without replying. He had learned how useless it was to talk with his daughter, had seen her grow from mastery over herself to mastery over others, permitted himself no expression of opinion except when he was deeply moved. He felt keenly the whole incident, but realized that it was still too early to worry about the whereabouts of Giovanni. The hot afternoon had developed into a stifling dusk, filled with the redoubled street sounds that mark the summer evenings in the city. His old eyes shut, as he ran his gnarled hands over the deep-cut wrinkles that filled the hollows of his face.

"He'll come back, and then. . . ."

The old man raised slow, scared eyes to her. He knew the tone of her voice and how capable she was of carrying out the implied threats.

"What a bold thing to do, the scoundrel, the scoundrel. . . ," she repeated as she set about giving her father his dinner. There had grown a custom in the family for the old man to have his meals alone after the others had finished theirs.

"You have made your pile," he unexpectedly remarked as he put his spoon into his dish of peas and onions. "But what has it got you? You have more money than all my family since Adam put all together. You're no better off, you're no happier. I was glad to get my bit of cheese and wine on the other side. . . ."

"You keep quiet," commanded Agnese.

The hours passed. Agnese sat at the window gazing out upon the boxed-in yards and the men playing at *palle* or *tocco* in them. She made an attempt at crocheting. Her father had gone downstairs to sit in his chair before the barbershop, and carry on interminable conversations with other old men of the block. It was partly his duty to sit there and answer all questions of those who came inquiring for this and that from Agnese and Michele. He was to say, "Come in the morning," or "Come this afternoon," or "Nothing, nothing yet!"

Zi' Matteo sat like a torpid turtle on his backless chair, a long reed pipe in his mouth, its red clay bowl reaching almost to the sidewalk; on the step of the shop door sat Mastro Gaspare, earrings glinting in his ears, toothless, his nose no more prominent than any other ridge of the deep wrinkles that cut in an aimless way the length and breadth of his countenance.

"Where's Michele, Don Gesualdo?" asked the latter.

"Oh, upstairs, sleeping. . . ."

"Sleeping? This hot night. . . ."

"Well," chirped Zi' Matteo, taking an extended puff on his pipe, "you don't blame him, what with a young wife and all. . . ."

"Oh," answered Zio Tonno who had worked for more than six years now as a street cleaner, and affected the white trousers as an evening dress, "it isn't that . . . he's made a fortune, he has, and he takes his sleep like a signore. . . ."

"This is what happened," began Gesualdo suddenly. "You know Giovanni. . . ."

Just at this minute Agnese appeared like an apparition in the dark doorway. Her father broke off his story as if a harsh hand had been clapped over his mouth. The noises of the streets became like the sound of a torrent in his ears. The elevated trains plunged deafeningly into the growing dark. He heard the watermelon vendors lift raucous songs into the ceaseless hubbub. His old eyes puckered into pinpoints, and the fear that his daughter filled him with became a mumble on his lips and a heat in his cheeks.

"What are you sitting there for like a useless dog? Don't you know Giovanni has not got back from school? Go and fetch him. . . ."

The hot evening wore on to a hot midnight. The cressets before the three special household saints of Agnese burned steadily in an airless room, making, with the faint glow in the stove, will-o'-the-wisp shadows on the walls.

Giovanni had not yet come, and Agnese sat at the window still as an image looking out into the night. All the neighbors had been sent out on the vain search. They had come and reported and gone home, Agnese offering no encouragement for anyone to stay on. Gesualdo nodded and blinked in the rocking-chair even more quietly than Agnese. From the room inside they heard the hard, steady breathing of Michele fast asleep. Occasionally across the room coursed the red shadows of the nearby gas house as the flames from its huge chimneys roared explosively into the night, and only after that became clearly audible long glad voices of young men singing in chorus.

What went on in Agnese's mind no one could divine. She herself had gone out with the rest in the fruitless attempt to find Giovanni. She had stopped all the boys she knew as his friends and inquired of them simply, "Have you seen my son?" She had talked to all the policemen she met. She had gone into Crino's private bank and announced to the corpulent, smooth-skinned moneymaker, "Giovanni ran away from home, and I can't find him."

Crino stepped out from behind the brass cage that pretentiously screened him off from the rest of the world, but seemed to have come out only to remark, "Well, well, ran away. . . ."

"Try to find him," she said.

"I'll call up the police station. . . ."

And Agnese left him shaking his head with the usual bewilderment she always threw him in.

Talk had been warm all the night, and no one was careful to hide the amazement at Agnese's concern over Giovanni. There was hardly anyone there who was not informed of his origin, and all had seen him grow up more or less looked after, but certainly not loved. Not that there was any trace of sorrow either in her voice or in her eyes. The same determined handling of this situation marked her actions as of every other she had to meet. A child had to have a home, and if lost, was to be brought back. Had she not had a commanding position in the neighborhood Agnese's treatment of Giovanni would have been overlooked. The fear in which great numbers held her inspired a concomitant scrutiny of all her acts, and though she could move about with greater freedom than any other housewife, she subjected herself to more insistent, unkindly comment. In this situation she evoked no sympathy — only amazement.

"Who ever thought she loved *o' pretuccio*?"

"Oh, you'd worry over a cur. . . ."

Agnese looked out of the window, and to all eyes would have seemed to be counting the white shadows of the clothes hung against the unlighted night. Very few Italian mothers would have foregone the luxury of the complete outlet the incident afforded to the crowded, tumbled feelings in their routinized hearts. Her father turned his wrinkle-plowed face to her, and time and again shook his head and stealthily made the sign of the cross.

Agnese was aware of nothing. Her experience in the grotto, her fantastic appearance in the church, her management of her life since, had all required unremitting fortitude, an iron self-discipline, and she was not the one to relax now. It was evident to her that Giovanni was bound sooner or later to return. At the worst he might have met with some mishap. This she discounted, for she had gone through similar situations with other mothers and had assisted them in keeping up their courage while the police or a friend in good time returned their wayward son or daughter. Mishaps came soon to be reported.

Giovanni had obviously decided to bolt. There was too much of herself in him, she understood, for him to be fully in her control. But the sensitive, timid, affection-seeking components of his character she attributed to the strain that was his father's, and she despised it altogether, and made it her purpose to suppress, not to encourage it. This was the mainspring of her attitude toward his schooling and his insistence upon what she dubbed the soft things connected with it.

She almost shook her father out of the chair when she put her own in its place, and said in her determined staccato to the saints' images as much as to him, "He ought to have had a father. . . ."

Gesualdo was too astounded to say anything immediately. He managed to get up, however, and go to her and look steadily at her as he said:

"Well, whose fault was it?"

"A woman it was I married," she said with simple bitterness, and then quickly as if ashamed of herself, "Go to bed. I'm going myself."

– 5 –

The gas house flames flared up and enveloped Agnese as she turned the key in the door and went into the inner rooms. The old man feebly let down a folding cot under the image of San Biagio in the large kitchen, and prepared to go to sleep, shaking his head interminably, his eyes filling with tears. On the river a tug whistled in a thin, reedy treble, a treble that seemed to take up the diminishing clatter of the elevated train just passing out of hearing. Certainly the noises were clear enough in the hot night to drown out the sound of feet clambering up the one flight of wooden steps leading to the Dantone flat. But the knock on the door was too peremptory not to be heard.

Agnese had slipped a skirt over her nightgown and had already come to the door before Gesualdo could move out of bed.

"It's Luigi. Open. . . ."

The short, stocky form of Luigi framed itself against the doorway almost ludicrously, for Agnese had expected the thin, slight Giovanni, coweringly seeking admission.

"Whew, it's hot. Even at night." Luigi spoke in English, "Just brought down a lot of men from the job. We're putting them on the subway work. Just got in. Got something to eat?"

Gesualdo had meanwhile turned on the gas light, a single flame from a hanging central chandelier which sputtered and whistled yellow and blue by turns.

"Put it out," commanded Agnese. "I'll get him something without any light."

"Making money on this job," continued Luigi lustily, seating himself on Gesualdo's bed. "This is the third time we've transferred the men, big contracts each time. Damn the grafters, though. The rakeoff's too much to stand. They want me to be a dummy contractor this time. . . ."

Gesualdo was bewildered by both his children. This boy of twenty-six who had managed to put himself in control of so many Italian laborers that he had become an important factor in numerous large construction jobs fascinated him, much as he knew that it had been the quick resourcefulness of Agnese, acting upon suggestions of Crino, that had brought about the result. Luigi had measured up to it, however, and once he had plunged kept his head above water by his own skill. Children of his own loins Gesualdo knew them to be, but as unlike his resigned ways as the New World was unlike the Old.

While Agnese put out chunks of cheese and bread and a bottle of wine, black olives and peppers kept in oil, Luigi maintained an uninterrupted recital of how much he had made on the company store, how much on the men he supplied to the various enterprises, how much on the jobs he had contracted for.

"We're the ones that are building up this country, I'll tell you. These subways they're building now, what would they do without us?"

He drank his wine with noisy approval, stuffed whole pieces of bread and cheese at once into his mouth, and threw olives in after them.

"Oh, say, what do you know?" He stopped eating, and from the manner in which he sat upright, and then checked his words, Agnese realized that news of real importance to them all was in his mind. She had said nothing ever since Luigi's arrival, too taken aback by his coming so unexpectedly in the place of her son. She said nothing now, nor did she turn to listen as she busied herself with coffee on the stove.

"By the way, how's Giovanni?"

Agnese did not expect the question. Luigi rarely asked.

"Don't know. Ran away from home."

"Whew!" he whistled, and got up to walk the length of the room. "When? This is funny. Damn funny. When did this happen?"

Agnese had to tell him the whole story.

"Well, that's different!" and he sat himself down again, evidently much relieved, although shocked, too, by the thing Giovanni had done. "Don't know where he is? Did you look for him? Get the police? Why, we'll get the whole department. . . ."

They all looked at each other, and for once each one had a keen realization of how much they really cared for the boy who had come to them unwanted and who had been responsible for the complete change in their lives. Not a word of it escaped them, however, unless the movement of Gesualdo's lips over his gums might have been words.

"This is funny," finally said Luigi, "damn funny. Guess who I saw on the train, on the train coming here from way up Rochester?"

The silence took up the wail of a boat from the river and held it suspended on a high note for what might have seemed the applause of some invisible audience. The heat of the night had been redoubled by the fire Agnese had fanned in the stove, and the room was stifling. Both the men knew that Agnese's slight figure quivered as she turned to Luigi. Gesualdo was wiping his face with a huge red bandanna.

"You don't mean. . . ?" She asked simply.

"Yes, Padre Gelsomino, but not a priest this time."

"Well," interrupted Agnese without the slightest tremor in her voice, "what is it to us? So, he's come to America. . . ."

"But how could you tell it was him?" asked Gesualdo.

"Do I know myself in the mirror?"

IV. Giovanni

– 1 –

As he ran and ran, Giovanni carried a picture of Michele bleeding. He foresaw his mother's horror: a white face with the muscles taut; Michele's continued petty persecution only more righteously pursued; the relations between him and them rebuilt on a foundation even more strained; his abandonment of all hope to remain at school; no escape. There was no regret in his musings. He admitted that he had wanted for a long time to do some such thing.

He smiled. He would have a story for the boys he would be thrown with now, not the adoring crowd at school but the superior street gamins who looked down upon him. Naturally, he had no intention of saying too much, just a detail here and there. The rest would shape itself in the minds of his hearers and, later, his admirers. Without doubt, they would receive him in their councils, permit him to remain at night in the empty lots overlooking the river, filled with old discarded carts, a generation of tin cans rusted from the rains, marble slabs from the nearby stone-cutter's yard, iron hoops, boards that made capital material for improvised shacks.

One such shack had only recently been built in a secret corner of the lot behind a mass of slate and a derelict dump-cart standing on end with its side-poles sticking into the air like two gaunt arms. Its floor was laid with motley threadbare rugs salvaged from the junk dealer's stores in the backyard. Dubious pictures from the newspapers and gazettes made the walls a suggestive gallery. Several were photographs Giovanni had seen that disturbed him even more than Michele's eyes sweeping over his mother's figure. A dirty, cobweb-covered lamp hung from the ceiling. A heavy rug such as covered the floors barred the entrance, once the outdoor ramshackle door had been opened. A stove-pipe sticking high through the tin-nailed roof attested to a complete economy inside.

Giovanni knew the rules governing admission. He would have to make some contribution of substantial value, gleaned from nobody cared where.

Street cars rattled by, the elevated trains hurtled above his head. Push-carts innumerable and the noisy chaffering crowd absorbed him as he made his way down the avenue. He did have visions of the gang's accepting him eagerly. He kept walking nevertheless in exactly the opposite direction, with no intention of applying for immediate admission.

Just before dusk, after hitching on trolleys and trucks, he had reached the water front and busied himself watching the ferries to Staten Island load and unload. Crowds rushed down from the elevated structure, pell-melled into the ferry house as if driven by a wind from behind. He strolled over to the heavy wooden beams along the water's edge, sat down, and gazed out upon the traffic of the Bay. Something of the same feeling he had when he picked on the mandolin strings in the half-dark of his room quickened his eyes until they rested all at once on tugs puffing laboriously against the growing darkness, on the wooded cliffs with their houses peering over the tops now beginning to show pinheads of lights, on impulsive whitecaps breaking themselves against air, on a huge liner parading its lighted immensity in a frame of misting sky.

He had forgotten food and home, and the ache in his feet, the pain in his heart. The giant arms of the Bay, as they held the restless, noisy lands, held him too, lulled him into dreams with tricky changes and flashes of novelty.

Often had he sketched crude lighthouses on paper, or shown huge smoke-stacked steamers much too rectilinear and lopsided, crashing into shoals of angry monstrous rocks! Here it all was, magically multiplied, and given life and a voice that penetrated him. A spirit moved him to walk, as if he were a tight-rope performer, the whole length of the massive beams that marked the end of the paved streets and the beginning of the Bay.

Up went his hands to balance his swaying body, forward went a foot most carefully poised, to the left moved his body, and then to the right. How he wished that the whole school might see him now, the whole block, the gang in its shack on the empty lots! His was a perilous position — for below him he heard the roar of waves, above him nothing but darkness, all about him the sound of feet on the march. Even his mother, his father . . . the image of a white face with muscles taut, the memory of stinging knuckles across his face made him suddenly cold. He stopped his miraculous performance, and ran, ran fast across the crowded square, fleeing something, rushing somewhere!

– 2 –

As he was running across the cobbled pavements, unaware any longer of moving waters and tugs and the skies that held them in, conscious once more only of a bleeding face and the memories of persistent meannesses ever since his babyhood, he found himself beginning to whimper, tears blotting out the scene, the crowds about him huge Micheles jostling him, snapping their knuckles across his face. Another boy might have sat down and had it out in crying, in recourse to his mother's memory at least, comforting, sympathetic. Giovanni had only the habit of going off into a corner and nursing his hurt alone, brooding over it, failing to understand that it should happen at all. In his pain he remembered, too, his teachers at school, the club of which he was president, his drawings, the report cards that brought whatever was the trouble to a bitter head. The round of thoughts was the same again and again. He was sitting now on a park bench, a diminutive shadow lost in the dusk. Several street arabs had stopped to look him over, and at least one had spoken to him.

"Whacha doin' here?"

"Nothing."

"Ain't sellin' papers?"

"No."

"Ain't gonna shine shoes?"

"No."

"Whacha doin' here then?" Amazement, incredulity, and an obvious suggestion that in his eyes Giovanni was a fool.

"Nothing."

The boy was shuffling off sideways, casting an intermittent gaze back in puzzled unconvinced scrutiny.

"Well," was the last bolt, "don't let us catch you doin' none of them things if you wanna know what's good for you."

Giovanni returned the amazement of the boy, and forgot momentarily the hunger and the pain that were making him unhappy. It was several minutes later that four or five local newsboys and bootblacks came by, slapping their bare feet on the cement walk. Their movements were in evident concert, for one called out, "Not there. Here he is." They all stopped, and like a cavalcade of marauders collected in a knot and surveyed the scene. Before long they proceeded to take seats on the same bench with Giovanni, looking at him sidelong, or staring him boldly in his face. Giovanni merely marveled at them, and wondered how in several instances such voluminous pants could have been held up by one brace alone.

"Where you live?" one asked finally, and something in the manner made Giovanni feel afraid and uncomfortable.

The question was repeated by another boy with the added phrase, "You better tell us."

"Uptown," said Giovanni eyeing them each in turn.

"Whacha got in your pockets?"

The question surprised Giovanni but he recollected the same practice among the rowdy groups in his own section of the city. He realized instantly that he was in for a rough time with them.

"Come on. You'd better cough up."

"I haven't anything.

"Let's see."

And the group surrounded him. The pirates knew their game. While the rest of them formed an encircling wall to shield their operations against too easy observation, the leader began to make an immediate search of Giovanni's pockets. He was a boy with a mass of dirty, curling hair matted close about a preternaturally round head and, completing the design of black, a whole day's perspiration and dirt had spread over his features. His black eyes snapped as he thrust his efficient, long-practiced fingers into one pocket after another and threw to the next in command whatever objects he found: several pencils, a notebook, some cord tied up in knots of eight, a whistle.

"Got no money?" the desperado asked in great anger.

"No."

"You're lyin'. Cough up."

"Haven't any. . . ." He tried to sidle off.

"Hold your horses."

"Let me go. I haven't anything. . . ."

"Give the bastard the mitt. . . ," one of the others yelled.

Giovanni made an attempt to break through and run, but in a moment he was fighting the whole crowd as they kicked him and punched him amid jeers and curses. They left him bundled up on the ground as they ran in several directions. It occurred so rapidly that it was impossible for any of the passers-by to see what was happening. Giovanni raised himself to the bench again, feeling the bruises over his ribs and the sting of punches on his face, his whole body trembling like a dog panting heavily.

A man stopped. "What are you crying about, sonny?"

Giovanni looked up.

"What's the matter? Where do you live?"

"Uptown."

"What are you doing here?"

Giovanni's fear was even greater than when the young rowdies had begun to pummel him.

"Nothing," he said.

"Why don't you go home? What are you crying for? Haven't you your fare?"

Giovanni stared into the stranger's face. He saw it was kindly and interested, but hesitated nevertheless before saying, "No."

"Can you find your way home?"

Upon being assured that Giovanni could, the stranger put a quarter into the boy's hand, and directed him to the nearest elevated station. Giovanni made a dash for it. The night had transformed the city into a mass of lights that outlined vague rooftops and traced the elevated structures to their converging points in the density of buildings. Giovanni had halted at the foot of the stairs, and gazed blankly at it all, his mind on the scene that would ensue at home if he returned. It was a flash, the impulse that came to him as he saw an empty van plainly marked, "Harlem Express" pass by, rumbling over the cobbles. He jumped in, thinking that halfway up on the trip he would jump out and buy fruit and buns.

– 3 –

He woke up amidst the sounds of men and horses. He had fallen fast asleep and unnoticed by the driver had been allowed to remain in the van left for the night in an empty lot adjoining a series of stables close to the water front. His bones ached from the beating of the night before and the hard boards on which he had slept. There was nothing for him to do but jump out and run, take his bearings and make up his mind what plan to pursue. No thought of returning home entered his mind.

He was hungry, and he recalled that he still had the quarter. It was several blocks, he knew, to the nearest bakery. He was in the vicinity of his home but far enough away to walk boldly through the streets without fear of discovery. On his way, he stopped to buy fruit and recalled how simple a matter it was for the other boys to seize an apple or orange or banana and run before the standkeeper was aware of the theft, and he promised himself to try it, too, the next time. For this once he paid, and felt a righteous greatness in strutting up the street with a whole bunch of bananas under his arm, while he stuffed one into his mouth.

V. Further Adventures

– 1 –

Fear of policemen and truant officers kept Giovanni in the backyards and empty lots, and threw him in with perpetual truants or boys out of work. Two boys whom he had seen and known at school had suggested that they enter the cellar of one of the better houses in a district west of where he lived. Having done so, and found gloomy, clean expanses of cement and wooden doors marking dark lanes to cobwebbed windows in the rear, Mike Meany made a further suggestion. His stub nose gave his full-puffed, freckled cheeks the half-sinister expression of a cavern gnome, and he added to the general impression by talking in a hoarse, double-fluted whistle through apertures left by missing teeth.

"Let's break in one of them doors. I bet they got pewter and copper and lead. . . ."

There were three of them. The other boy was considerably older than Giovanni but thinner and smaller, with the sunken, long-drawn face of an emaciated child. So short-waisted was he that he seemed to be balancing his torso on his spindle legs and kept looking so steadily with little hazel eyes out of his thin face that he communicated his own fear that he really could not get very far no matter how hard he tried to walk. Pencil-thin as his whole body seemed, he nevertheless appeared to be carrying a burden, and his reactions were too slow for him ever to be a wanted companion. But then he was not wanted either at school or out of school, and it was much worse at school where he had so many more boys to contend with, so many to placate, so many to convince that he was their equal, that he could match their stunts, play their games, join in their fun. Mike Meany had dragged him out that morning, and by merely singling him out as a companion for the day flattered him immediately into truancy and later into actual physical prowess and daring. Giovanni had joined them on the chance remark of Mike.

"Better look out, kid. The school bull's in that block!"

"He'll get you, too."

"No he won't. I know where to go. . . ."

And so the three of them became associated in their common adventure of defying the authorities. Giovanni had misgivings about the continued wisdom of remaining away from home and school, and once or twice lagged behind the other boys in an endeavor to break away and carry out his repentant impulses.

"Say, whatdya wanna do, queer us?" shouted Meany.

– 2 –

And so they found themselves in the cellar. Giovanni's experience with cellars, even with the one in the tenement owned by his parents, was of piles of discarded furniture and rags, accumulations of hundreds of dwellers who had sloughed off the acquisitions that constant movings and removals made necessary. They were ill-smelling, humid boxes, sought out by the stray cats of the neighborhood. He had ventured in them, but always beat a hasty retreat, his romantic dreams extinguished by the dampness and the darkness.

Aside from the dimness, this cellar suggested spacious living, and his imagination glowed. He sensed that those who kept such a cellar lived in rooms which, measuring like by like, were as different from the rooms his family occupied as one cellar was from the other. Old day-pictures of a world altogether unlike his own to which he might go and find wonder and delight always lacking in his, swam back before his mind and swept on just as if he were standing in front of a huge aquarium and gazing at the colorful movement within.

What Meany had said they might do seemed to him now a wicked impishness, a desecration, and an affront. He turned to protest, to make a serious effort to prevent carrying out Meany's plan. But he held his breath as one does who knows that something dreadful but unpreventable is on the point of happening. He heard Meany giving forceful instructions in his fluted voice.

"Jump over, Sticks. Yeh, you can squeeze through. Won't have to break the door and make a noise. Jump in, go on, jump in. What you see?"

He had himself clambered up the door of the cellar, a foot on the lock, a hand on the top of the door, and peered into the pit of darkness within. He had presence of mind enough to turn his attention to Giovanni and say in a dramatic whisper,

"What you doing there like a peanut? Keep a look out so nobody comes. . . . Light a match, Sticks. Yeh, there's a trunk. Open it. . . ."

Giovanni had become too frightened to be able to voice the protest he felt. But it was not only protest he felt. He had become too involved to want to retreat. The fear itself had come to have a delight of its own for him. The chill that made him quiver, the hard pounding of his heart, the taut alert muscles, the sudden shock of the realization that he must defend himself, and his companions too, stimulated his imagination. He reconstructed whole scenes of Spanish maraudings in New World settlements, piratical assaults on defenseless towns, Indian massacres, besieged cities. . . . He stood transfixed, the blank darkness before him a kaleidoscopic movement, the quietness a mingling of desperate voices and cries of pain. Life had ebbed away from him, and all the books he had ever read became the reality of the moment. . . . He could see, hear nothing else.

And then he felt a huge hand on his shoulder, and another, bony, angry, forceful, across his face. . . . He shouted and ran . . . behind him the steps of Mike Meany and then . . . the shrill agonized cries of an animal being torn apart by another, a long-continued, undisguised, shriek of pain and fear and helplessness. . . .

"Poor 'Sticks!" he thought. "Gee, that man's killing him. . . . Meany," he shouted, "let's go back. . . ."

Meany had rushed past him and gave no indication of wanting to turn back. Finding it unavailing to call to the fleeing boy, Giovanni stood stock-still, the cries of Sticks ringing in his ears, coursing through his own body, filling all his muscles with pain. He wept. He remembered the bare round bones of Michele's knuckles and knew that the pain they caused was not so much physical as understanding too vividly how alone, how forsaken, how unloved he was, how laughed at, how unaccepted. And he saw the pathetic, unfed body of the boy they called Sticks, the boy who was the butt of the coarsest jokes and the meanest wit, the boy who was always left out of the games. He saw it held in the brutal hands of the janitor and shaken and kicked and tossed back and forth on the cellar floor. . . . Sticks who had been pleased to be invited on Meany's adventure, Sticks who was not afraid because he was being commanded by somebody too forceful to resist. . . . He must turn back and help him . . . he must take the chance of being himself as roughly beaten . . . maybe caught and given over to the police and taken home. . . . But the cries had stopped. He was now out on the street. He did not know which house it was. . . . He walked on. . . .

– 3 –

What was he to do now? To go to the Italian section in which he lived would mean a long walk. He had but a few cents left of the quarter of the night before. The suit he had worn to school had been clean, well-pressed. Now it clung to his body like a water-soaked garment, spotted with the stuff of the vans on which he had hitched. His adventures of a day and a night had revealed a world not too good, not too willing to accept. . . . Agnese was a controlling strain in him, however, and the more he thought, the more he was resolved not to return home.

But he must find a place to sleep, something to do to get food. He lived too near the sort of life that depends upon day-to-day labor not to have a keen sense of the importance of work. He was aware, too, that work could be had, that other boys not much larger and older than he had gone out to work, were earning money. He would do likewise.

But as he thought, the other side of the picture became clearer: the tatterdemalion crowds he was in the habit of seeing, their rough ways, their talk, their dirt, their constant trouble with policemen. After all, at home he did have food, he did have clean clothes, and it was a place. The box he kept under the bed full of drawings, a pencil-David after the picture in the history book, the heads of lions, the lighthouses and the ships bending to the waves; the mandolin that he had from Luigi with the strings that tinkled myriads of dancers out of the darkness and made the housetops into thick-leaved woods; the small cot in the dark room where he could be alone, and merely by willing arouse from regions millions of miles away a new set of playmates, a new group of schoolrooms, patient Miss Skinners, and clubs over which he presided brilliantly; the backyard where he would sit on the lean-to door to the cellar, and where alone he was able to think of his mother like other mothers, caressing, yielding, affectionate!

They filled his mind, slowed up his steps, made him restless and unhappy. If only the small mouse-like features of Michele with the patches of wrinkles right above his thick eyebrows did not cast their length across his dreams — the way he had often seen heads printed in advertisements over columns and columns of type.

And he was afraid to go home. Actual physical fear of Agnese become silently savage, her eyes flashing steadily, her movements as precise as a machine, not only strengthened in him the strain which was Agnese and which would not be compelled, but aroused the timidity which was Padre Gelsomino's and which would not allow him to face the reality. But, boylike, he was aware of all the street movements, and as he thought, his eyes kept up a ceaseless surveillance of all the passing wagons. In a moment he had hopped into one and was fast proceeding in the direction of his home.

He was down at the waterfront in a short time. The city was constructing a pier at the dock. Piles of lumber, huge granite blocks, stacks of bricks formed natural sheltering places for the boys' clothes. They were there in hordes, chasing each other over the glass-strewn ground, in between discarded cartwheels, refuse heaps, jumping into the water like rats, throwing the timid in, ducking others, shouting — anything to be moving, making noise! Tugs pulled with confident strength as they pulled tows of barges. In the near distance green-banked islands held aloft a huddle of red brick buildings. A white slow steamer moved by silently. In the far distance there was a silver-like shadow of sails, or the low-hanging trail of black smoke from a barely perceptible stack.

As usual Giovanni's look was more than a survey of the scene. It was a singing in his heart, the whirring of many pigeons, each a thought, or a picture that never showed the full-face canvas but only a side or a tilted angle view. The same softness and loss of strength came upon him as when he traced a laborious lighthouse in his notebook, or a tree meeting the full wind and yielding. His pictures were all out of books just as his strummed notes on the mandolin were all out of his head, and in both instances a denial of the present, an overthrow of the immediate, a construction of a delight that was, and could not be.

The cries of the boys, the flash of their naked bodies in the sun, the river and the boats and the touch of green landscape with its feather of smoke transported him from

what was nearest him, and he sailed away on a wave of color as he listened to the singing that was within. Along with the sensation of living in a world not the one around him, came an actual physical restlessness, the same feeling that had made him behave as if he were a tight-rope walker stepping high above roaring waters. What could he do?

His answer came quickly enough. He was surrounded by a group of boys, boys of the same school from the same block.

"Hey, there, where you been?"

"Your mother's after you!"

"You'll get the works!"

"Whatcha been doin'?" Giovanni realized that he had become an object of extreme interest if not of admiration.

"Hey, Peppe, Peppe. . . ."

All the boys took up the shout, and to Giovanni it was plain that they were calling Peppe Totillo, their leader, and his own intermittent friend. That, of course, meant surrender to his family, and his mind was made up not to be taken home. He was his mother's son and though in her presence he would have behaved as if afraid of her, far away he could rise to his full stature, and defy her with satisfied self-sufficiency and assertiveness.

Peppe Totillo towered above all the boys and was further distinguished from them by not showing any traces of being Italian. Fair hair and still blue eyes might have put him with the Irish lads of the neighborhood. His father had built up a large enough grocery business to qualify as a leading figure among the new immigrants, and with Dantone and one or two others formed the elite of the settlement. Totillo the younger took this standing with some seriousness, never questioned it, and moved among his fellows with an air of pride and authority which, coupled with his almost man-grown stature, commanded obedience and respect. Peppe in his turn had always admired Giovanni. Giovanni easily led the boys of the neighborhood at school where Peppe never shone but where more than anywhere else he wanted to shine. He had often been compelled to listen to Giovanni's praises as a scholar sounded by a father who was as proud of him as Michele could not have been said to be proud of the smaller boy. They had walked home frequently, and Peppe had borrowed the books that Giovanni had drawn from the library, had attempted to draw pictures as ambitious, had joined the literary club, had even been elected its president.

He walked up to Giovanni now. The whole of his fifteen years were written on his serious face as he approached.

"Well, *Giovannino bello,*" he drawled out in a mocking sing-song. "The cops and everybody else is after you. Where the hell you been?"

Anyone who employed a manner of authority could awe Giovanni at the beginning of any encounter, and Giovanni felt now that he would have to surrender to Peppe and be taken home. He merely smiled rather foolishly at the bigger boy and said nothing. And he said nothing when Peppe began a dire recital of all the efforts that were being made to locate him, of the consequences of his runaway, of his mother's anger at him.

"Oh, it's all right," he finally exclaimed. "I been home and just came out for a swim."

They believed him quite easily and in a short time he had his clothes off and was splashing around in the water. He managed to elude the crowd before nightfall and find his way to the shack.

– 4 –

Huts, mountain recesses, caves in the woods underground passages in crowded cities have from time immemorial been the escaping places of the hunted, or the haunts of the unsocial, even the home of freemen. The rowdy boys of Giovanni's district who could not learn at school, who found no jobs out of it, who had no place in their congested homes betook themselves to the empty lots and in the manner of the lawless everywhere built themselves not only a shack but a society with its own laws and regulations. The police sought them out, and history records the arrest of many of them and their incarceration in fabulous prisons to the north and west where the strap was used freely and dark pens held the more rebellious on a thin diet of bread and water. When a store was robbed in the neighborhood, or a peddler relieved not only of all his pushcart carried but all that he had had in his pockets, the first place the officers of the law searched was the empty lots.

Reports of the mighty exploits of these gangs trickled down to the younger boys always on the lookout for older ones to admire. Highly colored was the talk about them, and the news of a policeman assaulted by the gang or even murdered was not something to be horrified at but to exclaim at in admiration, to elaborate into a vivid story of brigandage and piracy. The adherents of these lawless gangs, as they walked down the street, distinguished by the insolence of their swagger, the peculiar cut of their hair, the slant of their caps, threw not only fear into the hearts of the smaller lads but also awakened in them dreams of courageous deeds, manly undertakings, battles with the strong. Many longed to join, and often translated their longing into hanging on the outskirts of the gang movements, attaching themselves to one or another of the members, fetching and carrying for them with utter fidelity.

Giovanni looked upon these older boys with their air of infinite, unabashed superiority as upon demigods. He had longed to be allowed to sit with them in dark corners. He admired their quick retorts to men who tried to drive them away. It was all so unlike the manner in which he was made to obey his mother and a father whom he did not love.

With the coming of night, the lot took on the appearance of a devastated region. One picked one's way cautiously amid the debris of outcast stone slabs, lumber, parts of wagons and harness. The noise of the river gave it a voice, but otherwise the silence was an all-encompassing cloak with the darkness.

On a cold night there was the light of a fire where a group of homeless men were encamped. Occasionally from one of the newly built shacks came the glow of a stove. But if the police were known to be on the search the night settled undisturbed on a forsaken land, and the murmur of the water mingling with the random wail of a tug only accentuated what was forbidding, melancholy, and doleful in the total obscurity. Lit up by the intermittent flare from the stack of the gas house, it revealed misshapen forms of unrecognizable articles, and to small boys frequently prowling about, of a mysterious life far more inspiring than the hobgoblin tales told their more fortunate brothers sent to bed early between white sheets.

Late in June the heat keeps the whole city out of doors, and on the night Giovanni had decided to throw in his fortunes with the shack-gang many a group sauntered even in the empty places facing the water. Giovanni had already bought himself a pizza with the few pennies he had left — a dough-cake flattened out and spread with anchovies, slices of tomato, and cheese, all seasoned spicily and baked on hot ashes. He felt terribly alone and sick at heart as he found his way to the lot. He avoided any contact with passers-by and walked more rapidly if any older person even cast a glance at him. Too many children were allowed out for him to become the object either of suspicion or sympathy, but he understood that some search for him must be on the way especially if one of the boys had seen his mother.

When he had literally kicked his way among broken glass and stones and cans, and had come to the shack, he found it entirely empty. He had expected a complete assembling of the lawless clans, his boyish imagination unable to conceive of their being other things for them to do. But undismayed he entered the shack and groped in the darkness for a place to sit or lie. The darkness and the lack of ventilation soon joined forces with his excitement, and he fell fast asleep. He knew it was still the dark of night when he heard voices outside.

– 5 –

"I tell you she won't come across. . . . You ain't got the goods on her."

"We'll get the goods." This voice was a quick, excited treble.

"Aw, how you goin' do it?"

"Yeh, how?"

There must have been three or four talking. Giovanni stood up slowly, and moved to the exit for he could see the fitful light of cigarettes.

"Listen here," spoke the one with the treble voice. Giovanni recognized him as the Kid, a foreshortened thin boy not upwards of eighteen whose face was always preternaturally screwed up to one side in a wan, unworldly scowl, made the more sinister by a pair of black eyes that stared quite innocuously from heavy lashes.

"Listen here. She's got a room on the ground floor on the corner."

Giovanni understood little or nothing of all this.

"She keeps her shade down all the time, see, and the men go into the cellar from the back door and she lets them in that way and the cops don't know nothing and nobody else neither. There ain't no use us trying to get in 'cause she won't let you and that's that, see."

"That's what I say. How you goin' get the goods on her?" The stocky fellow who said these words Giovanni recognized as the toughest one of the crowd with a reputation for being afraid of no one and for having already served time. He made a practice of going to a fruit stand and looking over the stock and supplying himself quite nonchalantly with whatever he fancied; he remarked to the dealer, "See you later," and passed on. Any attempt to check him resulted in a night raid that was complete in its results.

"See here, there's money in this. She'll pay by the week or we'll squeal and she'll move fast enough."

"Yeh, but how, but how?"

"Let's get one of the kids she don't know to go in, see, and then he'll leave our trade-mark, see, on a piece of paper, see!"

"She'll cough up if we squeal!"

"You bet, Stocks!" A third voice had joined in the conversation. Him, too, Giovanni knew. A slinking, stoop-shouldered lad, taller than either of the others, who always carried his hands in his pockets with his elbows close to his body, and had such hollow cheeks as to make his triangular face look like a skull. He was known to be in on everything the gang did, without ever once assuming the leadership or even taking a share in the culminating act of any enterprise. But he invariably shared in the gains, and made a case out for himself without raising his voice or boasting of his deeds. "You bet! But where's the kid?"

"Any kid'll want to get his first shot!"

"Yeh! Get the kid, I says!"

Giovanni felt his heart thump against his body and the whole shack shake along with it. What had been eagerness to join the gang became a chilling fear that he would not be able to escape it. The conversation had been a conundrum to him all along, but the undercurrent of meanness he detected quite unmistakably, and it unsettled all his notions.

Though there was no thought of going back home, he had already resolved that he must get away. The gas house shot up its noisy yellow flare, and silhouetted the three gangsters against a background that was a line of distant rooftops and a foreground of broken, misshapen shadows. For the fleeting second he saw their faces he witnessed no dread spectacle of demonic horror but quiet, solemn countenances bent upon serious business. He drew up close to the rug that hung across the door, hoping to slink out as they entered. But the Kid, who was the first to move the rug, felt his body, and jumped back. Giovanni watched him retreat with his arms extended to prevent the others from moving forward.

"What the hell!" he exclaimed.

Skully, of the triangular face, made a slinking movement away from the scene, but Giovanni saw Stocks close up on the Kid and ask in a quick whisper, "What's the matter?"

Without another word he had pushed the Kid and himself into the shack and Giovanni against the farther wall. Matches were struck at once, and then the laughter that followed was so genuine that even Giovanni felt somewhat reassured. Skully in the meantime had come in at just the point to join in the laughter quite naturally.

"I'll be a bastard!" shouted the Kid. "Why, the whole world's looking for you. The whole police department and the fire department and the street-cleaning department . . . the block's gone dippy looking for you — where the hell you been?"

Skully had lighted the dirty lamp, and as it swung its smoky flame slowly back and forth Giovanni's eyes followed, his mind far away, the shadows of the three men distorted against the newspapered boards, the only real images in it.

"You'd better git home!" The Kid laughed. "Don't keep the old folks up no more."

"Hell!" said Stocks. "We'll take him home ourselves and claim the reward."

"What reward?" inquired Skully eagerly.

"Aw, the old lady's got the cash and she'll fork up if we gets the kid back. . . ."

"Hell she will!" said Skully simply and definitely.

Giovanni had become alert, his eyes watching the movements of the trio, and his mind set on determining the best moment for a breakaway.

"Say," chimed in the Kid, "I bet she will all right, all right."

"Ain't gonna take no kid back home," injected Skully. "Think I'm gonna be taken for a kidnapper — that's what they'll do, I tell you."

"And I'm not going home," shouted Giovanni as he made a dash for the door. But the heavy rug slowed him up sufficiently to allow Stocks to jerk him back with nonchalant ease and throw him on the floor.

"Where you goin'?" he laughed.

"Let me go. I don't want to stay here. . . ."

Skully had meanwhile whispered something into the Kid's ear.

"Gee! Hell!" he exclaimed, and got up to move several steps.

"What d'you say?" Skully bent forward urgingly.

"Naw. Nix on that. Aw, hell, the kid's too young anyhow! "

Stocks had understood and come forward to put his head close to theirs.

"Sure, Kid, that's the tip. . . ."

"Naw. . . ."

The argument became heated, fast, monosyllabic — a matter more of gleaming eyes and paling faces.

"Hell, they got all kinds of dough," retorted the Kid.

"Well?"

"Put us in jail in a minute. He supports the club! Fat chance getting out!"

"Nothing to it," said Stocks with absolute finality. "Come here, kid! Don't wanna go home?" he asked quizzically.

"You do what we tells you, see, or you'll go home and worse. Understand?"

"None of that, Stocks, hell, d'you wanna go up the river?" the Kid almost wept as he pleaded.

Stocks ignored him as he proceeded to pull Giovanni near him with a ferocious hold on his arm. "Get me?" he asked, and laughed, as he noticed how the boy winced from the pain of the clutching fingers, straining quietly to get away all the time.

"Anyhow," he continued in a somewhat reassuring tone of great secrecy. "Hell, the bitch'll give you a hell of a good time. Ever. . . ?

Giovanni understood only across a roaring of voices, a deafening shout in his ears, a clatter of innumerable memories of sly guffaws, coarse asides, and his eyes blurred in a hot mist that left his cheeks and lips parched. He wanted to run, run fast, get to a quiet spot.

He made a movement to pull away but Stocks pressed his fingers closer around his thin arm, and Giovanni looked fascinated at the cruelly laughing eyes that mocked him as he made his timid struggles to wriggle out.

"Oh, hell, Stocks, drop it."

"Since when y'been sayin' y'prayers, Kid?" Stocks answered without looking up, and clutched Giovanni the harder. "Youse all gimme a pain. Why, what the hell's in it? We throws the kid in the winder, and he comes out and tells us what he got for his money and what the hell y'fraid of?"

With this, he relinquished his hold on Giovanni, drew him between his knees, and began in the gentlest words, as if he were caressing him in the sweetest affection, to tell Giovanni what he wanted him to do. Giovanni gazed at him without seeming to understand, held by the account of doings he had heard about only in veiled hints, or even more difficult expressions of frank obscenity. It occurred to Stocks that his captive was ignorant of what he had been so carefully explaining, and he burst into prolonged laughter. The Kid and Skully joined him once they knew what it was all about. It was so genuine and so long continued that even Giovanni, frightened as he was, gazing from one to the other, twisted his agonized mouth into smiles of amusement.

"Oh, chuck it, Kid, we'll be doing the kid a favor! Hell, let's go. Time she's closin' up shop. Easy t'get the goods on her. . . ."

He seized Giovanni's fingers and dragged him mercilessly out of the shack, out into the desolate darkness of the lot. Here Giovanni made a desperate effort to break away.

"Say, say, there, kiddo!" drawled Stocks as he pulled him close to him and brought his eyes to within an inch of Giovanni's. "'Tain't nothin' to be scared about. Everybody does it. Y'ain't committin' no crime. But you're goin' t'go, see, and if y'don't, well y'll get somethin' y'ain't never seen yet and y'll git it on the bean, too, and that'll keep y' awhile."

There were just two blocks to the corner of the operations contemplated by the gang. It was after midnight and save for the open saloons and the cafés with their knots of drinkers and card players the streets were deserted. They came to a corner house with the walls flaunting a painted advertisement of the drug store occupying its ground floor, a rough Aetna belching smoke . . . . A green dilapidated shed made a rude vestibule to the entrance. To the right was a low window with the shades drawn and so dimly lighted that only close observation revealed it.

"Listen, kid," said Stocks. "No squealin', no yellin.' Y' got the money I gives you. You jump in soon's I open the window, see, and asks what I told you. . . ."

The Kid in the meantime had jumped to the window sill and with a deft movement of the hand had cut a piece of glass from the upper pane right above a catch. Giovanni watched, fascinated. The lower window went up before he knew it, and he felt himself seized by Stocks' rough hands and soon found himself in a large, almost barren room. He had barely time to note this fact when he heard the cries of men fighting and blows exchanged.

"Give it to him, Stocks. . . ." He knew it was Skully's voice.

And the next thing Giovanni was aware of was a half-naked woman screaming as she rushed from an inner room, a man pulling frantically at the door as he was trying to get out, the face of a huge big-jawed thug who jumped in from the window. . . .

"What the hell? . . . ," was all he heard. He realized he had been struck a severe blow across the head, and kicked as he fell on the floor. . . .

VI. Gelsomino Returns

– 1 –

Disgrace was not a sentiment for Agnese to feel, and yet something akin to it developed into the sullenness with which she faced the visitors who came inquiring after Giovanni's welfare day after day. He lay moaning and tossing on his bed, moved now close to the window overlooking the street. There was not an acquaintance nor any man for whom she and her husband had obtained a position who did not regard it his duty to call. What one has given, one can refuse to give again or cause to be taken away. And so they filed into the large room in which Giovanni lay and, if Agnese would not talk, they talked. The women relieved her of every little task. They straightened out the sheet, they brought in the water, they fanned the sick boy. For each attention he had a nurse, for each nurse there was a helper. From each newcomer, too, there was a chicken to be boiled, or a bag of fruit, or a bit of dainty — fresh *ricotta,* a junket, a stew. The Dantones wanted for nothing during Giovanni's prostration.

For several nights after the policeman on the beat had brought Giovanni back, they sat silent and motionless. Agnese said nothing. Luigi came in repeatedly, attempted words of consolation only to be rebuffed by an even more sullen silence. Just what had happened to the child that he should have been black and blue all over his body, his lips constantly trembling without the ability to form a word, his eyes rolling uncontrolled or staring vacantly into space as if alighting on a fascinating horror? Agnese asked herself this over and over again, but of no one else. Giovanni himself was unable to enlighten one, the policeman she would not inquire of. She realized that he had recognized the boy and to save her the shame and the agony of the police station ordeal had brought him home. That was all she had learned. If Michele had offered to inquire she would have refused to listen. Of Luigi she asked nothing although she had a suspicion that he had investigated and learned the truth of the terrible episode. As they laid the boy on his bed the first night, all she did was to look at him, pain in her eyes, while she kept biting and biting the side of her hand. Not one word or cry escaped her. The doctor had come.

"What you think, Doctor?" were her first words.

The doctor understood her better than she knew.

"More shock than hurt, but bad shock. You'll be good to him, won't you?"

Doctor Grace had enough presence of mind to pat Michele on the back as he said this, and pretend that he had been asking his question of her father who stood sadly by, blinking and blinking, not daring to cry for fear of provoking Agnese into a sharp statement. All the while he was aware of a look of pain in Agnese's eyes that he had never believed possible.

"He needs lots of love," he continued. "Have his hands stroked, gentle words, you know . . . the poor kid," he added as Giovanni moaned and moaned.

Luigi had come in.

"Just heard the news in the café!" he cried, looking around for the boy. Tears stood in his eyes, his lips moved, and he would have wept as he knelt down by the side of the bed had not Gesualdo seized him by one shoulder and shaken him. But he kept saying: "You damn poor kid, you damn poor kid!"

"Get out of the room, all of you," suddenly Agnese said. "I'll take care of him. . . ."

Only Luigi protested. But she took him by the elbows and with gentle, steady pressure guided him out, relenting only sufficiently to say, "Bring me in a basin of cold water, very cold."

She was aware of people having come into the kitchen as she quietly and with sure tenderness undressed her son. She was aware, too, of his hurt, sick eyes following her painfully. She said nothing. With the water she bathed him without uttering a syllable or the slightest sigh. In the silence every street cry achieved the poetry of desolation. The clatter and thudding of the street cars reverberated as if endlessly megaphoning the inarticulate muttering of numberless hordes. The cressets on the wall blinked and with each shadow they disturbed, rose to a point as if renewed in vigor.

Occasionally one of the visitors tiptoed to the door and looked in with upturned eyes, eager to be of help. Agnese sat down by the bed and, holding Giovanni's cold hand, watched him slowly fall asleep. He could not have heard her murmur as she bent low over him, "Gelsomino, Gelsomino!" All night she remained in the same place, applying cold bandages, holding Giovanni's hand, giving him the medicine prescribed. The men had fallen asleep in their chairs, and only Concetta, the woman upstairs who worked for her occasionally, had stayed behind and had not fallen asleep.

– 2 –

For over a week now Giovanni had not come out of his coma. The doctor came every day, stroked his head, pinched his arm or cheek, smiled encouragingly at Agnese, and left. She asked nothing and he said nothing. Gesualdo had not been allowed to remain in the room, Michele never ventured in, and Luigi was too busy with his work to come for more than a few minutes in the evening. The faithful Concetta saw to all the meals besides supervising the management of her own household of four children and husband. But though they saw little of her, they had never fared so well since their arrival from Italy. The good things that were brought to Agnese sooner or later found their way upstairs, hidden under a voluminous apron, and carried with the greatest of haste. The neighbors came filing in, stayed an hour, a half-hour, a few minutes, shook their heads sententiously and left.

Michele's wound had healed, the patch had been removed, and his scar gave his mouse-like, timid features a kind of piquancy that moved even Agnese to a low laugh.

"Well, at last you look like a bad, bad brigand!"

Michele was so pleased with the seeming break in the tension that had filled the house with unremitting sullenness for so long that he ventured upon playful affection, a slight groping gesture for Agnese's hand. She tolerated it for a second and then remarked, "Don't be a loon."

The silence was resumed. They sat in the dark kitchen, Gesualdo already asleep in his let-down bed. Luigi had come and gone. Michele had finally so tired of the protracted quiet that he had managed to stammer, "The neighbors have been . . . nice . . . to . . . come in. . . ."

"Nice! Nice! I'll tell them all to go the devil," she cried. As usual, Michele looked up silently.

"Ah, how they lick your hands. And they never fail to ask is there work do you think on the track? Am I their keeper, I ask?"

"Well, you see. . . ."

"No, I don't see. Inquiring into my life, daring to say nothing above a whisper, sorry for the boy when in their hearts they think I wish him dead. *I* wish him dead! "

"Why, Agnese, you. . . ."

"You too, poltroon, you too. Yes, we've made our pile, you and I. . . . And now you think I wish him dead. . . ."

Michele held the seat of his chair with one hand, as he rose flushing in protest, his new scar a vivid red, incapable of controlling his stammer long enough to frame a word. . . .

"Say something, say something, tell your lie. . . ."

It was evident to Michele that her mood would not bear the added weight of the slightest contradiction or denial. He shrugged his shoulders, smiled helplessly, sat down and buried his head in his hands.

"Sit up," she cried, "sit up. Do you suppose I blame you? Why shouldn't you wish him dead? Why shouldn't I?"

"Oh, quiet, quiet, Agnese. Do you want him to hear?" moaned Michele.

"Hear? Doesn't he know? Doesn't he know? Why did he run away? Tell me, why did he run away?"

The kitchen windows lighted up with the red roar of the gashouse stacks. They were both too used to it to note the somber silhouettes, made grotesque in their momentary display, of huge dismembered bodies hanging motionless on numerous lines.

"He knows you hate him. He knows I have not loved him. He knows, he knows. The neighbors know, too. We have made our pile and they respect us, they fear us. But they know. . . ."

"We've done . . . we've done what we could!"

Her father rose in bed and, caught up in the quick flare of the gas house flames, resembled the embodiment of a grotesquely sinister purpose suppressed and risen to claim fulfillment.

"Why so much talk tonight, you who never talk, you have led us all into this pass? Are you finally ashamed of yourself? Is your heart aching now? You have done with us what you wanted. What do you torment us all for? Go and take care of your child and then pray, pray for us all, miserable sinners that we are . . . pray. . . ."

With his scar twisted by his wrinkles, his mouse-mouth open, Michele stared at the old man in wonder while Agnese rose to her feet but for once undecided, and if not frightened, at least stirred visibly by the unexpected outbreak.

"Yes . . . pray. . . ," continued Gesualdo, the tears glistening in his eyes. "I have been quiet too long . . . I have let you rule. . . ."

"*Tâ, Tâ!* Sh . . . sh . . . no more of this, no more of this. . . ," suddenly whispered Agnese, and stooping to him held him in her arms strongly, savagely.

"No more! You kill me . . . no more. . . ."

She put her cheeks to his, and sang softly. "No more . . . no more . . . sleep. . . ."

The solemn cressets wagged, and the smothered glow in the stove was a point of concentration for all their beams. The motionless curtains across the windows gathered up the shadows from the hot, dark night, and washed them a pale gray. The oil-cloth on the table was a broad spectral sheen darkened here and there by the uncertain reflections of the saints' images hanging on the wall. From immeasurable distances came the quickly lifted and then the slowly diminishing plaint of a tugboat cutting the dark.

Gesualdo stroked Agnese's heavy hair as he must often have done when she was a child, as he had never done since the year that they had left Italy with their burden, the burden that had sealed their lips to affection, had given purpose to their new life in America, and had changed the habits they had acquired from generations of forbears.

– 3 –

She left him and Michele as suddenly as she had risen from her chair and went into the outer room where Giovanni lay asleep. The long, black lashes were motionless lines on his pale skin, the thin lips a red marking. As Agnese stood over him, she was afraid that he might open either his eyes or his mouth, that he would speak either without or with words, and continue from where her father left off. But just as he had lain for over a week, twitching now one set of muscles and now another, giving no indication that he understood what he saw or could tell what he might have divined, he remained without movement, the horror of his pallor a mute recital of an agony that could never be voiced. Slowly she ran her hand over his forehead, combed back the fine black hair.

"Poor unwanted lad! Poor unwanted lad!"

She spoke as if only with the unheard rhythm of her pulse, as if her thoughts had found their way into her bloodstream and had been echoed in its beats, and so she was amazed when his lashes quivered with an impulse to uncover his eyes. She put a hand over her mouth quickly, in fright. Had he heard? What she had said in his presence, what she had said to Michele?

Directly opposite the child on the wall stood on a wooden shelf a clay image of the Madonna, in a red garment, the infant Christ sitting pale and smiling in the crook of her arm. At her feet on the same shelf was a small green shallow glass filled with water, a half inch of oil floating on the surface. In it moved slowly and around and around a tiny wick pulled through a cork. The cheerless yellow light glided up and down the clay figure with each slow movement of the flame, and as it reached the head of the Madonna a smile spread over the face of the patient Virgin, a smile more enigmatic than revealing, to be interpreted as the observer felt, a caress of affection and understanding, or a gentle but persistent reproof.

For the first time in years, Agnese became nervously conscious of the image, the smile, its meaning. She had placed the various saints and figures about her home just as she had continued feeding her family the meals they had been accustomed to in Italy. She would never have questioned its propriety. She could not have doubted the unimpugned wisdom of a practice hallowed not only by time but suggestive of quiet and peace, the soft aisles of the church, the beneficent guidance of a love from whose hand we sometimes flee unwittingly and only for a while.

Whether it was the opening of a door, or a wind that had momentarily risen, the wick burned with unwonted fullness, the light rose rapidly over the clay figure, the Madonna's stiff features were transformed into a benignant softness, an appealing smile spread over them, she seemed to part her lips, and a hundred bells from a hundred steeples joined in a soft clash as if Her own gentle hands had pulled the ropes to summon all Her wayward ones to prayer.

Agnese walked as if following a far voice, walked steadily and unrebelling, reached the foot of Giovanni's bed, and fell reverently to her knees, burying her head in the sheets, clasping her hands above it with fingers interlocked in a visible torment of pain.

"Oh, sweet sister, oh, sweet sister," she cried very softly, "now, after a long, long time, sweet sister, I ask you to pray for me. I have been strong-willed. I have offended. I have led one of the consecrated into sin. I have made him suffer. I have denied him and Christ and You. . . . Oh, sweet sister, mother of God. . . ."

Her suppressed sobs shook the bed. She was not aware that Giovanni had opened his eyes, and had looked at her and fallen asleep again.

"I have done what I could, sweet sister. Pray for me. Tell our dear God. . . ."

The light of the cresset seemed to have gone out. There was a darkness all about, a darkness that became heavy and oppressive. She felt it coming down on her shoulders. It became a living thing that was placed deliberately upon her. She rose and faced the tall, thin figure of Padre Gelsomino.

Not a tremor did she show, only a throttled horror. One hand she placed over her forehead, forcing back the hair, the other between her teeth as if to bite it. Otherwise she stood motionless, a stricken, a beaten thing.

If Padre Gelsomino had looked ascetic in his cassock and beretta, he appeared in ordinary civilian garb thirteen years later as if he had emerged from the lonely, starved life of the cenobite. His black eyes shot immediate rays of light through Agnese. She noted that they had no sparkle; the light was steady, penetrating. His smooth olive skin had become like a crumpled parchment, a parchment that told now a different story, the story of a timid soul who had fought with demons. A palimpsest, Agnese would have called it, had she known, a Catullan manuscript scrawled over by a St. Chrysostom. The lights of the cressets touched his high cheek bones and long thin nose and suggested that a bungling artist had attempted to change a masterpiece of frank, open portraiture into an over-dramatic chiaroscuro. He had made no attempt to grow a mustache, with the consequence that Agnese could not get a clear picture of Gelsomino as he was now without his clerical costume, since the loose hanging coat and baggy trousers lost their identity in her mind. The habit of silence that was hers constricted her whole being, and she could only gaze with unyielding stiffness upon the unexpected figure, forcing back her hair, biting the side of her hand.

"Agnese, forgive me. . . ."

Whatever had been rich, soft, caressing in his voice had become even softer, richer, more caressing, but lacking vitality and force. It was the voice of one who has cried out futilely in the night into a silence that not even an echo has broken.

Agnese ceased biting her hand, made suddenly the sign of the cross.

"What are you doing here?"

"For thirteen years have I fought against it. . . ."

"What do you want?"

"I came to see you. . . ."

"Go away . . . what do you want?"

"Agnese. . . ."

"I don't know you. Go away. . . ."

"For thirteen years. . . ."

"I have forgotten you. What do you want of me? Go away . . . go away. . . ."

Agnese spoke in a whisper.

"But I have not forgotten you. You know what has happened. No other thought, no other woman. . . ."

It might have been the content, it might have been the pain, it might have been the tearing away of the flesh that enclosed his feelings — something there was in the speech that aroused her to anger. She paled perceptibly, but her outstretched hand and finger pointing to Giovanni was a vehement gesture.

"There is a sick child in this room. Do not talk again. I want you to leave. Our lives have parted. . . ."

"Only to the eyes of the world. . . ."

". . . and cannot come together again. Go back to Italy, to South America, to wherever you have been, to Canada . . . I don't know . . . go away. . . ."

"Agnese, Agnese," cried Gelsomino sharply, seizing the hand away from the bed and holding down her arm close to her body. "Agnese, I swore never to see you again, nor any other woman, as I saw no other before you. I prayed in my heart for thirteen years, prayed even as I worked in the mines, on the railway tracks in the burning sun. I set upon myself a severe penance . . . I have suffered. I want nothing of you. . . ."

"Go away then . . . go away. . . ."

She made no struggle to withdraw her hand, to move away from him, to evade his gaze that was becoming steadier and steadier, a shaft of light from a burning lamp sheathed in charred flesh, that burned her as it had burned him. . . .

"I came to look upon the child of my loins, the symbol of our torment, my torment, my torture. . . ."

Tears would have filled the eyes of another woman. To Agnese the words of Gelsomino, the visible sweat of a body in agony, signaled all the forces of restraint she had developed, bugled to the suppressed motives that had animated her appearance in the church, her departure to America. The slight tendency she had shown to weaken, to feel that she had sustained the full shock of an outrageous battle long enough, vanished with suddenness the moment she was aware of it. Her whole body stiffened, a mockery played in the surface wrinkles about her eyes, disdain trembled in her lips, and her voice gradually deepened as her composure became surer. With renewed self-confidence, she succeeded in releasing her hand so easily that one could never have realized that the fingers had actually swelled from the savage hold Gelsomino had on them.

She looked away from him, and though she saw the benignant image of the Madonna flushing with the ebb and flow of flame in the cresset, she gave no indication that the soft tide of sorrow and pain, and possibly remorse, that had swept her body to her knees had ever risen to a full swell. Not only did she see the image and understand what it had meant but a few moments before, but she gazed at it with emotionless eyes, either insensitive to the call of her all-encompassing kindness, or else defiantly indifferent even to her call for at least routine reverence.

"You are a cruel woman," Gelsomino almost shrieked, sensing the change in her feelings.

"You have no right to talk. You have been a cruel man. . . ."

"I was a priest. . . ."

"I was a child. . . ."

"You were the incarnated witchery of lust. . . ."

"Enough . . . our ways have parted. . . ."

"And, I repeat, only to the eyes of the world."

Neither was aware, so intense had become their feelings, that Giovanni's eyes had opened, that he had raised his head, had seen, had heard what had gone on.

An elevated train shattered the gathered silence of the midnight. A voice, raised in the melancholy-humorous sing-song of a Neapolitan popular ballad, emerged out of the noise of the rushing cars and hung poised in the silent skies. Giovanni's breathing made a low, sad accompaniment to it all, much quieter but dominant, persisting, clarifying.

"You will not listen to me! Why tell you, you obdurate woman, what I have suffered? I did not come really to see you, but this child, this child of mine. . . . It was wrong to have made you suffer . . . it was wrong to have wanted to hide my shame as a priest from the world. When you left, I thought I should find peace, diminished pain, forgetfulness. . . ."

Agnese interrupted him.

"Will you go? Will you waken the boy? Go, I say. I do not wish to hear your story. . . ."

Gelsomino looked at her with open jaws, incredulous, stupefied. It was evident that the quality in her that had aroused him in his youth still clung to her movements, to her voice, to her gestures. It was evident that though he had come to satisfy an unbearable longing to look upon his son. He was now overwhelmed by the same bold beauty, the heavy plaited hair, the languorous full eyes with their undertone of amorous laughter, the self-assurance that evinced itself as a challenge to break her spirit if one dared.

"Agnese . . . Agnese . . ." he whispered, shrinking from her hard, unrelenting stare. "Oh, the pain it has been, the agony of the damned . . . the years with rough, lustful men, in mines, in the fields, on construction work, in the holds of ships. Everywhere I worked . . . everywhere drudged until my whole body came near to breaking . . . worked to forget . . . drugged myself with the sweat I sucked in with my lips . . . black sweat of the mines . . . dirty sweat of ships . . . sour, stinking sweat . . . and all the time your face, your eyes, your arms, your breasts . . . Agnese. . . ."

Agnese had turned halfway from him, and as he called her name turned only her head to look at him with her cold mocking stare and low, resonant laughter.

– 4 –

Gelsomino moved closer to her. Her disdainful eyes danced, her head shook slightly in undisguised contempt, and she placed her arms akimbo in defensive unconcern. Giovanni had risen higher on his pillow. The cresset flame wagged unsteadily as the oil line sank nearer and nearer to the water. There was a stir of feet on the dark stairs outside, and a woman's voice saying in importunate, horrified whispers, "*Zitto, zitto. . . .*"

It was followed by a clatter of drunken shoes, and a man's quavering broken singing, *O' fiore d'arancie . . . oi ne!*" But Gelsomino was too intensely insulted in his own anguish to hear or see.

"You have suffered? You have drunk bitter sweat? You come like a coward seeking sympathy? You forget the grotto to which you let me flee. You forget the words you said when you knew I was with child. . . . You could not stain your cassock. . . ."

The drunken feet shambled by the open door. The man's voice came cracked and smothered through hands held forcefully over his mouth. Neither heard, nor did they have eyes for Giovanni, who stared at the two like a weary, solitary lizard at a strange thing molesting its retreat.

"Not as a coward, not as a priest, as a man, as a man. . . ."

He seized her in his arms, threw his whole body over hers, bent it backward till it must break in two with a bit more pressure, strained his parched lips on hers. His breathing was audible over the invading rumbling of the trains, the unrestrained singing of the drunken man upstairs. At first her arms were flung loosely over his shoulders as if she were yielding at last to a force too ecstatically demonic to be resisted, like a sapling in a dark storm, back and back without the power to straighten again. Her most desperate efforts, however, could not loosen his embrace, for she had become conscious of Giovanni sitting up in bed, and whether she might have softened in her lover's savage arms or forced herself free despite this new turn, she knew she must send Gelsomino away. But as she pressed closer to him in an attempt to throw his body off, he tightened his arms about her, sought her neck, her eyes, with lips, with teeth, becoming himself driven, overpowered, defenseless.

Agnese heard every word of the drunken song quavering down through the dark, and she could even think that she must give these tenants a severe talking to.

"O fiore d'arancie . . . oi ne. . . .

O che vuoi che ti faccia, brutta bestia — a — a — a!"

Memories of Giovanni growing up when he looked most like his father flashed through her consciousness. She recalled in queer distinctness meals she had prepared for Michele, altercations with men from whom she had bought her houses and who had tried to drive a hard bargain. All the while so encasing was this pressure of arms about her, become not so much a tangible thing now as an impalpable shadow developing mist-like about her that she was compelled to think of definite ways and means for escaping, shattering it, throwing it off.

"O fiore d'arancie . . . oi ne. . . .

Non songo bestia ma non songo monaco . . . o . . . o"

Agnese felt herself pushed back further and further, back to the broad trunk that she had placed under the image of the Virgin. She managed to put her hands between herself and Gelsomino's chest. She struggled to straighten herself. She dug her fingers into his coat, feeling for his flesh. . . .

"Agnese, che ti voglio, oh che ti voglio," she heard him cry in bitter agony; felt his tears touch her cheeks as they fell.

She knew he was weakening. She knew she would weaken, too, but Giovanni was crying, crying as she had heard him cry when they brought him back to her that horrible night.

With no further hesitation she gave Gelsomino a desperate push with both hands. She saw him stumble backwards. She followed him, and pushed again, and she knew he had fallen outside the door as she pulled it to and locked it. For a second she stood gazing at it, paling in the uncertain lights of the cressets, but the next second she had thrown herself on her knees by the side of the bed and was holding the frightened, weeping child in her arms.

– 5 –

Concetta found her asleep with her boy still in her arms.

"*Santa mia!*" she exclaimed, putting one hand over her mouth and tiptoeing to open the windows. . . . "Poor blessed things . . . they should both sleep. . . ."

And leaving them she hurried to the kitchen, aroused Michele in his dark, airless room, shook Gesualdo out of his sleep, and bade them both be quiet and come to their coffee.

"Leave her alone . . . get your breakfast and then go downstairs both of you . . . she's asleep . . . asleep with Giovanni in her arms . . . the blessed thing . . . sh!"

The men were sufficiently impressed with her manner to make no effort to disobey her, but were also completely overwhelmed at hearing what had happened.

Agnese asleep with Giovanni in her arms! It was incredible. They gazed at each other over the edge of their saucers, articulating their surprise only in the increased noises of their ingurgitation!

Michele, timid man that he was, literally said less than nothing. He appeared like one whom a heavy wind has deprived of hat, umbrella, and parcels, and left standing in no condition to move another step. The world had changed overnight. He had been living for a long time incapable of imagining an item displaced in a fixed landscape, an eternal combination of trees and hills and watercourses with the human touches of house and haycocks as immutable as the blue of the sky. Some force beyond all divination had arisen in the hours of his sleep, and with a quick hand had re-arranged the furniture of the sky and hills. From seeming slightly foolish at first and provoking a smile on Concetta's pinched face, he had become a pathetic figure. Even Concetta noticed how he left the table with frightened steps, not daring to look around, and hurried downstairs to the barbershop.

"What's happened to him?" she asked as Gesualdo ran his rough hand over his mouth and mustache. "He got pale, and the scar so red!"

"What could have happened? Nothing."

And as he gazed with a sort of reproof at the ever-inquisitive woman, he packed the red clay bowl of his pipe, and Concetta could notice, unabashed, that the last dexterous push on the tobacco seemed a sighed expression of finality. "At last. . . .!"

– 6 –

But Agnese's sleep was destined to be cut shorter than Concetta had planned. Evidently Gesualdo had not been sitting in his accustomed chair outside the shop, guardian against all importunate seekers after favors.

A woman had burst into the kitchen. Her breasts were so utterly flat that they arrested Concetta's attention at once and caused her small, thin face to pucker in agonized surprise and even caused her not to note the heavy kerchief tied securely under the woman's chin on so hot a morning. The fright in the woman's eyes was an embodied fear.

"Where's la signora?" The woman had stopped short, and asked in a piteous whisper.

"She's asleep. Come again later. After the noonday!"

But for reply the woman sank to the floor, evidently unable to hold herself erect, and it would seem that the sobs eventually crack the thin frame.

"*Ma che c'è? Che c'è?*" begged Concetta stooping to her.

Agnese had heard, and was standing in the doorway. Concetta saw her and began at once to make excuses for the scene, noticing the uncommon pallor of her cheeks, the restless eyes without their hint of laughter.

"But, signora. . . ."

The stranger woman on the floor did not rise, and her sobs became fainter.

"What is it, Concetta?"

They both helped to raise the woman to a chair.

"My husband . . . he came home . . . two weeks ago . . . his ribs, his knees, all mashed by a big stone on the job . . . we have six children . . . we have no bread . . .

Madonna, Madonna mia . . . what are we going to do? We have no friends . . . they said come here . . . they said you would help. . . . *Dio* . . . *Dio.* . . ."

If Concetta had been taken aback at the sight of Agnese asleep with Giovanni in her arms, she was left stone-cold with surprise at the figure of Agnese stooped over the disconsolate woman, holding her, too, in her arms, speaking softly to her, caressing her gently.

"Concetta, pack up some things . . . a bit of pasta . . . cheese . . . anything we have . . . go home with her. . . ."

"It's this wretched country," spoke up the emaciated woman as Agnese made her drink a cup of coffee. "We should have all stayed in Italy."

"Too late now," answered Agnese sadly. "Some come away for one thing, some for another, and no one who hasn't her cross to bear. . . ."

"Yes, we all have, Lord knows. But you have made your pile here, and we are still struggling. . . . What can my husband do? He works on the tracks, he works on the new houses, he works anywhere . . . and he used to have his own piece of land. . . ."

Concetta was ready with her package. The woman got up, stooped and would have kissed Agnese's hand.

"When your husband is better . . . bring him here . . . we, maybe, will find him work. . . ."

"*Dio t'aiuta, signora, Dio t'aiuta!*" she kept repeating as she was led out by Concetta.

Gesualdo had hurried upstairs once he heard the sound of voices.

"How did she come? I did not see her. . . ."

"*'Na poveretta! Lasciala sta!* Sit down. I want to tell you something."

Gesualdo sat down, and Agnese felt that her father had never been quite so willingly obedient as now, and she realized that whatever had coursed through her had flowed on throughout her household. Giovanni for the first time since his illness could sit up and smile. Gesualdo seemed to look upon her with an air of expectancy that heralded its own reward.

"Last night I thought it all out," she said simply. "We are going to move. We have made enough money. Why should we live in this old house? I am going to buy a house on the block with the Americans, and we are going to live like them, and Giovanni is going to grow up. . . ."

And for the second time Agnese let herself be held by her father as she wept tears that would not stop!

– 7 –

To Michele the moving did not come as a surprise although he had no word in it. Gesualdo had casually announced Agnese's intention, and had been careful in so doing not to let his gaze linger for even a second on the flushing features of his son-in-law. Dressed in his barber's white coat, he sat a mournful figure in a huge chair, the red contour of his newly acquired scar an outstanding incident in the general change that came over his countenance. If it can be said of any being so constantly quivering in every nerve and muscle as man, that he could become assimilated to the essential inertness of the chair in which he sat, it might have been said of Michele.

Ever since the morning when Gelsomino had once more crossed the paths of his life, his spirit had undergone a transformation. In the shop for years he had been voluble as the proverbial followers of his calling in all matters not of particular importance to the variegated modes the Dantones had developed for amassing a fortune. For more than a month, while the process of purchasing one of the brownstone houses now changing hands so rapidly from the "English" to the Italians, he had become disturbingly morose and sullen.

There was no variation from the normal routine of appearing in the shop in the late morning, keeping steadily at the intermittent activities it entailed, going up for a late dinner and the only substantial meal of the day, returning to work until long past dusk. Work consisted largely of entertaining the local politicians and their henchmen, playing at *tocco* in the backyard, or concocting with Luigi and Agnese further devices for squeezing more and more out of the immigrants who came to them for jobs or for assistance in dealing with the courts or the police or the school authorities. The only deviation was a foreshortened period of talk with Agnese, a studied if frightened avoidance of her gaze, a distinct if timid display of a hurt personality unduly, cruelly outraged. Between him and Giovanni communication of all kinds had ceased save for the unavoidable necessary words of ordinary life.

He could finally stand it no longer and one night asked Agnese to listen to what he had to say. They sat in the kitchen, still filled with the heat of a declining August day. On the table were the remains of the family meal: a bottle of wine, a *provolone* jagged rather than cut, olives, and bread. Michele kept removing first one, then another of these articles, or sticking the end of a huge carving knife into the oil cloth here and there.

"He was here one night last month," he said slowly, with averted eyes. "When the boy was sick."

Agnese looked squarely at him without making the slightest effort to reply. The flare of the gashouse flame took the pause for an occasion to throw into crimson relief the shining faucet, the washtubs, the stove and Gesualdo's bed against the wall.

"You won't deny it?" he questioned eagerly.

Whether by way of answer or of allowing him more time to elaborate his accusation, Agnese had lighted a match and climbing on a chair lighted, first one, then each of the other two cressets that were kept under the three saints' effigies in the kitchen. It was a routine gesture and no more of religious exaltation or devotion expressed in it than in the movement of a middle-aged sacristan with his thoughts on the young widow he would give his middle finger to persuade. Michele followed her movements with the same devouring passion in his eyes that she had evoked ever since her girlhood, and he knew that it would be useless to continue. However, his impulse had yielded a modicum of unaccustomed courage, and the feel of it was intoxicant enough to give him energy.

"Why did you see him? Is it fair to me? I thought he had been lost, had died somewhere. Where was it, in China or Africa or some place? Agnese, speak to me," he suddenly cried, rising from his chair and seized with a desperate fear. "Don't ignore me. Don't treat me like I was nothing to you. I shared your tears and your misery. I shared the hard work of making a way for ourselves in this country. I took, I took. . . ."

He fell back into his chair, putting his hand over his eyes to hide the tears that were coming.

"My shame," answered Agnese in a low laugh, completing Michele's sentence.

"Oh, Agnese, Agnese, don't say it. You know this is the first time the word has crossed between us."

"The last time, big poltroon, you!" said Agnese, laughing more cheerfully now, and going over to her husband.

Michele looked up at her as a child who, by making a clever remark, has just avoided being slapped.

"You still love him?" he could not avoid asking.

"We will not talk. What use is talk? People who talk soon hang from the gallows. . . ."

Whether any affectionate caress would have accompanied her words it would be difficult to say, for at this point Gesualdo, who had been out walking with Giovanni, still easily frightened at the slightest unusual noise or movement, unceremoniously threw open the door, already half ajar, and remarked loudly, "Well, wasn't that watermelon good, hey, you young loafer!"

VII. The Brownstone Front

– 1 –

The single brownstone house with its brownstone stoop and brass knobs, the broad sidewalk in front with the catalpa or maple adding a quieting dignity, neither the apartment house nor the automobile had as yet disturbed. Many streets north of where Agnese had founded her success, stretched rows and rows of these houses from the East River to where the still-wooded cliffs of Morningside Heights rose to block the apartment resident from easy access to the Hudson. They furnished a series of sturdy if maiden-like preserves for the prosperous merchant and the well-to-do professional man, and had become a symbol in the eyes of the Italian and other immigrants to the south of the culture and wealth of the United States. To live in one was the ostentatious ambition of anyone among the newcomers who had achieved some material place in the community.

The pressure of the ever-increasing numbers who came in search of bread and fortune gradually prepared the conditions which transferred the holdings from the established Americans to the north into the hands of the upstart peasants to the south. Agnese, who had been one of the first to wrest a fortune, no matter how dubiously, from the chaos and bewilderment of the city, was also one of the first to obtain possession of a coveted brownstone house, and to establish herself as an equal among those of the "English" who could not yet afford to move out or who did not yet feel the sting and the stigma of having for neighbor a "dago" family.

The barbershop was sold, and with it the activities of Michele underwent a complete metamorphosis. In place of the shop, Agnese had purchased a share in the city dump on the river not far from the empty lots in which Giovanni had attempted to make romance eke out a precarious reality. With it had to be bought and put under a measure of control a whole series of junk shops in the neighborhood, and gradually there developed, almost without the assistance or the desires of either herself or Michele, a brisk business in old papers and old rags, in bottles and bones, and the various fetid off-scourings of massed people.

Michele now marched off in the late mornings to inspect the dumps and to dicker with the numerous junk-cart dealers. Agnese herself found much work to do in going the rounds of her many tenement houses, collecting rents, listening to complaints, acting as mediator in the squabbles among her tenants — in fact, assuming duties in their essence manorial and attaching to her by virtue of the transfer to the new soil of customs and attitudes of the old. She made a determined effort to accord her husband a measure of deference so that he might attain a dignity and weight of his own, and backed by this assurance Michele displayed a front of golden chains, too heavy to rest easily on his swelling person.

"Look at the clodhopper in a swallow-tail!"

He never overheard the remark, but it was whispered and bandied about in laughter as he passed knots of his countrymen. But when he entered one of the countless cafés to get his cup of coffee with just two inches and no more of rum, they made way with effusive alacrity and no one but shouted a ringing good morning.

"Eh, Don Michele! Oh, for a day of shooting in the woods back of Villetto! What say?"

"And what will Don Michele have this bright morning?"

"Try the new anisette! *Ma, ch'é fino!*"

It was a triumphal progress. He forgot Gelsomino. He almost forgot his precise relation to Giovanni. He went even as far as to stroke the lad's cheeks in a warm, benignant superiority.

Gesualdo could not be weaned from his long clay pipe nor from his position in front of the house. Conscious of the enormity of his conduct in the eyes of the outraged "English" to the left and right of him, he insisted upon placing his chair immediately outside the iron railing fencing off the downstairs entrance, and making every effort to hide the pretentious brownstone behind a cloud of smoke as thick as it was ill-smelling. And he took the rise to eminence without any haughtiness of demeanor whatsoever and let these "English" know it by a democratic good morning on any bright day. To anyone interested he offered a recital of his daughter's remarkable accomplishments, stopping only for lack of language at praise short of the miraculous. But as usual, on the appearance of Agnese, he became a silent effigy placed as if for an ornament before the door.

– 2 –

Space extends the emotions and leisure refines them, and even in the relation of mother to son do these calm and gracious influences bring a light that seems of the spirit only. For now that Agnese could go to an indefinite upstairs where Giovanni had a room to himself looking out upon a backyard which he could cultivate as his own, it seemed a simpler matter to stand by him as he traced laborious drawings or copied innumerable figures into notebooks. Giovanni had become as taciturn and homekeeping as he had been vivacious and roaming before his running away. His long black lashes rested now on cheeks that never lost a pallor, a pallor which did not quite become his olive tinge. His form had retained the thinness to which it had been reduced by his shock and illness, and the light that used to illuminate his whole being had been withdrawn into the quiet centers of his personality. As he looked up and smiled at Agnese, she did what for many years she had never done, stooped to stroke his forehead or to kiss him gently without palpable emotion.

She had taken to tiptoeing into his room after she was sure that he had fallen asleep for the night, and stood gazing into his features in the pale glimmer of the cresset below the Virgin Mary she had placed above the head of the bed. Few words passed between them, but at these moments when he lay deep in slumber and she stood silently at his side, some communication there must have been, a sharing of a secret half-joy and half-sorrow in a light that came not from the dim wick overhead but from the center of hearts that could flame without being consumed. For she lingered long at his side, and often his hand moved to where she could take it in hers and hold it, and as a sad tremble overspread her lips, a quiet, unhastened smile touched the corners of his mouth.

There was no more mention of Gelsomino. Everyone had been made a partner in the change produced by his coming, and yet each one tacitly acknowledged that in mutual silence lay the greater happiness. To seek to clarify the situation would have roiled waters that had sought and found their level in a still basin, covering a bottom that contained growths better left unexposed. The change to the big one-family house, the development of their new enterprises, the feeling of expansion and power that came in the wake of these, absorbed the attention, transmuted the embittered emotions into dynamic adjustments, and left no energy for brooding, reproach, or regret.

Gesualdo hopped about in a perpetual to-do over this and that, became voluble with Michele, showed an intimate if helpless interest in Giovanni's solitary doings, and spoke up to his daughter as if he were a bad boy, the most loved and the most unmanageable in the family. Luigi, who lived with them, they rarely saw, and when they did it was to listen to strange accounts of the tunnel he was driving under houses, tales of blasts and accidents, the number of men at work, the money being made.

"No more going way upstate for me. Gee! what work! You're in mud now and then standing on a rock and you got to be careful or you'll be blown up. All the *paesani* are in it, got a job for everyone, could use all that come over."

Gesualdo stared at his son and followed him around the house, was at his beck and call, lived in his shadow, related his doings as he did those of Agnese. The gloom that had been so persistent an accomplishment in his life before this seemed to have been dispelled. Light-hearted and gay as the old man now appeared to be, however, he was careful to study Agnese's reactions, and by a kind of control he had acquired over Michele and Giovanni could manage to maintain the new equilibrium and composure established in the family. Yet he knew that at times the energy with which Agnese drove herself was but the hasty motions of one who has been discovered in the act of possessing something not his and is seeking clumsily to hide it.

– 3 –

Giovanni's long summer vacation was now at an end. He had become strong again but quieter, in physique so much slighter as to seem younger; but so self-controlled, so thoughtful, so in-drawn that he appeared to have sprung into a premature adolescence. Ever since he could go out alone after his illness he had been going to the library, had come home with huge books, had sat alone for hours reading them, or drawing, or writing. Agnese was indifferent to what he did, not understanding what it was all about, but supremely content to see him actively seeking happiness in his own way. Michele hardly noted what the boy was doing, but to Gesualdo it all seemed a miraculous display of magical powers of intelligence and understanding of the deepest arcana of existence. Luigi was more vocal.

"We'll make a doctor of him, or a lawyer, hey?"

The only time he talked about it with Agnese he discovered that her views were as vague as her contentment with his quiet ways was pronounced.

"Why a doctor? Why a lawyer? Why so much study and reading? There were no books in our family. Did you read books?"

"No," Luigi confessed, fingering the huge gold locket hanging from his chain. "Yes, you're right. But if I had!"

"Well?" she inquired simply, allowing the inflection to convey the greater part of her doubt. "I only knew one who studied much. . . ."

Luigi whistled softly to himself, and gulped the last inch of wine after biting vigorously into the cheese and bread before him. He had begun to understand.

"What'll you do with him?"

"Put him into your business, or mine. We have property. What does he need with study or work for that matter? In this country everybody must do something. He can go into your work. . . ."

"Suppose he don't want to? Besides, he is not so strong. . . ."

The matter rested there until the week before the opening of school.

Giovanni had returned from the streets but instead of stopping in the huge kitchen on the ground floor had proceeded stealthily upstairs and so aroused Agnese's curiosity that she tiptoed to the foot of the landing and stood stock-still to listen. There had for a long time been gradually coming to a head in Agnese's thoughts a disquieting suspicion that Giovanni not only had heard what had passed between her and Gelsomino but had learned in other ways further details of their relationship. The absence of all noise after the boy had entered his room, a stillness that impressed itself upon the house as if it were the echo of movements in a central hollowness, brought a quick thrilling flush to her cheeks.

There flashed to her mind at once the question that had strengthened her determination for many years, "Why should I be afraid?" But her hold upon herself had been broken by Giovanni's illness. She had realized then with a pointedness that was akin to a sudden stab by an unknown hand that her outward indifference to her son had been merely a form of inverted gratitude to Michele.

And the weeks that followed, despite the renewed vigor she had put into her enterprises, despite the sense of a new accommodation she had made to her life which Gesualdo and Luigi both had interpreted as a final suppression of all doubts of her conduct and a complete acceptance of her plans, the weeks that followed had poisoned the wound. For a second on the night of Gelsomino's appearance she had wavered, had felt the force of the passion that had moved her in the beginning, that had, in fact, meant summit moments in her life, would have yielded herself gladly to embraces which, though enflaming, brought peace and slumber to unruly nerves, taut muscles, heaving thoughts. But years of struggle, of cautious devisings, of intricate contacts had developed the habit of wariness and she knew that the more substantial portion of her life was the wealth she had accumulated, the houses she owned, the standing she had among her fellows. Her successful resistance, prompted as it might have been by the movements of Giovanni, still was a symbol of a rich life. But in her heart she alone knew that it had at the same time been a hypocritical denial of volcanic desires at the core of her emotions.

"I have embraced an ass," she told herself as these thoughts racketed in her mind, "and I have been as an image of stone, but though I have sinned in the eyes of my neighbors, I have not believed it. They do not believe it now. . . ."

And she followed Giovanni upstairs, conscious in an acute way of the presence of the interdicted lover that had been his father, his soft cadenced resonances in her ears, his manner of pausing before he spoke, his disarming intentness to all you said. And as she climbed the carpeted narrow stairs leading to her son's room, palpable proof of her indomitable purposefulness, she knew that the suspicion she had been forming would, must be verified, and a fear entered her heart that her material successes would in a short time be as water held between one's hands.

"Surely I have loved Giovanni all my life. What did *he* know of the anger against that other not meant for him? Giovanni, you must understand. . . ."

– 4 –

She entered her boy's room without knocking on his door, but whether he heard or not he kept his position at the window, seated on a chair, his elbows on the windowsill, his head in his hands, quiet, motionless. At her throat was a tightening that in another woman would have been the signal for tears, for clasping the boy in her arms, holding him fast in the surrender of love. She merely called to him, and she knew as she spoke that he was struggling with the fear that her voice contained the dreadful accents of a never-subdued anger that had been constantly menacing in the days before his illness and the coming of his father. And yet she could not change it.

"Why did you pass me by?"

Giovanni looked at her in the amazement of one who does not quite believe what has actually happened.

"You went right upstairs without stopping to talk. Concetta was with me, and she said, 'How rude!' I had to blush."

"No," said the boy simply, shaking his head.

"You should not do that."

"No."

"What were you looking at out of the window?"

Agnese noted the rapid flutter of the eyelashes, the head suddenly achieving what seemed an immobility, the darting flash of unsettling inquiry in his pupils. She knew again that she was reawakening all the fears of a black time far back, and yet she could not check herself.

"What was it?"

"The clouds . . . the wind . . . it's going to rain . . . the light . . . it's nice to watch it. . . ."

"But why did you come upstairs so quietly? You want to avoid me. Why?"

"No, mama, no mama," Giovanni answered in a frightened whisper. "It was the storm. I wanted to see it. . . . I wanted to draw it . . . like an artist. . . . I saw a man drawing a storm . . . there was a big tree he was painting. . . ."

"Where?"

"Oh, mama, mama!" Giovanni had burst into tears. Agnese had seized him in her arms, was brushing his forehead, crooning to him, her breath coming and going with the same anguished sobbing as was shaking Giovanni.

"No, my little child . . . no, my little child . . . it's no more like before . . . Giovanni, it's no more like before . . . you must not be afraid. Why be afraid of your own mother? Giovanni, no, no! Not that way. You hurt my heart. . . ."

They clung to each other unaware of the thunder, the rising blackness, the alternate flash and sudden shadowing of the cresset. Standing at the window, close to each other, they could not help but look out, but their eyes were fixed not on the glare of the windows opposite, nor on the waving of the few trees in the backyards, nor on the big raindrops that splashed on the sill and jumped with quick recurrent thuds into the room. One was searching into the other's heart for knowledge of his true thoughts of her, the other for some confirmation that there was truth and reality in this new love that could hold him so close and yet seemed incapable of stilling a yearning to be loved.

"Mama!" he finally ventured very quietly, very timidly.

They had half shut the window. He stood near it with his face pressing the pane, she seated on a chair close to him, holding his hand.

"Mama," he said. "Really, I saw a man painting, painting a storm. He made you see the wind. You were afraid if you looked."

"Why, how silly," she smiled. "Who could paint what you can't see?"

"But he painted it. A big tree was bending in front of it, and there was a man and a woman running away. . . ."

Into Agnese's peasant ways had never entered the consciousness of beauty caught out of the heavens and made permanent in a color, a line, a word. The images of the saints foregathered out of her imagination vague outlines of semblances which had become real only because they were on the lips of everyone, appealed to, prayed to, taken for granted, and with these outlines constructed material contours. This she knew, and she had watched as a child the old man who carved wooden statues for the churches and the shrines in the immediate vicinity of Villetto, and she had all the while believed that he was working with God's hand on his, guiding the knife, instructing his fingers where to move, how deep to cut, how bright to make the eye, how sharply to chisel the nose.

The old man with his small rheumy eyes set deep in cups of wrinkles kept sliding his bearded lips over toothless gums as he worked, saying never a word, frightening her with his unbroken intentness. But she had watched him only several times, and had not revisited his shop placed on the flagstones before his green-shuttered sun-beaten house at the foot of the hill on which Villetto hung.

For the last time she had watched him, he had carved slowly into the inert wood and out of it had come an expression, a look, a stern gaze — the unrelenting eyes of Saint John, and she had felt a presence that had not been, a conjuring of a life from the infinite beyond to which everyone constantly alluded.

She had run fast without looking back, believing the old man more akin to the bodiless spirits than to her friends of flesh and blood. And now this thing of painting the wind, the invisible movement of water and sky and foliage! It was as if there were those who lived not on the earth really but behind the things we see and know and hear.

"But he could not paint what isn't anywhere, Giovanni. . . ."

"It was such fun, you know, watching him paint," he continued, smiling uneasily. "I was even afraid, once. . . . He was putting on colors fast . . . the wind seemed coming out of them . . . it was making a noise . . . and then I thought I heard it speak. . . ."

"Just what happened to me once, in the old country. . . ."

Giovanni could not have heard her words, for the rapt expression of his eyes as he was recreating the scene that had stirred him was uninterrupted. His hand lay loosely between her fingers, his body pressed against the jamb.

"I was afraid . . . I didn't move a bit I was so afraid . . . and then the wind did speak. . . ."

"What a silly boy . . . If there's nothing. . . ?"

"But it wasn't the wind . . . it was a man . . . I thought I knew the man. He stood in front of me. . . ."

For all her strength of mind, Agnese still retained the naïve literalness of the peasant face to face with a reality that is really mystery to him. She looked up at the averted head of Giovanni, intently observing the movements of his neck and cheek, attempting not so much to understand as to take in the feeling whose intensity had made of the boy a statue-like dreamer uttering explanations as each detail evolved out of the fantastic mass that was his thoughts, streaming, unchanneled, uncontrolled.

"I thought I had seen him once . . . once when I was sick . . . and when he spoke I trembled . . . the old trembling came back . . . I was afraid. . . ."

It was Agnese now who was afraid. She clutched so hard the loose hand she held between her fingers that Giovanni looked back quickly. The full force of the storm had driven black masses over the housetops and out of their gloomy profundities rolled the slow rumble of thunder. The long beaded ropes of the rain swung back and forth, and what the clouds did not hide of chimney and cornice they uneasily, desperately curtained and recurrently exposed.

"All he said, though," continued Giovanni, as if reassuring his mother, "was, 'It's like God to be a painter.'"

"What did he look like?" asked Agnese without concealing from Giovanni the agitation that she communicated to him through her fingers, her voice.

"Tall, thin, and he spoke softly like a priest but he wasn't. . . ."

"What else did he say?"

"Just 'Why did you look so scared?'"

"Nothing else?"

"No. We just talked about the picture the man was painting. You know where it was? In that store-like, one flight up the white stairs where the trolley turns."

"Oh, see the sky!" said Agnese. "Yes, I know. The wind's blown over. . . ."

"Yes, blown over, and the sky's all blue. . . ."

"Giovanni," suddenly said Agnese, rising as quickly, and putting her arms about his shoulders. "What do you want to become?"

The boy was so surprised at this question as to raise blank eyes to her.

"Why . . . go back to school. . . ."

"And then?"

Recent impression more than any other impulse or cause must have prompted him to reply, "Paint, draw, be like God as the man said."

But though Agnese had come to her son with the dominant intention of making him understand the hidden agitation that was the core of her life, subdued and ordered by an uncompromising mind as it seemed to others, she had too little perspective or understanding of the manifold values built up by a cultured society to be able to grasp completely or sympathetically this notion of her son. Once more he receded for her into a misty retreat beyond the confines of her mind and heart, became associated once more with symbols that had become threats of control over her spirit, her desires, her very body. She pushed him not altogether ungently and she saw not without some vicarious satisfaction the features of Gelsomino in the thin countenance of Giovanni pulling as if with pain. A little staccato laugh escaped her, sufficiently hard to cause the sensitive lad to wince and pale. She was too aware of the agonized change and too near to the new sweetness that had come between them for her to do anything more than take his cheeks in her hands and kiss him, saying, "Well, you must go to school and then we shall see."

– 5 –

As she moved about the house, receiving the numerous visits that had become a fixed routine in her life by now, no one suspected the crisscross of winds that were her emotions within. Concetta spent most of her time with the Dantones, leaving to her daughter, not much older than Giovanni, the management of her household. She was the only person besides Luigi who had ever quite dared to set herself boldly against Agnese, speaking up when another would have shrugged his shoulders and departed, making the sign of the cross inwardly and invoking a variety of saints.

"I'll be blessed, and that before dawn," she exclaimed when Agnese had come downstairs, and she made a sign of the cross more as a jocose gesture than a solemn expression. "Has the storm frightened you?"

"Yes, you goose," replied Agnese, pushing her aside with a movement of the hand.

"You must have seen a ghost, instead, to be rushing by like the storm," answered Concetta as she followed her mistress into the kitchen. "And this veal you're roasting might just as well be his charred body. Good thing I let my house go to the dogs while I come here. You'd squander yourself out of food and home. . . ."

Michele had come in at this point, so wet that his face steamed and the scar showed up like a moon through mist.

"Whew, what a storm! Was on the dumps! Soaked everybody. It might have melted you right into the muck. . . ."

"Evidently you enjoyed it. Go upstairs and stop your chatter. . . ."

The important Michele shriveled into a mere point of gazing eyes and open mouth, but he made no reply except to look his consternation for Concetta to see. He went upstairs at once like a little obedient boy, once more conscious of an Agnese that had for a while only become maternally indulgent of him. She could hear his startled intermittent whistle as he mounted the stairs, and she must have pictured his mouse-like face extending itself into the elongated protrusion of his lips.

Other than this outburst of what was at best but petulance and irritation, she went about her tasks with her usual suggestion of mastery not only over herself but over others and the situation immediately in hand.

– 6 –

Antonio Farinella, the building contractor, came in as he did every evening now that his family and the Dantones were neighbors. It was not long after Agnese had bought into the exclusive "English" section, that other families that had thrived in America imitated her display. It had been evident that for some reason or another Antonio Farinella had been actuated by motives of jealousy in his feverish attempts to achieve a conspicuous, a startling success in America, a jealousy that centered in the desire to outshine the Dantones, if possible, and certainly to parade before Agnese each item of achievement.

And if anyone suspected that Antonio's feelings for Agnese were not altogether those of a business rival but had become merely an intenser if quieter continuance of those he felt for her on board the ship that had brought them to America, he took care not to reveal his suspicion despite how many others, who knew, happened to feel the same toward Agnese. Besides, with such a husband, the thinking went, who would not have taken a lover? No one had so much as remotely hinted at such an event in Agnese's life. But if one there was, if it was not the English Doctor Grace, then it must be Antonio with the eyes that never left you when they were fixed on you.

He fingered a ponderous golden locket in the shape of a Maltese cross, bejeweled heavily and making his unashamed portliness the more conspicuous.

"Got one of the subway contracts," he told Agnese as he lifted to his lips the wine she had poured.

"Luigi get it for you?"

Obviously whatever advantage obtaining the contract had meant to Farinella must have been minimized by that much.

"Yes, you old *civetta,*" replied Farinella, laughing and shaking his head in a sort of controlled tremble as he gazed fixedly at her. "Yes, if you must know. He does have the big drag with somebody."

"He knows how. He is a boy yet, but he knows a thing or two. Take my boy now. How he dreams! What can be made of him?"

"At least your boy minds and is good. Oh, I know what happened. But who has not kicked up once or twice? The children know more than their parents. You can't do a thing with my Tessie. You know. . . ."

Antonio offered an exposition of the waywardness of his children. The oldest girl had already declared herself grown up, would put up her hair, insisted on long dresses, a watch to pin on her bosom, money to place in her purse.

"They think you pick up the money on the streets. They don't know how we have slaved. . . ."

"Now, now, *compare bello,* not so fast. After all, it did come easy. What would you have been in Italy? What would we all have been? What would they have made of me? Here I have been free to do what I pleased. I came with a bad name. But it's not a name here. It's what you can do. I wish my Giovanni would understand it. It means making money, piling it up. But they give you a chance.

. . . They do not throw you out. . . . You are not damned. . . ."

A queer excitement possessed her. Antonio moved uneasily in his chair, clutched the empty glass with nervous fingers, pulled at his mustache, stared at Agnese, attempted to interrupt. But she had risen to her feet, her hand brushing back her hair, the other between her lips as if to bite it, and gazed, it would seem, through the walls of the room. Was it to the dim foul grotto in the hills, or the lone room with the huge fireplace where Gelsomino had beseeched her to go away, to leave him the peace of his parish, to leave clean and unsullied the holy cassock he was wearing?

"You are not damned here. You live and let live, the wicked and the good in one place. And why not? Why not?"

"Well, well, Agnese. Take a seat. Why all the anger? I don't question you at all. Of course, of course. . . ."

Agnese sat down as quickly as she had risen, smiling at Antonio as if she had said something foolish and was asking his indulgence.

"I want to make something of my boy. Here is a big business his father and I have built up. We want him to take it over, learn all about it. He talks about school and going to be a painter, an artist. What do we want of an artist, people who read books and books and books, and get notions that there is something sacred in it and we are nobodies? Tessie wants to put up her hair, Giovanni wants to go to school. . . ."

"Nothing wrong with that. . . ." Antonio got up from his chair, his olive features flushing with an embarrassment he could not control. There was a trouble implied in the nervous staccato sentences of Agnese which reddened her face, threw a peculiarly vivid light into her eyes, and communicated itself throughout the room as if a hidden force were dominating not only her, but him, too, and the very positions of the chairs and table, the unceasing ticking of the clock on the mantelpiece and the hissing of the gas flames in the colored globes.

"Of course, let him go to school. What's wrong with going to school and knowing what's in books?"

He was conscious of Agnese looking up at him and for the first time in the decade since he had known her and, as people said, would have given the nails on his fingers to possess her, he was aware of a central feminine weakness in her, of a need for support, for a man upon whom she could lean, whose words she might listen to with willing acceptance. He moved toward the chair upon which she was sitting and placed his hand on hers, stooping ever so slightly over.

"You are all excited, Agnese. . . ."

She remained silent and immovable. He had, meanwhile, become keenly sensitive to the heavy plaits of brown hair that shone in the gas light, the liquid flow of the shoulder line as it lost itself in her bosom, the troubled heaving of her breasts, and with a gesture that was that of an unfulfilled youth, still intense and vibrating, he pressed his lips upon her head, then drew it back toward him and kissed her feverishly.

He raised her from the chair with a brusque, violent pull of her whole body and, unaware that she was neither struggling nor yielding, drew her whole body to him as if the fury of a lifetime must find immediate outlet in one minute's wildness.

"Antonio," finally spoke Agnese, "enough . . . enough . . . look at me."

She smiled, and he could see in her eyes the never-ending light constantly hinting of a passion that yearned but could never be stilled, of a force which challenged and denied, of a power which controlled and could not be moved.

"Since the night of the ship, since the first day I saw your eyes looking over the waters. . . ."

"Antonio," she interrupted, "they are playing *tocco* in the yard, my father and other men. Go and join them. You know what I have always said. I have been unhappy, too. Do not tell me about yourself. . . ."

She sat down again and as she busied herself with slight adjustments of her hair, her dress, she turned her head halfway to him and asked, this time quite calmly as if she knew the answers would be genuine and impersonal, "So, you would send him to school and have him become an artist?"

"Yes. Why not?" He left without another word, but with the memory of the smile on Agnese's lips which doubled up his fists and brought his jaw muscles grimly together.

Agnese sat quietly in her seat, apparently a gentle figure in whom all doubts have been cleared, who gazes out upon serene vistas, and sees the day come to a close in a satisfaction that will bring pleasant dreams. But in her eyes stood tears, and as they fell on her cheeks a coldness crept over her, and the thoughts that were in her heart were of the days before the grotto, of a cadenced voice that made the darkness tremble with music.

– 7 –

It had become dark. Concetta had gone, Michele as usual had left for his cup of coffee and game of *tre-sette* in the café, the sound of the men playing *tocco* in the backyard mingled with the rumble of the surface-car passing the door. Agnese knew that Giovanni must be asleep, and as was her habit now she went softly to his room.

The moonlight following the stormy afternoon was all the more like a silver powder that filtered in through Giovanni's room and hung in shining halos about the cresset of the Holy Virgin, and touched with gold the brass knobs of the bed-post. It streamed in upon the boy's bed and gave a sad thoughtful distinctness to his thin features. He was not asleep but Agnese sat down, nevertheless, on the bed beside him and took his hand in hers. Not a word passed between them, but their thoughts could not have been far apart.

The scene with Antonio had awakened in her impulses and memories that had slept for years, and as they became clearer and more insistent to her mind and heart they built up images that she had been ruthless in shattering and casting out of her consciousness. Giovanni had been too affected by the words of the stranger in the painter's shop not to have before him the memory of the pale, sharp face, the kindly eyes, the soft voice. Their long years of unfriendliness, of living apart the nearer they were drawn together, had made both Agnese and Giovanni capable of a mutual insight which in these moments of love was too sharp not to hurt. Agnese realized with a poignancy that registered itself in the deeper silence she maintained that Giovanni had recognized in the stranger of the shop the same man who had held her in his arms while the boy lay suffering that hot, sad night in June. Giovanni never once raised his eyes to his mother but was willing to lie with his hand in hers, quiet and contented, a solacing contrast to the troubled, sorrowful years that seemed to have gone as darkness goes. And yet on his lips there was forming a question which in his heart he feared to ask and yet must ask.

They remained thus sleepless and nevertheless thoroughly relaxed despite the fear that each had, and might both have fallen asleep had not the doorbell in the basement jangled violently into the silence. Michele was coming up the stairs, Michele who would soon call Agnese away. Giovanni grasped with ever the slightest pressure his mother's fingers.

"Mama!" he said softly, opening his eyes. "That man who was here, who was with the painter . . . tell me, mama . . . tell me, mama. . . ."

"What, *figlio mio*. What, *figlio mio*?" she asked, pressing her lips close to his ears.

Michele's steps resounded through the big house, and as he passed the shut door they heard him knocking insistently yet timidly with loose knuckles.

"That man is my father . . . and not this one?"

She had no answer for him except to kiss him almost savagely on his lips, his hands, his eyes and then with an abrupt, decisive movement she left the room. Giovanni smiled as he watched a thin cloud of smoke spiraling slowly upwards and crossing the serene disc of the moon.

VIII. MICHELE

– 1 –

Michele lay in bed and thought. It was a huge bedroom, two windows at one end through which he could see the street, paneled closets with a washstand between, a fireplace with a black tile hearth and a dirty-looking marble mantelpiece. He never failed to look around the room. It had become a manner of religious observance for it fed a longing and it stilled a question. He delighted in admiring the rug that ran up to the hearth in streaks of color and got lost under the heavy brass bed. The curtains swayed like a gentle breeze across his consciousness, cooling a fever of doubt that had hurt him now for months. As he made out the broken images of the serried brownstones across the street, he luxuriated in their solidity. The fixed world in which he had moved so long would not soon collapse although it did seem still unreal, not enough of his own making to abide.

He recalled the stone-flagged room that he had shared with his grandmother so many years ago — stone flags and stone walls, a low sooty fireplace always piled with burning ash, the dinginess, the thick air, the pile of straw for the pig in the corner and the two hens. He had left the old woman to occupy the room alone and to die in it with no one by, only the pig at her side grunting for the mash it was accustomed to getting. He remembered how he had wept when he heard of it, and how he had to have his grief alone — for what could it have meant to Agnese?

This was Agnese — this flowered wall-paper, these huge, green plush chairs, and the brass-handled bureaus in a room that would have seemed the Queen's to the old woman. There was pride in the thought that he had married her, that he had achieved what he had longed for since his earliest boyhood. She had smacked his face, a hard blow that made him wince and cry aloud, and for nothing at all, just for staring and staring at her when she kept asking him, "Have you seen my baby brother?" And he had gone quietly to his grandmother and sat down on the hearth, raking the coals and saying to himself that he would fix her, and the thought had been so pleasant, the mood so sweetly soft, that he had repeated and repeated it only to find himself, as the years grew on, capable of thinking of nothing else and of no one else. He planned furtive meetings with her and was excited if he could see her pass by even if she gave no sign of noticing him. He had once contrived to sit on the same bench in church and to creep slowly toward her and feel her close to him and his thoughts were on her and not on God, although he prayed loud and with lips wide open sat watching the blessed movements of the priest.

These thoughts and similar ones he took from his memory every morning as he woke and especially in the last months when the whole structure of a life too much of her making and not enough of his own seemed threatening to fall about him. And so it was that he inventoried as he awoke the solid features of the huge room, and knew that as long as he awoke into it at least the outward appearances of his life would remain, conscious that Agnese was still his, that she had only a short time before she left his side, that she was downstairs busy with the multiplying details of affairs that had themselves multiplied so fast that he seemed forever unable to keep up with them.

Ever since the night of Gelsomino's return, his life with Agnese had become more and more complex, and he was aware that it was further and further reducing him to a nonentity without purpose in the scheme and of little or no help. As a barber with a daily routine and a constant stream of men who daily kept his importance like a lighted image before his eyes, he had had a place of his own, he had moved not as a puppet pulled about and shoved here and there or put in a corner and forgotten. He had had few words to say but what he said had been listened to and the replies were respectful. And how fulfilling a delight it was to go upstairs to his meals in the dark kitchen with its glowing stove and rude furniture. The dinner had been prepared by Agnese and she was there herself to serve him and to eat with him and to talk over their accumulating wealth and their new schemes for adding to it. And Giovanni was kept in his place and was not the center of their life together — the priest's brat. How he lorded it now — a strutting intruder, a priest's bastard!

On this particular morning he had need of a large draught of the hurt-allaying ichor of the room. Last night an incident that again made his position in the family seem of actually no importance had recurred with a kind of special sting in it, and he was resolved to make a beginning of asserting himself. What a damnable country this was after all! Despite his timidities and his self-suppression he had never entirely subscribed to its code of conduct. It was not so much the male, he had perceived for many years, as the quality "male" in man, woman, or child which commanded the respect he thought due only the obvious species. He realized what he owed to Agnese, but he cried aloud to his own heart that she was as much obligated to him. Had he not driven underground where its roar could do no harm, the open river of talk? Was he now to be told to stand by while she planned and planned a future for the puling, whimpering bastard of a whoring priest? He was not allowed, in actuality, even the crumb of overseeing the dumps. How the workmen laughed at him behind his back, and the words they used and the open disregard of his orders and the guffawing in the cafés when he permitted himself the luxury of expanding upon the theme of the growing Dantone wealth!

Farinella, whom he had bitten in the neck and humiliated before the whole steerage years ago — that man, their next-door neighbor now! He made free of his home, he and his three ill-mannered brats! He not only made free of his home, but what could all the snickering mean, the veiled remarks in the café on the corner, the business associations he and Agnese had developed, their constant meetings here, there, and everywhere?

"Have you heard?" These were the first words that greeted him as he sat down to a cup of coffee and anisette the previous night in the café.

"Heard what?"

A card player thumped the table as he laid down an ace, and a demitasse fell to the floor. The fat Don Gaspare, always good-natured, instead of answering Michele, laughed: "We'll have to charge you double for that. Good thing it wasn't the rum!"

And letting the cup lie in the sawdust, he turned to Michele:

"Nothing of importance, Don Miche', a little bit of a buy-up of houses."

A shout of laughter that to Michele seemed to fill the whole of the spacious corner store followed immediately as Don Gaspare, raising his tray clear above his head, minced toward the counter. What could it mean, thought Michele? Had someone said something funny at another table? Was the laughter for the words of Don Gaspare or for his grotesque nimbleness? Was it general or confined to one table? Were they laughing at him? But why? But why? He dared not look around. As he gazed out of the curtains to the opposite side of the street and felt the silk quilt over him, he made a wry face and all but stuck out his tongue as he might have done when a boy. But the moment in the café when the laughter roared in his ears was like a blow of a fist, the blow of a dwarf, puffed up with sudden grandeur and lording it over his former master. He recalled it and winced.

"A buy-up of houses? Well, what's that? He repeated and repeated the question.

"*Whey, Farinella bello!*" The whole-hearted greeting stabbed into Michele.

Farinella waved his hands to this man and that man in the style of the grand signor, his face beaming.

"Don Gaspare," he cried, "treat the crowd on me."

"*E bravo, e bravo!*" The shout was taken up all around.

Cups tinkled in their saucers, hands clapped, feet stamped, a wag jumped on a chair and cried for silence while in one of the corners the crowd broke into a ribald popular song.

Don Gaspare lifted his voice above it all in a lugubrious tenor and demanded to know, "What will the signori have?"

In the meantime Farinella, having seen Michele, burst into a merry greeting:

"*Whey, Miche'!*" and, drawing a chair up to his table, added, "We certainly put it across. We start work next month."

Michele stared at Antonio stupidly, his face flushing, his eyes blinking.

"Well, what?" He asked.

"Why, I thought you knew. No?" He scratched his head thoughtfully and came down with his open palm on the table. "That's funny."

"What's funny?" Michele fairly shrieked.

"Agnese never told you?"

"About what?"

"The tenements. . . ."

"Well?"

"Luigi, and she, and me. . . ."

"Of course. . . ." Michele tried to laugh it off.

"Why, we bought up all the row of houses opposite yours. . . ."

"Of course. . . ."

". . . and we're going to build a huge house six stories, eighty families, baths. . . ."

A crowd had collected around the table.

"*Evviva, evviva l'Italia!*"

They shouted lustily, and stamped, and yelled. A group seized hands and clamped around the table at which Michele and Farinella sat. Don Gaspare raised his tenor voice in song:

"And when it comes to brains . . . who has them?
The dagoes have them, yes they have all right, you bet!"

– 2 –

As he lay in bed looking out of the curtains Michele heard the shouting. He knew he had not deceived Farinella. Farinella knew that Agnese was shoving him aside. But the houses were there behind the curtains. They had not yet come down. They stood there, the symbol of the life he and Agnese had built together. She had dominated the situation but they had struggled together, and no one could claim the whole of the result. She could not toss him out of the world they both had constructed. The curtains blew, and across his heart a soothing wind passed and it made the whole of the room echo with the memories of barbershop and dark kitchen and long nights together.

He jumped out of bed and ran to the pier glass between the two windows. He clenched his fists at the image of his growing corpulence and the scared face above it.

"What's the matter with you? Have you lost all manhood? Are you the poltroon she calls you? Did you do nothing for her? Did you let her be called a whore and be treated like one, she and her rotten brat? Are you going to stand for this other man? Is he going to have his fill of her, too, and toss her back to me? Are you a fool? Are you a beast with horns? Ah, there are your horns! There, there!"

He placed his hands to either side of his forehead and stuck out his thumbs, and stared like a frightened child at the grotesque night-gowned image in the mirror.

Agnese entered at this moment.

"Well!" she cried. "Blessed be all the saints. Michele Dantone!"

Michele turned with a start, his face white, his whole body shaking, his jaws hanging loose.

"What's all this mean?" Her quick staccato utterance made him writhe with the agony of her long years of domination. But he could not say a word.

"What's all this? Say something! Are you dumb or crazy?"

"Crazy, Agnese, crazy." He shouted and wept together, and lifted up at the same time his pitiful mouse-like face to hers, coweringly, beseechingly.

"You must be. Get your clothes on. You'll catch your death of a cold."

"Why should I care for that?"

"Oh, quiet you, quiet. What's got into you? Get dressed."

She took him by the arm and escorted him to the bed.

"Why, you're shaking all over. Be quiet. Here are your clothes. Get dressed quickly and go and get shaved. You have to come to the lawyer's."

"To the lawyer's?"

"Yes. To sign a contract. . . ."

"Contract?"

"We're building. . . ."

"I don't know a thing . . . don't know a thing . . . What's all this?"

"What do you have to know?"

"So? What do I have to know? Is this all I am now?"

"Don't be a lout!"

"Why should I sign then? Why should I sign? It's as much my money as yours. I worked as you worked. . . ."

Agnese left him without another word. He stared after her in the dumb way of a beaten animal, shrinking into himself, hands in his hair, his scar a vivid blot on his cheekbone. He realized that affairs had come to a point for him, and that he had better decide once and for all to play the part of the unwanted but tolerated partner, accept the bounty of the good fortune that had happened to them, go back to the humble role of knocking at the door, entering, bowing to the insults. At least he had Agnese, proud, selfish woman that she was! He had done nothing to the scoundrelly priest. He would do nothing now . . . he would do nothing . . . he would. . . .

He had dressed and gone downstairs.

"*Whey, Miche'!*" came the hearty greeting of Farinella. Luigi sucked in the last gulp of his hot coffee and did not look up.

"Take some coffee," said Agnese simply, filling his demitasse and pouring in a small amount of rum.

"We'll make America yet!" shouted Farinella. "Hey, Luigi? We'll show them a thing or two. Why, Miche', we'll build the biggest houses they ever saw. . . ."

The stolid silence of Michele finally reduced his gayety and good spirits. Putting a shawl over her head, Agnese led them all out, Michele saying not a word, never looking at one or the other, casting on the whole enterprise an ominous gloom.

– 3 –

Agnese had given orders for a huge dinner to be served that night, and had told Concetta to spare no expense. Concetta had spared no expense.

The upstairs room had been cleared of furniture, all the tables in the house had been put end to end, the mantelpiece, filled with bottles of wine and liqueurs, made a dazzling rainbow of color as it was reflected in the mirror behind. Twenty chairs had been set, and before each chair was piled a pyramid of plates, one for each course. "Thank God!" said Concetta. "A monastery could eat their fill and have enough left over for a bit of charity."

In the room below another table had been as plentifully laid for the children, some of the old men of the neighborhood, and for whoever was not too ashamed to worm his way in. All the gas jets flared and as the intermittent wind of the warm September night blew in, the curtains swayed dizzily and the jets whizzed and roared. The contracts signed, sealed, and recorded were to be appropriately baptized in an orgy of eating, drinking, and merriment. Michele forgot the wound aching at the depths of his pride, and in the general abandon even rose to further heights of self-importance.

Don Gaspare, who kept the coffee shop, had made himself master of ceremonies. Peter Doolan and Michael O'Farril contributed the link between immigrant and established settler and provided a spectacle of generous approval of whatever was eatable and drinkable. Antonio Farinella, sitting next to Agnese, became not only flushed with the wine he was drinking but showed that he was permanently capable of the gypsy romance that had flashed in his eyes years ago in mid-sea. Luigi ate with the rest, noisily and happily, proud of the success that had been theirs, prouder of the success still to come, and so completely elated with the function, symbol of the wealth and the standing they had acquired, that he could watch the drunken flash of desire in Antonio's eyes and say nothing. Michele ate and drank unceasingly, shoulders bent over his plate, refusing to lift his eyes, to see anything, taking the slaps on his back and the shouted compliments as meant genuinely for both him and Agnese. He, too, realized the importance of the occasion. He did have quick glimpses of the still hot night on the ship when he had dug his teeth into Farinella's neck. But he knew he must accept the new situation, suffer Farinella to express desires none too honorable, none too subdued, not only in word and in the fire of eyes dancing with wine but in open gestures. Don Gaspare had saved the situation time and again. He would lift his glass on high and shout, "Everybody now! Everybody! Up with them, up with them, and repeat my words . . . *Evviva Agnese* . . . (shouts) . . . *Evviva Michele* . . . (shouts) . . . *Evviva l'Italia* . . . *Evviva l'America* . . . and drink . . . drink . . . drink it all down . . . every bit. . . ."

The children had come upstairs despite the repeated orders to keep out. They crowded in at the doors and watched eager-eyed. For the tables had been removed, the cask of wine had been placed in one corner, the huge trays of confetti and *dolci* in another corner, and a mandolin, a guitar, and an accordion filled the room with music. Catarina Farinella and Antonio, Agnese and Michele were to dance a tarantella.

Concetta was standing in the doorway keeping the children from crowding in, her face smiling with satisfaction, happy to be a party to so great a celebration. Luigi stood next to her, slightly intoxicated, laughing to himself, and now and then stamping his feet in time with the music. Gesualdo sat near the window looking on with a pleased smile in his old wrinkles, making soft gurgles of approval. Giovanni leaned on him, quiet, thoughtful, withdrawn. Occasionally the old man would stroke the child's hands and mutter something about how grand it all was, they certainly had "made America," and weren't they all to be proud of Agnese.

"Well, let's have it," cried Don Gaspare. "Come on, there, the music, and put into it the soul of our beautiful Italy. . . . Oh, make way . . . make way. . . ."

– 4 –

Once again the tarantella was to end in anger and savagery.

The four couples had faced each other, moved back and forth, saluted, and turned. They had exchanged partners and danced the first slow figures. They had held hands aloft, the four of them, and whirled like a pinwheel gathering greater and greater speed. They had come once again through a maze of gyrations and exchange of partners, and Farinella, overanimated and more vigorous than usual, twirled Agnese about and about, but in his turns with Catarina spun her mechanically without abandon of gesture or word. He shouted in tune with the music, stamped his feet, snapped his fingers. Once, as he passed Luigi, he pushed the young man against the wall.

"What, a little wine, and you're done for. This is America. Wake up!"

And he seized Agnese and whirled her about, her feet off the floor, her face warm with the exertion.

All this was amusement and glee to the onlookers. They clapped their hands and shouted their approval.

"A great boy, that one," Peter Doolan confided to Michael O'Farril.

"You bet, but I'm looking to see his ribs caved in for him," answered Michael, filling himself another glass from the barrel.

The dance had come to where partners are changed, and the couples dance singly. Catarina and Michele turned about and about and suddenly stopped. Agnese and Antonio remained on the floor. . . .

"*Bravo, e bravo. . . .*" Everyone shouted and applauded.

"We'll show there's the blood of youth in us yet," cried Antonio, seizing Agnese about the waist and whirling.

Her laughter sang above the music, unmistakable in its sense of joy. Michele winced as he heard it, his face instantaneously robbed of the color given it by the dance. But the perspiration remained and ran down his cheeks like cold tears glistening in the gas light. He had rarely heard her laugh with such heartiness, such lack of reserve, and such a sense of joy and youth and eagerness. His lips quivered but he remained immobile, fascinated.

Antonio and Agnese had interlocked elbows and stamped in a rhythmical gyration as everyone shouted. They sprang apart, faced each other and, placing their hands on their hips, looked into each other's eyes, their faces flushing, their bodies tense with excitement.

Slowly they bowed to each other, face to face, then to one side and then to the other. She took her place in the center and he moved about her, stamping his feet deliberately, calmly, as if teasing her into response, while she followed his movements, raising her head with tantalizing vigor, and again they interlocked and whirled. And all the while it had become increasingly patent that they had eyes for no others, had cast aside all thoughts of others, had found in each other something they had longed for — not the contracts they had signed, not the houses they owned, not the positions they occupied.

The elemental had burst through dams of routinized attitudes. Energy not meant to be harnessed had become loosed. Fire not meant to smolder unused had softened iron sinews. The poppy seed of passion had burst into flaming petals which swayed to the music of tumbling waters and hot winds. The musicians had caught their spirit, had redoubled the tempo, raised the sharp cries of their instruments to the pitch of pagan ecstasy. . . .

Catarina, stout, slightly perspiring, her face, like Michele's, chalk-white, stood biting her lips, looking on, feeling forgotten, cast aside, trampled upon with every movement of Antonio's feet.

"Grand to watch them," whispered Concetta in her ears. "I never knew she could dance so. She's like fifteen. See the way she moves like a flower. She's got no flesh. She's quick. . . ."

Giovanni had moved closer to his grandfather with his face half-turned toward the dancers. He had never seen his mother so happy, so gay, and as he gazed almost wild-eyed his lips twitched as if in pain, for he sensed something in his mother he would never know, would not want to know. It was at once savage and yielding, intense and pliant, restless and subdued. And he was uneasy, and he clung close to Gesualdo, unhappy, hurt, fearful. The desire to escape was in him, and as he sent his quick eyes about the room he knew he must, for he felt ashamed. How could his grandfather keep mumbling to him?

"She was like that, really. Like that before she had you. Full of life, a rose, a summer's day. . . ."

– 5 –

Agnese saw no one, neither Michele with his blanched face, the stout Catarina with her sad eyes glowing, Luigi leaning back against the door jamb smiling drunkenly, Giovanni clinging close to his grandfather as if afraid. The music had quickened again for the dance together, she had allowed herself to be taken quickly into Antonio's arms when he bent his head over her and without warning forced her head back from the chin with his hand and kissed her. There was a shout, half of intense joy, half of outrage. Catarina had thrown herself between them, and with savage fury had slapped Agnese first on one cheek, and then on the other.

"*Civetta . . . bestia . . . putana. . .* ," she screamed.

"What are you doing?" cried Antonio, seizing her and pushing her to the wall.

"Doing? I'll tell you what I am doing, you dog, you pig. So, so, that's the contract. . . ."

She flung herself at him, punching him with her fists, trying to bite him, tearing herself away if he tried to hold her.

Agnese had put her face in her hands, and stood motionless, her whole body limp, shame flowing over her like a torrent so that she seemed to sink lower and lower and draw closer to herself to avoid it. Michele had no idea what to do. He stared at his wife. He stared at Catarina as she struck and struck at her husband. He stared stupidly at Luigi. No one dared to interfere.

"Pig of a dog. You stinking brute. Let me get to her. I'll pull her eyes out. She's done this too much. She has put horns on her husband. She won't do this to me. . . ." Catarina screamed and screamed. Her joyless years of work, the animal-like docility of her life, the dammed-up imagination that had been hers, had found the only rebellion they were capable of. She had torn herself loose from Antonio and had flung herself on Agnese, shrilling incoherently. Tessie, her overgrown daughter, hair done up on her head much too adult-like, was attempting to pull her away.

"Mama, mama, don't do that. What a disgrace! What shame!"

Agnese had finally recovered her composure.

"Catarina," she cried, "what are you doing? Will you make a little thing big? What's happened has happened. Look at this crowd. Will you start all their tongues going?" She had put an arm about the enraged woman and was holding her tightly. "Go home. . . ."

"Go home!" shrieked Catarina. "Go to hell. . . ."

And she pulled quickly out of Agnese's embrace, ready to turn violently upon her rival. Antonio broke between them, caught his wife in his arms and, lifting her completely off the floor, carried her out as she burst into paroxysms of tears.

Several of the guests were preparing to leave.

"Better make a bee-line out," Peter Doolan whispered into O'Farril's ear.

– 6 –

"Where are you going?" asked Agnese, calm, collected, as if nothing had happened. "No time to leave yet. Here, Don Gaspare . . . pass the *dolci,* the liqueurs . . . start up the music. . . .Where are you, Michele? Don't look like a mouse. Come out of your hiding. The cat won't bite. And Luigi, Luigi! You should have brought the American girl. You could have danced the American dances. One for me, there, Don Gaspare. Don't you know that *Strega*'s my drink? See that Giovanni gets some of the sweet little cakes. Giovanni, where are you?"

Gesualdo, her father, took up the cry, "Giovanni, Giovanni!"

"Oh, he went upstairs . . . ran quickly, quickly like a dog," said Concetta. "He must be asleep by now. . . ."

Agnese said nothing. Concetta, alone, who knew her well, saw her lips quiver and her face momentarily go white, and Concetta crossed herself without the visible gesture, and prayed.

"And now, Filippo Terrabella," Agnese addressed the accordion player in a shout of voluble cordiality, "now is your turn. Do that promised jig as you play the accordion. Don't forget all the fire of Vesuvius. I want the old country life back again. We have conquered America. We build its houses, we clean the city, we lay the rails. Show them we have the fire of volcanoes in us. Look, Peter Doolan, this is the way to live. . . . Come, Filippo! Pass the wine there, Don Gaspare. . . ."

A circle was made in the hot room. There was not the spontaneous gayety of a quarter of an hour earlier. Some of the guests had gone out despite Agnese's entreaties. The rest had huddled back to the walls and made a quiet, subdued group of spectators, awed by the power of their hostess, so unperturbed, so dominant she appeared.

Filippo came forward, a tall, thin gypsy type, eyes blazing in a swarthy foil, fine matted hair pulled down on both sides from a center part, his accordion swung debonairly over his shoulders as it alternately quavered and wailed.

He shuffled quickly on both feet and as quickly returned to his original starting place only to proceed struttingly back while his instrument raised a monotonous appeal to a satyr god hidden in a distant mountain grotto.

"Oh, flower of the fig, sweet you are,
But not the sweetness of my passion flower.

Oh, flower of the jasmine bush,
Her fragrance is the spring's, it never dies.

Oh flower of the orange growing wild,
What, what do you know of beauty when she's by. . . ."

Filippo was the only gay person in the crowd. There was no mistaking the genuineness of his performance, an undulation of body in time with the persistent merrymaking of his accordion. As his voice broke in upon the strains of the accordion in a running improvisation of stornelli, the audience applauded, shouted, and called. The jig had proceeded rapidly to an unexpected climax of fast-moving feet, swaying body, and passionate voice, when the sound of quarreling broke in from the outside door.

"You will not come in."

Luigi's angry shout cut off the young Filippo in his wildest moment. Everyone had rushed to the door.

"What's all this, good people?" cried Agnese. "For shame, for shame. There's nothing. Get back. . . ."

"You're drunk, and you'll cut up no more in here," yelled Luigi.

"For the sake of God, Luigi, let me in. . . ."

"No knife, no knife. . . ." The screams were terrifying. Every pretense at keeping up the party was cast aside. The door was jammed. Some of the people had rushed to the back and were going downstairs into the kitchen and out the back way. Others were trying to break through to get to the front door. Agnese was caught in the struggling mass unable to make her way out. When she was finally able to get through and had come to her brother's side she was in time to see Antonio go rolling down the brownstone stoop to the sidewalk. She gave a piercing scream.

"Why did you do it, Luigi, why, why?"

-7-

Disturbing as the evening had been, overcome with the excitement and the fear that it inspired, tense with the need for keeping up an unperturbed appearance, Agnese nevertheless realized how ominous the possibilities were. She had sunk practically all of her money in a common scheme with Farinella. It was he who had the technical knowledge of building and upon him would ultimately depend the success of the undertaking. To antagonize him now, to open up a breach between the two families, to make an enemy not only of Catarina but of Antonio too — all this she perceived with instantaneous horror would be the end of her success in America, a tragic, costly conclusion to a bitter struggle without joy, without love, without sweetness and the inward serenity that smiles even upon hardship.

A large crowd had collected in the streets. The dark night had sufficiently hidden the identity of the fighting men to keep from the curious too detailed a knowledge of what had happened. A large enough number had assembled at the foot of the stairs to make it impossible for Antonio to rush back precipitously and engage Luigi in the savage grip he longed for. If he had had a knife in his hand, he was now unarmed. He rose to his feet and made a frantic attempt to pull away from the restraining hands that held him and the little mob that blocked the sidewalk.

Agnese in the meantime had pushed Luigi aside and with superhuman effort had closed the front door and occupied a position immediately in front of it.

"What do you all want here?" she shouted. "Move off. Is there no policeman around? Get away, get away. . . ."

Antonio had disengaged himself and was mounting the steps.

"Get this crowd away, Antonio," cried Agnese. "Can't you see this crowd is breaking up my party? Help me to drive it away. Antonio!" she called after a pause. Antonio stood stock-still, gazing at her, utterly stunned by the power of her calmness. "Antonio, help me, help me. Don't look so savagely at me." All this she spoke in an agonized, terrified whisper, and then she raised her voice menacingly to the noisy crowd at the foot of the steps. "Get away from here, I say . . . away . . . away. . . ."

"Let us go inside," whispered Antonio close to her, "and they will go. Come. . . ."

Someone behind her had meanwhile been making attempts to force the door open. Agnese had exerted all her physical pressure to keep it shut as she was putting all the power of her will into withstanding the crowd below. But at Antonio's words she seized the knob with a suddenness that surprised those inside and, taking Antonio by the hand, quickly drew him after her into the house.

– 8 –

Everybody not in the immediate family had already taken his departure. Michele stood behind the curtains looking out, devoid of the power to act, his whole body bent in an impotent huddle. In an armchair Gesualdo sat, helpless, too, his face flushed with anxiety, his knotted hands brought close to his chest as if straining to him something infinitely dear that was not willing to remain with him. Luigi was behind the door as Agnese and Antonio came in, lost in shadow, an irresolute figure, torn between impulses of which he was ashamed and a desire to assert himself angrily to the full.

"Listen, everybody," cried Agnese, but, not instantly perceiving Luigi, asked, "and where's Luigi?"

"Luigi," she spoke confidently, deliberately panting as if for breath; however, her eyes were vivid and alert as her father had rarely seen them. "There has been too much bad blood tonight and there is going to be no more. Old times are gone. We are not in the hills with peasant louts now.

"We're in America and they do things differently. We're not young, either. We have got business, big business ahead of us. I have suffered enough, do you understand? I have suffered enough. I suffered when I was a child and had my baby alone, far away from everybody, in agony, in fright. You have never suffered like that. You all say you love me. Each of you. You love me for one thing or another. I love you. I am a woman, too, and a mother, and a wife. We're not going to spoil the things we've done in this country."

She continued in shrill staccato, her face flushing crimson and growing pale again, her whole body quivering where she stood.

The men gazed at her in amazement, speechless, unable to glance at each other for fear of revealing the intense shame of being so forcefully controlled by this woman who seemed to have found a diabolical method of imposing her will upon them all.

"We're in America, do you hear? In America? We're going to make our life here to the end of our days. We're going to die in our beds and we're going to die rich. Come close to me, all of you! Michele, I say, close to me! Here, Luigi, give me your hand, and yours, Antonio, and here, papa, yours, too. One upon the other . . . come. . . ."

They obeyed, if without alacrity or zeal, at least without open protest or murmur.

"And say after me . . . all of you . . . 'God is good and we will be one in friendship, in business, and we will make America and no one shall stop us, enemy or friend, love or hatred. . . .'"

They repeated the words after her, smiling stupidly, heads bowed, their voices scarcely audible above the panting of her breath.

"And now, we shall drink each a glass of the wine I have from the home town. It's not your home town, Antonio, but it's nearby. We have been neighbors all our lives. Pour it, *tata* . . . no . . . no . . . not in glasses. Go downstairs and get the *fiaschetta* that came only last week." Gesualdo hurried to get it while Agnese continued her stream of nervous, excited talk. "It's a seasoned one, Antonio, made from the finest ash. Tight as a ship. Fits right in the hands, too. It's joy to hear the wine come blub, blub. . . ."

Gesualdo had brought the diminutive cask, soundly hooped with birch root, with a thin long spigot on its flat side.

"I'll take it first," she cried, seizing it and raising it far above her head. Tilting back her head so that her mouth was directly under the spigot, she allowed the wine to trickle through and bubble musically into her mouth. The sound it made as it slipped into her throat was like the dropping of beads down a flight of stairs. The men marveled at her as she drank and in the marvel of her performance saw the strength of her will and forgot their anger. Each in his turn drank and when they had finished Agnese turned to them all again, and cried:

"Tonight has been and is over. What has happened, has happened. Don't forget, the houses must go up. The people they must look and cry out, 'What a sight! What a feat!' And now good night, good night. . . ."

IX. ANTONIO

– 1 –

Antonio said good night as hastily as Agnese.

He found Catarina kneeling in the attitude of the deepest contrition, almost of humiliation, before a plaster figure of the Holy Virgin. She did not turn to look about as he entered nor did she stop her solemn half-suppressed wailing. The features of the Virgin, cadaverous white over her stiff mantle of stark red, betrayed over the slightest smile, an effect produced by the shadow thrown from an oil lamp swinging above her head.

The room in which Catarina had placed this statue was similar to the downstairs dining and living room of Agnese's and of the other brownstone houses in the neighborhood. Sunk below the level of the street, long and narrow, a door cut through the back leading into the kitchen through a washroom and pantry combined, with a ceiling unusually high. The room gave the impression of a crypt. All the lights were out with the exception of the swinging lamp. Its light made a shadow rather than an illumination across the whole length of the floor, and evoked out of the mirror over the dark marble mantelpiece fantastically distorted replicas of the Virgin, the chairs, the hat rack in the corner, suggesting a series of other statues along a dim, strange corridor without end. Into this medley of lugubrious forms was thrown the silhouette of Antonio's head and body as he stood holding the door half-open with his left hand and gazed at Catarina kneeling at the other end.

"*Porco Dio Santo,*" he exclaimed under his breath, gritting his teeth with such vehemence that the sound was heard above the lamentation of his wife. It was not the first time he had seen her in this position, nor the first time that he had sworn under his breath the sacrilegious oath. "*Porco Dio Santo! Bestia Madonna.*" He banged the door after him and his impulse was to throw her flat upon the floor and dig his heels savagely into her face, her breasts.

"Drive my wicked thoughts out of my head, *Maria Vergine di Gesu,*" Catarina intoned. "Drive the wicked thoughts out of my head, *O Dio, O Dio!* For my children's sake! Let that beastly creature drop dead in the street, let her drop dead in the street! Blessed Virgin, Mother of God, help me hold my head erect, for my children's sake, Mother of God, blessed one!"

"*Porca madonna santissima!* Get up from there, get up!" shouted Antonio.

The fierce intentions he had suppressed broke the full volume of his voice and reduced it to a brutal, throaty whisper. "Get up from there . . . get up . . . get up. . . ."

Catarina was well aware of the deep current of superstition in her husband's character despite the outward bravado, and she had long before learned just how far she could go with her prayers without bringing on a violent physical assault which she could not have withstood. Swaying her body back and forth, her hands held tight between her knees, she lifted her thin wail in a desperate sing-song rhythm:

"For my children's sake, have mercy upon me. Blessed Mother, have compassion upon us all . . . drive my wicked thoughts away. . . ."

"For the love of Almighty God, stop it, stop it, stop it," shrieked her husband in wild crescendo.

"Oh, let me alone, Antonio, let me alone. . . . It's for my sins, it's for my children's sake. . . ," she answered meekly without turning round. "*Dio c'aiuta. . . .*"

"For the last time, Catarina. . . ."

– 2 –

Catarina knew she had won. For many years she had realized that Antonio had not loved her. But she had found him a faithful husband in his own way. Her demands upon him were few and modest. She was content to have him return from his work, sit at the table, dispose of his food without so much as looking up, bragging all the while of his exploits on the job, put his children on his knees after the meal, peck at their cheeks, laugh with them, drive them away after a few minutes, take down his pipe, smoke away at a rapid rate, move around the room banging with his fists on the tables and the chairs as he kept fighting first one, then another, of the men that worked for him or with whom he had any dealings, swear at all the saints in the calendar as he did so, only to fall into a chair as a finale and sink into a deep, noisy sleep.

Those were the happiest moments of her day. Immediately after his sudden slumber, which would last for an hour at the most, Antonio made a fastidious toilet, pomading his hair close over his head, pulling up the ends of his mustaches to points directly over his cheek bones, and without stopping for a word of good-bye left the house unceremoniously to return within two hours, go to his bed, and, undressing, fall fast asleep.

There were nights when he stayed at home, but these nights were not so quiet. They were the nights devoted not to the search for business away from home or in cafés or in the residences of other contractors. They were devoted to the sacred scanning of the numerous plans and blue-prints, specification sheets, cost catalogues, bills and memoranda with which the desk in the corner of the dining room was perennially littered. He quarreled with the children, he quarreled with Catarina for permitting the children to be noisy, he quarreled with himself as he failed to work out his sums, or found himself in tangles of calculations. On these nights he was awake long after the others had gone to sleep. Catarina had made several attempts to sit beside him as he worked, busy with crocheting or lacemaking, only to discover that the sounds of anger, the loud imprecations to this saint and that, the brusque shoving back of a pile of papers were all manifestations of irritation at her presence.

"Get to bed. Can't you leave me alone? Do you have to meddle in everything? *Per l'amore di Santo Stefano!*"

– 3 –

Their marriage had been arranged between friends. Catarina had remained in Italy after the first contingent of young men, some with brides but the majority without, had left their coast town of San Giovanni a Mare to make their fortunes in America, and to leave the young women in a desperate frenzy of speculation as to who would be called away first to become a bride in America.

Catarina had been the first to be called. She had not known Antonio save when she had seen him on his return from the army, tall, spare, and straight, a red sash across his belt, and a fatigue cap, with a tassel saucily dangling from the side.

He was known as a moody, quiet youth. A sort of forced glitter in his eyes and flashing teeth had brought quick merriment and laughter among the girls. But there ensued an instantaneous suppression of it, all the more apologetic for it was not unmingled with fear. The reports that he was a blaze of strength in the tarantella, that he grasped one with a determination short of the ferocious and whirled one about in silent vehemence were like torches to their imaginations, and though more than one made a motion of shoulders and head as if to say, "no, thank you, not for me," he was thought of as an excellent catch. Especially was this so when there was added the undoubted confirmation of his industrious habits, his skill as a workman on the houses that had been built in the town, and the great love and affection he had shown to his mother ever since she had been widowed. So Catarina was called the lucky virgin and they all promised that on the night of her wedding in New York they would build a bonfire in San Giovanni that should light up the whole sea — and show her that they were dancing about it to her happiness. And against the wedding day they had all been busy on a huge lace coverlet for her nuptial bed with a design of grape clusters in delicate canisters, even now the admiration of her friends.

The first year in New York had been a money-getting year for Antonio. Never out of work, he had gathered handsome wages but had not given proof to his friends of ability to spend them wisely. It was one girl after another, and not Italian girls who could not be had for the purposes he intended, but the "English girls" who were after one's purse, change and leather and all. For several months preceding his spendthrift days, he had gone to Michele's barbershop in the evening and while the men outside played at *tocco* or bemoaned interminably the lot that had brought them to America, he lounged against the door, a disconsolate, morose figure, hungry for a sight of Agnese with her slim form and braided hair. But Agnese had not encouraged him and more than once the ire in Luigi's glance had provoked him to a wry, challenging laugh that forboded possibilities none too wise, and his *paesani* had begged him to give it up.

"What do you want with that little bitch?" Barto Losanto asked him one night as they walked under the clattering elevated trains to their rooming house several streets up. "What do you want to get mixed up in a row for? *Fattite l'America* and then, you know you can have the best of them. Listen to a friend, Antonio. That's what I'm doing. I ain't got your luck. Been out of work more days than working. But I'm sewing it up in a bag. Got money in my pocket now. Going to send for my father and little brothers first, and then for the girls and my mother. May take me two years. But I'm sewing up the cash in my pants. Let her alone. She's married. She's a bitch, too. That ain't his child. You know the story. Get a good girl. . . ."

"*Porco diavolo,* Barto, shut up. . . ."

But Barto kept hopping along with his larger companion, a short, thin little fellow with distressed, beaded eyes and a face that came all to a point at the tip of his nose.

"Oh don't show your temper to me. Remember Catarina. . . . Catarina, you know, the daughter of o'Papariello Solimano . . . the priest chaser who made the bricks . . . she's a pretty thing too. . . . We'll arrange it. . . ."

One night Antonio had gone to the barbershop as usual and learned that Michele was out, and that Luigi had left with a gang of men to "work the tracks" somewhere upstate. He ran up the stairs to Agnese's room, knocked on the door and forced his way in. Agnese confronted him calmly, the baby Giovanni in her arms.

"Well?" she asked simply.

"I've come. I can't keep away. You've burned up my heart."

"Go away now. Did the neighbors see you?"

"Why should you care for neighbors?"

"Go away now. . . ."

"Agnese, you are a fire in me. You have burned up my heart. When I first saw you on the ship I wanted you. I let myself be bitten and did nothing. I did nothing because you asked me. And now we are alone. I can't go away. We'll go off together. This is a big country. . . ."

"Antonio, if you love me, go away, go away, I say. . . ." She came forward pushing him against the door, exerting a fierce, animal pressure upon him without touching him. "I'm no good for you, Antonio. They will all tell you. I must fight my way here alone with the man I chose. There's no more love in my life. There's to be no more love in my life. I'm going to fight it out with my man. He was good to me . . . I'm his now . . . you were not there when I wanted . . . no . . . no . . . I would not have taken you . . . no matter how strong, no matter how savage . . . you would not have taken me, what's more . . . you know the story. Shall I tell you the story that you know? I can be nobody else's . . . not even this man's . . . I am cursed with something . . . it makes you love me . . . I can't love . . . go away. . . ."

"Agnese, it's fire I live in . . . it's fire . . . ."

Resolutely, coldly, Agnese came forward, turned the knob of the door, opened it.

"Go away now . . . do not come again . . . the future is long. Who can tell. . . ."

"You're a hell witch . . . a she-devil. . . ."

"Yes, I know . . . they all call me that . . . but why will you?"

Antonio covered his face with his hands, bent his head in defeat, stood weakly at the door, let himself be firmly, steadily pushed out. He ran downstairs, to the street, up the avenue, ran until he was exhausted, stopped, stood like one struck violently by an unexpected blow, stood as if he were whirling about too fast to fall, and then he laughed, laughed aloud. A small crowd gathered about him of which he was altogether unaware. It was Barto who had first brought him to his senses.

"Are you crazy, Antonio? What's the matter?"

The little fellow took him by the arm and made him walk along with him. His face was all screwed up with anxiety.

"You act like a madman. You're the way you were in the army the night the girl slapped you in Florence. . . ."

"Barto, for God's sake, let me alone . . . don't take me home. . . ."

"All right, where'll we go?"

"Where? Where would one go in this God-abandoned country? Where? To hell. Let's go to hell together, hey Barto? To hell?"

Barto became frightened. "Don't, Antonio! You're sick, you're sick. What'll happen to you in this country, all alone, living with men only, no women folk to care for you? Brace up . . . go home . . . go to sleep. . . ."

– 4 –

From that night on Antonio spent his money with a recklessness that caused the *paesani* to put their heads together and determine to put an end to it. He had barely acquired enough English to be understood on the job, but he was forever seen with an "English girl" hanging on his arm. They knew too well where he made their acquaintance.

The city in those days was a blaze of open saloons with their dives in the rear, dingy sawdust-covered holes where men sat for hours until they were either thrown out in drunken stupors or emerged in the tow of smirking prostitutes. Often they were left to face the dawn, their money gone, dirty, stupefied or even blood-soaked from blows of thugs.

Antonio, like other Italians, was not accustomed to hard drinks. One glass sufficed him, and one look to determine his choice of companion. And he was home early and to bed in time to get up sobered and ready for another day's work on the mason jobs on which he was employed in various sections of the city.

During the year he had saved a sum of money which in the old country would have placed him on a par with Don Eduardo, the lawyer and banker. Like the rest of the men he carried the money in a roll or in gold pieces in one or more of the pockets of his suit.

The feast of *Sant' Elena* was in full swing. Arch upon arch of colored lights running to an even more brilliantly lighted crown in the center spanned half a mile of streets. Under them in full fanfare marched and marched again, the band and its tail of a procession, stopping at every street corner for long ropes of fireworks to be fired in rapid, deafening succession. The streets were lined with pushcarts displaying innumerable festoons of dried nuts, tinted cakes, pastry rings glistening in the light, pictures of uncounted saints, candles, and candlesticks for the devout to take to the church. The whole colony had emptied into the thoroughfares, jostling, guffawing, shouting, shuffling back and forth following the procession. To the confusion was added the clatter of elevated trains and the clanging bells of the surface cars, cursed again and again as they forced the sacred line of marchers to halt and make way for them.

Barto had seen Antonio plunge into the crowd and soon lose himself, his shoulders thrown up with violent self-approval. Before leaving he had taken out roll after roll of bills, several little linen bags filled with gold pieces, a package of letters.

"I got enough in this pocket, see, Barto," Antonio had said. "You keep the rest for me. No matter what happens, hold on to it. Send it to my mother. . . ."

Barto sat dangerously tipped over on the edge of his chair. He looked with blank amazement at Antonio, his eyes blinking with immeasurable rapidity.

"Antonio! Antonio, when are you going to end this? It's almost a year now . . . be sensible. Take a little man's word. . . . What do you mean by all this? Sounds like a lot of foolishness. . . like a little baby. . . ."

Antonio jumped from the bed on which he had been sitting, his feet hitting the bare boards of the floor with such a noisy impact as to convince Barto of the uselessness of further argument.

"You're the baby! What are we getting out of all this? Work, work, work all day. A little *tocco* at night, a gulp of wine, and to bed! Bah! Worse than the army. Tonight's a gay night. I'm going to Doolan's."

Doolan's had acquired a reputation more evil than it deserved. For Peter Doolan made it a point of honor to see that as soon as a man was visibly drunk he was forcibly ejected from the saloon. He had another honorable objective in his management and that was to allow only what he called "select girls."

His windows were, in a sense, decided manifestations of the impulse to artistic expression. By day they blazed with the unnumbered rainbow effects of the hundreds of variously colored bottles on display beneath a chandelier hung with crystals iridescent in all lights. By night, the chandelier shed a fairy effulgence of forever changing color upon the rich array of liquors so that, though the neighborhood children had been repeatedly warned against loitering near the wicked saloon, they stood gazing into the window open-mouthed with astonishment and wonder. Half-swinging doors, each one a mirror with an elaborate design for border, allowed passers-by to catch a sight of feet resting on a highly polished brass rail, of brass spittoons in a sea of finely powdered sawdust, of three-legged tables. A discreet door of heavy, dull-finished oak, marked in large gilt letters "FAMILY ENTRANCE," permitted admission into an anteroom and beyond that into a foul-smelling replica of the larger room in front where the "select" feminine patrons of Peter Doolan could sit and sip their whiskey while waiting for the inevitable customer of the evening. The night of the *festa* Doolan's illumination was outdone by the glittering colored lamps swung across the streets, and whether because of this or the feeling that something solemn and religious was in the air, it stood out only feebly and seemed ashamed to be ogling one in a manner like a painted lady smirking in the dark.

– 5 –

Antonio might carry his shoulders high and smile gaily, but Barto's beaded eyes looked all the more distressed, for he knew that Antonio was cursing himself for a fool the while, blaspheming under his breath the most blessed saints and hoping throughout it all for someone to whip him out of his stupid big-boy bravado. Barto opened his lips wide and brought them together again with an inaudible snap, stood thinking motionlessly for a second, put on his hat in a frenzy and rushed after the swaggering Antonio.

But Antonio had walked fast and sat now with one leg thrown out, hat at an angle, and a huge hand flat on a table in the backroom of Peter Doolan's saloon. Before him stood the huge glass of beer he had ordered. He was fully aware of the young woman, arrived for the *festa,* who winked at him as she tossed her head and smiled the sign manual of her profession. But he kept his leg stiffly out, balanced his hat carefully on his head, moved two or three fingers to an inner rhythm of anger and memory and bitter debate.

Outside there arose the voices of several young men intoning in sad falsetto, "I'll fight the world. I'll fight them, for you're my sweetheart now." The woman leaned over her table and tossed her head with undisguised directness. She sat in a corner but Antonio could see the gold in her teeth, the big feather-hat flopping over her bleached hair, the full bosom forced higher than its natural lines by tight-fitting corsets.

They eyed each other now and then, but neither changed tables. They might have gone on in this fashion for the whole evening, ordering drinks and making no other attempt at stirring. The entrance of two young men who took seats with the high-bosomed prostitute must have been a signal. Antonio could not distinguish the rapid whispers in which they talked, but he could not fail to see some connection between them and the woman rising and undulating toward him several minutes after the young men had left. But he was more conscious of their shining patent-leather shoes with thin points, tight-fitting trousers wrinkled above the ankles, and their dancing, shambling walk as they left the room — he was more conscious of these than of the smiling woman as she took a seat at his table and placed her hand caressingly on his.

"Let's make it a beer again, or whiskey, hey?" she simpered coaxingly.

The waiter had already placed two whiskeys and water in front of them. Antonio thought it peculiar but said nothing, nodded and, without looking at his companion, took her cheek between two fingers and twisted it, laughing throatily the while.

"Alla righta, we dreenk," he cried, and poured the glass down.

"You got the big, black Italian eyes, kiddo," she laughed.

Antonio turned a pleased grin to her.

"You gotta — you gotta — the gold tootta." They both laughed uproariously.

"Another drink, hey, *paesano?*" She waved her hand, and the waiter placed two more glasses before them.

"Sure . . . me paya all . . . two more . . . sixa more . . . you gotta . . . you gotta. . . ." He made a movement indicating that her bosom was ample and expansive, and they laughed again.

"You're sweet," she said pulling him to her with one hand. "Bet you got a nice sweetheart."

"Na, na. . . ," he shook his head, and gulped down the second glass. "You . . . you . . . gonna be my switahearta . . . com'monna . . . we go. . . ."

He rose unsteadily, his black eyes dancing from the unaccustomed liquor.

"Oh, no. Take your time. What's the hurry? The night's young, kiddo.

Let's have another. . . ."

"No!" he cried hotly. "We go now. . . ."

"Oh, Tony boy, you're in a goddam hurry. . . ."

"We go outa now . . . no more dreenka for me."

But she had waved her hands again. Fresh drinks had been placed on the table as if by magic.

"All right, you hot devil," she said, poking his ribs and rising. "Just this one more drink, see."

She raised a glass to his mouth.

"Go on, sweet boy, drink it down, drink it down," she cried, laughing drunkenly, as Antonio, trying to avoid the glass, slipped further and further back. The tight-trousered young men were standing in the doorway, and he thought he caught the woman winking at their tense, leering faces.

He slapped the glass swiftly, dashing it to the ground and spilling the contents over her dress.

"You goddamn. . . ."

"We go now," he cried hotly once more, seizing one of her arms under his, and dragging her forcefully with him as she screamed and laughed and swore at him. "Whadda hell you teenk me dreenka lika peeg?"

All that he recalled after that was a glimpse of the young men coming from behind, a quick, soft blow on his head, and then waking up in a dirty, foul-smelling alleyway several blocks from the saloon. He omitted no detail which he recalled as he narrated his story to the *paesani* gathered about his bed.

"Barto found me there. No better than a pig I was. Remember the pigs in the mud back home? They banged me up for good measure when they found my pockets empty."

"His face was all mashed up, blood, dirt. . . ." Barto opened his mouth as he gazed first at one and then another of the visitors and, having made his point, snapped it shut.

"It's the last of it, sure as the Angel Gabriel is in Heaven," swore Antonio.

– 6 –

And so it was decided to send for Catarina, the brown-haired, plump little daughter of the brick-maker. She would make him a sensible wife, and he had strength, and a good trade, and money saved up.

Catarina arrived just in time to make the wedding a merry pre-Christmas event. Aside from the *paesani,* who considered themselves her constituted protectors, she was alone in a vast country, as the Italians phrased it. Not even one of her relatives had found it possible to accompany her on the voyage, and her desperate mother was in the end compelled to seek the assistance of the parish priest, Don Matteo, who never was without knowledge of someone or other about to set off for America. Don Matteo had frequently been called upon to give his blessings to young men and old men, young women and old women, departing to make their homes in that far-off land.

"I am glad you are going," he would say, "and I shall pray and do always pray to our Blessed Mother that you keep well and mind God and his church no matter where you are. But, but, my child," here he would lay his hand on the traveler's head and utter a series of deprecating sounds with his lips, "I do not approve of your going. I do not approve of so many going away to that land. Gold it may have, and wealth it may bring you, and may you enjoy it. But they say it is a godless land. They have forgotten their duty to the church and cast from their homes the sacred effigies of Our Lord. Few are the edifices erected to the glory of Our Savior and fewer those who visit them. But to the willful who would depart from the protection of our happy, quiet towns, I say, 'Go, God be with you. Leave us in our poverty. Hasten to the gold-paved towns of that monstrous country in the great distance.' And now," he would add, changing his tone of voice to one more matter of fact, "don't forget to buy a scapulary of our patron *Sant' Elena* and have it blessed, and leave a candle on the altar."

To Catarina Bassardino he spoke these words and more.

"You are a brave girl to go alone. Father Rocco is a dear young priest, devoted to his work, and he will accompany you to New York and not leave you until your friends there take you out of his hands. You are fortunate, my young one. You are fortunate, most, most fortunate. You are getting a sweet, good man. He was my favorite altar boy, and he was always faithful and gentle, and he grew to be a handsome lad. Ah, Catarina, a great big piece of a man and the handsomest in his military class, and he will make you a good husband. You will prosper. . . . God be with you. Don't forget. Buy a *Sant' Elena* to wear around your neck. Place a candle on the altar. . . ."

Catarina had always been plump so that the long wearisome voyage did not even soften the color which shone on her high cheekbones and gave her round, full face a girlishness that not even the long skirts and ample bodice could conceal. At seventeen she was already grown up, especially marked out, as she thought, to set an example of industry and devotion to the other girls who would soon be sent for. Although she was plump and red-cheeked and had teeth so small and white that her mouth seemed perpetually expressing a childish pleasure in everything, Catarina was essentially a timid, submissive, even unhappy soul.

She gazed with sidelong eyes at Antonio as he stood in a corner of Zia Cristina's kitchen, drinking with the men. Zia Cristina had promised to house her for the few days before the wedding. Zia Cristina had made a regular practice of doing that very thing, and many were the girls who were married from her home, weeping silently and copiously for their mothers left in Italy to pray for them on their wedding day. It had been just a friendly act at first, but as the years wore on and more and more new brides made her home their temporary headquarters, she had begun to expect that the little favors of ten dollars or five dollars and full orders of salami and *prosciutto* and nuts and oil from the *grosseria* as a gift from the happy bridegroom would be forthcoming as a matter of course.

"There are all kinds of ways of piling it up in this country. No wonder she's as big around as her stove. Sure she ought to keep laughing. She's the virgins' friend, she says, and the Virgin will be her friend, but she tells them enough to send herself and all of them straight to the devil himself."

Barto sipped her wine, and ate her *tarrallini,* and played *tocco* with her husband, and he was quite right in believing that she would fill Catarina's ears with spicy bits out of Antonio's life, and put the young thing on her guard against that "*malandrino* of a gypsy" as she called him. And so it was. No sooner had Catarina been allowed to shake hands with Antonio, bow politely, her head dropping with its weight of blushes and embarrassment, than Zia Cristina cried out to her, clapping her hands, "Inside now, and take off your things. Here, let me have that shawl. Ha! shawls are pretty . . . this one for instance . . . not like the hats here . . . they're like flower-pots on your head. . . . But your shawl . . . oof, oof, why the tears? Plenty time for tears . . . he's a handsome boy . . . isn't he handsome? Some handsome, I always say . . . lucky girl that gets him, said I lots of times . . . he'll be good to you . . . there . . . there . . . there. . . ."

She gathered Catarina into the voluminous folds of her arms and bosom and rocked her back and forth.

"Oo-oo, little girl's afraid . . . afraid . . . afraid to be no more . . . a maid . . . a maid . . . a wee bit, lovely maid. . . ." She sang to the tune of a popular song.

She sang and she slapped Catarina on the back, and she laughed.

"Plenty time to be afraid . . . afraid . . . there! Oof . . . oof . . . silly . . . silly tears . . . stop it, child, stop it! Don Rocco's a pretty little priest, isn't he now? He's been drinking with Antonio, and he likes him, and you will like him . . . you will love him . . . he's a catch, I tell you. . . . Sure, he has had his fling, and you must have heard . . . well . . . of course . . . who hasn't heard . . . and whose mother's son has not fallen under that woman's foot . . . and . . . sure . . . young men . . . must have their wild days . . . Antonio's no exception. . . ."

Catarina burst into a fresh fit of weeping and clung with both her arms to Zia Cristina's neck. She was finally quieted and went to her dinner in the large kitchen, her tiny white teeth and her brown-cherry eyes, to use Cristina's phrase, giving her face its only animation. She sat next to Antonio, who kept awkwardly urging her to eat, but she ate nothing, said nothing, rarely raising her head, not even smiling, although the remarks became bolder and bolder as glass after glass of wine disappeared from the table. And she was married two days later, and went with Antonio to the three rear rooms of a tenement. They had been fitted out with several round-backed spindle chairs, a highly polished oak table, a rough *bur-ro,* as they called it, a white, iron bed that was to have the elaborate lace blanket good enough for the nuptial bed of the princess herself.

She wept when the door closed behind her and her husband, and felt more terribly alone than even when, standing on the deck, she had viewed nothing but water, white, noisy, and restless as far as the eye could see. Try what devices of word or gesture he might, Antonio did not succeed in getting her to cease weeping, silently, continuously, her body shaking and trembling, shaking and trembling. That night remained clearly in her memory for the rest of her life. And Antonio never forgot it either; it became so intolerable a memory, indeed, that at the slightest sign of her weeping he was seized with an uncontrollable fear that there would be a repetition of it and he bent all his energies to prevent it. He promised anything, did anything, swore to anything just so long as she in turn promised not to cry.

"Per l'amore di tutt' i santi, Catarina, Catarina, don't, don't!"

She had made a good wife. While he prospered, she became rosier and rosier, although never lively, never assertive. As the children came, a settled air of determination, as of facing courageously unexpected hardships, brought out the essential timidity at the bottom of her nature. But she gave herself to her tasks with wholehearted energy, scrubbed, cooked, looked after the children, anticipated fearfully, pantingly, all of her husband's wants, followed his every suggestion as if it were the order of a tyrant.

Like the Dantones, they, too, had prospered. From a mason's helper he had risen to a mason, saved his wages, took over small contracts, finally became much sought after. His work was thorough, dependable, accurate. After the tenement had been torn down, they moved into one of the newer houses, adding to their furniture as well as to their family, sending for his mother (who died before she could enjoy the fullness of this blessed country, as she put it), finally for her mother and father, both of whom, as if it were in the book of the good saints for it all to happen, died, too, after several years. Catarina became more and more frightened and less and less assertive. She failed to learn the language of her new country, had no interest in acquiring a taste for its styles in dress, its new foods, its new ways. But in this she was like countless others and was not at all peculiar. However, she was different in that she made no effort to make friends, to entertain, to spend in any pretentious display the money her husband was making. Her children and her husband were the complete inventory of her desires, interests, activities. She dressed the young ones like replicas of the smart children of the "English" whom she occasionally saw on the streets. This was the only exception to her practice of doing only those things which were to her like the old country, familiar, heart-warming, reliable. The results were at times grotesque but she was unaware of it.

Antonio minded his own affairs, seemed to have forgotten about Agnese, although he spoke of her to Catarina, admired the fortune she and her husband were accumulating, and knew all that she was doing. Catarina, who had been told about her husband's infatuation for *la civetta,* winced at the mention of Agnese's name and inwardly made the sign of the cross. The next day she ran over to Zia Cristina to hear what she could hear, and immediately followed this visit with one to the church and a confession of mean, wicked thoughts that made her unhappy.

"Thoughts that are daggers . . . they hurt. The milk in me sours. . . ." Invariably she heard nothing. Antonio had achieved and was maintaining a reputation for sound business habits and for incomparable family ways. Even when he stayed out later than usual, and Catarina heard him in the kitchen pouring out his nightcap of red wine and munching on figs or cheese while she lay trembling in her bed, she knew that there had happened nothing to break the soft monotony of her ways. The latter years of her married life had become years of trust in minding her own business, doing her work, providing for her children. So it was not altogether with dread that she approved of moving into the big brownstone house next to *La Dantone*. Moreover, Zia Cristina had assured her that the talk had died down.

"He works too hard. A man that works too hard has no head for women. . . . And he loves you, too, my little fat potato, and his tiny ones. Who would run around chasing women when he has a brown-eyed Tessie?"

– 7 –

But the experiment of living in the big house next to *La Dantone* brought bitterness into Catarina's thoughts. Tessie ran in and out of both houses, and the curly-haired straight back Ciritillo plodded after, screeching to be taken along, and Rosinella, the baby, remained behind, her fists churning and churning her eyes shut. Catarina rarely visited, and when she did go with her husband, made a quick bow, and sat down smiling, saying "Yes" or "No" to this and that, and hardly more than three words the whole evening besides.

Agnese noted the signs of fear in the timid woman, and despised her for it. She in turn rarely addressed Catarina except to say, "The wine is not what it was in the old country, hey?" or other remarks that might be answered politely enough no matter what one said. The occasions for visiting the Dantones seemed mercilessly to have multiplied, particularly since Agnese never came with her husband to visit them, and Catarina more than once had remarked about it to Antonio.

"Well, why doesn't she come? I'm nobody, I know. But she might come in and say a few words, and eat something or other with me. But I am glad she doesn't come!"

"You have only housework to do, Catarina. She has a big business. She takes care of it all. . . . Her husband. . . ."

"Is soft as a squash. You could run a finger through him. . . ."

"The ass! What a man for a husband . . . what a man. . . ."

At these times Catarina realized she had made an error in mentioning

Michele at all. The look in her husband's eyes became indrawn and sad, and, to her so perturbing that she made the sign of the cross under her apron and mumbled a prayer to the Holy Virgin.

And then came the question of the contracts and the large building job that Antonio and Agnese had undertaken in common. Even less than Michele, Catarina had contributed little or nothing to the growth of her husband's construction business, and was so rarely taken into his confidence that she knew nothing in connection with it. She had sensed, however, with the intuitiveness of suppressed fear, that this new ramification contained the elements of disturbance to herself, her family, and Antonio, too. She submitted, nevertheless, to the more and more frequent ordeal of going to Agnese's house if for no other reason than to be present when Agnese and Antonio were together. It was inevitable in the course of time that the details of the enterprise would become so numerous and need such attention as to bring Agnese and Antonio into each other's company again and again, and Catarina was too simple to perceive that of the two there was less to be feared from Agnese than from Antonio. She had begun to make hesitating little protests and even to kneel before the statue of the Virgin in her dining room in the hope that the evil consequences she feared might be averted by human or divine interference. And, besides, she went more and more to church and to confession.

The day when the contracts had been signed Antonio had returned home in high spirits, and yet Catarina understood him too well not to catch a hint of a frustration more thoroughgoing than his delight in the huge new job ahead. She was dressing for the dinner and the party at the Dantones' when he surprised her weeping softly.

"*Porco diavolo,* what's the matter now?" he had shouted, painfully revealing his irritation.

He stood behind her, put both hands on her shoulders, and shook her with some decision.

"What's all the crying about? Aren't you happy that we have got this big job and all the money that's coming with it?"

Catarina wept and said nothing. Antonio paced the floor and added neither word nor gesture to the situation. And as she wept, she continued her dressing.

"Are you going to wear that shawl? Aren't you ever going to learn? Didn't you buy a hat like an American? Why. . . ."

But Catarina had sat down on the edge of the bed, the shawl in her hand and partly spread over her lap, a white cashmere shawl with alternate red and yellow stripes pencil-thin but vivid and gay, and silken golden fringe fine as hair.

"It's the shawl I brought with me. It's the shawl. . . ."

Antonio went out, leaving her to weep alone, and shouting as he shut the door, "It's beautiful, *Porca Madonna,* wear it. . . ."

And now after the party with the disgraceful scene in which both had participated so ignominiously, there she was on her knees, the children shouting for her in their rooms, screeching her damned prayers to the Holy Virgin. He felt too guilty not to throw the greater part of the blame on her.

"For the love of. . . ." His oaths were too incoherent for her to understand them. "Stop it . . . stop it . . . go to the children. . . ."

"What will become of us, what will become of us?" Catarina fell into a chair, put her head in her arms upon the table, and wept.

"Shut up!" yelled Antonio. "A fine way to carry on after. . . ."

"After what I did? Say it, say it," she snapped, her tears gone, but her voice still soft with melancholy and not with anger. "What do you mean? Are you going to chase after that witch, and in my presence and before the children kiss her and embrace her and shame us all and yourself? Was I to stand by and cry 'Hurrah' and let you. . . ." Her tears came afresh, her whole body shaking with their impetus.

Tessie, who evidently had been trying to put the other young ones to bed, called out, "Ma . . . ma! Rosina won't mind. . . ."

"What do you care about your contracts?" Catarina snapped again. "We got enough money. We have everything we want. We don't starve. More money, more money. . . . Why, why, why? She's got you by the neck. She leads you by the nose. She knows you're soft. . . ."

Tessie continued her shouting. Antonio kept staring at his wife, his face in rapid motion, his hands clutching desperately at the air in stupid uncertainty, realizing his guilt but perceiving likewise the deeper reasonableness of his desire for Agnese, a reasonableness neither his wife nor any other could understand.

The night noises had entirely hushed. An occasional trolley car banged and hurtled by. The room was still in its fantastic semi-religious darkness. If Catarina said another word and the children still kept calling, Antonio knew he would be incapable of restraining himself. The years had not brought him the peace that comes in the wake of routine. More compelling than all other feelings was this residual passion which had had no assuagement and which kept an intermittent fire burning in his heart.

"Listen, Catarina," he suddenly shouted, seizing her by both wrists. He took enough time to cry angrily to Tessie and the other children.

"You children stop it, stop it . . . go to bed, *Porca Madonna!*"

They knew too well this sharp anger not to mind.

"Listen, Catarina," he shouted throatily, his face close to hers. "Listen, *Dio Santo.* You're my wife. I married you long ago. You have done your share. We have worked and made our way in this country. We can hold our heads up, I know and you know, and it's you and me, too, that did it. And you have been good to me and I have been good to you. I've been, haven't I been, haven't I?"

"Yes . . . yes. . . ," she stammered, standing still, making no effort to move, her eyes fixed on his face in fright and wonder both.

"I've been good, and you know it, and the world knows it. All Italy knows it. And I've been good though I didn't want to be good . . . didn't . . . didn't . . . they made me marry . . . settle down . . . and it's not been bad . . . it's been better . . . yes . . . they said it would be . . . but listen . . . listen. . . ."

He raised his wife's hands to the level of her face, still keeping his hold on her wrists, and pulled her so close to him that she could feel the breath of his mouth move about her eyes, her nostrils, like the heat of a candle flame.

"But my heart burned all these years . . . it burned to possess another . . . to hold her body till it should crack in my strength. . . . I bore an insult for her . . . deep in my heart there's the scar of it . . . men know about it and I have said nothing . . . Why? Why, Catarina, why? Because I have wanted her and for years I have said nothing . . . stuck to my trade . . . built up the business . . . reared a family . . . been a good husband . . . but the fire in me was hot . . . it kept up and up . . . and now . . . and now . . . Catarina. . . . You understand . . . you understand . . . you will say nothing . . . you will do nothing . . . you will not get on your knees before that saint . . . *Porca Maria del Carmine* . . . you do . . . you do it once . . . understand . . . *santissima. . . .*"

He shook her back and forth, still holding her wrists until finally, exhausted himself, he sat her down gently in the same chair she had used before, and stood glaring over her, panting heavily, an unwonted sullenness on his features. Catarina gazed up at him, too terrified to speak, her round plump face rendered child-like by the open eyes, the half-open mouth, the turned-up chin.

Then, as if stirred by a remote impulse, with a gesture such as a baby might employ, he took several strands of her hair in his fingers and felt them over and over, pulled them slightly, patted them down, rearranged them in perfect silence all the while.

"You understand?" he asked, at length. "You understand. . . . You see I should have strangled him on the boat . . . that squash-head . . . that baby-idiot . . . he bit me on the neck . . . the scar you ask me about so often . . . that was his bite. . . ."

He spoke quietly, as if finally he had found someone to sense the full import of a secret too profound to divulge. Catarina remained immobile, the experience far too unusual for her to have a defensive reaction.

"She made me promise, and so I did nothing. There was a look in her eyes, a witch's look . . . it burns through me. . . ."

"What vile nonsense!" suddenly cried Catarina. "You're just a low beast that smells a bitch in heat. . . ."

The unexpectedness with which she spoke and her precipitous rising from the chair changed the current of his thoughts and feelings too sharply for him to say another word or do anything.

"I'm an ignorant woman," she cried. "I have not bought houses on my own and gone into business and met men in cafés and saloons. But I know you and her kind, too, and you're married to me. You're my husband and she'll let you alone and give peace to me and my children or . . . or . . . I'll do what that puling whelp of her husband. . . ."

She screamed with such ferocity and shrillness that the children were disturbed, and first one and then another began calling to both mother and father, "What's the matter . . . ma . . . ma. . . ?"

But Antonio had clapped a hand over her mouth, and thrown her back into the chair, shaking her again and again with such desperate and mechanical rhythm that she should have elapsed into insensibility had he continued it.

A few minutes later Tessie, her hair still in braids hanging down her back, her childish face pale and frightened, entered the room. She was barefooted and in her nightgown. Catarina saw her first, and made a violent effort to wrench herself loose from her husband's savage assault.

"*Ta . . . ta. . .* ," said Tessie, placing her hand on her father's arm. "Totonno wouldn't sleep . . . *Ta* . . . listen. . . ."

Antonio slowly relinquished his hold of his wife's mouth and head, and turning around gazed stupidly into the face of his daughter.

"Totonno won't go to sleep. . . ," she said simply, and took his hand as if to lead him upstairs. But Catarina snatched her up in her arms, and half-weeping and shouting she faced her husband.

"Mad beast . . . mad beast . . . mad beast . . ." and stopping suddenly, as if momentarily endowed with superhuman strength, ran out of the room and up the stairs with the child in her arms. Antonio remained stock still, smiling wrily, and then he walked over deliberately to where the Madonna's image stood in the half-shadow of the cresset and struck it so hard a blow that it fell from its pedestal with a heavy thud. Beneath the two windows at the front was a stiff black mohair couch. He made his way to it with slow long strides, sat down thoughtfully, then stretched himself out his full length, and shut his eyes.

– 8 –

Next morning he was awakened by the bright early sunlight, but nevertheless remained stretched out as before. He did not move. Catarina, he realized, was stirring upstairs with the children, and he noted, too, that outside on the sidewalk had gathered a group of workers. Some had brought along boxes with mason's tools. Others had pickaxes and shovels. Several had carpenter's chests. They had all come attracted by the prospect of many months' work ahead on the buildings that he and Agnese had planned to put up. He smiled, and studied them all with a look of amusement. The September day was going to be unusually warm, but the men would stand for hours in the sun waiting to come in and be signed up for work. The thought pleased him. Vaguely another thought, a painful, writhing memory, tried to twist itself into his consciousness. He struggled with it and forced it to go as he willfully brought into his recollection days when he, too, stood outside contractors' offices waiting for a job. Gradually his mind took him back step by step to the time of his boarding the ship for America, his meeting with Agnese, the dance on board, the incident of the bite, his stupid, drunken bouts and the women. . . .

He jumped to his feet as he heard the outside bell ring. The ring was so peremptory that he went to open the grated door without stopping to realize that his hair was disheveled, his face unwashed.

A thin young man, faultlessly dressed in the style of the day, took off his shiny brown derby and placed it in the hand that held his slender knotted cane.

"Is this Mr. Farinella?" he inquired with a slight bow of his head.

"Yes. . . ."

"Ah, then, you're the man I want to see." He spoke in soft, ingratiating accents with a winning smile that puzzled Antonio because it seemed to be made with the mobile upper lip only and to move without control to one side of the mouth. He had time to notice that the stranger's face was sharp, of a green pallor, but well barbered; his features were quick-moving, and the eyes in particular shifted between two slight slits as narrow as the pencil-like eyebrows.

"Mrs. Dantone said to come here. She will come here, too, she said, in a few minutes. Maybe we better wait for her."

Without a word, too puzzled to understand it all, Antonio let him in, motioned him to a chair, and then went to the foot of the stairs, and whistled very softly.

"All right," he heard Catarina answer. "I am coming right down."

Going into the other room, Antonio recalled that he had broken the image of the Madonna. He picked up the pieces slowly, and made a small pile of them in the corner where they had previously stood in their entirety.

"Broke last night," he explained to the stranger who had turned to see what Antonio was doing. He was still holding in one hand both hat and cane.

"What a shame, what a shame," he said in his soft voice. "They say it's very, oh, very bad luck." He made the sign of the cross just as Catarina walked in, bowing stiffly. The young man returned the bow without rising.

"Get us some coffee and that bottle of cognac," said Antonio almost gruffly, staring full at his wife. "Agnese will be here in a few minutes. Very important business."

"That's right," interjected the young man, as if he realized that his words must necessarily conclude the arrangements.

While Catarina was in the kitchen preparing the coffee, the doorbell again rang, and Antonio called out that he would open the door. Agnese came in, her skirts as usual moving to the rhythm of her hips, on her head a bright red kerchief.

"*Whey, Donn' Agnese bella,*" exclaimed Antonio in his ordinary voice of aggressive business man without the slightest trace of embarrassment or suggestion of anything out of the ordinary having occurred. "There's a young man here. . . ."

"Yes, I know," she answered sharply, "a pretty business . . . Oh," she cried, seeing the stranger, "you are here quickly. Well. . . ."

She sat down and, noticing Catarina walk in, she turned in her chair.

"Good morning, Catarina," she said very sweetly. "Oh, don't put yourself out. Had coffee. Oh, if it's with cognac . . . well!"

As Agnese was in the act of sipping her coffee and cognac, she turned abruptly to Antonio and said at once: "This man's name is Paul (she used the English form) Variglia. He has a business, too. He protects buildings just going up. The police are not good for that — that's what he says. And he wants us to pay him for it. Only one percent of the cost — that's what he says. He must pay his men."

Variglia kept a fixed even gaze upon her, made not the slightest movement or gesture. The only evidence that he was interested in her remarks was the continuous smile on his shifting upper lip, a smile that finally provoked Agnese to turn her attention to him with a vigor that that gentleman had obviously but rarely encountered.

"And he sits there smiling. You smile as if you were somebody." She addressed herself to him directly. "Smile if you must. You will not get a cent from me." Her voice had become sharp and high and there was no mistaking her sincerity.

"It don't matter who pays up."

"You will get a cent from nobody, not a cent from that building. There used to be snakes in my country that looked at you just the way you do. I looked back at them, and if they moved I killed them. I was not afraid then."

Variglia shifted his smile to the other corner of his lip.

"We always get paid for this service. Ask any contractor with a big job. Ask Farinella." He turned to Antonio with a movement that seemed pivoted on his cane and hat which he still held in his right hand. "He knows how important it is. There are fires that happen in the night, and sometimes whole carloads of material are stolen. The policeman has a big beat. You know. You heard the other day how that wall caved in on the house they are putting up the other side of the Elevated. It was a big job — almost ready. Cost the contractor all the profit and more. He can tell you how important. . . ."

"Enough," cried Agnese. "We got watchmen for that. . . ."

Variglia shrugged his shoulders and smiled.

"Maybe we had better. . . ," interposed Antonio.

"Better nothing. We got all our money in this thing. We aren't making too much. . . ."

Variglia smiled again, and suggested "Strikes happen, too. . . ."

"Let them. . . ."

"Very, very well," concluded Variglia as he rose.

He bowed stiffly, adjusted his derby with great deliberation upon his head, moved his cane to his left hand, slipped his smile to the other extreme of his lip, and walked out.

Antonio and Agnese discussed the matter at some length, Agnese finally bringing the talk to an end by slapping the table with the palm of her hand.

"They're robbers and brigands. I'll not pay a cent. . . ."

She turned to Catarina.

"Catarina, I want to talk with you. Let Antonio stay . . . why should he not stay? It's about last night. Don't be angry. You have always been a dear — *mi sei molto simpatica* — you know. Don't let us quarrel. Last night was my fault — mostly my fault — Antonio loved me before he knew you. I had a husband . . . I have a husband . . . and a child. . . . You may know the story. Who cares about that now? We're in America. Here things are not the same. Here it's your work . . . what you do . . . what you are . . . I have made America . . . people all know that I have worked . . . and I have made money . . . I own houses . . . have the dumps . . . nothing else counts. . . . Do you understand, Catarina? Don't you, too, sit there smiling at me and getting pale and red and angry-looking. The thing's over now. The men shook hands last night. Antonio will forget. . . . We must put up those houses . . . we have all got to make America . . . that's what we came for. You hear that, Catarina. . . . You understand? You will forget? You will forget?"

She talked earnestly, leaning over the table, looking eagerly for a sign from Catarina.

"Did you come here to torment me?" asked Catarina as if frightened.

"No, Catarina, do believe me . . . by the Virgin. . . ."

"By the Virgin! By the Virgin no less! Listen to that, Antonio — by the Virgin! By which Virgin? By the Virgin there?" she pointed a vivid trembling hand to the shattered remains of the statue piled up in the corner. "The Virgin he broke with his fist? There will be no more peace in this house after that. . . . He does not care for Virgin or me or God or children . . . but for you . . . you . . . you who bewitched him on the boat . . . bewitched him in this country . . . the way you bewitched. . . ."

"*Porca Madonna* . . . shut up . . . shut up. . . ," yelled Antonio, going to his wife with both his hands uplifted and trembling menacingly.

"Antonio, sit down . . . sit down. . . ." Agnese spoke in hardly more than a whisper. "Listen to me, both of you . . . Catarina," she added deliberately, quietly, as they took seats and became still, "I forgive you, Catarina. You have said harsh, bitter things to me . . . and of your husband, too. . . . If you say so, I did bewitch him . . . that's how you say it. But I did not know . . . I am a woman like you. How should I know what is in men that burns them with such stupid feelings? Believe me . . . it is all over . . . Antonio understands . . . we're in a big business . . . it must be a success . . . it must . . . for your children's sake . . . for all our sakes . . . Catarina . . . Catarina. . . ."

Her voice had become high, rhythmic, almost a prayer. She had got up from her seat, held her hands out before her supplicatingly, advanced toward Catarina. "Let us make peace . . . let us forget . . . forget . . . forgive. . . ."

Something insistent, hysterical, too demanding in Agnese's speech seemed to cast a fright over Catarina. She rose slowly, watching every move of Agnese.

"What's there to forget? What's there to forgive?" Her questions came like quick echoes, almost inaudible, and, having asked them, she brushed suddenly past Agnese and ran upstairs.

Antonio and Agnese looked at each other.

"Why did you have to do all this?" asked Antonio with an unmistakable tone of contempt in his voice.

"Listen, Antonio. What you feel, I cannot help. I do not feel it. Understand at once. Something there is in you I like . . . *e ti voglio bene* . . . and you know it. But no more. It was there only once in my life. Now there is this thing . . . this work . . . nothing must prevent . . . I have no love . . . I have no home . . . I have no child . . . really I have no child . . . I have this . . . this work. . . ."

Antonio had taken a step toward her. She raised her hand to stop him.

"You must not say anything. . . ."

"Must not say anything?" cried Antonio. "Nothing about that night on the ship? Nothing of the serpent in you that gets into my soul? Nothing of the promise in your eyes when you made me give up cutting the throat of that poltroon husband of yours? Nothing of the fire in your eyes that lights up mine? Nothing of the feel of your body against mine as we danced last night? Nothing of the agony of wanting that. . . ."

"Nothing, Antonio, nothing . . . nothing. We have work to do . . . we must do it . . . we must . . . do you hear? We must. . . . You gave your word last night

. . . you took a vow . . . you drank to it. . . ."

"You're a witch . . . a damnable witch. . . ."

He could say no more. Agnese had already left. But no sooner had Antonio turned around than the doorbell rang, and Agnese reappeared.

"Antonio, there's a whole mob outside. Send them away or tell them if you have work. . . ."

X. THE DANTONES AGAIN

– 1 –

The night of the celebration and the ill-fated dance, Agnese had left the men and rushed up to her bedroom exhausted. She ordered Michele to "go off somewhere . . . anywhere . . . out of my sight. Why do you stand like a pig?" Michele shambled out, his lips twitching, his face flushed, resolutions to put an end to humiliation and contempt pounding in his heart.

Agnese lay face down on the pillow, her arms spread out, clutching at the sheets with her hands. Not a tremor passed over her body. She was as inert as a frozen log, but in her raged the fever of her assertiveness. The shame of the repeated smacks on her cheeks in the presence of her guests coursed through her like a molten metal. She saw Antonio, Catarina, Giovanni standing clearly before her. There was no motion of her face to betray the agitation within. She singled them out individually and spoke to them.

"Tonight, Antonio, I could have you. I felt I could have you. Why did you not strip my clothes from me? I wanted you to throw me down on the floor . . . dance over my body . . . crush my breasts in your hands. . . . It would have hurt. I wouldn't have screamed. I should wait for your arms to hold me all round, for your body's weight on mine . . . I have wanted it for years. Look at that husband of mine . . . the simpleton . . . the skull-face . . . the corn-cob. He has held me, would you believe it?"

She spoke quietly, distinctly. She seemed to hear the unformed accents filling the room, but she continued in spite of it. She even had a feeling that Michele had not left, was nearby in fact, and could overhear the thoughts that came to her like well-uttered words.

"Yes, I have let him hold me. No, not often . . . at long intervals . . . when I feared the agony of want would shrivel me with its flame. Oh, then I undressed before him. I watched his mean eyes dance. He came toward me like a big, awkward boy. I had to tell him, "Kiss me here . . . and here . . . don't be so eager . . . can't you take your time . . . now, hold me tighter . . . not that way. . . . Oh, the wild pain! He could not quiet it . . . I thought of you as he held me . . . yes . . . and of Gelsomino, too . . . the soft hands that he had . . . a true priest's hands . . . do you know, Antonio? They were gentle hands but hurt me when he laid them on me . . . a keen, long hurt. . . . Not what yours would be like. Yours are calloused from your work, and knotted. They would bruise. Why do I want to be bruised, to have you bruise me? Your body would hold me down. I could not move. Gelsomino held me down, too . . . so forcefully but so gently, too. If he came tonight in this room, I should have him. Do you hear, Antonio? I should have him . . . and you . . . and this Doctor Grace . . . and Michele, too . . . long afterwards . . . when I was exhausted . . . and I would not know what he was . . . what he was doing to me . . . I have thrown him off me . . . again and again and . . . I pity him for no one else will have him. . . . He is a simpleton. . . . You must not abuse him. . . . Yes, some day. . . ."

There was a long pause in her thoughts. She smoothed the pillow with one hand with a back-and-forward movement over and over again. Otherwise she remained immovable.

"Some day . . . Antonio . . . but the priest will come back first. Why didn't he throw me on the trunk when he came last spring? It was a hard trunk. My ribs would have been hurt. . . . But he could have had me then. . . . He can have me now. Do you think he will come to me, Antonio?"

The singular fact in Agnese's life had been that ever since her confronting Gelsomino in the church she had not once wept. She did not weep now. But the impulse was present in her. For the object ahead of her, this building enterprise that seemed so important, appeared utterly foolish, almost without point. It was like a flash of understanding. What would she do with them when they were built, all these houses, one after one, red brick like a mountain wall? She had made America, they would say of her. But what was that? What was that? The agony of all these years, making believe she was happy, happy, happy with that corn-cob, that imbecile, who took her when she was somebody else's, when she never once let him have her really, never once felt the millionth part of that pain that was like infinite music when Gelsomino . . . blessed Gelsomino. . . ."

The tears might have come now. She bit her lip, however, and sat up. She looked steadily ahead of her.

"And you, Catarina. . . ," she said drily and shook her head. "You really have a right to be afraid. But I won't take your man away. I will go on with the building, and I will make both of us rich. And we shall get old. And it will mean nothing, only a dirty story then. Zia Cristina will tell it, if she is still alive . . . how you smacked my face just when Antonio would have thrown me down and I should have let him have me. . . . Yes . . . but no more now . . . Catarina. . . . The houses must go up . . . you must help too by just keeping out of it . . . like Michele. . . ."

She rose and went to the window. Tomorrow would begin the work of tearing down those brownstone fronts where the "English" with money had lived. Tomorrow she would make sure of Catarina. Meantime she must go to Giovanni. What a reproachful look had been in his eyes. She would talk to him and make him happy, lie down beside him, let him put his arms about her neck. Why was it she had not known that in him would be love, understanding of life, something better than making America? And she must drive that reproachful look from his eyes.

– 2 –

She went to his room. A light was shining in the dining room downstairs. It must be Michele waiting to be called up. She raised her voice.

"What are you doing there? Come up to bed."

She entered Giovanni's room, and shut the door quietly after her. She heard Michele climbing the stairs, slowly, slowly. A trolley car passing by accentuated the labored thud of his shoes on the thinly carpeted stairs. She approached the bed and stopped suddenly. It was empty. She stood still with fear. It had come quickly, the fear that he had run away again and would be brought home limp, helpless, staring at her without seeing her, trembling all over as on that night in the early summer a year ago.

She opened the door and called, "Michele . . . *Ta* . . . *Ta*. . . ."

"What is it?" asked her husband who had hurried up at her cry.

"Giovanni? Where is Giovanni?"

"Well," answered Michele with a sort of mockery on his face, "Well. . . . Is that all? Why, where could he be? He's in bed. . . ." Michele was starting to leave her.

"No . . . he's not there. . . ."

"Maybe upstairs . . . drawing . . . you know the little artist. . . ."

Agnese was aware of a peculiar attempt at ignoring her feelings as he spoke, in fact, not so much ignoring them as being indifferent, even a trifle anxious to aggravate them if possible. She had not been so overcome with the events of the day as not to realize that here was not altogether a manifestation of something new in her husband but the expression of a cunning she had always been sure he possessed. She looked at him in the half-darkness but noted that the sharpness of her glance did not completely disconcert him as at such moments it generally did.

"What are you saying?" she rapped out.

"Well . . . well . . . there you are at it again. Can't you speak civilly to me anymore . . . at no time . . . nowhere?" he asked in a tone of great personal offense. "I tell you he must be upstairs, drawing, painting. He always does that when things hurt him. You know. . . ."

He made a motion to leave her and was in the act of placing his hand on the knob, surprising Agnese by the coolness with which he did so. Michele had never quite lost the awe he felt for his wife and even in the most trifling occurrences showed it so grotesquely as to make Agnese burst into laughter if not into anger.

"And what should he be hurt at?" she inquired firmly.

"Why should he not be hurt?"

"Hurt? Hurt at what? At what? Don't stand there with your mouth open. Say it . . . say it. . . ."

"There, there you go again . . . again. . . ," he stammered.

"What was he hurt at?"

"Hurt at your shameful ways. . . ." He stammered it out hotly. "At the shame of it . . . do you hear . . . the shame of it . . . in the presence of everybody . . . you keep on making a fool of me . . . put horns on my head in the sight of the world. . . . You saw me this morning. I'm going crazy. Do you hear, I'm going crazy . . . . You will make me crazy. . . . Do I want to do anything desperate because I love you so much. . . ? You don't love me . . . I know . . . I was a fool. . . . But I saved you from all those tongues. . . . Why do you twist your mouth at me like that? I'm not nobody . . . I'm not . . . you ignore me . . . you and that man I bit . . . why did you pull me off?"

The contempt which Agnese felt for her husband came out in its entirety in the rapid glance at his whole body and the short dry tone of her command which followed the longest speech he had ever made to her.

"It's about time you went to bed. . . ."

"I . . . I . . . won't . . . I will . . . will speak. . . . Do you hear?"

"Too much, Michele. You are certainly in a fever."

"You laugh at me. You keep laughing at me. . . . Will you drive me crazy?" There was no mistaking the sincerity of his words, uttered as they were in fear of some thought that was driving him against his nature.

"Michele . . . that's all over tonight. . . . Go to bed. . . ."

"I will cut his neck. . . ." He was turning the knob of the door. Agnese had made a gesture as if to seize him by the arm when the doorbell rang, timidly at first and then quite smartly.

"What's that?" exclaimed Agnese.

"Let me go and see. . . ."

"No. I'll go. . . ," and she hurried downstairs.

Outside the door were Padre Gelsomino and Giovanni.

"Pardon, Agnese," said the Padre very naturally, "Giovanni came to me late tonight, and I have brought him back."

– 3 –

He turned and hurried down the steps. Agnese was too stunned to understand it all at first and watched the retreating form of her old lover as he moved rapidly down the street, not stopping once to look back. Giovanni stared at her in amazement. She stood watching Gelsomino and seemed to have forgotten his own presence completely. The expression in her eyes was like nothing he had ever noted in her before. It was a light rather than an expression, a burning of old faggots someone had left in a heap and forgotten, and for some inexplicable reason burning, burning brightly.

"Ma, ma," he whispered in timid agitation. "Come upstairs, why are you standing there?"

– 4 –

Michele, who had followed Agnese, had in the meantime opened the inner door of the entrance and glared, both perplexed and exasperated, at his wife and step-son. He had not seen Gelsomino and so could not divine what could cause Agnese to remain so fixed and seemingly so engrossed in an object in the distance, while her son like one dumbfounded held her hand and gazed into her face.

Cruelly unassertive and submissive though he was, Michele was not so dull-witted as to fail to perceive that for many months now a change had been coming over his wife. He attributed it partly to the return of Gelsomino, but nevertheless felt that Antonio was mostly responsible for the rapidity of its growth and the intensity of its effects. Even at this moment he could not help giving vent to the anger that the thing had wrought in his soul.

"She has no use for me at all. It's the others and the brat. Why does she stand there like a person dreaming? She forgets me. She forgets I'm here, her husband. She never trusts to me — but, God . . . God!" he cried desperately in his own heart, "she will not turn me away! She will not turn me away."

At this point Agnese, hearing Giovanni's call with great suddenness, stooped over and seized him violently in her arms. She kissed him repeatedly, muttering words of the tenderest affection, words such as Michele had never once heard spoken to himself. Quick anger made him turn pale and wince. An unspeakable hatred of the boy followed in its wake, his fingers closed furiously, his whole body leaned forward. He was seized with a violent desire to slap him hard on both cheeks over and over again, over and over again, to laugh at him while he wept, and then to stamp on him with both feet, and laugh, laugh, laugh. Instead, he turned about and shuffled morosely upstairs to his room.

Giovanni clung desperately to his mother.

"You are not hurt. You are whole. You are here. You frightened me. My son," she cried. "My darling!"

Not realizing where she was or how late it was, she sat down on the step before the door, and drew Giovanni close to her. They were silent for a long time, conscious only of each other's warmth and the joy of their embrace.

"Where, where did you go?" she asked softly, kissing his ear.

"To my father," he replied. "But he brought me back, see. He brought me back."

"Yes, yes . . . but why did you go . . . why? Tell me. You know I love you. You know I love you." She held him so tightly that he could hardly catch his breath to answer.

"I love you, ma . . . I love you . . . ma."

"Then why, my son, then why?"

"I hate all these men . . . Michele, Antonio . . . everything here . . . everything."

He pressed his head to her breasts. Something in the pressure, the warmth of the position, gave him a sense of being understood at last. He raised his hand to stroke his mother's face, ran his fingers over both cheeks, put them, baby-like, on her lips and enjoyed the sensation of having them kissed, nibbled.

"I hate those men. They take you away from me. Remember when you first loved me, when I was sick. I loved you then, too, for the first time. I love you now . . . so much . . . so much."

He threw his arms about her neck and kissed her on her neck, her cheeks, her lips.

"My son, my son," she kept repeating. Once again she felt the impulse to weep, but she was not in the habit of tears. She held his face away from her and looked into it with beaming, moistened eyes. "But you want to leave me now that we love each other?"

He answered immediately with a seriousness so real that, despite the fear it inspired, she could not help smiling, and then bursting into a quick, short hysterical laugh. Giovanni did not seem to mind it at all.

"No, ma, I don't want to leave you. But I hate these men — Antonio especially. I hate him." He paused. A vivid flush came to his cheek.

"I don't want to see him kiss you. . . ."

"My little boy, my little boy," she said in great excitement. "How you talk! What do you know of all this?"

"I hate him to look at you the way he does — I ran away when he kissed you. I ran away . . . ran to my father." (He said it without hesitation.) "But you see he brought me home again. My place is with you, he said. I wanted to stay. I did not want to come back."

She crushed him to her and kissed him feverishly, stopping the flow of his words. In the pause they held each other tight. Trolleys had passed. A passerby had occasionally glanced up. One had stopped for a second to watch the curious scene. At this point, Agnese heard an object falling with a heavy thud, followed by the sound of a crash. She arose to her feet as if frightened out of a deep sleep.

"Giovanni," she almost laughed, "look where we are! What stupids we are. Come in."

She opened the door quickly and hurried in.

"Go to your room, quick. I will come too. I will put you to bed. You will go to sleep."

Giovanni had become accustomed to his mother's new attitude, her constant attention to his wants, assisting him in a hundred ways as she had never done before, even when he was much younger. As she helped him to undress, put his clothes away, prepared his bed, he recalled how it had always been Gesualdo, his grandfather, who had always put him to sleep and sat by him holding his hand, stroking his forehead. He recalled, too, her morose, stubborn silence when he said good night, the hang-down head, surly, almost hateful good night Michele said. And he could not help believing that since all this had changed ever since his true father's return, it was not his illness alone that had made it possible but something that had taken place between Agnese and his father when, more than a year ago, he saw them facing each other in the glazed light of his feverish eyes.

He crawled into bed, a sleepy, tired smile on his face. Agnese sat down beside him and stroked his forehead.

"Ma," he said. "I would never leave you again. I like my father," he added, as she kissed him. "He likes me to come. We sit and talk. He's been all over, in China and places. . . ."

"How much does he know?" thought Agnese fearfully. "Is this the time to tell him? Has he told the child?"

"He told me an exciting story once," continued Giovanni. "About two Chinamen. They were sailors in the same boat and they slept in the same place, and there were only about thirty sailors. The boat was dirty and old. Only a few white men were on it. Miserable men is what he said they were, and these Chinamen always gambled and then one night one Chinaman had lost everything to the other one, even his knife and shirt. And then one night, there was a terrible storm, and they knew the boat was going to be smashed and sink and everybody was ready to get away and my father, he said, he went to the bunk, he didn't know why, and he found the Chinaman who had lost all the things had cut the other one's throat and was stuffing his pockets with everything."

"My child, my child! What a story to be hearing," whispered Agnese.

"And then the next thing he knew, he was in a hospital and he didn't know what happened to the Chinamen."

"But has he asked himself why . . . Michele . . . why I?" Agnese kept revolving in her mind as she listened.

"He went to South America, too, and he worked on a big farm there!"

She kissed him and hugged him and said finally, "You must go to sleep."

"He went all over," the boy rejoined. "He has an Italian school, you know, in the room behind that painter. . . ."

"Yes, yes," said his mother. "But sleep now. . . ."

"He's going to give it up, though. . . ."

"Why?"

"He has too few pupils and he is going to work in a big saloon as a waiter. . . ."

"Go to sleep, dear, go to sleep. . . ."

"But, ma, ma," he suddenly cried, sitting up in bed. "Why doesn't he live here with you?"

Agnese took Giovanni into her arms and clutched him to her with such force that the boy cried out.

"Ma, ma."

"My boy, my own boy, you must not ask that now, not now, and not your father either. Promise me. Promise me." There was the thumping of a fist on the wall. Agnese started. "What can that man want?" she asked herself. She got up, composed, strong-willed as usual.

"You will learn some day, Giovanni. But now you must not ask . . . no one. You promise?"

Giovanni's eyes looked big and uncommonly bright as he fixed them on his mother.

"You are too young," she continued in the gentlest tone he had ever heard her use. "Too young. You must be good . . . good to everybody — Michele — your father." This she said in faint, almost terrified whisper. "Some day you will know."

She bent over, kissed him, tucked the sheets about him and left quickly.

– 5 –

Agnese, however, was not through. She found Michele sitting on the edge of the bed, his face bloated and pale, the small hole of his scar a vivid red spot. His lips twitched as he looked up at his wife. His eyes were filled with moisture as if he had been weeping. His whole body shook as if he had been surprised in an act that terrified him.

"Well, not in bed yet!" was all that Agnese said. She went to the heavy mahogany dresser with its big mirror and slowly let down the long, firm braids of her hair.

Michele's eye followed her, an unwonted anger shining in them, but an anger not unmixed with a kind of desperate pleading, an unvoiced demand for affection and sympathy, for acceptance of himself as a man, as her husband.

He jumped up with sudden violence, walked quickly to Agnese and cried in a hoarse whisper, "I will kill him yet!"

Agnese turned quietly, still taking the hairpins out of her hair. There was not a trace of emotion. She looked calmly at her husband and allowed a long pause to intervene before saying, "Don't make a fool of yourself. We had that all out tonight. Go to bed."

"So you laugh. So you laugh at me," he shouted in tears. "Laugh, laugh . . . You will see. . . ."

Agnese took him by the arm. His whole body shook and his mouth twisted in vain attempts to utter thoughts that he could not put into words. Agnese led him to the bed.

"Go to sleep," she said gently. "You, too, are tired, and I am tired. This will all work out all right. We have lived a long time together. We have made money. We want to build. . . ."

Her words were drowned in the wild cries of Michele.

"To hell with building . . . to hell with the money. . . . It ain't building, it ain't money. . . . I'm all alone in the world . . . they all despise me, ignore me . . . you, too, ignore me . . . put horns on me . . . despise me. . . ."

He became incoherent. His head sank in the pillow as his whole frame shook with the spasms of his sobs.

Agnese undressed slowly, and, as she went to bed, reflected that in only a few hours, she must go to see Catarina.

But she could not sleep. She lay back and thought.

She had more sympathy with Michele's attitude toward the building and its value than he would have believed. The pyramiding details of her life were too loosely joined. The main ingredients of love and understanding had not cohered. The walls must topple. She was beginning to realize all this in a sulphurous gleam of fear as Antonio, and then Giovanni, forced her feelings from their crypts in her will, and as these feelings more and more reached out for something to grasp, and that something she knew was not Antonio, not altogether Giovanni. The soft, sibilant voices calling to her, the low cadencing love-words she knew . . . she knew this was not a dream . . . this gentle hand. She lay on her back, her eyes partly open, but she knew she dreamed.

– 6 –

There was a forest through which she was making her way painfully, for she was burdened with an armful of sticks. "I have no use for these sticks. Why do I carry them?" At the best, they served as a means of breaking away through the heavy brush, the innumerable dry twigs, the blankety cobwebs drawn across them. Hardly any sunlight penetrated the intense gloom of the thin lane; she was forcing a path through the trees and bushes. However, she could discern here and there the broad petals of a huge, red flower, damasky soft and hanging droopily, hard yellow berries and tall green cones standing apex up. She would have dropped her bundle of sticks to gather the colorful blooms. She wanted so much to play with them, to make necklaces and shawls, but the weight of the sticks was becoming unbearable. She must get through. She must deposit them somewhere.

And then something prevented further progress. A huge hand was bearing down upon her, crashing through the treetops, and as each branch fell the huge, red petals, the yellow berries, the green cones fell, too, changed to flames and disappeared. The immense hand was upon her and she started back. She could see each individual hair on the fingers, the fallen lines like gaping crevices filled with the foul decay of leaves and underbrush, the pores, grotesque, fantastic pits . . . what disgust! what horror!

Michele's hand was timidly, feebly stroking her body, her breasts, and as she was not moving away, and curling up her body in defense as she had done these several months past, he had been feeding an eager, feverish hope.

He had drawn close, put his face near, forced, but slowly, his other hand under her body. The half-open eyes were like those of a woman exquisitely slipping into soft ecstasy. They had the subdued drifting light of passion and the mouth had severed in a smile that was joy and unvoiced laughter. Michele lay his hand firmly upon her breast and, his heart laughing, his whole body radiant with warmth, placed his lips to hers.

She woke with a start, nauseated with fear, the sight of the monstrously oversized fingers causing her to shrink with a rapidity that multiplied, enlarged her feelings. She sat up sharply, staring with unbelieving eyes upon the frightened-looking Michele. The chilled impulses had arrested the suppressed muscles of his face and now it had a sly but apologetic satyr expression of passion turned to lust by the unexpected thwarting.

They gazed at each other motionless, one, horror-stricken at being denied, the other, bewildered at being wanted when she did not want.

Her nightgown had slipped off her shoulders and on the exposed breast the light of the cresset above the bed revealed its still firm roundness, the hard red pointedness. Michele's eyes drank it in greedily. His whole face quivered. He clasped his arm about her and pressed his lips upon the naked bosom. Deprivation, the bitter agony of being further and further thrust away and out of her life, had not only given flame to anger, but had imparted heat to his desire, and in frenzied persistence, he clung to her, the adamant, the unwilling.

At first she made no move. She allowed herself to be held. She was still too close to her dream. With dizzying lucidity, the events of the day past, the return of Gelsomino, the continued importunings of Antonio, her long damned-up yearnings leaped into her consciousness. She thought of them and her mind shot back to her primitive childing in the grotto, to the sweet abandon of her love for Gelsomino — the bitter prospects, the willing Michele, the life in America — the money.

She had come to herself. She gazed down upon Michele as he kissed her, kissed her as a soldier in a sacked town who has at last, at last come on a woman — what matters it that she has fainted, has become lifeless from horror, fear, disgust?

She gazed at him, feelingless, unstirred, as if she had swooned but could look on helpless, without sensation. It was no longer than a second. The pressure of his lips she could distinguish, the flushed cheeks, the throbbing blood. . . .

"Agnese, Agnese, *mia, mia, mia,*" he cried, choking with smothered, hysterical sobs, his incoherence saying all too clearly what he had so long left unsaid.

She stroked his hair. "Why, why do I do it?" she asked herself.

The utter unexpectedness of the gesture drowned Michele in a flood of heat. He relaxed, his whole body covered hers, lay on hers inert from too great feeling, waiting to be stroked again and again, held, and accepted utterly, utterly.

And then he raised his face to hers, his chin close to hers, his hair falling back, his eye glinting with moisture, on his lips a smile so self-pleased, so assured of conquest, so grateful.

Disgust poured its hateful tepidness all over her. She felt clammy, in a cold sweat — and yet pity and sympathy and gratefulness, too.

She allowed him to hold her more tightly, but her flesh crawled. She shrank as in her dream. She shivered in the conflict of her emotion. She placed a hand on his shoulder to force him off.

He understood. He jumped up, drew the sheet off the bed with savage emotions, kept twisting and twisting it around his hand, while the other swayed in long movements helplessly at his side. His whole face wept silently.

All she could do was to stare.

"So," he whispered. "So . . . So . . . you laugh at me. . . ." He stammered helplessly . . . and then he shrieked in horrifying pain. "You despise me . . . so!"

He fell in a grotesque heap on the floor.

XI. CATARINA

– 1 –

Agnese did not sleep that night. She did not even think. Her eyes open, her hands crossed over her breasts, she lay quiet. Picture after picture passed before her mind: the lake at the foot of Villetto, the public square with the chattering women washing clothes in the fountain, the old cathedral Campanile, standing like a white sentinel in the hot morning, the men crushing grape with their feet for the new wine. There were sharp flashes of evening scenes with Michele and Gelsomino sipping their *moscato* in silence as if to determine who could remain speechless for a longer time; the long days on board ship, the first year in America, the dirt, the choking air, the cramped street, the labor-drugged men stumping into the barbershop seeking work.

She passed no comments. She seemed without sensation. It was as if one movement of hand, or lip, or eye, a stir of the body, might cause the orderly procession of pictures to tremble into a shrieking medley that would render her altogether insensible. She held herself particularly rigid at the point when she appeared to be gazing at herself barely turned fifteen, her brown eyes filled with the still light of devotion raised to return the gaze of Padre Gelsomino. He was looking straight into her face, and the direct intensity of his look broke into radiance the quiet light of her eyes. And then he lowered his lips and with them touched her hair and she saw the little girl shudder; but the scene changed as soon, and there was the filthy horror of the grotto. She saw herself crouching in a crypt which she had cleared of dirt and mildew and slime — cleared it with her hands and then filled it with leaves and grass and hay. . . . She shuddered. The picture crashed and fell. She had moved. Michele had crawled into bed.

There was light in the room. The dawn wind had puffed out the curtains. She looked out, and saw the long row of brownstone houses, murky dabs against the sky, empty, now, useless-looking. Michele evidently was asleep.

"Poor man! Let him sleep," she thought. "But he must bear his own cross, *Gesù, Giuseppe e Santa Maria!* I am bearing mine and who knows how much longer, how much more bitter it is all going to be."

She was careful to make the heavy braids of her hair even firmer and to pile them up behind the part in decided, coquettish circles. To make certain, she took the yellow and red kerchief only recently imported from Italy, folding it into a triangle and placing it on her head with a long pin and comb to hold it. Cocking her head, she looked at herself and smiled. She went downstairs to Concetta's black coffee with rum and, having refused further debate with the immaculate Paul Variglia, went to Antonio and Catarina.

– 2 –

Michele, however, had not slept. He had followed every step she had taken, and as she smiled into the mirror his own lips contorted into a wry agony of a smile, and the scar on his cheekbone burned crimson.

"So," he said to himself. "So, she can get up so calmly, fix herself up to see that bitch's son of an Antonio. So. . . ."

He decided to make an end of this farce of being ignored, trampled upon, discarded. He would go to the "dumps." At least he had charge of those. Surely he had to submit all his plans to Agnese, simple as they were, and all the accounts passed through her hands. Today, however, he would assert himself. He would. . . .

But he sat still in his chair, one sock on, one sock half pulled up on his leg, his fingers clutching it frantically.

"After all, what can I do?"

The question blanked out his mind; it stunned him into activity. Only his lips twitched and twitched.

He leaped up in a kind of automatic fury, doubling his hands into nervous feeble fists.

"He won't, he won't, he won't," he shouted aloud. "I'll cut his heart out and feed it to the cats."

This outburst seemed to calm him, for he resumed his seat and his dressing.

"I'm somebody," he kept thinking. "'Don Michele Dantone.' They all call me *Don*. They take off their hats. I can carry a cane. . . ."

Before going out he ascertained that Agnese had gone to the Farinella's. The information seemed to invigorate him for he stepped briskly down the street. The September day was warm and bright. The workmen assembled in front of Antonio's had made way for him. Some had doffed their hats with the greatest show of respect.

"They do take off their hats," he thought with pleasure, and he quickened his step, nay, gave a jaunty jerk with his arms now and then.

– 3 –

As he passed the long rows of pushcarts lining the curb on the avenue, he felt an inordinate pride, and he most easily justified to himself the elevation at which he carried his chin, the slight expansion of his chest.

"*Whey, Don Michele bello!*" he heard from vendor after vendor and many a buyer.

He stopped at one cart to finger the grapes.

"*Ma, che sono belle,*" he cried, holding up a cluster to catch the light. Several women had gathered about the cart, and nodded approval.

"They're good to look at, sure," one ventured, "but they're nothing like the grapes we grow in Varino, not a bit, not a bit. Ah, those were grapes. . . ."

"I can believe it," answered Michele, and was glad to see how pleased the woman was that he, Don Michele, had agreed with her.

"We grow them fine, too, big as walnuts. Each one makes a pint of wine, and what wine," he added without a stammer. "Hey, Filomena," he cried in glee, addressing the owner of the cart. "You remember. . . ."

"Remember!" answered Filomena in her small cracked voice. Her eyes, sunk in caverns of wrinkles, beaded with light. She raised a cluster of small white grapes far above her head, her leathery, knotted fingers trembling with age. . . . "When I did this with a bunch, I shut out the sun, and all around me became cool. . . ."

They all laughed.

"Save me five pounds," said Michele importantly, "and put in some of those peaches, too, and anything else you have. Here's the money," and as he handed her a bill, he shook his head sadly. "Money, money!" He made a clucking sound of deprecation. "Give me the grapes of my Villetto *bello* and this country can keep all its money!"

"You you can say that," shouted a sodden-faced gaunt woman with a sickly looking child in her arms. "Yes, yes, you have made America. You own houses. You put up houses. But we starve, see, we starve. . . ." Her shrill voice was becoming bitter and Michele took his change, and hurried away.

"She starves," he thought. "I'm starving. I'm starving." But the feeling of exhilaration came back, for he felt himself slapped on the back, taken by the arms and propelled affectionately along.

"Don Michele!" shouted Doctor Pastrocchi, newly arrived from Italy, a high pointed collar throwing his chin up perforce. "What things we hear of you in

Italy! Villetto is proud of you! Imagine the little barber's apprentice! Why he's a gentleman . . . a *Don!* Ah!" He put his arm deeper into the crook of Michele's. "You need not be ashamed of yourself? I'll tell you, Don Michele!"

Don Michele drank the words in with glowing avidity. He could say nothing. He knew his stammer would return. He did not even look at the florid rotundity of the doctor, the faded cutaway, the frayed cloth buttons, the spotted black cravat that labored to reach the soaring points of the collar. Don Michele was too simple to understand the voluble doctor's motives, did not realize that his impecunious companion hoped to employ the Dantones to establish himself in a lucrative practice. . . .

"America's the place." His reedy voice aspirated the sound. "Talent in this country snatches gold out of the air and turns it, not into a sordid ornament, but into an alchemy, Don Michele! An alchemy that transforms characters, makes the butcher a king's minister, nay a president! "

The doctor had become excited with his own speech, withdrew his arm with unexpected spontaneity, jumped a foot in advance of Michele, and took the pose of an orator.

"You have achieved a pinnacle, a high place, a high place," he said solemnly, lowering his voice. "And I . . . well, I have just arrived. But we are *paesani!* We shall know how to be of help to each other! Ah, Don Michele. . . ."

Once more he introduced his arms under Michele's, and with more subdued but just as persistent vigor propelled Michele along. All the while Michele had been conscious of a sensation that varied from the exhilaration of self-satisfaction to the dubious warmth of feeling himself needed by one as much in need of a prop to his ego as himself. He nodded to the left and right as pushcart vendors and housekeepers cried out, "*Whey, Don Michele bello!*" They reaffirmed the assertion of his spirits, and he could turn to Doctor Pastrocchi with a smile. There could be nothing so stupid, so inferior in himself that he must be shoved aside. He would make a beginning of asserting himself, claim his rights by a firm display of his virtues. Thanks to the good doctor, he had a view of himself that was truer to the facts than Antonio or Agnese suggested.

They had come into the shadow of the enormous gas tanks, staring red cylinders upraised against the sun. The noise of the hawkers was many blocks away. Now the river, hitherto suppressed by the sprawling streets, the din, the tenements with their innumerable windows blinking dazzled eyes in the sunlight, lifted its sharp thin whistles. Don Michele's accustomed nose could catch the advance odors of the garbage dumps, the concession that he and Agnese had bought and that had taken him out of the menial status of barber and elevated him to leisure and to a Don.

"Good morning," he stammered, taking the doctor's hand. "Good morning!"

"Don Michele!" the doctor answered, stepping back and raising his hat obsequiously. "*Lo saluto!*" He bowed to the ground, trailing his voice with him.

– 4 –

Michele turned quickly to hide his flushed countenance and began to move gingerly toward the river. The street was the residence of junk-cart owners. On one side rose the cylindrical balloons of the gas tanks, darkening the sidewalks and gutters. A row of squat, white houses with brownstone stoops ran the entire length of the streets on the other side. Out of the windows hung streamers of red peppers set out to dry. On the sills and fire escapes sat shallow wooden platters filled with brick-red tomato paste which sent an acrid odor down the wind. Numerous pushcarts stood on their tail boards, their arms thrust unceremoniously into the air. Within the small iron enclosures in front of the basement windows knots of old women with bright kerchiefs over corrugated foreheads, full-bosomed young women, boys with shirt fronts open and eyes blazing keenly, sat on haunches and hams and sorted rags which they pulled from a central pile. The men yanked apart old stoves and chairs, salvaged nails and the copper bottoms of old boilers.

Again Don Michele nodded left and right, stopped for a word with one and then another.

"Not like putting out the figs to dry, Don Michele," shouted an old pinched woman in a hoarse basso, and in a dialect he barely understood. "But what can you do in this vile land?"

"What's the hurry, Don Michele, what's the hurry?"

"Oh, we understand, Don Michele! You're a man of affairs now. What a change from the old country! God continue to be good to you, Don Michele!"

Every *Don* exploded like a Roman candle before his eyes. He could confess to himself in the intimacy of his own heart that he had decided on this walk for the antidote it was to the degrading happenings of the night. No plaster saint ever moved in procession through more revering groups. Who was essentially better than he? “Oh, Agnese, Agnese, what foulness are you practicing on me? Come and see me in my glory.” And by now the taps of his heels had taken on the rhythm of a swagger.

Ahead of him he could see the first outlines of the “dumps” — low-lying barges slung amidships to the pierheads, piled up with refuse that steamed malodorously in the heavy sunlight. Men, potato sacks wrapped about their feet, raked the mounds of offal to the level of green pastures. They were followed by women with their skirts raised up and knotted above their buttocks, carrying bags. Now and then they stooped with the quick motion of birds, seized an object out of the putrid mass, and put it into their bags — ancient gleaners in a new world. Their silhouettes against the skyline of the river island with its brownstone edifices, domed and spired, crawled like enormous fantastic spiders. Michele quickened his pace.

He felt his coat seized from behind, and he heard the sounds of a man out of breath.

“Don Michele . . . Don Michele!”

He smiled before he turned around. It was an old man with red eyes without lashes, crisps of white hair straggling over his neck and ears, innumerable wrinkles, and toothless gums. A length of rope barely kept up his bags of trousers.

“Don Michele,” he cried timidly and held up clasped appealing hands. “Well? You promised. . . .”

“*Ma sí, ma sí, Zi’ Chele.* I know, I know,” answered Michele in his lordliest fashion.

If the other greetings had been relishes to his fears of self-approval, this was a banquet. The old man had asked for work some days back, and here he was pleading for it with staring eyes, open mouth.

“How are we going to eat in our old age?” the old man whistled despairingly, twisting three fingers like a pinwheel in front of Michele’s eyes. “You won’t let us starve? We came three thousand miles, the old woman and I. . . .”

“I know, I know, but. . . .” And as he answered, he was thinking, “See, see how they depend on me . . . these . . . and others.”

“They put our oldest in prison, Don Michele. The other died . . . the only two left . . . *Don Michele bello, per L’Amore di Dio Santo, Don Michele!*”

“But Zi’ Chele, patience . . . patience.”

“Patience!” The old man’s face moved all in a piece. “I’ve had seventy-two years of patience! I’ll do anything, Don Michele . . . run my fingers through the worst dirt piles . . . little pieces of gold sometimes, a bit of brass . . . something gets in . . . you know . . . I'll earn my money. . . ."

"But Zi' Chele, Zi' Chele, you see I can't. . . ."

"Don Michele . . . Don Michele!" The words had fallen like a blow. "Don Michele!"

Michele was enjoying it, surely not the old man's distress, but the light it put him in, the feeling that he counted for something among the *paesani.* For he was keenly aware that he could not have employed the old man without first consulting Agnese, and Agnese, he knew, would have only one answer. "Are we to feed the starving? We'd starve ourselves." He started to go.

"Come tomorrow!"

The old man followed, trying to hasten his steps in his grotesque impotence.

Michele had spoken with unwonted force and decision, with not the slightest stammer. He could not help a feeling of warmth although there flashed into his memory men in Villetto beating with whisks of fresh twigs their old mules and laughing as they watched the fantastic efforts of the beasts to move. When he stepped on the gang-plank from which the garbage carts emptied their contents into the barges, the thick smell of decay assailed his nostrils without the usual disgust. It was not incense, but it was welcome. A dozen barges, heavy with the off-scourings of the huge city, lay quiet in the sun, one filled with cans, flashing in the light, one with paper scraps too dirty to be baled and sold, one with the mixed peelings of vegetables and fruit, floating with grease oozily melting in the warmth of the day. On each one moved oily looking men and women, sorting, leveling, gleaning. . . . A group had burst into song. . . .

"*Se ssta voce t'sceta inn'a nottate. . . .*"

"*Nun pensi a me. . . .*"

The strain was gentle and melancholy, and the leading voice clear and long-sustained.

"All this I control. All these people obey my orders," thought Michele, and he nodded warmly to the foreman who was sloshing his way to him. But his satisfaction was not too great to render him deaf to a remark one of the workers had made to another.

"The old corn-cob, what's he hobbling around for now?"

Michele was sure he was meant although he let himself think it was Zi' Chele standing behind him. . . .

"Don Michele . . . Don Michele. . . ," the old man almost whispered.

"Not today, not today, I said," he snapped back, pleased at the sharpness of his voice. "That'll teach them to respect me," he thought. "It'll make them understand my mood."

However, a revelation was in store for him. He seemed vaguely sensitive to a change in the work, the movements of the workers not altogether solacing to the wounds of his pride. Nevertheless, up to this point he had experienced an abundant sensation of triumph. His heart did pound with anger at the "corn-cob" he had heard. Still, he was conscious of a real warmth suffusing his spirit. He had intended making certain changes in the way the barges were lashed and in the disposition of the various workmen, and was glad at the alacrity Gaetano, the foreman, was showing. A tugboat had chugged up close meantime and the levelers and gleaners had jumped off one barge to another while the boatmen were belaying.

"It's pretty early," said Michele, nodding toward these maneuvers.

"Sure early, but that's my idea now," answered Gaetano. His almost girlish voice lacked its customary note of respect, thought Michele, puzzled. The foreman towered above Michele, a stalwart figure, a mass of jet-black curls on his head, his open shirt revealing a wrought-iron musculature almost frightening in its strength. But his blue eyes were soft and troubled-looking despite the long mustachios drooping below the corners of his lips.

A string of barges had been belayed to the tug, the tug had given a shrill peremptory puff on its whistle, and barges and tug were starting lazily down the river.

"What do you mean, it's your idea now?"

"Well, you see, that's how I figured it out to save an extra cent or two. I've got to, you know."

Gaetano's voice was confidential and soft, but certainly not the voice of a subordinate. Michele looked at him quickly, almost with fright, his lips moving rapidly so that he knew he must stammer as soon as he spoke. He heard the water slapping the barges, the splash-slosh of the workers' feet, and the song resumed in a lustier key.

"*. . . dormi a suonno chieno . . . o . . . o . . . o*"

"B-b-but. . . ," he stammered, gazing directly into Gaetano's eyes. "But . . . who . . . who gave you orders?"

"Orders, orders?" repeated Gaetano in blank amazement as he stroked first one and then the other of his mustachios. "Why, nobody. I give orders here," and he continued talking as he realized that Michele was staring at him too dumbfounded to utter a word. "Why, since the lease, you know. Donn' Agnese and I signed the lease the other day. I pay her so much and I make what I can. That's why. . . ."

– 5 –

Only the sense of triumph as he strode through the friendly respectful crowd that morning had supplanted the pallor that a sleepless agonizing night had brought on. But that was gone now as he sharply felt the stiletto of this development thrust into his consciousness. His face turned weakly pale save for the small vivid disc of his scar. He looked up helplessly, without a word, his head feebly moving left and right, left and right. The quiet waterfront became a place of noise and confusion. Whips lashed through the air. The docks rose and sank. The singing workmen dizzied about him in perpetual circles. Old blear-eyed men poked livid points of tongues into his vision. He was so weak he could not close his hands.

"S . . . s . . . so!" he said finally. "So. . . ."

He turned about with the sudden fury of despair, ran and walked, ran and walked. Then he stopped, stood stock-still. He was in front of the stoneyard that occupied the empty lots adjacent to the row of brick houses. A stone-cutter was carving an inscription at the base of a monument hewn in the shape of a tree stump. He watched the man at his work. Then he felt Zi' Chele behind him, feebly, timidly tugging at his coat.

"Don Michele, Don Michele, *per l'amore di Dio!*"

When he reached home, forgetting to pick up the grapes on the way, he rushed into the downstairs room where Agnese was at table eating. He came to a sudden stop. The only object he was conscious of was a soup plate with a thin tomato sauce in which *baccalà* and peppers were heaped up.

"Concè," shouted Agnese, " a plate for Michele!"

She had noted at a glance the speechless agony, the complete demoralization, of Michele's spirit. Her irrational mixture of warmth and harshness revealed itself in the command to Concetta and in the cool way she proceeded with her meal.

"Sit down, Michele," she said. "This is very good, just enough sting to it.

I might have made it myself. . . ."

Michele obeyed. His was more than a love for his strong companion. It was a tribute to a force that could hold him firmly and at the same time cradle him in a safety that made his timid heart cease its restless beating. It was the sensation of the cradle dropping through space and his consequent fall inevitably to follow, that was stifling the efforts he was making at self-assertion. But he had been too cruelly hurt at the "dumps" for much resistence now. He sat down.

"Gaetano has taken over the 'dumps,' you know," she said calmly, dipping a huge crust of brown bread into the sauce of fish and peppers. "On a lease. I needed quick money. The workers have to be paid immediately. Work starts today. I didn't want to be bothered with the 'dumps,' too."

Concetta had come in with a more than ample dishful. As she placed it before Michele, a trickle of the red sauce spilled on the flowered table cloth. . . .

"Oh, what a trembling old hand I'm getting," laughed Concetta.

"You fill the plates . . . so!"

"Why not?" she snapped back in her rich self-pleased voice. "What else have we in this world, and especially in this country? Let's fill up, I say."

Michele was slowly inspecting the hot stew with the tip of his spoon. In another second he was eating. But he did not say a word throughout the entire meal. Nor did Agnese.

Outside they heard with great distinctness the noise of the wrecking crew at work.

– 6 –

When Agnese had had her small cup of black coffee, her piece of *provolo* and her apple, carefully, almost painstakingly, peeled and quartered, she ordered Concetta to be sure to have enough for Gesualdo and Giovanni.

"Save a dish for Luigi, too," she suggested. "He'll be here late tonight."

"What a woman, what a woman!"

Concetta clucked her admiration, shook her head. "So many things on her brain and she sticks her nose into my affairs! I've worked for you two years, now. The Madonna be thanked, two years, and I don't need to be told, not the slightest thing, you hear, not the slightest. Get out to your business and be careful a brick don't open up that pretty head of yours. Why. . . ."

Concetta would have sung her litany, as Gesualdo called it, all afternoon, knowing that Agnese would not have spoken a word in reply except possibly to say, "Oh, let's have an end of it, you old owl." Agnese cut her off, however, this time by calling out to Michele in a soft, almost kindly voice. But she could not sense that it seemed so strange to him that he felt his flesh crawl and go cold.

"You haven't slept much, Michele. Go upstairs and take a nap. . . ."

"That's an idea, a good idea," Concetta affirmed as Agnese shut the grated door behind her. "Why don't you? 'Closed eyes are happy eyes, and shut lips tell no lies.' That's a jingle-jangle of my own, and it's what I always say."

But Michele had shoved away his dish, had laid his head on the table between his arms and was weeping quietly.

"There! Why, you are sleepy! Who wouldn't be after last night's party? Oh, as for Antonio and all that! He'd be a ninny who thought about it twice. A fig for it all! Why, he was drunk and who pays attention to a drunk?"

As she talked, she noticed that Michele's shoulders were throbbing with what must have been smothered sobs, and she clapped both her hands to her mouth.

"*Gesù, Giuseppe e Santa Maria,* glory be to God," she exclaimed in an undertone, her chestnut eyes wide open in stupefaction.

Just then Gesualdo bustled in. These days he was always well dressed. (Concetta said of him he seemed always on his way to his own wedding.) Today, his neat if baggy serge was covered with a layer of powdered plaster and minute shivers of wood.

"Oh, they're coming down, they're coming down!" he almost sang as he slapped his coat and trousers. "Michele, I tell you it's a sight for these old eyes of mine! How fast they work! Bang goes a sledge, down comes a wall. Woof! Pull a hook, and down comes the house. Plaster here, bricks there, and what noise and the shouts of the men! Why, Michele, no wonder there's gold in this land. . . ."

"Hope a cornice'll mash your top in some day," shrilled Michele, rising in a fury so spontaneous that Concetta and Gesualdo stared at each other in fright. "On you and the lot of you, damn you all. . . ," and he hurried out of the room, through the kitchen and into the backyard.

"What's happened to the goody-good all of a sudden like?" asked Concetta.

"*Zitto, zitto, per carità, Concè,*" whispered the old man. "You mustn't, you mustn't. . . ." Gesualdo's eyes were shining, as he flicked a particle of dust off his collar with deliberate uneasy slowness. "I shouldn't have said a word! You mustn't put the whip to a chafed flank . . . what a cross he is carrying. . . ."

Perceiving, however, that he was possibly revealing too much as he noticed Concetta cocking her head in the manner of an eager confidante, he suddenly shouted, slapping his hands before him, "Come on with the soup, and hurry, there, hurry, there. Don't stand drooping like a wet hen."

– 7 –

The backyard displayed the most revolutionary transformation of all the portion of Agnese's new and imposing residence. Thanks to Gesualdo, in less than two years there had been transplanted to it a miniature Italian vineyard. A pergola of unpainted sapling trunks with the bark shaved off ran down the middle, flanked and roofed with broad-leaved grapevines heavy with gleaming clusters. In the hot September afternoon the perfume of the ripening fruit was like a warm odor of new fermentation and under the canopy of leaves the shadows were dense as in a crypt. A marble basin held a green mirror of motionless water, flecked and checkered with the delicate flitter of the leaves overhead. At either end rough-hewn rustic tables with unbacked benches told the story that the pagan gods of wine and the feast could wink you an invitation even from behind the corners of a brownstone front. Gesualdo had done his work well. The yard had become a rendezvous for many of the *paesani,* and the sounds of men playing at *tocco* and the clink of glasses completed the narrative.

Michele sought it because he could reach it without having to pass in front of Gesualdo and Concetta. Even he realized that his explosion was for him unnatural. Once in the garden, he had a chance to be still. Something in the coolness of it fell like a light wind filled with sweet suggestions of his sheltered, timid childhood in Villetto. He recalled the moss-covered slab of the old well into which they lowered the wine flasks when his father lived. It had once been covered with snow . . . the only snow that had ever fallen in Villetto. He remembered how he had taken a stick to trace lines on the slab. How he stood wondering at the cold powdery white, and how suddenly. . . .

But there was someone at his side! A door had been cut in the fence between the Farinella and the Dantone yards, a door hidden from view by a smaller pergola itself drooping with grapevines. Catarina had entered, taken him by the hand, and pulled him under the roof of leaves.

"Sit down," she said in a hurried whisper. "Sit down. I want to talk to you. . . ."

– 8 –

Catarina had practically dragged the stunned, unresisting Michele to the nearest bench. She sat opposite him, rested her plump bosom on the table, and vigorously leaned her head toward him until the storm in her eyes could communicate itself to Michele and raise him out of his lethargy of self-depreciation. Fright, a wild plea not to be driven too hard, a frantic protesting of blinking eyes, unquiet lips against the horror of determination in Catarina's energy, kept him seated uneasy, despairing.

"You know I love my children. May they be saints! And so you will understand . . . as I love these fingers, I love them. I would not bite off my nails, would I? So, I would not hurt my children . . . I would let no one pull my nails out, would I? I'll let no one hurt my children, do you understand, do you understand?"

Her voice thinned and broke; but at the same time it threatened, dominated. Michele put out two mercy-pleading palms, turned a pale countenance to her, begged with fallen shoulders to be let alone.

"You ought to know . . . I can't talk to that . . . to that. . . ," Catarina choked on her sob. "She's a devil's witch, and you know it . . . but you're her husband. . . . Let no disaster come upon us! I beg of you, Michele, for my children's sake . . . let her watch her step, keep her feet out of my home . . . let her keep her dirt to herself. . . ."

The chestnut strands of her hair had left the heavy combs stuck in a circle about her head, and cast stringy shadows on her cheeks, her eyes. She kept brushing them back with her thick, short fingers.

"Antonio's a good man if he's let alone . . . you better warn her. . . . *Vergine Maria Santa* . . . should we all suffer for a witch? You put her in her place . . . you're her husband . . . I don't have to tell you what to do."

Michele made no answer. Not once did he attempt to stop the torrent of her words, to offer a remark of protest, to calm her . . . he blinked, squirmed on his seat, and simply stared at her, stock-still.

"I love peace, Michele, and I love friendship, and respect the world and everybody in it. I beg you, Michele . . . keep an eye on your wife, let her mind her step . . . or . . . or. . . ."

She placed her hands over her eyes and shuddered, fell back into her seat, and, her head in her arms on the table, wept convulsively. It was the weeping that roused Antonio to fury and finally reduced to impotence the energy of opposition. Michele could only look at her in speechless amazement, and then gaze about him, wondering. Her sobs and tears continued. At last he placed a hand gently on her head.

"I'll know what to do. . . ," he stammered. "I'll know what to do. . . ."

However, before his eyes leaped visions not of the treacherous Agnese whom he never could make out, but of Antonio whose intentions he understood too keenly, and whom he had hated ever since the night on board ship over thirteen years back. The impulse that had unleashed the jealous anger in his heart he could feel now, hacking like a dull knife at his long habits of quiet and constraint. The happenings of the day and the night, this bewildering collapse of another person, abject almost as his own, had brought on a physical debility which he sensed in loose joints, tired eyes, fear of stammering if he dared talk. And with it the anger of his very impotence, the need to shout to the world that he was no simpleton, no fool, was seeking an object to break on. Little did Catarina divine of the course on which she had set his mind.

"I'll fix him yet," he thought to himself.

He put a hand on Catarina's shoulder, and like one much stronger pressed down assuringly.

Catarina raised her head with a sudden jerk, so vehement indeed that one of her combs fell, hit the table with a thud, bounced and rattled on the stone flags under the benches. The sound startled them both. It gave them both time to recover slightly from their mood of bitter despair.

"We were happy," said Catarina simply, wiping her eyes with the side of her hand. "Now this!"

"We were happy, too!" said Michele as simply.

"Nothing must happen."

"Nothing," assented Michele.

"You'll know what to do."

"Yes, I'll know what to do."

– 9 –

The door in the fence had opened and Barto Lo Santo was standing in the shadow of the vines.

"*Che diavolo,* Catarina," he cried in a humorous lilt of his thin voice. "I've been upstairs, downstairs . . . in the cellar, in the bedroom, shouted and called and whistled and coughed, and here you are. . . ."

He stopped, held his mouth open for a second, as usual, shut it again and blinked.

"Well?"

"I got a message for you . . . from Antonio. Inside's a whole box of grapes, a mess of live eels, two big *provoli* . . . I don't know what . . . I had to cart them . . . He said cook all you can. . . . He'll come late. . . ."

"Late? Why late?"

The tone astounded the good-natured Barto. He looked at her quickly.

"He and Donn' Agnese and I don't know who. . . . *Dio,* how am I to know? Went somewhere . . . some business . . . I don't know. . . ."

Catarina's eyes flashed a bewildered message to Michele. She had not become accustomed to the necessities of a business requiring a woman and a man to be thrown together constantly. She could not understand why a woman should be involved in business at all. There were men for that. And in the recoil from the spectacle of it she had the disconcerting sense of an abnormal, almost immoral, strength being employed to wrest from her and her kind who minded their home and children, the dearest possessions of their souls . . . a quiet retreat, peace in routine, the assured expectation of affection. . . .

"Barto! Barto!" she exclaimed, weeping, "Barto. . . ." She went to him with her hands outstretched, her lips quivering, her eyes wet. "Keep that woman away from him . . . keep her away. . . ."

Barto held his mouth wide open in utter consternation, and fluttered his eyelids with indescribable rapidity as he always did when excited.

"Catarina. . . ," he pleaded, "Catarina!"

After all, there was the husband of Agnese. What could he say?

"And it's not talk, Barto. It's not talk! I know. You saw last night. . . ."

Her voice was shrill, frightened, hysterical. There were people looking out from the back windows of the square of houses that outlined the block. Concetta had come out. . . .

"For the love of the good Saint Peter, what's all this shouting?" she cried, superbly unconscious that she, too, was shouting. "I heard what you said . . . away inside, too . . . and look, the whole world's leaning out of the windows. . . ."

"What do I care for the world? I'll shout it so they'll all hear. . . . She's a witch . . . *'nna putana . . . 'nddiavolata.* . . . That's what . . . she and all her money . . . what if she has made America? She's a witch. . . ."

"Oh, shut up. . . . Don't whinny around here . . . get inside. Have some shame." Concetta turned to her with great disgust. "What's happened? What's happened, I ask you? Nothing . . . nothing! Last night? Why, Antonio was tipsy . . . that's all. . . . She's a good woman, I tell you. . . . She makes the whole world good. . . . She's a saint, and I know it. . . ."

"A saint! A whore I say . . . a whore!"

"*Dio Santo, Dio Santo!*" exclaimed Concetta, her hands in her hair. "What a country! What a country! What are we coming to! Hear that woman!"

Barto blinked and kept his mouth open, looking from woman to woman with a mechanical precision. Michele attempted to break in between them, tried to exhort them to make an end. But every time he opened his mouth, he began to stammer and was too late to prevent a fresh outburst.

People here and there called out from the windows.

"Shame, shame. . . ."

"Stop your shouting. . . ."

"*Dio Santo,* what disgrace. . . ."

"This is America. . . ."

"Oh, ho . . . there . . . the *ricconi!*"

And finally there stood up on a fire escape a stick-like shadow of a man, with a belt tied so tight about his waist that a long end dangled between his legs like a tail. He was in shirt sleeves, with no cuff buttons, and so his sleeves flapped as he waved his hands up and down in mock imitation of a band leader. He was Lippo Nardi, the halfwit son of Mastro Paolo, the ice and coal man who had made so much money that he owned the house he lived in.

Lippo shouted at the top of his lungs:

"America, America, gnash your teeth and wail.
There goes the rustic jackass.
A-swishing of his swallow-tail!"

By this time Barto had recovered from his confusion. He took Catarina by both arms and shook her.

"Stop it Catarina, stop it," he whispered. "Go to your own place. . . . It will be all right. . . ." He pulled her through the door. She struggled but allowed herself to be taken away, shouting all the time.

"Tell her to look out, the bitch . . . tell her to look out. . . ."

– 10 –

Michele rushed back into the house but his cup of bitterness was not yet full. Concetta pursued him with an anger that mounted to the pitch of fury.

"What a man! How could you stand there and say nothing? Have you no respect for yourself? Let your wife be talked about like that! A dog would bite back! But you . . . you . . . shame, shame. . . ."

Gesualdo was hurrying downstairs.

"I had gone to take a nap. . . ," he said. "But all this noise . . . what was it!"

"A horrible scene! That woman next door . . . in the backyard . . . shouting . . . the vilest names about Agnese . . . the disgrace of it . . . and that man . . . that man. . . . Her husband. He stood there, hung his head . . . in shame no less . . . took it all in . . . seemed to believe it . . . what a disgrace!"

"*Zitto, zitto, Concè, zitto,*" kept interrupting Gesualdo, "not a word more . . . go into the kitchen. . . ."

"Shameful, I say . . . stand like a stick . . . his own wife . . . a queen of women, too. . . ."

"Inside with you," commanded the old man in a whisper, and succeeded finally in quieting her, and shutting the door after her.

Michele had dropped into a monstrous leather chair, still shining new, as if it were an article of furniture not naturally welcome or favored in such a home as Agnese had built up. His elbows on his knees, his head in the palm of his hands, he sat, a disconsolate figure, no straight line anywhere in his posture, a fallen sack.

Gesualdo, his wrinkled face all concern, had poured out cognac in two small glasses.

"Michele," he said quietly. "You look terribly pale. Seems like you'd been in the earthquake. Take a swallow of this. Will do you good . . . come . . . here. . . ." He put one arm around Michele's shoulders, and with the other hand held the cognac.

"No, *ta,* no . . . just let me alone . . . I'm at the end of it all, *ta* . . . at the end. . . ." His utterance was a subdued sing-song, a whisper, and so he did not stammer. "No, I can't drink, *ta,* I can't drink. How could I say a word to that woman in the yard? How could I? No one knows what has been done to me. It has been ever since Antonio and his family moved next door. . . . Cursed the day I gave up the barbershop . . . that life was good . . . good . . . *ta* . . . *ta* . . . what's going to happen to me? My heart keeps pounding out 'Be a man, be a man . . . you know what to do. . . . You know what to do. . . .' Night and day . . . shall I sneak up to him with a knife in the dark?"

He sat up stiff.

"I'll go crazy," he yelled. "Crazy, do you hear? I'll cut . . . I'll rip him open . . . from the navel down, like a fig. . . ."

His hands trembled. His whole body shook. His face had turned white. With lips stupidly open, quivering, he gazed intently at Gesualdo as if in the presence of a fear that had taken a mysterious but unmistakable shape.

"I don't want to do it," he chattered convulsively. "I don't want to do it."

Gesualdo was too overcome to do anything but repeat, "Take a sip . . . just a sip . . . just a sip. . . ."

Michele was sitting on the edge of the chair, his whole body in the throes of spasmodic horror. "*Ta, ta,* I don't want to do it. . . ."

Heavy beads of perspiration appeared suddenly in queer spots on his face, blinking and dancing, running precipitously down his cheek, or standing perfectly quiet in the pale hollows. Gesualdo became frightened, especially since the voice of the suffering man lost volume and strength, became dry, cracked in his chest. He put down the glass, and turned about to put Michele back into the deep portion of the chair. Michele, however, had stood up, a trembling loose mass, with horror-stricken eyes, and cried like one with the gallows-rope about his neck protesting to the saints his desire for life.

"I . . . don't . . . want . . . to . . . *Ta*. . . ."

And then swaying, shaking, he fell to the floor as he had done during the night. Gesualdo shouted for Concetta, bent over him, calling his name with the ineffectual iteration of those who do not know what to do. Concetta and he finally managed to carry him upstairs.

"Like a sack of crushed grapes, he was," explained Gesualdo later. "All knots and soft places and mashed-like, you know, and limp. . . ."

XII. ILLNESS

– 1 –

Gesualdo it was who nursed him back to health. It was he who induced Giovanni to sit for several minutes a day by the side of the bed and ask, "How are you? Are you better?"

He would not say *ta* for many days, but on one occasion caused the pale helpless Michele almost to jerk his head with electric suddenness and look intently at him. Gesualdo, who was standing by, looked too, puzzled. He had said in a shrill forced voice as if someone had pinched him until he uttered the word:

"*Ta,* daddy, are you better?"

They did not know that Giovanni had been talking about Michele's illness to Gelsomino and that Gelsomino had said, "You are wrong there, Giovanni. Maybe he expects you to say it. He is hungry for kind words."

Gesualdo kept the room dim, almost gloomy, the windows shut tight, except when Doctor Grace was coming, the house noiseless. He fed Michele from a spoon, holding up his head with one hand. Agnese would sit close by on these occasions, straighten out the sheets, pat her husband's hands, make inquiries in a voice, gentle, really, although anxiety in it had been replaced by attention and interest only. But it was low and soft if not caressing, and Michele opened slow, weary eyes, covered with a moist glaze, and he would stare at her weakly and long without answering a word. It was the same when the two were alone.

She busied herself with putting things in place, the image of Saint Francis on her dresser, the crochet-covering on the big trunk in the corner, the pillows on the bed. For days and days Michele had been unable to speak, nor did his lips ever move; it was as if the mind that stirred them refused to have them shape any expression at all. Gesualdo, in spite of Doctor Grace's order to the contrary, would bend over him, and urge him to speak.

"Can't you talk, Michele . . . you can . . . I am praying to Saint Biagio for you . . . he will loosen your throat . . . something dried up your throat and closed it up? But try . . . try . . . say one word. . . . We all want you to get better . . . say, 'I'm fine!' Just that. . . . Maybe you can pray . . . *Dio Santo, prega nobis.* . . ."

Agnese, however, would take his hand after she had completed the little tasks she deemed necessary and ask, "How are you, Michele, better, maybe?"

And Michele would turn his head feebly, open his sad-looking weary eyes and stare at her.

Neighbors filled the rooms downstairs all day long, bringing their quota of gifts for the sick: *ricotta* and fruit, live chickens, a mess of broccoli. Most of them could not afford it, but no one would have dared come to pay his respects without some "little bit of a nothing," as they phrased it. Curiosity spurred them to ask over and over, "Could I just peep at Don Michele, poor man . . . say one word?"

They thought themselves entitled to at least that much in return for coming and for the little bit of nothing always wrapped in newspaper. They could not understand the order to keep them out. Agnese sat down with them and exchanged a word or two, but vouchsafed no extended attention to any of them.

"What a country! You get sick, the Lord only knows how."

"Yes," Agnese would answer.

"Imagine . . . losing his speech! Have you burned a candle to San Biagio?"

"What a pity, Donn' Agnese! And you with all these big tasks on your hands. I pray to the Madonna for you!"

"Oh, we poor just have little troubles . . . a slice of bread only in bean soup with pasta, and a chew of celery, maybe! But you . . . an enormous house with so many things . . . your business . . . it's a pity, sure, it's a pity, poor man, and you, too, Donn' Agnese. . . ."

"Well," smiled Agnese, "we all have our trials."

– 2 –

Luigi rushed in, the night Michele was put to bed, and went close up to Agnese. His eyes gleamed intensely as if a vigorous blaze of suspicion had flared up and then stilled itself into a steady flame.

"Agnese," he demanded, "nothing happened?"

"What could happen?"

"You know. . . ."

"Are you crazy, Luigi, to talk that way to me?"

"Agnese, I have the Italian in me yet. I'm not American, money or no money, and you're not either. . . . I've kept still too long. Once I wanted to cut a priest's throat with a sickle. You remember."

"Well," said Agnese, giving him back a steadier and more prolonged gaze, so steady and so prolonged that it pierced him like a heated lancet, "you are talking too much, too much. The man's sick . . . that's all. We all know our places. We had it out last night and you pledged . . . well? And besides, you will look after yourself. This is not Italy, and I'm less of an Italian now than ever. . . ."

Brother and sister looked at each other, understanding the strength of each other's will. Possibly had Agnese lived in Villetto where the penalties for such behavior as Luigi had hinted at were immutably fixed in the customs of the community, she might have winced, for his eyes laid bare the suspicion he entertained, and made clear that he had not changed his attitude. The old habituations were coiled up like sleeping snakes in the warm sun of the good fortune in America. Agnese could see their sinister power in the tense muscles of Luigi's face and, although she was not one to fear, she had a flash of the monstrous tragedy that might eventuate. She realized that the brother in him would drive him, for the stupid vengeance he would exact, to quarters where the catastrophe would be more poignant and unforgivable. And so she was the first to perceive the dangerous values in a speech such as she had made, and sufficiently shrewd to change her tack.

"Luigi, don't be an ass," she said, smiling. "You never had long ears. He's sick, that's all, just as certain as the Holy Virgin. Get your foolish thoughts out of your head. . . . Concè," she shouted, "bring out that *baccalà,* and that new *Gragnano* Gaetano brought!"

– 3 –

A cold October had set in. Blustering east winds swept the chill from the river through the crowded streets. Michele had lain so long in bed, either incapable or undesirous of leaving it, that his illness had lost its dramatic appeal to the sympathy of the family. Although he began to show an interest in the doings about him, he still lay stunned and exhausted.

"Oh, I don't know," said the long-legged Doctor Grace, holding the glass of *Strega,* yellow-green, where the light could dance from it in rainbows. "Oh, I don't know when he can get up . . . it's nerves, you know, a real shock, lost his steam, don't you see . . . the machine can't keep up. . . ."

"But he get up?"

Agnese inquired fretfully, and yet the doctor noted the signs of an anxiety not altogether without an enfeebling effect upon her own spirit. He placed a hand on her knees.

"Agnese," he said, "you're not going to worry. . . ."

"Oh, no, no, no . . . not much worry for me . . . for him. Why is he sick so long now?"

"He will get well."

"But when . . . when?"

"Hard to say. You know what, though," he said suddenly, but thoughtfully, throwing his legs out slowly and putting his fingers together before his eyes like a screen. "If he got really, but really sick, he'd get well . . . oh, broke a leg, got pneumonia . . . would take his mind off what's worrying him . . . see . . . but," he laughed, "that can't be . . . so . . . well, patience. . . ."

"Yes, patience. . . ," assented Agnese. And then the doctor held his inclined position as if transfixed, his small blue eyes held still by the look in Agnese's. He wanted to speak, to take back what he had said. But Agnese had gathered the lace cashmere shawl, the white of which accentuated the flushed olive of her features, put it over her head, and, as she drew it under her chin, rose slowly.

"He must get well . . . everybody is getting sick too . . . see . . . you'll give him some good medicine . . . no?"

He jumped to his feet with a sort of humorous alacrity and drawing the heavy lace curtains aside looked out. He could not have continued to gaze another second into her eyes.

"Well, they're getting along, aren't they, now!" he drawled. "The old brownstones are coming down fast. What a change, Agnese! What a change, and all your work! You're a better business man than a hundred Americans, I tell you."

"You think so, hey?"

"Oh, you're a keen one," he almost shouted as she stood by his side and gazed out with him.

"Oh, you little devil, you know it," he added. "Think of it . . . buying Judge Colston's house to make room for a dago tenement. That's rich. I tell you . . . a peasant wench, you might say! Why, I remember the old judge sitting out there on his stoop on a hot night . . . girls and boys on every step . . . seemed fixed there for eternity! And you come along, Agnese, and you say, 'shoo-fly' and they 'shoo-fly' all right. . . . Rich, I tell you. . . ."

The houses that once had stood in dignified serried ranks were now gaping walls, a confused mass of plaster and shivered timbers, piles of broken bricks and dirt. In coming down they had exposed the rear of the tenement houses on the other street, unpainted, with fire escapes strung with peppers and long ropes of bright red new sausages, piled up with boxes and bedding, radiating clotheslines that flapped their burdens in the brisk wind. Tall, leafless branches thrust like yardarms into the air, a single acanthus tree rose solidly out of the ruins. The wind danced furiously in the wrecked area, gathered the powder of plaster and brick, the loose scraps of paper and slivers of wood, whirled them off into vortices and deposited them all on window sills and sidewalks. Doctor Grace had no sooner finished talking than a particularly animated gust had flung across the street and rattled against Agnese's windows.

"The wind's not too cold? I'll keep his window open, hey, doctor?"

"Well, that was a kick-up, wasn't it, now? Oh, no. Keep them open, do him good. . . . You know," he turned to look down at her, "I can't get over it, just can't get over it, what you have done!"

He put out a finger and held up her chin.

"And you're a beauty, too. . . ."

"You talk funny, you know. . . ."

She put a hand on his shoulder.

"You funny man!" She laughed a rich subdued laugh that echoed and re-echoed in his ears for days afterwards, as it always did.

"There!" he said with an air of nervous conclusion. "I've kissed you. . . ."

"You funny man!" she repeated, but her laughter had become thin and shrill, and as she placed her head on his shoulder he was not certain that she was not weeping and laughing both, in hysterical explosion. She was not weeping, but her laughter was not of happiness, not of joy. She began pounding his shoulder with her fist, not hard but with a slow irregular beat. The gesture was so sudden and unexpected that Doctor Grace drew back in a kind of fright and consternation.

"This sickness, see, it's on my nerves . . . maybe, I made him sick . . . see . . . maybe . . . see. . . ."

He had no opportunity to answer, for Agnese had left as if an instantaneous impulse had ejected her from the room.

– 4 –

It had been over a month that Michele lay sick, and the whole family began to show the inevitable signs of depression and irritation that accompany prolonged illnesses in any group. No one had foreseen, however, the startling development that set in several days after Agnese's talk with Doctor Grace. She had insisted that the windows in her husband's room be kept open night and day. One night the wind had been so strong that it blew out the lights in the cressets beneath the Virgin, Saint Francis, and, worst of all, Saint Blase, patron saint of throat diseases, guardian against lung trouble, easer of the voice.

"*Giorno maledetto!* That we moved in here," cried Gesualdo to Agnese. "See what you have done. You and your American doctor. The man's dying I tell you . . . dying . . . red like a beet with fever . . . coughs . . . spits blood . . . been up all night. . . . *Madonna mia d'u carmine,*" he shouted after a pause, since Agnese sat in the leather chair sipping her coffee and rum and making no reply. "The man's half a corpse, Agnese, and you sit there. . . ."

"*Ta,*" she said finally, "he'll be better soon . . . I know it, I know it . . . *Dio Santo!*"

"Doctor Grace says better . . . you say better . . . and he'll get better! May God be good! After all he's a Christian, too, like you . . . you can't pour poison into his heart and then. . . . It's a disgrace, a disgrace!"

Agnese put her hands on his shoulders and shook him into silence. "Will you kill me too! Pour poison into me! *Zitto* . . . let's hope . . . I know . . . I know he'll get well. . . ."

Gesualdo was taken aback. The color had fled from her face and in its place was the pallor of a strain that measured an inward agony in no way physical. Her father realized keenly now what he had often wanted to believe, that much of the cold ways of his daughter, much of her hardness and determination, was a willful sinning against herself.

He stepped back.

"*Gesu, Giuseppe, e Santa Maria,*" he mumbled, made the sign of the cross, and went upstairs. . . .

– 5 –

The windows of the dining and sitting rooms just below the street level were grated and across them were drawn white curtains heavily designed in bouquets and jardinières. The gray day was like a murk filtering down into the streets. Agnese stood between the curtains, holding one in one hand, the other in the other, pulling them nervously. She looked across the street and saw the men already resuming their task of carting away the mounds of the debris cleared to make room for the structures she had planned. They looked like reapers on an early dawn in the fields outside Villetto when the fog was still low. There was Antonio, athletic, heavy-set, commanding. How he moved among the men! Why wasn't he the one instead of that . . . she did not frame the insulting expression. Antonio would not have consented, although he was willing now, even now. . . .

She stood as immobile as a waxen image. Her eyes were aware of the trucks pulling away. She saw the rapid figures of the passers-by. She heard the trolleys clatter, knew dimly that there was an early snow flurry eddying and dizzying about.

However, there was a grayer day in her heart, and a great gaping space, too, where a tall edifice of hope had lifted spires and colored windows in the brightness of her girlhood, and all her numerous chilling doubts like the flakes whirled slowly over it. As she pulled at the curtains she must have realized that pedestrians would glance at her and wonder why she stood there so quiet. It mattered little. Smiles played about the lips that retained their fullness and their redness. Bitter smiles they were, flashes of conclusions to problems that had of late begun to vex her. Why be worried over what questions strangers would amuse themselves with? Never had such things as neighbors or strangers caused her to hesitate on any line of conduct.

As the flakes lazied through the air she followed them with her eyes as she pursued query after query in her mind. She had never discussed her plans with anyone, but she had never failed to debate them with herself. Her will had dominated her mind and heart. In the eyes of Villetto and the world hers had been an act of willful impiety to allow herself to become the enamored of a priest. By her own act of withdrawal into the grotto, she had known what loneliness could be, and she had determined to go it alone before she was stoned out of society; but to be alone like a spire, built brick by brick, by devoted hands, to stand out as a monument, an object of respect, at least a somebody to whom all would look up and if not love, certainly not despise openly and with impunity. . . .

Two horses, black and gray beasts, huge and powerful, were straining at a rope. They were pulling down the old stump of the acanthus.

"How solid that was," thought Agnese. "That's how I was going to take root in this new soil. But what did I do? In the first place, I committed a sin. I have confessed it to myself, oh, how many times. And then a crime, worse than a sin. I led that poor . . . (she could not say the word "fool") to marry me . . . oh, I knew what was in my mind. . . .

"And now there he is sick, and I torture myself. For I have made him sick . . . I know it. . . . What could I do? What could I do? *Vergine Santa Dolorata,* what could I do?

"And now I have done worse! *Dio, Dio! Dio!* . . . But it was Doctor Grace! 'Open the windows,' he said. He would get well . . . let him be really sick . . . pneumonia . . . open the windows. . . .

"That night I did . . . wide . . . all . . . and the wind blew. . . . He had not said one word for weeks. . . . How shall I forget his face when he woke, shivering, and he whispered, 'Agnese, Agnese, do you want to kill me?' Did I? Did I? . . . *Madre di Gesu, Madre mia pietosa* . . . did I? Did I?"

She kept straining at the curtains, and looking out with wide scared eyes, her mouth open, her face getting paler and paler, in a cold spasm of sudden terror.

"His face! . . . every muscle twitched. . . ."

There was a great shouting of men; she watched how the horses were making a final desperate effort. As they pulled, she hung more steadily on the curtains, her body bending with each movement of the animals, her lips shouting silently with the men.

"Is that Antonio holding the rein? Make them pull, Antonio, make them pull, Antonio, make them. . . ." Her mind kept repeating it, repeating it. . . .

"Ah, there . . . ah, there. . . ."

She grasped the curtains more firmly; there was another shout, another heave, a lunging forward.

"*Madre mia, madre mia.* . . . Did I? . . . Did I? . . . Did I? . . ."

She screamed in horror, the horses had plunged forward so suddenly!

Concetta, Gesualdo had run to her. She had pulled the curtains down, rod and all, and lay a huddle of dresses, curtains, shawl, insert, eyes wide open, lips framing a question. . . .

– 6 –

In the afternoon she was sufficiently herself to go downstairs into the kitchen where Gesualdo and Concetta had got into a brawl that was heard throughout the house.

"What's all this fuss about?" she inquired sharply.

Although Concetta wanted to ask, "What are you doing here, pale as a ghost?" she said quickly. "Your father here . . . what a fool! Wants to call in Filomena, you know, the pushcart woman. . . . Says she knows a charm . . . a charm from the old country . . . lays hands on him . . . says . . . '*Birribirriba*' and *teccoti* . . . she's cured . . . bah!"

"And I say it can't hurt . . . Agnese, it can't hurt. . . ." The old man had tears in his eyes, and his lips moved with the slowness of sorrow. "He's done for. . . . Doctor Grace said 'no hope.' . . . It can't hurt, Agnese. . . . He doesn't know anyone now . . . shakes the bed with one cough . . . Agnese, Agnese. . . ."

Gesualdo sobbed.

"Of course it can't hurt . . . try anything . . . anything. . . ."

Filomena came, but before entering Michele's room, demanded that all the windows be shut, the room made dark, all the crosses and saints' images removed, all the cressets extinguished. . . .

"*'Nna stupitaggine. . .* ," mumbled Concetta.

"One doesn't take a chance with the devil," whispered Filomena as she tied her black shawl under her chin with trembling knotty hands. "There must be another person with me. . . ," she confided. "But he must not call on any saint, say no prayer . . . not even in his heart. . . ."

But though she hobbled about the bed over and over, and laid her rough palms on Michele's brow, on his hands, on his chest, and though she murmured numerous incomprehensible incantations, the sick man showed no improvement.

She had no sooner gone than Concetta ran out of the house to summon the priest. "At least he won't die a pagan beast," she snapped.

"How is he?" asked Agnese of Gesualdo. "How is he, *ta*? He must get better . . . he must get better. . . ."

"Yes, my daughter, yes," answered the old man consolingly, taking her hands in his. "Do not let us say 'no hope' like the doctor. . . . 'It'll be a miracle,' Doctor Pastrocchi said. . . . I called him, Agnese. . . . I thought it might help. . . . A miracle like the saints worked. . . . There will be, Agnese, there will be. . . . You must not put pain in your heart. . . . 'A miracle,' he said. . . . There'll be a miracle . . . there . . . child of mine . . . there. . . ."

"*Ta,*" said Agnese, finally, putting a hand on her father's cheek as a child might who is asking a favor, "I am going to the church . . . to pray. . . ."

"*Lodato sii o'Signore. . . ,*" mumbled Gesualdo, and crossed himself.

Agnese had not been in church these thirteen years.

XIII. GELSOMINO

– 1 –

Giovanni's story to his mother of the man who had likened the painter to God the creator was not complete. He had not failed to suggest that he had some feeling that the stranger was the same person whom he had seen through his sick feverish eyes, but he did not reveal the companionship that had developed between them.

Ever since Giovanni had regained his health and had returned to school with his heart filled with the new love that his mother showed him, his whole nature, as happens in boys that grow rapidly, had undergone a transmutation, an enrichment of the impulses that were fundamental to his make-up and not held in common with all other youngsters in the world. And this transformation was not entirely of his own devising — not entirely the expanding perceptions and understandings that had come out of his ill-fated adventure at independence and assertion. It was in large part due to the friendship he had contracted not only with the stranger whom he knew in a vague way to be his father, but also with the artist, Gino Birrichino, into whose shop he had drifted one day, attracted by the artist himself and the paintings displayed in the windows that bore the large printed legend: Studio of the Fine Arts and Painting. It was in a street lined with innumerable grocery and butcher-shops, each dingy and dirty as the dark mud-caked street itself.

Gino was one of those men who have not made and cannot make the necessary distinction between the reality of the present and the dreams that hover over it and around it. Why he persisted in painting nobody could tell, for he was perpetually and precipitously dangling over the brink of a poverty that already had reduced his frame to pencil-thinness, but had not, at the same time, chilled the fire that burned within it.

Gino painted al fresco, sitting conspicuously at the foot of the limestone steps leading to his colorful shop, an easel in front of him, placing his colors on the canvas with multitudinous gestures. Invariably he wore a purple vest, a purple beret with a tassel, no coat, and shoes that reached with sharp points into the infinite. Groups of men and boys, women big with child and carrying oil-cloth bags filled with their marketing, stood around gazing at his work.

"*È bello, hey?*"

"Sì, oh sì, ch'è bello!"

The most extravagant comments left him unmoved. In fact, he turned to his onlookers himself and vouchsafed his own judgments.

"You thought it would be impossible to make that nose appear pock-marked?" he asked, the first day that Giovanni had seen him at work. "Not at all. But here, here is where skill counts."

He stopped to flourish his brush in his ductile fingers and then to bring it down smartly on his palette.

"Signor Pittore," Giovanni said almost in a whisper, pulling at the artist's shirt sleeves, "may I stay close? I want to see. . . ."

"My child, you must be the kernel of a poet. Stand close, of course. I'm flattered. Here's a box . . . not a royal seat, but a seat."

Giovanni sat down awkwardly, his face flushed with excitement.

"Sit and learn," the artist continued. "Took me years — under the finest masters in Naples. You see, I have to hide that ear under the curls of his hair, and yet you must know the ear is there."

As he stood up to accomplish this astounding feat, he revealed how completely his buttocks had slipped into this shank-like thighs, and how his back curved out beyond the posterior lines of his hips and waist.

"Don't breathe to hard," many a one would say, sensing the smiles of amusement that rippled through the crowd. "You'll drive him through the picture."

But once Gino had turned on them his sea-green eyes, slightly bulging, but not altogether quiet, something in the nature of a gentle holiness fell on the gathering. They did hold their breaths, and opened surprised mouths as he talked. They forgot the hollow, puckered cheeks, the mustaches curled like glistening tendrils, the long nose that took a sharp bend almost perpendicular to the line of his brows. The lesson in appreciation became an event in the day of the casual passerby.

"This picture," he would say, "a country girl at a well . . . note it carefully. She how she bends her neck. You must not make it too stiff. You must not let it strain. . . . And the eyes! They must tell you the water is cool, but you can't see the eyes — the lids cover them. And the color! The green skirt, the yellow stripes, the peasant bodice of lace and linen! It's a joy . . . a bit of the lane behind my place in Soddo it reminds me of . . . ah, *che paradiso bello* . . . the artist catches it . . . so!"

His *bottega* was the front room of a railroad flat in what once had been a pretentious limestone edifice, judging from the brass knobs still remaining on the heavy paneled doors, the brass bells that did not ring, the brass letter boxes with their plate glass shattered beyond use. The marble mantelpiece topped by a mirror overhung an open hearth now the receptacle for castaway tubes of paint, old brushes, and old rags. Reproductions of Michelangelo's *Adam,* Da Vinci's *Madonna of the Rocks,* Baldovinetti's *Madonna,* attested to his discrimination, and various unfinished originals to the end of his effective self-confidence.

"Ah, Gelsomino, the art of painting! The joy of it! To catch the spirit of Angelo, of Titian, of Correggio! Only reproductions? Yes . . . but who can hope to equal the gods? I tremble to lay my hands on the doors of heaven."

At night the room was the rendezvous of the literary lights of the community, and the scene of heated controversies: Italian lawyers now working as the makers of skirts or allowing themselves to be supported by admiring relatives, jobless men who had taught school on the other side, doctors who had failed to establish themselves. Gino led the talk while Gelsomino sat interested but silent.

He lived in the back room, where Gino kept a stove, and cooked the meals for both of them. An accident had brought them together, and necessity had joined them. And together they succeeded in eking out a thin existence on coarse minestrone and idealistic vaporizing.

Who Gelsomino was had not become known. The *Villetani* who had been acquainted with him in Italy were few and far between. Gesualdo had made no attempt to seek him out, Luigi had reasoned that it was insane to poke into a dying fire, and Agnese would never have been the first to arrange a meeting, and the last to talk about him.

– 2 –

After Agnese had left for America, Gelsomino had continued to perform his duties as if nothing had happened. But camps had formed for and against him. And there were massed enemies in his own heart, the camp fires of passion in conflict with itself. His face, his step, his voice showed the evidence.

"Why so pinched today, *padre*?"

"You ought to take a trip, *padre.*"

"Let me bring you some soup, *padre,* chicken broth with rice and new dandelions."

"You ought to change that slop-jar of a servant you have. . . . I'll come for a while . . . get you up some real dishes. . . ."

There were the sentimental women who forgot their religion in the flush of the excitement. Others were bolder in their comments. Oh, of course, he was human, and could one resist a willful girl who flung her shoulders at one with a motion that . . . well! They had known of *padri* who managed things quite discreetly, oh, quite. One would not dare talk openly.

"But if you come closer, I'll whisper it in your ear. Remember, though, a dead secret. Why yes . . . huh-huh! His wife! . . . Would you believe it? She's hoping now that this young *padre* . . . as if he has not been given a hard enough mattress to sleep on. . . ."

"He's taken his horns in like a snail. . . ."

"Oh, he has, indeed, and crawls around like one. Good as confesses!"

"Poor thing, he's awfully pale . . . like a lemon. . . ."

"A fool, I say, let me cross myself! Why, he could have . . . a brood by now! . . . he, he, he!"

"There's the young padre in Melfina . . . they say he has a whole family already. . . . So help me! . . . sure . . . sure. . . ."

"And if this pretty one wanted . . . well . . . now . . . he, he, he!"

Men handled him more roughly, and those in the habit of stopping for a chat with him after their day's work hurried home. Zi' Giacomo, so old and so hard-working that his head hung below his shoulders as he dragged his legs along, had never missed a Sunday in church, and would not now. But every Sunday after mass he spat on the pavement with much conspicuousness, making unmistakable sounds of relieving himself of a foul discomfort. Then holding his nose, he said in a loud voice that cracked on the last note: "Begging everybody's pardon, but it does stink around here."

"You couldn't blame him, could you, now," a foppish young blade remarked in the café. "A pretty bit of flesh like that. . . . Oh, I tell you, a priest's life . . . oh, it beats the devil! But we — we starve for a kiss in the dark. . . ."

A group of the bolder lads put on the long robes of funeral mourners, white sheets with skull-like hoods of the same material, and with mandolin and guitar serenaded him in ribald songs under his window.

Over their coffee cups in the only café in the town, the older men exchanged casual remarks, not protracted discussions like the women, no sotto-voce laughter, no slow vicarious tasting of romance on the tip of the tongue.

"So the saint turns rake, hey!"

"Knows how to pick them! What an eye!"

"And don't have to marry her!"

"Luigi ought to have sheared his head off, the cheap little pope!"

The remarks all got to Gelsomino's ears. He became quiet, aloof. His spare figure was no longer seen walking about the town, stopping here to chat, there to receive some newly lald eggs, at another place to lift the new baby into the air.

– 3 –

His nights had become torments. Always the emaciated figure of Agnese with her baby in the crook of her arm! He flung himself at the feet of the Holy Virgin, lifted agonized lips to her serene face, held out trembling palms in prayer. Words of forgiveness would not come, the ecstasy of contrition did not shake him. How he had preached to sinners to fall on their knees in penitence, tear off the garments of the flesh, raise the agony of their hearts in prayer! Only he, he could not pray, could not even mutter one word . . . only raise pained, pleading eyes!

The services he performed began to be empty gestures, blasphemous caricatures. What though his heart said: "You have confessed . . . you have suffered . . . your sin is forgiven . . . cast aside the past . . . let your thoughts be now forever of God and of the Church. . . ." He knew the truth was not in this formula. Forever as he stood before the sacred altar, nay, as he touched the ark of the Sacrament, there, there . . . see it floats before my eyes . . . her naked body . . . her breasts.

Ten months was all he could endure. He must fly.

– 4 –

One night he was startled out of a sound sleep. He had sat up in bed motionless as an image of stone, peered bewildered into the dark as if the resolution framing itself in his mind were being reflected in the distant shadows, and then had risen deliberately, put his clothes into a portmanteau — he still had it with him, green canvas with brown leather straps — and left the parish. He had given no one the slightest intimation of his intentions, sent no word to his mother, did not inform his bishop.

There had been a fair in the fields outside the town, and many drivers were packing up and leaving in the early hours of the morning. As a boy, he had taken part in these fairs, packed fruit, pottery, salami, cheeses into huge wicker baskets, and laid them out on straw mats for sale. The stamping horses, the braying mules, the jingle of harness bells, the acid odor of the animals' bedding, the gray moving forms, the shouting men, the smoldering charcoal fires, the carts lined up on the road, made his gentle eyes flame.

He inquired for a peasant who might be headed toward Bari, and offered to assist in return for a lift.

It was at the quiet unhurried seaport of Bari that he got his first berth on a ship. Taciturn, but never sullen, hard-working but never a pace-setter, loyal but never toadying, he was left unmolested by all the crews with whom he sailed. Mysterious stories circulated about him. His sallow complexion and long delicate features caused one of the most superstitious of the men on the British freighter to remark to a crowd one night, "Aw, I tell you he's the Wandering Jew. . . ."

Gelsomino knew they were talking of him. He smiled and left before they could become aware of his presence.

"He ain't no priest now. What would an anointed priest be doing among sailor men?"

A comment like this meant that at the next port he would sign off if he could, or abandon the ship. From that time on, his companionship with members of the crew became an intolerable striving to keep his identity even more securely hidden. For he did make friends, peculiar attachments more sentimental than he had suspected possible, although for the most part one-sided. Men came to him to complain of their hard lots, to let loose the sadness of lonely souls too full of memories, to obtain his approval of pet theories of creation or of the formation of certain headlands or of the causes of storms, the hold of women on men. Something in his nature induced the spirit of the confessional, and his intense manner of listening was so gentle withal that the men felt at ease, solaced, and comforted.

– 5 –

While on a Portuguese sailing-vessel he had fallen in with a sullen member of that race, grotesquely pockmarked, and with an underlip that had been cut loose from his jaw in childhood and sewed back by inexpert hands. The canines and the molars on the left side were constantly exposed, and that whole side of the face pulled far down and altogether immobile. The young fellow hated everything, blasphemed God and the saints in such ribald terms as to have turned even an unbeliever's stomach. He professed to despise anything remotely resembling a woman, and yet had been collecting for years the lewdest cartoons and pictures, and photographs of himself and prostitutes in the most obscene poses. . . . Money he professed to despise with an insane hatred.

"Money," he said, "is God's contraption to make men stink. So he could hack up their bodies and souls without conscience. Money is a dead soul rotting with worms, see. It's offal from saints' carrions. . . . A bitch in heat enough to draw the angels. . . ."

Gelsomino listened to him, said nothing. Their languages were different but they understood each other.

One night he had just returned from his watch. There was no fog low down, but no moon and no stars. He could hear the sea moan with a kind of yearning, more musical than the sounds of instruments. The four hours were lonely ones, the only hours when the desire to pray became an agony of frustration. It was then that Agnese came to him . . . her warm, soft skin, the eyes that closed gently as he kissed her and opened again like dim pools in a silver dusk, the rich laughter that was like the bells of festal afternoons! Ever and again the damp in the air was like a cold compress on his forehead, his cheeks. As usual he said as few words as possible to the watch that relieved him and walked rapidly to his bunk.

An uncommon weight of sadness seemed to have settled upon him. Why had Alexandra sworn at God, at Christ, at all the saints? Why had he pushed under his nose, as it were, the putrid facts of his own life? What business was it of his to ask, "And the girls? What, never? Are you a priest or a eunuch? Oh, you good man . . . let me see your tonsure!" And he had remained with the wretch, sat listening to him, looking into his eyes, watching the distorted face struggle as the lips failed to meet! The large deep pocks on his nose, under his eyes . . . how revolting they seemed.

"Ah, Agnese, *Agnesella!*"

He hurried to his bunk. He was about to crawl under the blanket, clothes and all, when his neck was seized. Fingers clutched it. He was thrown to the floor. Alexandro dug a knee into his chest. . . . "You crawling fish of an angel!" he spat into Gelsomino's face. "Where's that damned wad you carry? . . . Not a stir, there, not a word . . . . We're all in on this, see. I've searched everything . . . can't find it. . . . Where the hell is it?"

After several minutes, Alexandro realized that it was impossible to extract any information by choking his victim. Gelsomino said nothing, made no effort to extricate himself. He rose quietly and stared deliberately into his assailant's eyes with the gentle intent look he always had.

"Alexandro," he said finally, "were you afraid to choke me? You saw I was not afraid. I would not have fought you, and had you killed me, you could have found the money here in my pocket. . . . You say the gang wants it. . . . Call them . . . let them all come here . . . I'll divide it with you. . . . Why not? . . . I don't need it. . . . I don't spend it. . . . I have no one that wants it. . . . Call your friends. . . . Why not, Alexandro?"

Alexandro glanced at him with his motionless eye, while his shoulders sagged in a mean droop.

"Try none of your sainty-saint stuff on us, you God-infected bastard," he drawled out through his exposed teeth. "Damn it, can't you talk like a man? Always that syrupy voice of yours. . . ."

"Alexandro," Gelsomino repeated, "call the men, as I said. You all need the money more . . . or do you want it all?"

Alexandro jumped forward, and made a movement with his hand to seize the small linen bag in which Gelsomino had his money.

"Why, there it is," he said, "if you want it all. . . ."

Alexandro for a minute was evidently in a quandary. He finally raised his head sullenly, and gazing fixedly at the priest, gave a low prolonged whistle. Several men came forward: one nonchalantly pulling up his trousers, one shambling and grinning, another stepping briskly, his pipe in his mouth. . . . They stopped short when they saw the two men, made a circle and cautiously craned their necks forward. Alexandro told them. Their eyes glared with surprise in the darkness. . . .

"Who the hell ever tipped you off we wanted his money?" inquired the oldish man with the pipe. "What are you trying to do . . . get us in on another job of yours, hey?"

Alexandro made a movement as if to pull a knife.

The man with the pipe spat on the floor of the deck and grinned into his face. . . .

"You don't say, you bastard. . . ."

Before another word could be said he had struck him a violent blow on the jaws. Alexandro fell in a silent huddle. A trickle of blood oozed over his hanging lip. . . .

– 6 –

At the next port, Bahia, Gelsomino left the vessel. The oldish man with the pipe had dug an elbow into his ribs one day and said, "You're a god-damn ninny, see. . . . Take a tip from me, too. Stick that wad in the bank, see, or somebody'll knock your block off yet. . . ."

In Bahia, Gelsomino followed the old sailor's advice. He mailed the money to Naples. He made his way into the interior, finding work in out-of-the-way villages, in mines, on river boats. He managed to reach Buenos Aires, and from there wandered into the wheat fields, to the ranchos, and finally across the Andes into Chile. He sought work where only men were employed and as far as possible in lonely places far removed from cities, from families with women.

It had been easy enough to avoid them until curiosity, a deep-seated desire that had stirred his heart from the beginning, a longing for a sight of Agnese, of Giovanni, led him, by steady stages, into the United States.

– 7 –

In a small wooden trunk he kept under his cot in the dark center room of Gino's flat he had a large gold cross attached to a black chain of heavy silk strands. It was tied to a black Calvary Cross with a silver Christ, a sagging sorrowful form, too keenly executed to have been merely a symbol to the maker. These were the only objects he had taken with him . . . these and the torn shreds of a scapular of crocheted silk with the St. Chrysostom whom he so much loved. The scapular he had worn about his neck continually until his experience in a small mining town in Pennsylvania.

It was the work of Agnese. She had spent all the spare time she had in the making of it. She had used the finest strands of silk in many colors and had woven into the thousand delicate stitches the vigorous hands, palm to palm, the fragile but firm chin, the high determined cheek bones, the steady protuberant eyes with their long well-defined lashes, the black, string-like hair combed in the form of a halo. And the chain that held it was also of the neat painstaking crochet work. At intervals of half an inch was a disc, then a diamond and then another disc, and in each of these forms was a symbol — the rose, the chalice, the mitre, the staff, the holy book — each clear, almost jeweled in its colored strands. No one but Agnese and he had ever laid eyes upon it, and he often recalled how they had both started when they gazed upon it one evening.

The hearth-fire in Agnese's flagged peasant cottage cast the only light in the simple room. They had taken the scapular to see it better in the glow of the slow flame. Gelsomino was sitting on the three-legged stool close to the hearth, Agnese on one knee at his side. Not like ordinary lovers did they gaze upon it, with laughter and words of sweet silliness, but with smiles that were like the steady flames of altar candles when no wind stirs. Long they gazed upon the saint's sharp features softened by an inner heat of conviction. Then Agnese whispered:

"*Caro, caro,* do you know?"

And the whisper was one almost of fear.

"Yes?"

"He looks just like you."

Gelsomino looked at her, quickly moved, then his lips loosened into smiles that were the beginning of laughter.

"You pretty goose . . . you followed the picture in the book?"

"Of course. But my thoughts . . . they were yours, and my fingers touched your eyes and your lips and your chin as they snip-snapped, snip-snapped!"

And then, as happened frequently, he had stood up, his eyes fixed and sad, his fingers at his side loosened, closing, loosening, closing . . . Agnese understood. She bent over his hand, her knees still on the floor, and with frantic passionate vehemence pressed her lips upon it.

– 8 –

For more than a year the daily round of the miner's life had dragged him into a heavy fatigue that left him without thought, without memory. He had found a room in the cottage of a miner above the average in steadiness and sobriety, Luke Malone, kept for him by a sister past middle age.

Her tall body was vigorous and full, and in her tight-fitting calico wrapper preserved the vestiges of a youthful suppleness. Had it not been for two items — the small myopic eyes which she kept constantly half-closed in an attempt to focus them more steadily, and the heavy-set nose with its large moving nostrils — her pompadoured hazel-colored hair, her straight long neck, would have been attractive and still provoking. But she was even more reticent than Gelsomino, moved about her tasks with the nervous energy of one who suffers in silence the pangs of inward rebellion, and, as the men ate, stood over the table with a determined look that would have rendered uncomfortable everyone else but her brother and the gentle Gelsomino. In consequence, she had not kept a boarder long, nor had she managed to hold the attention of any man. Gelsomino had been with her for more than a year when the strike which kept him home idle began.

They had not learned much about each other. Labor-drugged and without interests that compelled the general talk that throws to the surface the hidden qualities of personality, they had been content to regard the existence of each other as a sufficient fact, and attempt no further exploration. One morning, however, something disturbing had occurred in Gelsomino's room and, because of it, he already had been considering leaving the work and proceeding to another town.

Waking up suddenly, as one does at times, conscious of a something unfamiliar in the room, he saw Martha at his bedside, her lips making the first movements of speech. Her small eyes were half-shut but Gelsomino saw an expression that puzzled and frightened him, penetrating, lingering, eager.

"Get up," she said, and hastened out of the room.

– 9 –

The strike had now lasted for three weeks. There had been bloodshed, riots. Feeling had risen to the pitch of warfare. Luke and Martha approved, but took no active part in the struggle. Gelsomino stayed home. He had occasionally bought a book and had learned to read in several languages. Martha fingered the dozen volumes, turned them over and over, Greek, Italian, Portuguese, Sanskrit, and wondered more and more at her somber taciturn boarder, especially during the three weeks of the strike, sitting at the window, reading, reading. . . .

Luke had gone to a meeting. The air was rife with rumor. State troops were being rushed to the scene. The men were arming. A number of houses had been fired. It was known that a gang had been organized to demolish the water pumps.

"You sit there reading" — Martha had come in from the railed-in porch — "and here they say a big fight's on. . . . Good thing we're on a hill-like. . . . They won't be minded to come this way. . . . You won't be going out?"

"No," said Gelsomino quietly, and resumed his reading.

"'Fraid sort of, hey?" Martha bulked over him, arms akimbo.

"No," he answered, looking up quickly, "no, no," he repeated so convincingly in his gentle manner that she trembled with embarrassment.

"You're a strange one . . . you keep to yourself. . . . You ain't a miner of course, not for life. . . . I've been wondering what you are. . . . What are you?"

All these remarks had been delivered singly, after pauses. But Gelsomino, although he had lowered his book and met her look directly, stirred uneasily at this last question. The soft light in his eyes shook like the gleam on moving water.

"You're strange! You're like someone with a secret. Maybe you killed somebody!"

"Martha," he cried, sharply, but still in his gentle voice.

"Yes, you keep things dark. If you ain't killed someone, you're running away . . . you're hiding, you're ashamed, you're afraid . . . you don't say nothing at all . . . you ain't made friends with Luke . . . with none of the men . . . you ain't said much to me either . . . ain't looked at me like I was a woman . . . you ain't put a hand on me . . . it ain't natural . . . it ain't natural . . . you're a dark one . . . maybe you're a saint. . . ."

With a horror-stricken face, Gelsomino rose from his chair. The sentences had come like bullets, from the rifles he had been hearing in the valley. He tried to speak.

"Maybe I ain't seen what you wear around your neck! You was sleeping and I seen it close then. . . . A picture of yourself. . . . You *are* a saint! Anyway you think you are! I took it in my hand and looked at it and I heard you talk in your sleep . . . some girl's name you mentioned. . . . I wished it was mine. I wished you called me. . . . I wanted you to look at me . . . to want me. . . ."

Alarmed, Gelsomino stared at her but with his usual quiet gaze. To Martha, however, it seemed inspired by the soft impulses she was awakening.

Her small eyes imbedded in pits between her high sharp nose became radiant points of light that spread over her features a suggestion of eager hope fulfilled. She could not divine the utter revulsion that swept like a wind-tossed torch through the whole of Gelsomino's being.

Nevertheless he could not leave her, or speak with the decision that would arrest her frantic, her mad intention. Instead, his habit of listening kept him standing in front of her, unnerved, bewildered.

"You're made of flesh, too," she said, this time in an oversweet voice. "You ain't no real saint . . . I put my hands on your chest when you slept . . . I kissed your forehead . . . you came back from the pit that hot night, you remember, tired like a dog . . . you fell right asleep. . . ."

"Why can't I talk to her?" Gelsomino kept asking of himself. "Why can't I make her stop? Why can't I run away?"

"I came into your room . . . I turned up the lamp . . . I threw off the sheet. . . ."

Martha drew in her breath as if to shout. She laughed instead — the laugh of an insane person sufficiently lucid to realize the effect she was producing. . . .

"Just that picture around your neck . . . your picture! Oh, I wanted to put my mouth on you . . . kiss your body like a mother kissing her baby. . . . Gelsomino!" she gasped, "let me take you in my arms . . . let me kiss you . . . let me hold you. . . ."

"Martha," said Gelsomino finally, "you do not know what you are saying . . . you are a sick woman. . . ." His voice was tender and soft, such as he might have employed in the confessional.

"I ain't no sick woman," she cried, aware that she faced immediate frustration. "I ain't no sick woman. I'm burning up, see . . . you got to take me . . . you got to take me. . . ."

"Martha!" was all he could say.

"You ain't no saint . . . you had women . . . you call them in your sleep . . . you want them, too . . . like I want you. . . ."

"I must go away, Martha," he said almost inaudibly, still gazing at her, "I must go away. . . ."

"You ain't going . . . you ain't . . . you can't leave me now. . . ," she cried.

"I can have no woman, Martha, no one. . . . Once there was one . . . she made this. . . ."

He drew the scapular through his open shirt front, held it between his fingers.

"It can't happen again, Martha . . . it is a long time now. . . . It can't happen again. . . ." He pressed his slender hand over his forehead, through his hair weakly, dreamily. . . .

"You must let me go away," he added.

"Oh, forget it," she cried, trying to seize his hand. "Forget it."

"This," said Gelsomino, "will not make me forget . . . ever . . . ever . . . ever. . . ."

"Then tear it off . . . throw it away. . . ."

An insane light leaped into her eyes. Laughter flew up the sides of her cheeks like a flame newly fanned. . . . She seized the scapular in her hands and with a convulsive jerk tore it away from his neck. Her laughter filled the room. To Gelsomino it sounded like the laughter of countless women — amused at his helplessness.

Her leering face brought back to his mind the monstrous face of Alexandro, the drunken sailors guffawing over their lecherous nights in town, the laughter of the men in Villetto as they talked about him. And as the insane Martha shook with laughter at his frightened face, there came, too, the vision of Agnese with her brown plaited hair, the rich sound of her voice ringing like holiday bells.

He held out a gentle hand. "Let me have it back."

The late August sun had dropped below the straggling chimneys in the valley below, and the room had darkened.

"Here," she laughed, "take the bitch's present," and tearing off a piece of the silken chain with its delicately crocheted symbols, she threw it at him. He stooped to pick it up as it fell.

"And this," she cried, backing up and rolling the table backward.

He stooped to pick up the second piece.

"This too," she laughed, still backing up. "And this. . . ."

As she threw piece after piece on the floor, he bent over and put it into one hand, and followed her, afraid to look up at her, afraid to miss the slightest shred.

"On the stairs," she called. "See . . . there. . . ."

He could barely make out anything. He ran his palm over the uncarpeted floor. He knew he was climbing the stairs, but her laughter, diabolic in its persistence, and the determination to gather the patches of the sacred symbol, had given his motions continuity and coherence. They seemed the best defense he could make against her, the simplest way of letting her expend the fury that possessed her.

"And here," she cried finally, going into her room still backwards, "here's your picture, your picture. See, I got it in my mouth. . . . I'll chew it up and spit it into your face. . . . The saint! The saint!"

The early dark of the night was still sufficiently gray to outline the large figure of Martha in the doorway. He saw her raise her hand and take the scapular between her teeth. Her lips opened in the cunning smile of a halfwit aware of a strange acquisition of power.

"Why bother with it?" he moaned in his own heart. "Why bother with it? It's so many years . . . I'm a lost wretch . . . why bother?"

But he stumbled forward in a frenzied eagerness to pull it away, to save it from the foul destruction that threatened it. And he realized both as he did so and as he moaned in his heart that it had become to him more than a sacred symbol. It was the only garment that could clothe his body before his own soul.

"Drop it," he cried frantically and made a quick movement to seize it.

She laughed in her throat, and her small deep-set eyes condensed into rounded lights. He came closer to her. Instead, however, of stepping backward as she had been doing she stood still. He had caught the scapular in his fingers, but as he tried to pull it away, she drew it deeper into her mouth and closed her teeth upon it. He had been gentle hitherto, and still continued to be gentle; but he held on to the crocheted silk with his fingers, jerked at it, now to the right, now to the left, beseeching her pitifully to let it alone, to give it up.

But as he exerted all the strength of his fingers to release the scapulary from her teeth, with one hand she banged-to the door, and then with her fingers she tore at her blouse, her corsets. After a second, with a suddenness that surprised him she opened her teeth and he fell backwards with the scapular in his hand.

"Martha!" He screamed.

There she stood before him, her breasts, her torso glistening white in the soft gray of the twilight.

"There," she laughed. "There . . . you dassn't say no now . . . you god-damn saint you . . . you god-damn saint you . . . ha . . . ha . . . ha. . . ."

In his ears her laughter was like a wind stampeding in the tree tops, crashing branches about his head, running off into a whistled lament, softening into a whisper of despair, and then increasing into the mad volume of exultant energy. There was no stopping it, nor the torrent of the obscene comments she made on him, on her body, on her breasts.

He stood staring at her helplessly, too stunned to act. For a minute he felt himself dizzying, a sensation of his head and body revolving frantically and then slowly, frantically and then slowly, while his feet remained steady and fixed in one position. And as he gyrated, he seemed to be peering into a multitude of windows set about him in a circle, and in each of these windows was the form of a woman exposing her torso. Each torso was different, but the head above it . . . could it be, could it be Agnese, Agnese?

"Lord God," he prayed. He could hear his voice above the storming wind that brawled and wailed. . . . "Lord God, have mercy, a sinner stands suffering before Thee, hold out Thy hands to him, hold out Thy bleeding palms, blessed Jesus, sweetest of men and my God, my brother. . . ."

He ceased suddenly. He heard the door downstairs thrown open, the sound of feet, the voices of men.

"Hey, there, Martha," one called up anxiously. . . .

Martha heard, too, but instead of answering, she burst into another spasm of laughter. Gelsomino, thrusting the pieces of his scapular into his pocket, hurried downstairs. A group of sad, shoulder-drooping men raised their heads as he entered. One of them had lighted the lamp on the oil-clothed table and Gelsomino saw Luke's body stretched out on the black mohair sofa.

"Where's Martha?" asked one.

The sound of her voice rang through the house . . . a rise and fall of coarse sly laughter.

"Her and the dago," growled one of the men, "been hitting it up."

Several of the men looked at each other. Their sad faces distorted into weird expressions as they sensed the import of the remark.

"Call her down," one of them commanded. "Her brother's been shot . . . dead. . . ."

But there was no need. There she stood before them.

"Hell!" cried one of the men.

"What the hell? She's crazy!"

"I'll be damned."

She leered at them all, and laughed softly in a kind of sustained gurgle.

"Your brother's been shot . . . dead. . . ."

She looked frightened for a second, but only for a second. Then she advanced toward the speaker, a simpering lustful leer on her face. . . .

– 10 –

Soon after, Gelsomino left for upstate New York and there worked for several months with a railway gang.

After the scene with Martha, he had enjoyed few nights without the recurrence of the horrifying nightmare of the circled windows. He feared to go to his cot in the abandoned freight car that formed the sleeping-quarters of the men. He feared to sit around with them as they related the stories of their wives and sweethearts, of their bought pleasures in the town.

Gradually, however, the dream changed in detail. The lighted windows became glowing plaques bordered with the torn shreds of his scapular. The plaques revolved about him now, slowly and musically in a rhythm that lulled him into quietness. And as he lay inert and withal relaxed, he unshaded his eyes, and looked eagerly into the glowing oblongs. In each was the head of a boy, black-haired with dreaming, steady eyes, and a mouth that quivered in sadness.

He woke one morning after the dream had been more persistent than usual to find the bare fetid box-car emptied of its laborer sleepers. The nearby village doctor was holding his hand. He lay in bed for many days. When he was well he packed his bag and trunk, carefully laid away the torn scapular in a small linen bag, and went to New York.

XIV. FATHER AND SON

– 1 –

When Gelsomino left the railway gang, he had but one immediate purpose. He had fought against it for years. Now, however, he knew that he must see Agnese and the child that was theirs. After that, nothing else would matter. The eleven years of utter isolation would gather into an incandescent moment, be burnt up — the offering of a contrite heart.

"God, my Savior, my immolation has been complete! Thou knowest it, Lord Jesus. The thoughts that tortured my flesh — like gadflies I drove them away. Desire filled my dream. I drove it away. Only a glimpse of them I seek! Nothing else of the flesh is in me. I shall be but the spent carcass of my youth. . . . I shall be fit, then, oh Lord, but only then . . . once more . . . Thy will accordant . . . once more, Lord, to enter into Thy temples, to live in the shadow of Thy palms stretched in blessing over me. . . . Lord, sweet son of God, have mercy, have mercy!"

Had he not overheard occasional mention of Agnese and Giovanni, Michele and Luigi, possibly the plan might never have suggested itself to Gelsomino. Many of the laborers among whom he worked owed their position to the Dantones; others knew about them. Luigi was at the head of several gangs working in remoter sections of the track.

"She's piled it up, I tell you. . . ."

"From a barbershop, no less. . . ."

"She's a wise old owl, now, if you want to know. . . ."

"A dark one, I say. . . ."

"You heard about? Sure, not his son at all. . . ."

These and many other remarks were like quick shutters opened and shut on the lives of the only ones that bound him at all to life. The glimpses he had were all too fitful and even terrifying. Dared he go? Dared he seek them out?

– 2 –

After his struggle with Agnese in Giovanni's room, Gelsomino walked rapidly and aimlessly. The night was hot and many people still crowded the streets. They moved like noisy shadows past him. When they jostled into him, they seemed to lack force and bulk. The lights of the stores were like huge torches, and yet he knew he was groping in a vast nave where no candles had been lit on a day of rain and storm.

"The niches are empty," he kept saying to himself. "The saints have left their places . . . the niches are empty. . . ."

The open cafés roared with flame as he passed by, as if the doors of huge furnaces had snapped open. He hurried his steps. There must be quiet places. . . .

He did not know that he was walking toward the river. After a short time he realized that the houses had become fewer, that there were no more stores, that there was only an occasional straggler. But he was not prepared for the dim serenity of water barely touched by wind. . . . Its sounds were low and softly sustained. They fled and returned, and mingled with the silence. He knew he was on a dock. He was standing on planks. Between them he could see the water beneath, striped and moving. . . . It was cool. It was soothing. Here was quiet. Here one might sleep. . . .

"The temple doors are closed against me. The niches are empty. . . . The saints have fled. . . ."

The next morning Gino Birrichino found him sleeping on the edge of the dock. Gino had come early to paint the East River with its little huddle of islands just as the sun splashed and shattered in the water.

"No beauty in this country? Bah . . . it's only country louts that can't see it. . . ." It was one of his favorite themes. "I'll paint the beauty . . . and then lo and behold they see it!"

They talked. They met again. They took up their living together. . . .

"I knew from the beginning . . . you're not one of these *caffoni* . . . rings in their ears, and swallow-tails to their buttocks."

Gino took every occasion he could to explain his own clairvoyance.

"But what you are, Gelsomino Merlino . . . well, it will take the devil himself to know. . . ."

"And I have told you a thousand times, Michel Angelo Buonaroti, that I was a teacher in Italy and then sailed to the four corners of the earth."

"But this boy, here, you old pepper-nose . . . this Giovanni, that comes so often. . . ."

Gelsomino lived too close to the artist not to be drawn into conversation. As far as he could, he avoided subjects that threatened to become personal, and on his side Gino came soon to understand the wishes of his companion and respected them. The group of dilapidated intellectuals that frequented his *bottega* took both of them for granted. Although the silent listening ways of Gelsomlino perplexed them, they made only occasional mention of it.

– 3 –

For fully a year Gelsomino had attempted to make a living by giving lessons in the Italian language. Gino had painted elaborate signs announcing the presence of an Italian teacher in his studio, had placed them in the windows of drug-stores and barbershops, and swore confidentially that if signs ever fetched scholars his signs would gather them in by the droves.

"The ferrule in one hand at his side, the open book in the other, the raised eyebrows . . . a perfect symbol. Ah, and those rascals in the other corner: the touch of an ideal shining in their eyes . . . *Gelsomino bello* . . . it will fetch them . . . it will fetch them!"

But at about the time that Agnese's houses were building, both Gelsomino and Gino were compelled to acknowledge defeat. . . .

"They have forgotten their fatherland," shouted the artist. "The beautiful tongue of Dante! What do they know of beauty . . . the simpletons . . . the louts!"

"They make so little money, those who still love the ways of their old country," said Gelsomino.

"Well, you have Giovanni at least. . . ."

"Ah, the blessed little man! You have him too! He comes to see you paint, to learn and to paint. . . ."

"There's a mystery there! What a keen eye, what ideas! Let him once have a bit of technique, learn the ways of the master! How could a boy, now tell me, you're a learned man, how could a boy, a barber's son, a peasant-wench's son. . . ."

Despite the long years of self-control, Gelsomino winced at these words. His face turned white and then red, quickly. Not too quickly, however, for Gino to notice. . . .

"Every time I mention that woman," he thought to himself, and then aloud, he continued, "but it is remarkable that he should. After all, what is she? Made money? Who hasn't in this country if he is enough of a lout? Well, feel hurt and show it! I don't know why you do it. . . . I say again there's a mystery there! Good thing the boy comes though! He gives me courage and gives you something to do!"

"Gino," said Gelsomino, "he is the only scholar left and he comes without being sent. I get no money for it!"

"Oh, we'll get along, if the filthy louts will buy a picture or two."

"Yes, but it's cold in this studio of yours, and there'll be no beans for the pot tomorrow."

"We'll build a fire of these," cried the artist gaily as he pointed to his pictures.

"But I insist on providing the beans . . . and so tomorrow, I shall begin to work. Only this morning I made sure of having a job. . . . Remember a banker, Crino? He and Mr. Doolan are opening an Italian restaurant for the Americans. . . . I am going to be head waiter. . . ."

For once Gino was stretched out in a chair, his pointed shoes reaching out to the farthest point possible. The *bottega* was cold enough for a fire, but since they had not built one in the small charcoal stove on the hearthstone, they wore their overcoats. Gino manoeuvred his hands in the pockets so that his overcoat blanketed him tighter than ever. . . . Then he whistled long and gaily.

"A waiter, a head waiter! Well, no doubt you'll eat."

"Both of us, Gino, both of us. . . ."

– 4 –

Ever since Gelsomino had taken up his duties as waiter, he had seen less and less of Giovanni. Immediately after leaving school, the boy hastened to the painter's studio. He had begun to acquire a definite reputation at the school as a dreaming lad whose head was always in the clouds and his feet trailing after. The year following his illness had brought about a transformation that delighted his teachers and did not so much disgust as perplex the boys. Seriousness and quietness marked him now, and despite this disheartening fact they insisted upon electing him president of the Athenian Literary Club, the highest honor the student body could accord. Many of the boys waited to walk home with him; several wanted to study their lessons with him. His drawings and paintings became sensations. One of the boys went to Miss Skinner:

"You ought to see, Miss Skinner! Giovanni — how he can draw! He painted a picture — an old monk! You ought to see the eyes . . . they look at you like all over . . . and he's walking along and there's a big gas tank. . . ."

It was this picture more than any other single event that had brought father and son closer together. Giovanni rarely followed the irksome routine that Gino insisted upon . . . quadrating the canvas, making a single line outline of the drawing, making thumb-nail sketches, trying out color combinations. One afternoon while Gino painted on the sidewalk, Giovanni had found a study of a young monk in brown hood and cassock, evidently the work of Gino himself.

Elbows close at his sides, hands thrust out with palms up, the cord pulled tight around a starved waist, high cheekbones tinged with fever, eyes absorbed, wide-open, gazing into a nothingness that he explored futilely for meaning, the monk presented a picture of intense hope and moving despair, affirmation and negation, bewilderment and understanding. Some subtle element of color or content had aroused the interest of Giovanni. He had found a dirty canvas partly used, put it up hurriedly on the easel, fumbled through the brushes, and began to paint.

It was late spring. The strong wind blowing from the river had cleared the dark street of its odors. Sounds entered the room; the shrieks of children, rattling of wagon wheels on the cobbles, the vender's cries lifted into shrill laments. As usual a crowd had collected around Gino, and he worked rapidly, talking to the onlookers.

Giovanni heard nothing, so rapt in his own painting had he become. Something in the countenance of the youthful ascetic called to impulses in his own heart. The rapidity of his brush strokes, the certainty with which he placed a line here, a color there, the painstaking intentness with which he applied himself to the eyes, the fingers, would have astounded Gino. They plunged Giovanni into an unrelenting silence of concentration. Neither the street noises nor the creaking stairs, the shouts in the backyard, the persistent barking of a dog in a nearby alley way, distracted him from his task. He did not hear the door open, did not hear Gelsomino enter, did not know his father was standing near just as intensely interested as he himself.

"That is very good, Giovanni," said Gelsomino after a long time.

The boy started.

"I didn't know you were watching."

"It has been so good to watch you."

Giovanni looked up quickly, and then cast his eyes down, and shifted his position uncomfortably. But a smile slowly spread over his features. His father's form was a slender shadow against the north light of the late spring afternoon. He was hidden in the lessening brightness so that Giovanni could not see the rapid movement of the muscles, the flash of the eyes, the mouth eagerly opening as if to speak, the head thrown forward to scan and to listen. Had he noted these things, Giovanni's smile would have become a serious expression. His heart would have pounded with redoubled fear. He would have thrown himself into his father's arms as he had longed to do, so often now. . . .

"I . . . I . . . didn't know you watched me. . . ," he repeated.

"Why don't you finish?"

Gelsomino pointed to the canvas. . . .

"You see I put gas tanks behind the monk," said Giovanni very seriously. "Gino says, 'Always put a background behind a portrait the way they did years ago.'"

"Yes, but gas tanks, Giovanni?"

"He's a poor monk . . . I don't know . . . I can do them . . . but see, behind them I have the river, too, and the dome, see. . . ."

From that day on the two met more often, talked a great deal. Occasionally Giovanni stayed to eat with the two men. After their meal — Giovanni liked best of all the *polenta* with tomato sauce — they walked.

– 5 –

One night Gelsomino and Giovanni were alone. They strolled to the river. A recreation pier had just been built on which a band played on weekday nights. Its blaze of electric lights cut a golden block into the dark, and cast on the waters a shimmering golden plaque. To the south and north extended vacant lots, stone-cutter's yards or areas piled with bricks and lumber. At first the pier had been frequented by whole families, the women with their hair drawn back tight from a central part, or done in firm and full pompadours, the men in shirt sleeves, long-stemmed clay pipes in their mouths. It was a gala stroll they took, like walking out into the country, happy in their noisy children. The young women walked with their parents, but the grown-up boys formed boisterous groups of singers and merrymakers. The wilder ones among them, those who had combined into vicious gangs, stood on corners under electric lights, guffawed self-consciously, made obscene noises by blowing into the sides of their fists, deliberately jostled into respectable family groups, especially if there were young girls in them. To have started a fight with one of these groups meant serious consequences. The fathers glared, and swore under their breaths, but the mothers shrilled.

"Don't pay attention to these loafers! What beasts! But, it's this country!"

Occasionally the women snapped back, "You good for nothing! You gutter wretch! You vile snake!"

For their pains all they received in answer was a torrent of abuse and catcalls. At times, these rowdies threw one of their crowd headlong at the shrieking women and for minutes there was turmoil.

Father and son walked leisurely, both a trifle conscious of being in each other's presence, as if aware of an intimacy that was too secretive — forbidden even. They were like lovers first sensing the mutual sweetness of their joy. Whenever Gelsomino stopped for a second, he put his arm around the boy's shoulder and his ear close to catch the quiet words. Giovanni flushed perceptibly, he felt himself overwhelmed with a soft warmth that became a sweet pain in his heart. Gelsomino understood, and with the understanding came a pang of bitter longing that never turned sweet. At such moments he quickened his pace, unmindful of the boy, his mind recasting in swift confusion the events resulting in the sadness that was on them both. The mood vanished almost the instant it was born, though it left the original longing from which it sprang even more definite and insistent, a yearning that was agony for the first time when he could take the boy in his arms, and whisper the frantic secret, "My son, my son!"

And Giovanni in his turn understood, too, and with his understanding came similar impulses, not aggressive ones, but a simple desire for the affection he had always lacked. They had come to the pier, and instead of going upstairs where there were brighter lights, where the band played, and the couples danced, they chose the dock-like structure beneath, long, dark and low. Barges were moored to it, filled with bricks and sand, bags of cement, and lumber. One contained bricks dipped in tar, erected into a triangular prism that made a black splotch against the darker sky, and insinuated into the air an odor of foul stagnant waters drenched with the intermingled fragrance of decaying wood and flowers. Gelsomino was ignorant of the fact that the toughs of the neighborhood reserved the dock for their special rendezvous on hot summer nights. Nor did he note that on this particular night, the barges themselves had been requisitioned by groups of them. On the barge with the tar-bricks Giovanni had seen a huddle of men's forms, dense shadows in a semi-circle, and when the music of the band fell into less vigorous rhythms, he heard whispered talk, restless, impatient, uneasy.

The intermittent blaring of the band, the soft whisper of the water eddying around the barges, the laughter of people in the distance, the shuffle of dancing feet, made a subdued music in the night that transformed the ordinary drabness of the city streets into a resting place for hearts in need of loneliness and silence.

"This is like the nights aboard ship, Giovanni," said Gelsomino, leaning on a steel capstan and gazing out into the black sky beyond the gold shadow of the pier. "You city people can't imagine how sweet is silence . . . and," he checked himself. He had it on the tip of his tongue to add, "bitter too, so bitter. . . ."

"I used to come here," answered Giovanni. . . . "I'm glad you brought me . . . ."

"Why, don't you love it now? Gino swears by all the saints this is a true home of beauty."

"The houses look like shadow-forests. . . ," whispered Giovanni, drawing close to his father, loving the intimate quiet of their talk together. He had never had companionship like this. The affection that had sprung up between him and his mother had an element of primitive love, the warmth of bodies sheltering each other in a bleak storm. It had been engendered in fear and in pain, and grew as all the other values seemed to lessen in his mother's heart. Dimly, but steadily he perceived how she shouted for gladness in her soul that she had found him, for his own need of love had taught him to understand those without it, and young as he was he knew the place he was occupying in his mother's life.

But there was a different quality in this love between Gelsomino and him, a gentleness amounting almost to timidity, a shadowing of the blaze in their hearts by the fear of their unknown relationship. They were closer because they were so far apart; they were so far apart because they did not dare get closer. Gelsomino did not know what Giovanni knew, and Giovanni owed to his mother the duty of silence. However, here, on the pier, in this removed spot, like a quiet chamber in a house of many activities, they were drawing nearer and nearer. . . .

"Many nights, Giovanni, I looked over the water. I seemed far above it, out of the world. It was as if I were living beforehand the ghost I am to be. . . ." The strange expression for a moment chilled the light in Giovanni's eyes.

He looked in amazement at his father. Then he said, "That makes me afraid. . . ."

"Why no, child, no," the older man almost cried.

"Because sometimes you seem so far away, even now."

"But I am here."

"I know," said the boy echoing the laugh. . . . I'm glad. . . ."

Then he stood closer, and put out a hesitant hand, feeling for Gelsomino's arm. It was a gesture that touched his father like the slow warmth of a candle flame, a warmth that must soon melt the reserve of the older man. So Gelsomino thought. But it was more than a gesture inspired by love; it was a gesture of real fear.

The huddle of men on the barge had caught Giovanni's attention from the very beginning. He had dismissed them from his mind at once, but their whispers and their movements constantly brought them back into focus. Then he heard a voice, a familiar voice, sneering and laughing and at the same time metallic and commanding, filled with meanness. He knew it too well.

"Ah hell, punch the god-damn lights out of him."

"Jesus Christ, Stocks, Jesus Christ!"

"Cough up, then. . . ."

"Don't . . . don't. . . ."

Gelsomino heard too, now, put his arm around the boy, held him close. Giovanni clung, his body quivering.

"What is it, child?"

He moved away, Giovanni close to him. The band had burst into a massive brass movement, insolent and gay, like the march of returned soldiers roughened in the war. A tugboat struggled to raise its shrill complaint above the uproar. And then as the music of the band softened into the merry squealing of clarinets and flutes, the tugboat's whistle lengthened into a thin querulous wail.

"How fortunate," thought Gelsomino. "There, there," he whispered to Giovanni, "you can't hear them now."

He realized that the voices had awakened memories of great pain in the sensitive boy, and that he was reliving an experience of agonizing horror. Giovanni's body was pressed close to his as they stood still, thinking they were out of earshot. He could feel its soft flesh quivering, and as he stooped to wrap the child in his arms there came to him a sensation of tenderness that loosened his joints, pulled away the dams from his emotions.

He all but shouted even as a lover might, "*Figlio mio . . . figlio mio . . . benedetto!*"

Giovanni pressed his head against his father's breast, placed his hands on his father's shoulders, hung and clung at one and the same time. The tugboat whistle had not ceased. It had become sharper. It had become human. It was the cry of physical pain. It was one of the men on the barge shrieking as he was kicked and stabbed.

Gelsomino seized the boy in his arms, and ran. Crowds had hurried down from the upper level of the pier. The music had ceased. There were the incoherent sounds of pain in the dark.

– 6 –

He took Giovanni to Agnese at once. As he retraced his steps home, he had the illusion of walking through tunneled stone, the walls glistening with mildew and damp, here and there bursting into phosphorescent sprays. For the lighted stores, the multitude of windows, the noises of the street had changed into the detail of a dungeon keep from which his soul longed to flee.

The slender hope of effecting some sort of union with the two persons who bound him at all to the active world was losing color and form, becoming the shadow of a substance. And coincident with it was growing a desire that was acquiring the force of will, and yet a will that could not dictate nor direct. The one meeting with Agnese had shown him the impossibility of an arrangement which would erase the bitterness of their separation long ago and the dreariness of the intervening years. And he was beginning to see, too, how difficult would be an intimacy with Giovanni that would make his life in New York bearable and fulfilling.

"Gino," he confided to the artist when he got home, "has it ever occurred to you how much of a carcass is the life about us?"

"Birrichino was pouring wine out of a straw-encased bottle. On the dirty table in the kitchen, was a plate smeared with tomato sauce, and piled with the bones of a chicken. A huge brown loaf and a half *provolo* nearby caught the unsteady reflection of the whistling gas-jet. The room was barely lighted by the single flame. The iron sink, the disorderly dish shelves, the stand-up bed in the corner were ill-defined black splotches. Gelsomino looked around, and smiled wearily.

"The people are like worms born of the decay."

Gino poured his wine into his throat with a rapid noise.

"Well," he said, half-choking, "well, I had to get that down before I could take in what you said. The picture is not pleasant."

"No," affirmed the priest, "no, but it seems so. . . . What horrors of men and women are about us! They crawl all over each other. If they can, they sink their feet into you, coil like slime around you. . . ."

"Whew," whistled the artist. "You're in a mood tonight. Better have a glass of this! One of the good ladies sneaked it in and a whole dinner with it . . . took compassion on a poor artist! Ever see her? What a body!"

Gelsomino smiled again, and then dropped into his habit of silence, all attention to Gino. He let the artist spin a long narrative of an affair that was beginning to seem like real business. But though he seemed to listen, he was thinking, and in the process he had come to the resolution that had been slowly shaping itself in his mind.

He was weary of his loneliness, weary of the secret which set him apart. He had sought the hidden ways of one who escapes from the contempt or the indignation of his fellows, and had found neither the peace nor the beauty shed by a heart that accepts. Friends he had not made, and certainly he had found no meaning in the tumbled variety of life. The episode that had chilled the warmth in Giovanni, and brought terror into his eyes, was a symbol to Gelsomino of the basic quality of life. In a panorama of silence, in the haunts of beauty, in the hours of labor there was a center of viciousness, emotion compacted into cruelty ready like a charge of powder to blow the whole fabric into bloody shivers.

Often he had recalled the even days of his life as a priest, and often he had longed to return to them. But he was excommunicated. True, he had sought to prove his penitence in the pursuit of labor that would numb him, reduce him to the level of the imbruted. Yet he had sought it outside the channels prescribed by the church, had sought it even with a reservation in his heart, a hope that he might in some fashion regain Agnese and become united to his son. Now he was ready for complete immolation. His prayer had been a lie, and he knew it. Now he would write to his bishop, and seek entry into a monastic order, the most rigid and withdrawn he could find.

"You know, *Gelsomino bello,*" Gino broke in on his thoughts, "good wine is the best philosophy. It warms the heart, quickens the blood. You should drink more. It'll bring the red to those yellow cheeks of yours. . . . You think too much. Thinking makes you old, sir, dries up the juices in your joints, and, if the wine is brought to you by another man's wife, and she pours it for you, why, let me vouch for it — it is the elixir of youth! This wine now, Geraldina, upstairs, you know . . . what a body! In my ear she whispered it, Gelsomino. 'Tonight . . . very late . . . listen as he goes down the stairs. . . .' Ah, ha, ha! Look around there, you old angel. Life a carcass !" He poured himself more wine. "The devil or the church has told you that. By the complete calendar of the holy saints of Christendom, so long as there's wine, and cheese, and an apple, life's a gay lady with rounded breasts and quivering thighs. . . . Take a glass, and drink, my friend . . . her favors are all too few. . . . Ah, ha, ha."

Gino stopped short. There were steps on the wooden stairs outside. He rose, poured another glass, pulled down his purple vest, ran his long hairy fingers over his mouth. . . .

"Take it from me, Gelsomino, a bit of flesh, a bit of wine and sweet art as a friend to hold by, and life is no carcass . . . there, the door! He's gone and *la bella Geraldine* is waiting. Good night, dear friend, good night!"

– 7 –

Noises crashed about Gelsomino's head, the gas jet seeming to shriek its way to the top of them all. He heard voices shouting all about him, lewd and sly and lustful. There was laughter . . . the laughter of women, the coarse hollow laughter of men in passion. He stood up, his whole body flaming. He put his hands to his ears, but the sounds redoubled.

Was it the gas jet? How its thin irregular flatness shook and trembled like a hand that one placed on a woman's body! With nervous, eager fingers he turned it out!

But the room was flooded with light. There were windows all about him, brilliantly illuminated! He covered his eyes with his hands . . . but there they were . . . the women exposing their breasts. . . .

He stumbled over a chair as he ran into the center room, dark, ill-smelling, narrow. He fumbled for his trunk. He found the crucifix, the cross, the scapular! He brought them all to his lips. He kissed them with frantic energy. Then he sank on his knees and placed the Calvary cross with the drooping Christ on the flat top of the trunk, and beside them the scapular and the golden cross. The silver and gold glinted in the dark as he gazed at them. The noises roared in his ears. The windows circled and circled about him.

"Holy God, Jesus my deliverer," he cried, "lift me to Thy side. I am Thine, Thine and no other's. My heart also bleeds. . . . Take me in Thy arms. . . . Console me with Thy love. . . . Make me whole again. . . . I am Thine, Holy Jesus, sweet Son of God, and my brother. . . ."

His voice was a quick, unsteady whisper as of one in fear.

"Here, now, and forever, I dedicate myself to Thee anew . . . I am Thine . . . take me to Thyself. . . ."

He stopped, exhausted. Perspiration gleamed in silver beads on his forehead, his cheeks. He grew cold. The air in the room was motionless, heavy, hot . . . he felt dizzy, he reeled . . . he threw his arms on the trunk, and brought his head down between them . . . the noises had died away, the windows had become dark. . . .

A little later he rose, lighted the gas, shoved the bread, the cheese, the sauce-plastered plate to one side, and wrote to his bishop.

"I am Gelsomino Merlino, priest thirteen years ago of the parish of Villetto. I abandoned my parish, unfrocked myself, and went into the world. Permit me now not to relate to you my experiences. Allow me to say simply that I endeavored in my own way to lead a life that should be a castigation to my flesh. Now I seek to return to the bosom of the church, a penitent sinner. You will know best what discipline to prescribe, what penance to undergo. I await with eagerness and hope your counsel and your forgiveness. If it is possible, could it be arranged for me to enter the sacred order of the Trappists since I desire a complete withdrawal from life?"

– 8 –

While waiting for the reply to his letter, Gelsomino had begun a systematic regimen of purification. The money he had saved was not so considerable, he calculated, to make possible giving up all form of work. It might be a month or it might be a year before the bishop's answer arrived and all the necessary forms and arrangements concluded. But within the limits of his routine he planned as complete a series of holy devotions as would be possible.

In Doolan's and Gino's pretentious café and summer house no breakfast was served. The three waiters employed arrived for work at ten in the morning, left at three in the afternoon, reported again at five, and one remained until two in the morning every three days.

The long hours suited Gelsomino. They kept him away from his rooms. Only occasionally would he see Giovanni, and then for only a short time. It was imperative to prevent the affection between them from becoming a worldly chain which he could not break without too great suffering to himself, and particularly to the boy.

The work in the café was sufficiently heavy to keep him on his feet almost continuously and so to fatigue him that he could drop off to sleep immediately after it was over. But no matter how exhausted he was, he found time to go to the church, kneel, bow his head in prayer, and only when his whole body ached with drawn nerves and twitching muscles would he go home to his bed. Before dawn, he was in church again, on his knees for hours. He had become a familiar figure in the church before a month was up. But he avoided meeting Father Donato, the priest of the parish.

"What are you up to," asked Gino. "You're looking like a ghost."

Gelsomino smiled, and listened. With Gino, too, he avoided protracted conversation.

It was at this time that Michele had taken to his bed. Giovanni had been persuaded by his grandfather to enter the sick room every day and inquire of Michele himself how he was doing. It had become an irksome duty, and he performed it only because of his love for Gesualdo. Yet he knew too that it would please Gelsomino, and so there was another reason for continuing it. Nevertheless, he detected not only in his own manner but in the surprise expressed in Michele's eyes how hollow and insincere the act in reality was. He had resolved to talk it over with Gelsomino and, despite his promise to his mother, learn from Gelsomino's own lips the truth which he had known but which he was compelled to keep as a secret.

One day Giovanni had hastened to the studio immediately school was over.

"Where's Signor Merlino?" He inquired. . . .

Gino whistled.

"That's a strange bird, Giovanni," he replied. "At the church most likely.

He's like a ghost around here, flits in and out, and not a word from him. Better get to work on these heads, young man. You'll do only heads for a month — none of your ambitions! Learn the details first, now you're young. An eyelash is the study of a lifetime. When I studied in Naples. . . ."

The artist was in one of his talkative moods. He was altogether unaware of the sadness in Giovanni's manner. The boy did take up his drawing board, sit at the window, and with crayon, and pencil, and charcoal attempted head after head. But it was listless drawing. Mostly he was looking out of the window. And he did not listen to the continuous chatter of Birrichino.

Several minutes before five, Gelsomino came in. The streets had darkened. The light in Gino's studio was a heavy pervasive gray. The chill of the late October day had not altogether been dispelled by the charcoal stove burning in the old marble fireplace. The room looked more like a bleak stone quarry with its piles of canvases back to back than the studio of a painter.

"Well, *Gelsomino bello,*" shouted Birrichino, "welcome back to the living!" He laid his palette on the mantelpiece and took his long reed-stemmed pipe from his pocket. "There's Giovanni been waiting hours. Seen Doctor Pastrocchi? Came here this morning. Thinks you're doomed if you don't look out. Giovanni, can't you make this man change his ways?

Gelsomino turned to the boy.

"Giovanni," he said, "I always look at the drawings you are making. . . ."

The boy stood up, and looked awkwardly in the direction of his father.

"I leave them for you to see. . . ."

"He thinks you're a new Murillo, young man, soon to outdo his master," cried Birrichino, lighting his pipe with a piece of charcoal. "Anyhow, I won't deny it, you've got it in you and where you get it from is a mystery . . . peasant father, peasant mother. . . ."

"He's a barber and my mother is not a peasant," retorted Giovanni with some heat, resenting the term "peasant" since he knew it was usually accompanied by "lout" in Gino's mind.

"Oh, no offense, *Giovanni bello* . . . no offense . . . There must be rich blood in their veins . . . hey, Gelsomino?" said the artist, eyeing both of them down the long stem of his pipe which seemed only an extension of his thin nose.

"Must be," answered the priest calmly.

But Giovanni had reddened. His eyes danced as in a fever. His lips quivered spasmodically. He looked from the artist to his father. The gray in the room had silvered heavily, and then yellowed to a soft gold as the charcoal embers spread their even glow. The shadows of the men were ill-defined splashes on the floor. Giovanni could not make out their features but he noticed the brilliant gleam in his father's eyes, the gleam of the nervous exhaustion and the sustained tension of his last two months' unrelenting regimen. He looked steadily and fixedly as his father's eyes became more intense in their expression the longer the boy kept gazing. There was fear in them, too, sadness and the longing for the open love which he had resolved to suppress. Gelsomino cut the tense situation short.

"Your parents should be happy," he said to Giovanni so calmly that the boy felt his whole body shiver. "They should plan to have you devote yourself to painting."

"But they're not happy!" The words came out suddenly like a shriek. Giovanni trembled. He saw his father's head drop, the eyes close, the whole body droop into a helpless picture of sadness.

"I mean," he answered quickly, "I mean he's sick . . . very sick . . . now. Everything's upside down in the house . . . and he and I, we had a quarrel, and I never call him *'ta.'* . . . Should I, should I call him *'ta'*? Should I?"

"Of course, Giovanni, you must call you father, *'ta'* . . . always, always, especially now that he is sick. . . ."

– 9 –

At whatever hour he left the combination saloon and restaurant, Gelsomino first went to the church before going home. The granite building, many-windowed and spired, cut in two the wretched monotony of dirty red-brick tenements on the street. A long flight of marble steps led to massive oak doors carved into numerous panels. To either side of these steps, a series of four slate steps led to another door, painted green under and behind the pretentious marble stairway. This door opened into the lower church, floored in wood, and filled with three rows of crude wooden benches for the worshippers. It was the portion reserved for the Italians. Upstairs the benches were carved and cushioned, the floor was flagged with marble, the vestibule with mosaic. In contrast to the simple painted altar in the Italian section, the altar here was of marble, ornate in carving, with gold-fluted pillars. Everything else was in contrast, the ample stained-glass windows, the beautiful niches, the elaborate bas-reliefs of the Holy Passion, that made an intermittent frieze around the walls. The incense floated into the high-arched nave and did not cling as it did below to the low-rafted ceiling, leaving behind a continuous odor of something stagnant and acrid. On Sundays, two collectors stood at the top of the steps and received the offering of ten cents from each entrant. It was a curious custom to Gelsomino. He did not try to understand it. He felt, besides, more at ease in the lower church — so simple, so lacking in profuse adornment. Despite the vivid memories it brought by contrast with the eighteenth-century cathedral in which he had preached in Villetto.

He dipped his finger in holy water in the bronze ewer at the entrance, crossed himself, and rapidly walked to the altar steps where he kneeled. He took out his beads from his pocket, put his golden cross around his neck, and bowed his head. His eyes remained still, his fingers worked rapidly, his lips moved in uninterrupted sibilance. The lights of the church were blotted out, the soft tread of those who came and went made no sound in his mind, the growing chill of the unheated basement did not touch his flesh. Gelsomino in a few minutes had achieved complete oblivion such as a tired person obtains who lays his head on his pillow and falls off to sleep at once. "*Miserere mihi, domine,*" he prayed. "*Ave Maria's*" followed each other in quick succession, or each one in a continuous chain with no broken link. After a half hour he rose as from a trance, still letting his beads slip regularly through his fingers, and, like a sleep-walker, moved to another portion of the church; at the foot of a Saint Francis, a Saint Paul, a Saint Stephen. Before each one he repeated his prayer, or said another one particularly propitiatory.

Exhausted both from the work of the day, and from the long-kneeling posture, and absorption in his prayer, he stood up dazed and weak, feeling the muscles of his face draw, his eyes sink into twitching hollows. He breathed in the stale air laden with the stagnant odor of incense. Slowly he breathed it in as if he were standing on a hilltop where the winds blow free and the clouds swim rapidly aloft. And as he did so, his whole body shuddered, his face heated and glowed. He smiled sadly, and hurried from the church. Like the sounds of activity in the holy edifice, so the sounds of the streets were lost in the deepest current of his thoughts. He walked as through catacombs. When he reached the unmade cot in the unlighted room he occupied, he prayed once more, this time to the drooping Christ on the Calvary cross, and then went to sleep.

X. THE CHURCH

– 1 –

Agnese walked directly to the church. She had placed over her head a black cashmere shawl with long fringes. It covered her to the waist. She held it tight around her shoulders and breasts by clutching an edge in either hand and keeping her hands together under it. She moved with the rapid steps of a nun crossing the yard between her rooms and the church. Her eyes looked straight ahead, for the mind behind them was considering other things besides the obstacles in her way. The lazy snow flurry had changed into a wet powdery rain that hung halos of dark gold around the lamp-posts and sheeted the store windows with beaded silver lace. A penetrating chill fell with it. Others shivered as they hurried. Agnese felt nothing, her face filmed with the cold dew. She passed the iron fence in front of Doolan's and Crino's bar and restaurant, recessed over twenty-five feet from the sidewalk. An automatic barrel organ was wheezing a popular tune. But she did not hear nor did it occur to her that she might know the slender form of the man that had just come out, and hurried into the chill gloom of the night. . . .

"*Madre pietosa,*" she kept repeating in her mind, "*Madre pietosa,* do not lay this other burden on my heart."

The tall figure preceded her down the side street in which was located the church of Our Lady of Olivet. It was a dark street with no stores to cast their intermittent glow. The only lights were from the lamps in the tenement-house windows, and the two globes at the top of the church stairs. The tall figure walked rapidly. She saw it shadowing its way ahead of her. There was no reason for her to think of it.

"*Madre pietosa,* have mercy. . . ."

She entered the church. She had not been in it before, and did not know how to reach the point where the image of the Holy Virgin was. She saw a man's form, black and quiet, kneeling on the altar stairs. A vague memory of many years back rose like a cloud through her thoughts, and her body seemed to proceed quite as if she were living over again the sensations of that moment. Almost unconsciously she hurried with little running steps to the aisle along the wall and then, like one frightened at the strange warmth, the strange smells, the unbroken silence, the candles blinking in the dimness, she ran headlong the length of the church and threw herself on her knees at the foot of the statue she was seeking. . . .

"*Madre pietosa, madre pietosa,*" she cried in a hoarse whisper, "have pity on me, sinner that I am. Lay not this other burden on my soul, sweet lady of God. I led one into wickedness, stole him away from his duty to thee. Let not this other one hasten to his death. I did not know what I was doing. Say not that I pushed him to his death. Mother of God, have pity, Mother of God, Mother of God. . . ."

The shawl fell back over her shoulders as she raised her head to look directly into the Virgin's eyes. On the thick braids of her chestnut hair the light of the cresset swinging above the Madonna's form cast a soft illumination. Her brown eyes caught the gentle radiance. She clasped her hands under her chin, and lifted mute, pleading lips. Then the warmth of the church suffused her whole body. Her head drooped until it touched the pedestal, where she let it lay.

"Mother of God, full of grace," she prayed in low quick whispers, the words coming to her lips with the precision of things learned in childhood. She remained kneeling, her head on the pedestal, the black shawl over her body. The tall figure of the Virgin, in robes of red and green folds, rose stiffly in front, the cresset above her touching her high cheekbones with light, enveloping in soft yellow the head of the infant Christ in the crook of her arm. Agnese remained, reciting all the prayers that came to her memory. At the conclusion of a whole series, she raised her head.

"Have mercy. Thou knowest I did not do it. Keep him from death. Keep him from death, sweet Mother of God."

The statue of the Virgin was at the extreme right of the altar. Had it not been for the cresset above it, it would have been hidden in the dark shadows of a corner. Behind the statue was a door leading into the sacristy. Occasionally it opened. One of the priests had come in and was going out. He cast a rapid glance about, saw nothing unusual and went his way. The front door opened, now and then, and after several seconds the candle flames all leaned toward the altar as if the person who came in had blown on them. With that, the faint shadows flickered on the floor, flickered and then steadied again into their soft outlines.

– 2 –

Gelsomino remained motionless, a heap of black clothes. His knees rested on the edge of a wooden step leading to the altar, his shoe-tips touching the edge of the one below. His head was bent so far forward that his body described an arch the length of his back, not an easy graceful arch but one that pictured the agony of an unquiet spirit. His arms were pressed close to his body that the hands might more easily come together over the beads he held near his lips. A continuous rhythmic sibilance issued from them as he slid bead after bead rapidly through his fingers. No other motion or sign of life came from him. Even his black garments, rejecting the feeble light of the candles burning on the altar and on the images to his right and left, seemed a covering for an empty pedestal rather than for a living person. Absorbed in his prayers of contrition he saw nothing, heard nothing. . . .

"Mother of God," Agnese repeated and repeated, "give me a sign that he will get well . . . a sign, dear Holy One . . . a little sign . . . let but the light in the lamp burn until the midnight . . . Mother of God . . . here will I stay, kneeling, to watch it . . . if it goes out, I know I am guilty . . . I vow to Thee I am not, I am not, I am not. . . . Thou knowest it . . . *Madre Santa . . . Santa. . . .*"

Sobs choked her. She placed the side of her hand in her mouth and bit it to keep them back. Her body shook and trembled. After several minutes she stopped abruptly. Her mouth, her eyes opened as in a kind of fright. A wind had blown in from the door, the flame in the cresset had flickered, and wavered, and dipped out of sight.

"Mother!" she shrieked aloud as she saw the flame bound back to its straight position. Several persons in the church, kneeling at the sides of the benches, looked up quickly. But Agnese had bent her head again, and again she resumed her prayers.

"I meant it as a cure . . . Thou knowest it. . . . *Madre pietosa, piena di grazia. . . .*"

Gelsomino did not hear the sudden short shriek. He kept fingering his beads, still huddled over, still with his knees on the edge of the step. He had come to the end of a series of the acts of contrition. His lips were still but his mind spoke incessantly.

"My spirit, my body are Thine . . . I renounce the flesh and all the evils of it . . . I am utterly Thine . . . let me anew consecrate myself to Thee. Vouchsafe that I am worthy of the long wait until I can come to Thee, cleansed and sweetened by the mortification of this, my flesh . . . *Gesù, filio Dei.*"

He rolled the beads from finger to finger, praying rapidly in his murmurous sibilance.

For hours they remained so, he oblivious of everything, Agnese torn with agony, her mind and her eyes constantly on the flame which had become to her the voice of the Madonna.

The light rain had been caught up by a quick wind and tossed into every aperture. The chill of it had completely filled the church. All the other worshippers had left. The spacious low-ceilinged dimness was like a quiet underground crypt. The candles wagged and straightened, shut like eyes, and as quickly opened and glowed.

A young priest, a stout man with small steps, opened the door behind the Madonna, and went up to Agnese. He tapped her gently on the shoulders:

"*Sorella,*" he said, very softly, "you must go now. . . . Soon the candles will be put out. . . ."

Since she did not move, he bent down to her ear, and whispered, "Go now . . . your prayers will be heard."

She turned and raised her head, keeping her kneeling posture, and looked at him a trifle bewildered, unbelieving, frightened.

"It is late . . . the sacristan will be putting out the candles. . . . Your prayers will be heard. . . ."

"But I must stay," she cried out. "I must stay. . . . It's a vow . . . until midnight. . . ."

"It is almost midnight now. It will be getting too cold . . . is it so necessary?" His voice was kindly.

"Until midnight," she barely uttered the words, her face terror-stricken, twitching. "I must have an answer to my prayer. . . . The Madonna must tell me I am not a murderess . . . I am not a murderess. . . ."

The priest raised fat little hands in a gesture of horror.

"Father, father," she cried out, turning up her face full to his, but still on her knees. "Kneel with me . . . pray to the Virgin Mother that he live . . . let her give me a sign . . . a small sign . . . let the flame in the lamp burn . . . burn until the stroke of twelve . . . Father, kneel and pray with me . . . Mother of God. . . ."

Her head fell on the pedestal, as the sobs shook her body.

"My child, my child," the little priest kept whispering, himself as frightened as Agnese.

Just then the sacristan, opening the door with the decisive sound of one who has business to get over with, began at once putting out the candles in the brass holders along the wall, using a long pole with a shuffler attached to the end. He was obese, with a great paunch that wabbled as he shuffled, and a face with hanging jowls and loose puffy lips. He breathed so heavily that the lips trembled like a horse when it whinnies and the echo of the sound reverberated throughout the church. Evidently it was a sign for Gelsomino. For he rose immediately and, putting his beads in his pockets, hastened to the door while the sacristan continued snuffing out the lights. . . .

"My child, my child," repeated the priest. "Do not harass yourself so . . . I will pray with you. . . ."

Gelsomino had just opened the door, but the wind that rushed in was too strong for him to walk out at once. It came like a mob pushing with wet-cold hands, and raising a jubilant shout that ran the length and breadth of the church. The remaining candle-flames whirred as the wind pressed against them, shook and spread close to the wax. The cressets above the images near the altar swung with the noise of chains. The shadows blackened and grayed, blackened and grayed. . . .

Agnese jumped to her feet, her finger-tips between her lips, and gazed startled at the lamp above the Madonna, slowly swinging back.

"Mother of God . . . Mother of God," she whispered deliriously through her fingers.

Another gust of wind blew in. The sacristan shambled as fast as he could to the door which Gelsomino was still holding by the knob. The lamp retraced its arc, the light in it flurrying like scared eyes, and then suddenly darkening, and as quickly it went out!

– 3 –

Agnese shrieked, a high piercing sound of agony.

"*Figlia mia,*" cried the priest, going to her.

Gelsomino turned, wild-eyed, trembling: he knew the voice. Visions of a hot summer's day in the Cathedral of Villetto blurred his sight. His body once more chilled as when the shrill accusations filled the vault.

"But I did not kill him . . . I did not kill him . . . it wasn't me . . . it wasn't me. . . ."

"Calm yourself, dear sister," the little priest said over and over.

Gelsomino had hurried to her, stood at her side.

"Agnese," he called.

"Oh!" she cried, her hands in her hair . . . and stared at him stupefied. . . .

"You . . . you. . . ," she finally said in a hoarse undertone. "You . . . Did you hear? Did you know? . . . You have been following me then? You know he's dying."

"Agnese, Agnese, what are you saying?"

"From Giovanni you heard . . . perhaps you already know he's dead . . . that I killed him . . . chilled him to death."

"Agnese . . . listen to me."

"You come for me now . . . to claim me. . . ."

"For God's sake. . . ," he pleaded, the muscles of his face, haggard from his recent privations, drawn into taut strings. "For God's sake, Agnese. . . ."

"You . . . You!" She laughed in mockery. "You coward . . . you steal the boy's love . . . and now you come for me!"

"For the love of God, Agnese," cried Gelsomino in despair. He stood shaking and at the same time helpless, incapable of gesture, paralyzed by the bitter onslaught of accusations so unfounded and so surprising that he could not meet them.

The sacristan's fat face had solidified into rigid blocks. He looked at the priest, but the priest was too overwhelmed to do anything but thrust a hand out now and then and draw it back immediately in a vain effort to calm Agnese.

"So . . . it's the love of God now," Agnese mocked him. . . . "For the love of God . . . a priest without his cassock cries 'For the love of God.' You, you who pleaded with me that day . . . 'How can I? Take off my robes? Agnese, for the love of God . . . Marry Michele . . . Marry Michele' . . . And now he is dead . . . and you come for me . . . you vile rat . . . you . . . in a church too . . . I should have known it . . . a place for hypocrites . . . a messy place . . . a place that tortures you . . . what do they know . . . these saints? These saints? These less than men? . . . Tell me, you . . . you have been around . . . Do they help you . . . these painted lumps of clay? These saints that sit by the right hand of God . . . do they help you?"

"Agnese, Agnese. . . ," interrupted Gelsomino. His voice was quiet and patient though quickened by the intense suffering he was undergoing. "They do help, Agnese," he hurried to remark, hoping to calm her by a display of assurance.

"Liar!" she shrieked. "This one . . . this one . . . she laughed at me . . . she calls me murderess. . . . What does she know? What does she know?"

But she became quiet with the instantaneous silence of a clock that stops ticking. She had been gazing into Gelsomino's eyes. Whether moved by the unbroken kindliness with which he continued to look at her, or by a light that pierced through gloomy memories to sweet moments in the soft dusk of Italian summers, she changed her tone of voice. It became gentle, low, supplicating.

"Gelsomino," she cried, "Gelsomino . . . you believe me . . . I did not kill him. . . ."

"But what are you saying, Agnese . . . Agnese . . . *Agnese mia . . . mia. . . .*" His voice broke into tears. He had no conception of what she was saying, and understood only that she was in pain, wracked with thoughts of a deed that was too outrageous to allow her a minute's peace. All the impulsive sympathy of his nature flooded over him, and he longed to remove her out of the swift current of her despair. Something however in the mere use of "*mia*" fell like a sharp wind on Agnese. She shivered perceptibly and then she lifted wide, trembling lips.

"Gelsomino," she said slowly, pleadingly, watching him closely. "You don't believe me . . . I opened the windows . . . to kill him?"

"But Agnese, Agnese. . . ."

"Gelsomino, Gelsomino!" she cried, her face contorted with terror. "You don't . . . you don't. . . ."

"But Agnese . . . *Agnese mia.*"

With an impulsive movement Agnese placed her hands on his face. She was compelled to stand slightly on the tips of her toes to do it. She gazed steadily into his eyes, as if looking for the truth in the slightest flutter of the lashes.

"Tell me . . . you don't believe . . . like the Madonna there . . . that . . . I . . . I chilled . . . chilled Michele . . . to death?"

She pressed her hands upon his cheeks, as she spoke, and drew them down the length of his face as if by the gesture she could coax a truthful reply.

Up to this time, he had felt sufficiently removed from the central turmoil of her mind to pity and want to help. But this gesture tore away the barriers of the long years between them. It was as if she had drawn him into the dark centers of her pain, and made him quiver with its intensity and horror. And similarly he trembled with the perception, immediate and keen, that she had flung herself into the quiet wells into which he had poured his recent feelings, and that she hoped to emerge, soothed and cleansed of the horror that overwhelmed her now.

"You know, Gelsomino, I am not heartless. . . . They have called me witch and names too horrible to say. . . . I have made my way in spite of them. I have been hard and mean . . . Gelsomino, I say it here, in this holy place . . . to you . . . to these saints . . . to the world. . . . But I am not hard . . . not mean . . . not really. . . ." She paused.

She spoke hurriedly, leaning gently against him, with quiet urgency, as if explaining a proved case of guilt in the hope of receiving sympathy without which she could not face the future.

"Gelsomino," she resumed . . . "I did open the window . . . threw off the covers of his bed. . . . But you understand? It was not to kill him. . . . No, no . . . believe me . . . you believe me, don't you . . . don't you?"

"Yes, Agnese . . . yes. . . ."

"Doctor Grace said, 'Let him get pneumonia. Then I can cure him.' He was very sick . . . Giovanni has told you. . . . No?"

The young priest had ordered the sacristan to proceed with his business in the meantime, and leaving them alone, he knelt at the foot of the Virgin's image and seemed to pray. The greater portion of the candles were now extinguished, and save for the star-like glitter of the lamps in their red cressets here and there, the church was in almost complete darkness.

"Agnese," Gelsomino answered, "you are in great sorrow."

"I have prayed to the Madonna to save him, but she blew out the flame above her head there. See it . . . out. . . ."

"But is Michele . . . dead?"

"The light is out. . . ."

"Agnese, listen to me. . . . We do not know . . . the wind blew very hard . . . it is foolish to put too great trust in such a sign. Let us kneel again, you and I both . . . let us pray together . . . here . . . on this floor. . . . So . . . our hands together . . . on our knees. . . ."

Gently he took her by the wrists, and slowly lowered her to her knees. He knelt beside her. Holding out their clasped hands, they bent their heads to the floor, and prayed aloud, Gelsomino's voice ahead of Agnese's.

"Holy Jesus . . . Son of God. . . ."

– 4 –

The young priest had risen to his feet, perplexed and helpless. The fat sacristan had wobbled up to him with hands outstretched, inquiring. They were spared the difficulty of solving the problem. The door had rattled as if it had been shaken by a severe gust of wind. But it became clear that someone was tugging at the knob on the outside. Several seconds later he was pounding on the door, and shouting. The sacristan wabbled as fast as he could, followed by the priest. Agnese and Gelsomino, side by side, continued to pray.

It was Gesualdo, excited, drenched with the cold rain.

"Is my daughter here? My daughter, Agnese Dantone?"

"Slow there, old man, slow there!" wheezed the sacristan. "Think this is a stable? You shout so?"

The priest had come up in time, and begged him to come in.

"Follow me," he said, and led him to where Agnese and Gelsomino were kneeling.

"Agnese," he shouted, just as soon as he descried her form in the dark. "Agnese."

She jumped up.

"Come home. You need not pray . . . he will live . . . he will live . . . the crisis is over . . . you must come home . . . he spoke too . . . called your name . . . 'Agnese,' he called . . . and then closed his eyes . . . his fever's gone . . . his skin is so cool . . . he is sleeping now. . . ."

Gelsomino had stood up too, and had joined the group. When her father stopped speaking. She turned first to him and then to her old lover, speechless.

"You see," he said, "God has heard. . . ."

"Yes . . . God has heard."

She echoed his soft voice.

"Go to him now. He needs you."

"Yes," she said, staring at him.

"God has heard our prayers."

"Yes, God has heard," she paused, shook her head slowly to the right and left, and continued, "God has heard *your* prayers . . . not mine . . . he has seen too deep into my heart. . . ."

"Good people," the priest interjected at this moment. "You all must go . . . it is very late. . . ."

"Come, Agnese, come," Gesualdo kept urging. Having recognized Gelsomino, he felt vague fears crowding all about him.

But Agnese could not take her eyes from the face of her old lover. The prayer and the persistent regimen of self-denial had cut quivering hollows in his cheeks, deepened his eyes, and given them an expression of fervent searching. As she looked she saw what she had not seen in his features a year and a half back — something beautifully childlike that made him both timid and trustful, willing to believe and yet afraid, a lack of strength that was not so much cowardice as it was bewilderment. And as he looked at her, she was afraid. She was glad her father was calling. She knew she could not go back if he kept looking at her so, looking as if what his restless eyes were searching for he had found in her, peace in the center of the winds, calm at the end of the storm.

"Gelsomino," she whispered, and in her voice had come back the accents of her youth, the love and the wonder, the delight and the madness of her discovery of one so sweet, so dear to love.

"Gelsomino," she repeated, pleading once again as she had pleaded on the day they had parted. "Gelsomino!"

She knew he had breathed in the meaning of her cry. Words she could not have used to bring from their hiding places in her heart the dread impulses of her love for him. She knew that in the music of his name as she spoke it were the thoughts that only he could have understood. She repeated it again and again while he held up to her a face that bore the imprint of pain, but pain that was like a cloud colored with the light of the sky behind it.

She was glad that her father called again. She turned and hurried to the door, as Gesualdo labored painfully to keep up with her.

– 5 –

They walked in the chill the six or seven blocks to their home.

"Will he never stop it?" Agnese asked herself as her father kept up a continuous explanation of how they had saved Michele's life.

"Doctors don't know everything. 'Give him up,' they said. 'He's no better than dead!' 'No better than dead,' said I. 'We'll see,' I said. 'We'll see.' I had a donkey once and the military doctor said, 'Give him up . . . can't cure the old beast . . . he's good as dead.' But I, guess what I did, Agnese? Your old father don't give up. Guess what. I bought all the castor oil in Don Tocco's drug shop and soaked a peck of oats in it and I forced it down the old thing's throat. You ought to have seen him gag! It was a sight! But down the oil went, and out it came too the next day, and up stood the old fellow and he pulled many a load after that, I tell you. Good for dead! And so with my respects to Doctor Grace and Doctor Pastrocchi! 'He'll live,' I said. Apply heat — that's the thing in this pneumonia trouble — apply heat! I did. . . . Luigi came home on time and Concetta — she called me crazy — well, maybe I was, and we got all the empty beer bottles . . . more than a hundred . . . and we filled them with boiling water. You could hardly hold them, and we piled them up around him, on top of him, on his feet, under the bed . . . everywhere . . . and we kept changing them . . . it was up and downstairs with boiling water . . . one hour. . . two hours . . . three hours . . . four hours . . . then the stroke of eleven o'clock . . . sharp eleven . . . the wind was banging away at everything . . . like an old soldier gone mad it was . . . and Concetta kept saying, 'You're cracked. Who ever heard of beer bottles to cure anything?' 'Apply heat,' said I, 'Apply heat.' Luigi said, 'Oh, he's done for. Let's stop . . . see how blue his lips are.' 'Apply heat,' said I, and then the wind hit against the windows like a lot of stones. . . . You could hear it wail too . . . and then it stopped and we heard a voice like it came out of the wind. . . . Oh, what a blessed moment that was, Agnese. . . . Michele's voice it was . . . I leaned over him and he said, 'Agnese,' plain 'Agnese,' he said, and I came for you right away."

But it was not the figure of Michele that Agnese was seeing in her mind, nor was it his name that was in her ear, as he whispered it. Before her stood the thinned, haggard features of Gelsomino. In her heart echoed the sibilant cadence of his voice.

"He did love me!" she kept saying. "My damned self-will. . . . Marriage I wanted with him!"

She carried on a bitter debate with herself, hardly hearing the words of her father.

"You're not meant for a priest, I told him . . . vile woman that you are to tell him that. See how he has been punished! He has loved me all these years . . . and I have loved him . . . no one else . . . no one else . . . he has suffered . . . how he has suffered. . . . Other women had children the same way. Did they run off? Did they get the priests to leave the church and God? They stayed on . . . and they had other children. . . . But you . . . but you! What is all your money now? Your marriage . . . your houses! An empty barrel that smells of sour wine! An empty barrel . . . sour wine . . . drink your wine now! You pressed it from the grapes you picked yourself! You'll drink it, woman. Drink it to the last! You've been afraid all these years to seem afraid! Beans would have been enough and a crust of bread, and the third pressing of the wine! To have waited for his coming in the dark hours . . . and heard his voice . . . felt his hands upon my breasts!"

"We'll have to have a feast, Agnese," continued the old man. "Michele will soon be up! A great banquet in the big room. . . ."

– 6 –

Concetta opened the iron gate for her.

"You fool woman," she cried. "Hurry in. To be out in the damp, this cold! You ain't got the tough hide of Michele. The beer-bottles'll scorch your skin right off. . . . Sit down here. Let me get you some wine — hot wine with an apple cooked in it. Don't go up yet. Let me have your shawl. Take off your shoes! Heat up that wine," she called out to her daughter in the kitchen, as she knelt to remove Agnese's wet shoes.

Luigi was sitting in the large leather chair, his legs stretched out, in his shirt sleeves, his hands in his vest pocket.

"He'll live now," he said significantly.

"Live!" cried Gesualdo. "Sure as God he'll live."

"Well," answered Luigi, "hope he'll have more luck!"

"There ain't nobody had better," asserted Concetta, with an air of closing a book for good. She took the hot wine from her daughter, and slowly spooned it out to Agnese.

"But I don't want this, Concetta. Why do you make me drink it?"

"Sh . . . sh . . . you must . . . don't say another word. We can't be forever boiling up beer bottles."

She went to see Michele soon after. The small cresset at the foot of Saint Blase's image was the only light in the dark room. Agnese smiled wryly as she saw it.

"I might have prayed to that! I would not have met him again, and received the old pain."

Michele was sleeping quietly. The hard breathing had softened into the normal rhythms. His face, however, though it had lost the flush of fever, glared a dead white.

His hair, which had grayed considerably, seemed in the dull light but an extension of the pallid forehead and cheeks.

"How thin he's got," said Agnese to herself. "A ghost of himself! Like that other! Two ghosts . . . and I!"

She laughed a low, hysterical laugh, and as she did so Michele opened his eyes feebly. When Agnese stroked his hand, a smile overspread his features, a smile that turned painfully the corners of his mouth and slid like a sickly unwholesome glaze into his eyes. She drew back.

"He hates me," she said. "He hates me."

– 7 –

Her bitter thoughts were brought to a quick conclusion. Giovanni, who slept in the adjoining room, was calling.

"Ma . . . ma. . . ."

"Sit down by me," he beseeched her as she entered his room. "Stay here . . . I am afraid. . . ."

Agnese placed her head on his chest and clasped her hands beneath her chin.

"Your waist is damp, Ma," he said. "You're shaking so! Why, Ma?"

"Nothing, child, nothing. Maybe I am afraid, too."

"He will live now. He will live!" His voice was soothing and sympathetic, and he ran his hand with the softest motion over and over her back.

"Yes, he will live, he will live," she cried, and embraced him with a vehemence to which he was unaccustomed.

Giovanni mistook it for joy and happiness, and he laid his head on her shoulder, and said:

"He will be happy, too . . . my other father."

"Oh, my son, my son, my son," she cried and kissed him madly on his cheeks, his neck, his head. The unusual fury of her gesture coursed through his body like a fever. He was helpless in her arms, overcome with a wonder that was akin to fright. Only on the steps outside the door the night of the hateful banquet had he known her to be equally in the control of a force which seemed beyond the routine of daily affection. But this was even a fiercer display, and almost by instinct he began to sense meanings in it which he recognized as belonging not to him, but to another. With fear and horror he realized, too, that the wild affection she was showing him was a retreat from the horror of her real feelings for the sick man next door.

Then as she kissed him, she questioned and questioned without pausing, in a voice wet with tears though she was shedding none.

"But you will love me, Giovanni, you will love me, you will love me?"

Again he stroked her back, patted her hair, and with awkward pressure held her close to him.

"You're all I have," she said. "You're all I have."

She grew calm in his arms, and he laid his head gently on hers. So they lay together motionless, their beings transfused with a love that was deeply enough selfish to make each want the other, and withal so innocent and sweet that it hurt not but soothed.

– 8 –

Gelsomino, too, had hurried home through the chilling mist to the unheated darkness of his room. His agitation left his heart silent and bare as a wind does a field covered with autumn leaves, when it has blown wildly through it and then subsided. He was tired too, stiff from the long kneeling, and unawakened fully from the fearful concentration of his prayer. The shock of seeing Agnese and being brought back into the swift drift of her problems, had been too instantaneous, too unforeseen, too vehement for him to be able to think of it in the forced quiet of his walk home.

He kneeled at the foot of his bed, and prayed. "Help her, O Father, to take him into her love, and let her days be sweet. Help me, too, to drive from my thoughts the last impiety of my lust. Make me fit to enter into Thy temples, once again, in the name of the Father, the Son and the Holy Ghost! Amen. . . ."

XVI. THE NEW BARBERSHOP

– 1 –

Michele left his sick bed a well man but a taciturn one. He had announced to Agnese when he was first able to sit up, a plan which he soon put into action.

"Agnese," he said to her as he sipped his cup of hot chicken soup, "I will open my barbershop again."

He had selected a store next to the houses being put up by Agnese and Antonio, and at a diagonal from their home. A busy street meant business. With the exception of Doctor Grace, the Americans had all moved out, and many of the brown fronts now gleamed with store windows displaying boxes of macaroni of various size and shapes, loaves of bread, braided and twisted, in various lengths, or as thick and as big as cart wheels, strings of garlic silvery flaky in the sun, salami and cheeses.

As Michele sat in one of the revolving white chairs of the newest models, and tilted back his head by merely pressing a button on the chair, he surveyed in the broad mirrors his spotless expanse with considerable satisfaction.

"We shall see," he vowed to himself. "Here *I* am the boss."

His name in large ivory letters made him smile with a soft contentment. Not that he saw it backwards in the mirror but that it was his own — Michele Dantone. Passersby would read it and know that this shop was his, that his had been the moving force in its establishment, his were the superintending brains.

"I'll make my own pile . . . my own."

Trade had been brisk from the beginning. He was employing as his assistant Filippo, the accordion player. But Filippo had begun to complain that there was no time to practice.

"I'll go mad without music," he had said.

Michele worked steadily, without talking. As a matter of fact, he dared not talk, for, since his illness, his stammer had become worse, and in the effort to produce some words his face twitched so spasmodically that the red disc of his scar shifted like a movable light on his cheek. The pain of the process had become unbearable, and he maintained an almost complete silence except for a peculiar laugh of constant affirmation to everything that was said.

Antonio had been one of his first customers.

"Why, *Michele bello,* you'll make your own America, yet, I'm telling you.

What a place! Red and white pole whirling around like a sausage machine! Ivory chairs! Electric lights! Whew, you got the American way about you."

He threw out his feet in luxurious relaxation, leaned back his head, and as Michele tucked a clean towel under his chin, cried out, "Go ahead there, Michele, and do your worst!"

In his reclining posture, Antonio was in no position to note the slow wan smile that lifted the corners of Michele's lips. If he had been, he might have brought down with a thoughtful pressure of his palm and fingers the assertive ends of his waxed mustache.

"I could do it now," Michele yelled in his own heart. "This give-no-damn bastard'll get it yet."

"They're pretty nearly up, Michele," Antonio shouted while the barber paused to wipe the lather from the razor. "They'll be finished before the New Year! And what a celebration this new Italy will see then!"

One by one the old men who had made a rendezvous of his old shop trickled back. Behind the store they used the dirt yard for their game of *palle.* The clinking and the thudding of the balls as they struck and rebounded from each other, were a pleasant echo of contented days in Michele's memory. When he was not busy, he joined in the games, and was surprised to find that the paralyzing stammer disappeared.

"A hit," he shouted. "A hit there, Zi' Tonno. And now I'll smash your ball. *Peppino bello,* right into the fence."

"*Per Bacco,* you did it!"

"Oh, when I set my mind to a thing!" he answered in glee.

When they got together over the beer or wine, matters were different. The talk was spirited and took the form of good-natured fun-making at the expense of the men who had lost the game and were therefore compelled to stand the expense of the drinks and *tarallini.*

"Two more losses like this, Peppino, and you'll have to lay off your men."

"He'll go back to the pick and shovel."

"In fact, he needs a shovel now to hit the ball at all."

"But Michele there, he's the lucky man."

"Hits them every night."

Zi' Tonno, who still wore for evening dress his streetcleaner's uniform, remarked in a high-pitched, shaky voice, "He hits everything hard. Makes money with barbershop, the dumps, the houses they're building. Lucky man!"

"Oh, it's Antonio and Agnese that go it big," Zi' Vito added in accents of admiration.

"They're at it all day long. Wherever you go you see them, ordering this, directing that, haggling with the municipal officers. What energy! They deserve their success, I tell you!"

But the mild weather which permitted this outdoor pastime had soon gone, and the men congregated in the evening in the shop itself. Filippo collaborated with shoulders and feet to breathe the gay, lamenting music out of his shining accordion, and often raised a lugubrious tenor in accompaniment. They played at *tre-sette,* instead of *palle,* taking particular delight in slamming down a telling card so hard that each separate knuckle reverberated.

It was later than usual, on a night of quiet snow. Michele had had Concetta bring his supper of sausages and peppers, with huge chunks of bread and wine. The men had sat down in earnest to a long session of cards. In the back room Filippo, who refused to play, was coaxing whispered melodies out of his sad instrument.

"You'll see tonight!" Peppino announced, as he cut the long black cigar in two with his curved pocketknife. "I've been paying for the wine too long."

– 2 –

There was a sharp knock at the door, which Michele answered immediately.

"A thousand pardons," cried Paul Variglia as he adjusted his cane and hat and transferred them both into his left hand. "A thousand pardons, Don Michele. Don't let me break in on your game."

The stammer interfered with a prompt reply, and compelled him, against his will, to take hat and cane and coat put them away, and then offer a chair.

"Very stormy tonight!" Paul Variglia informed the group.

"Wh-wh-wh-what brings. . . ?"

"Just thought I'd drop in . . . a little matter of business . . . nothing serious."

"Bu-bu-bu-?"

One of the men dealt out the cards with a kind of forlorn motion, possibly just to keep himself occupied, knowing that the game would not be resumed for a long time. Others sat tilted back. One whistled the soft tune that wheezed out of the accordion next door.

"It's this way, Don Michele," Variglia began, smiling. Taking a small leather wallet out of a vest pocket, he handed it to Michele. "This is a new shop and a fine one . . . the best in Little Italy, got everything, steamers for the towels, electric cutter — a very fine shop."

Michele meanwhile had discovered that the wallet contained a small nickel crucifix, an image of Saint Michael, and another of Gabriel, blowing his trumpet.

"A little gift from me," Variglia explained, "wishing you success, one for each mirror. They'll bring good luck. The Christ for praying to, San Michele — well, he's your namesake, and Gabriel to announce the grand success."

"Ye . . . s, bu . . . t. . . ."

"It's a custom of our business — the Merchant's Protective and Security League. We give them to each store that opens up — according to the kind and the name." He smiled blandly.

Michele leaned forward to listen.

"We post one of these on your door, see — a sticker with our trade-mark — and our men protect you against thieves, fires, broken windows. The charge is very little. You never can tell what will happen. Your wife — ah, what a good head for business she has! Well, she don't want protection. It's her business. Maybe it's all right. But insurance is insurance, as the Americans say. Only a few minutes ago, while I was coming here, there was a fire — a fire in the new houses. Oh, don't get excited! A little thing — the policemen put it out. I offered them protection. The day I saw them Antonio had broken the image of the Holy Virgin. A bad sign, I told him, a bad sign. But no, no, they were not going to pay our small, our very small fee. . . . Well!"

"A f . . . f . . . fire in A . . . a . . . nt . . . tonio's building!"

Michele had jumped to his feet. The muscles of his face slipped and fell, slipped and fell, out of and back into their normal positions. The scar slid up and down like a flame point. The amazement was not concern entirely, as Paul Variglia intimated by his cautious side-glance and the amused puckering at his mouth corners.

"Might have got a start, and the wind would do the rest!" he added with solemn shakings of the head. "What a calamity that would be . . . almost all their money sunk into it, I understand."

Peppino stopped dealing cards to an invisible group long enough to ask, "Say, don't fires get started on purpose too?"

Paul Variglia was not in the least affected.

"A lot of low-downs, you know, coming in out of the rain or the snow. They got to warm up somehow, and then, whew! up goes the pile!"

The sticker appeared the next day on the pane of Michele's door. He never informed Agnese of his having joined the protective association, and never inquired whether she and Antonio had changed their opinions concerning the wisdom of belonging.

– 3 –

As often as possible Michele preferred to eat his meals in the barbershop. Concetta or her daughter brought them to him, not without some protest.

"What a grand signor you've got to be," cried Concetta. "Has to eat his meals in private! Give way, there, to my noble lord, give way, there," she announced, spreading out her apron as she had seen peasant women shooing away chickens.

"With a wife at home," she proclaimed on another occasion when all the card-players were present, "he eats here! And what a wife! The most beautiful, the liveliest soul — the queen of all of them! You fool you! Be careful or. . . ."

She stuck out her lips and put her two thumbs to her head as the symbol of the horns that might be prepared for him.

The anger that was flooding Michele turned into a chill that tied his tongue. Peppino came to his rescue.

"You old cat, jump off that fence or I'll throw my shoe at you," he cried in humorous indignation.

"Oh, well, what's the proverb say?" retorted Concetta. "As you make your bed. . . ," she shrugged her shoulders. "As for me, I'll sleep on four pillows, thank you," and she left with an impertinent swish of her voluminous skirts.

– 4 –

The barbershop was not proving the soul-soothing escape that Michele had intended. Timid to a fault, he had worked himself into a rage which, not finding outlet in action, turned into an inner process that had paralyzed his body, his speech, his waking functions.

"Why did I not waylay the puffed-up boaster months ago, string him up like a pig, cut out his stones and send them to his wife?"

These days he asked the question calmly and he answered it calmly, "I'll do it yet."

He consoled himself, however, with the thought that he was doing everything to avoid the bloody obscenity. After all, change places, change customs.

Had he not sought the seclusion of his own trade in the hope of bolstering up his self-respect, surrounding himself with friends of his own stamp, and so keeping clear of the complicated business of Antonio and Agnese? But it kept pursuing him. The expression on the faces of his cronies as Concetta made the hateful gesture! He shuddered as he thought of how tightly they kept their lips closed, how they hung their heads, and attempted to evade his scrutiny.

"*Madonna Santissima del Carmine,*" he whispered in his own heart, "and do I have to . . . do I have to . . . do I have to split his middle like a pig's?"

"Good morning, Don Michele," Catarina all but whispered one morning, and smiled painfully. "I brought little Ciro! Needs a haircut so badly! Oh, this shawl!" She almost wept her annoyance as she awkwardly extricated it from the door in which it had been caught. "And look at that little brigand! He saps all my strength. Get off that chair, Ciritillo, get off. . . ."

"It's all right, Catarina, let him stay."

The round, red-faced chunk had in the meantime climbed up and was surveying the marvel of the duplicated scene in the mirror.

"I can see you!" he shouted in glee.

"You take off that overcoat," Michele commanded, but he could add nothing else, for the dreaded stammer had come back with the memory awakened in his mind as he noted a tendency on Catarina's part to look him all over with an unmistakable air of contempt, faint as it was.

"*Porco Dio,*" he muttered inwardly, "keep your mouth shut. Don't start on the same question. Don't drive me mad again!"

"It's a mean life in this country in the winter! How cold, and how dirty!" Catarina spoke with the air of one who had suffered long.

The slip-slip of the scissors was Michele's only answer, but in his heart he was repeating, "Let her keep her mouth shut . . . let her keep her mouth shut!"

"That's the heaviest shawl! You could wear it on the coldest day! But here, you have to go dressed in a quilt, Lord bless me!"

"She's not going to speak," Michele thought. "What could she say?"

"You look well, Don Michele, a little thin, but well. I never can stop marveling. It all seemed like a miracle . . . your getting sick like that, falling in the grave like, and then coming out again . . . and the beer bottles and all. . . ."

"Hurry up, there!" shouted little Ciro. "Ma, I want to go home."

"Oh, the little brigand . . . the little brigand . . . he's always on the jump . . . Don Michele is so good to you, be quiet! Well, the houses are going up!"

"Y . . . yes."

"It's slow work."

"The c . . . c . . . cold!"

"I don't know what it is! I wish they'd be finished or burn down . . . or something! There hasn't been a day of peace in my house since they started! I never see Antonio from morning to night! Always the houses! Always the houses! And out he goes, he and Agnese! And long past dinner time I have to put the macaroni plate on a boiling pot every night. Then I see him, him and Agnese! They work hard there too, I know. Always together! But I am tired of it . . . tired of it . . . tired of it. . . ."

Her nervous excitement caused utter impotence of speech in Michele.

"She was bound to talk . . . bound to talk!" His head rang with the unspoken anger that could not come out in words.

"I'm a different man, there, lady!" He told her in a silent shuddering of his whole body. "Go careful! You'll tempt me to it! *Te le manderò in un piatto le scatole di tuo marito.* Careful . . . careful . . . shut up . . . shut up!" But he could not say the words aloud. They thundered in his thoughts and the noise of them shook the scissors in his hand.

He hurried with the task of making Ciro's curls part in the direct center of his head where Catarina insisted the part should be, hurried to shut the door behind them, hurried to sweep up the hair with such energetic strokes that he seemed actually to be sweeping up the last tangled memories of an incident he must, he must forget. . . .

– 5 –

Agnese and Michele had lost the habit of intimate talk together. He had acquiesced too readily in all that she said, and he had rarely opened a subject without having suggested a phase of it with which she would agree. They had both been content to sit with their separate thoughts for so long now that the rift that had been created by the events culminating in Michele's sickness had merely confirmed the situation, if painfully emphasizing it at the same time.

But the night of Catarina's visit, Michele had stammered through a long speech. Agnese had found him fumbling through the drawers of the clothes chest in their room, had stood gazing at his operation, but said nothing.

"L . . . look . . . ing for that old r. . . r . . . rabbit . . . knife of m . . . mine," he had volunteered without raising his head. "Got a b . . . b . . . bone handle . . . c . . . curved like a . . . a . . . a . . . new m . . . m . . . oon. I used to . . . to . . . s . . . skin rab . . . b . . . bits with it in V . . . V . . . Villetto . . . H . . . hope I c . . . can find it . . . F . . . friend . . . going to b . . . bring me s . . . some rabbits. Hope . . . I d . . . don't . . . have to use it . . . hate to c . . . c . . . cut anything . . . now."

"Oh, take them to the butcher!" Agnese answered sharply.

"Yes . . . maybe! . . . but I found it . . . see . . . I . . . found it."

He raised a scared face to hers, with stationary eyeballs that gleamed intensely in the gas light. The suggestion of fear was too spontaneous and genuine for it to have escaped the attention of Agnese.

"What's in his mind?" she thought.

As if he had divined her query, he let a thin self-conscious smile pass like something one licks from one corner of his mouth to the other, and shook his head slowly up and down with a deliberateness that both amused and alarmed his wife. Then he said:

"R . . . rabbits used to . . . eat up . . . everything in the g . . . g . . . gardens! We c . . . c . . . caught them . . . and . . . sk . . . skinned them and we didn't even b . . . b . . . bang their . . . b . . . brains out against a . . . a . . . wall!"

They had not exchanged so many words at once since his illness. Agnese had smiled at the last remark of her husband, had shrugged her shoulders, and said to herself, "He's getting queer besides!"

But as they lay in bed, both facing the ceiling and both with eyes shut, she kept asking herself, "What's happened now? Has anybody put ideas into his head?"

And Michele kept reiterating to himself, "I don't want to . . . I don't want to . . . I don't want to."

Even in his waking thoughts on the subject, he brushed away with mounting horror the sinister plan that his desire to avenge his wounded pride suggested and suggested. Certainly there was no happiness in his home, and the long afternoons in his barbershop, despite the merry wheezing of the accordion, seemed but a mocking replica of the emptiness and the solitude he felt whenever he was at home. He shunned and felt shunned. Giovanni had made an attempt at friendliness. But there was a memory of his being called "*ta*" while he was sick that angered Michele too persistently for him to accept the kindly gesture.

"The little brat . . . to call me *ta*! Laughing at me . . . laughing at me . . . when he hadn't called me that for years, for years!"

Luigi he rarely saw. Gesualdo annoyed him.

"Never stops telling how he saved me! Why didn't he let me die? Beer bottles . . . boiled beer bottles! Kept me alive! What for? Make my horns longer! *Maledetto Iddio! Maledetto Iddio!* I'll show them! I'm no simpleton! I'll nail both of them on her bedroom door!"

Despite his resolute self-assertion, Michele doubted, if not his courage, his physical ability to carry out the revolting design he had formed. He ran away from himself, never at peace unless someone were with him, talking to him, playing at cards, at *tocco,* at anything. The accordion replaced his cronies by day.

"Don't stop Filippo, don't stop. Play that jig again! Sing . . . sing to it."

Filippo wanted nothing else.

– 6 –

But when there was nothing to do, and the antic instrument had ceased its merry wails, Michele ran to the windows. The door of his house was visible . . . a cold silent mockery that said, "What do you know of what goes on behind me?" Then it was that he most wanted to shade his eyes with his hands, blot out the sight of door and house and street. But then it was, too, that before his eyes he saw the hateful bloody objects he had vowed to tear out of Antonio's body and nail up conspicuously for the world to see.

"I've waited too long! Oh, let me forget . . . forget!"

Zia Cristina caught him one day peering intently from behind his door. Her ample rotundities, like billowed clouds on the horizon, expunged the distant view. She knocked with her knuckles on the pane in front of his eyes.

"Whey, there . . . you're like an old monk who's caught sight of a naked girl bathing! Look up, there, let me in."

She crowded him back into the store, and carefully lowered her immense expanses on the edge of a round-seated chair.

"Like sitting on a ten-cent piece," she wheezed. "You ought to have chairs for all size customers, Don Michele! You're looking pinched again there, young turnip! You think too much. Thinking makes the hair white."

Michele, too overcome with her explosive volubility, could only stare at her and smile with feigned delight at her presence.

"Wh . . . what br . . . brings you here!"

"Out shopping! Saw you flattening your nose against the pane! Was there really. . . ?" She winked suggestively. "Thrilling to see somebody else at it, hey? You old lecher, hey? What things one does see in this country, *Michele bello.* What strange, strange things! Know that artist Birrichino? Well, I saw him, so help me God, with my own eyes, like a monkey going up the fire escape and into Geraldina's house. . . . Oh, I don't blame him. She's a nice morsel . . . a nice morsel! Her husband must have heard . . . and yet he does nothing! The poor corn-cob! He's a drug clerk, and he has the longest hours . . . and while he's away the little lass will play . . . he . . . he . . . a strange country, Michele, a strange country!"

She seemed to have produced the effect on Michele she wanted. She sat with her fat hands on her knees, an immobile mass, slyly staring at him from the fat recesses of her eyes, observing the pallor of his face, growing green, the pupils contracting, the lips twitching.

"It's a good thing, too, Don Michele, that we have dropped the ways of the old country. We're liberal souls here. Must be so. Business is the most important thing. Must keep going . . . oh must! Women go out like men . . . in company with other women's husbands. You can't keep cutting their throats can you, now? No business'd get done at all. And for the most part there's nothing to it. . . . Take yourself. You got your barbershop — a fine place too, needs your time! Take Agnese. Why, Donn' Agnese has a big business . . . what a head, what a head that woman has!"

Michele reddened, but with all that felt his body run cold. He wanted to jump at her throat, pull the blabbing tongue out of her mouth, throw her out into the street like so much offal.

"You're a gr . . . gr . . . great one . . . Zi' . . . Zi' . . . Cristina," was all he could stammer.

"Why, yes, Michele, new country, new ways. . . . So Agnese goes everywhere with Antonio. You mind your business. Catarina looks after her house . . . nobody gossips . . . the world goes on. But in the old country! Well, now . . . there'd be any number of stones nailed to many a woman's door, hey?"

– 7 –

That night Michele waited until his friends had gone. Filippo, who slept in the room behind the shop, had not yet returned. Michele put out every ceiling light, the lights in the windows, and pulled down the shades, the brown shades with the green and gold letters. "Michele Dantone — Tonsorial Parlor." Then he turned on the small light over the shelf in front of his chair. How the green and yellow liquids jumped into view, and ricocheted over the white sheen of the marble, of the chairs! They fascinated Michele, and for a second threw him into complete inactivity, spot-lighted in the mirror.

Then, just as if he were preparing a sharp edge for the next customer, he drew out the flat pumice stone in its wooden casing, lathered it carefully, and taking out the curved knife he had used to flay rabbits, began sharpening it deliberately. The silence intensified the slight shuffling noise as the blade moved back and forth over the stone, and as he wiped it now and then to test the edge, the single light caught up the brightness of the steel, and tossed it up and down into the dark mirrors.

XVII: ON THE ROOFTOPS

– 1 –

Antonio was too hearty a man to have allowed his failures to make headway in his love for Agnese, to depress him or lessen the vigor of his appetite for life and work. He superintended with unflagging attention every detail of the large construction enterprise. His voice boomed everywhere, his athletic figure sped untiringly from cellar to roof. He walked the unfloored beams with a carelessness that amazed the workmen — a carelessness that was the heedless cunning of confidence and experience. Sometimes his voice burst into a tune of the day, sentimental, long-sustained, jubilant, a fresh importation from the sidewalks of Naples.

Only one snowstorm and several days of cold weather had slowed up the work. The frame was completely up, the facing of yellowish brick had been carried to the fifth story. The paned windows, the bath tubs were piled up on the sidewalks.

"Now, Compare Barto," yelled Antonio, slapping his friend on the back and then rubbing his hands in glee, "a couple of weeks more of sunny weather, and we'll stick up the tree on top of the buildings, and there won't be enough beer and wine in New York to go around. . . ."

"I know," piped Barto Lo Santo, feeling the area on his back where the slap had landed, "I know, but the next time think how small I am and how big you are and that we're on the fifth floor with no flooring, and I have children and so have you!"

But the agile Antonio was running the length of a transverse out of shot of Barto's voice. In several seconds he was at the top — a rectangular crisscross of beams now in the process of being covered with the boards that were to be the roof. The irregular rhythm of so many hammers, the sight of so many carpenters on their hands and knees, sent the blood mounting to Antonio's cheeks.

"Just a month before Christmas maybe up, all up — ready to rent!"

He drew in a breath of the keen, sunny air.

"They're higher than anything else around! There's the river! What thousands of houses! How funny the clothes look wriggling in the wind! You could have seen the Adriatic in my home town," he mused. "Yes, but who could have put up these enormous buildings?"

And then, just as to Agnese, there came to him, too, the question, "Well, what's it all for? Oh, yes, we shall live well, Catarina . . . the children will have everything, but. . . ."

He was about to do what always injected new spirit into his muscles once he felt himself drooping — burst into a merry whistle, rush to a workman, dig him in the ribs with smart camaraderie, laugh heartily, and proceed to the next point of inspection. Instead, seeing the figure of Agnese coming up the ladder from the floor below, he stooped over and helped draw her up. . . .

"Good morning, Antonio, what a day!" she said. "If it only keeps up! The sun up here is warmer, and there is less wind too! For this sight alone, Antonio, for this breath of fresh air, the whole business has been good!"

She loosened the yellow-fringed kerchief covering her head and neck, revealing the liquid brown of her hair, and the glint of her gold earrings. Antonio could not help but note how soft was her skin, and how the flash of her teeth took up and verified the quick vigor of her passionate eyes.

"It's been good, Agnese," he said, slightly averting his gaze. "Just for the sight of this . . . and you alone with me!"

"The wind blows with a vim," she replied, as if she had not heard, slapping down with her hand her billowing skirt. "The men don't seem to mind it."

She stepped from one beam to another like one experienced in walking over the yawning hollows between.

"Careful, Agnese," Antonio cried.

"There's more fun doing this than gathering the grapes on Villetto's hills," she answered. "You can't picture it, Antonio, a hill, but a high one, covered from top to bottom and all around! Heavy vines on fences and poles! And every vine drooping with a thousand clusters. Your country is not a wine country. You can't picture the girls, the men, the donkeys, with baskets piled with red grapes. It wasn't easy walking! If you slipped! And the sun was warm, and the wind blew — like this! Oh, Antonio, I sometimes think how much better it might have been had we all stayed where God put us. But, there's more fun doing this! There's more danger, more life. . . ."

"Death, you mean," Antonio whispered, smiling nevertheless.

He was on the same beam with her. He had seized her hand on the pretext of assisting her, and held it down with a firmness that brought new color into her cheeks.

"Careful, there are the men there," she said under her breath. "And I have your word, Antonio!" she added beseechingly with a kind of forced gayety. "Look! How pale the fire out of the gashouse chimney is in the sunlight. . . ."

"Not in my heart, Agnese."

"Antonio — you promised! Do not torture me!"

"How many years it has flamed! Can I smother it now? Speak. Can I smother it now?"

"Quiet," she ordered sharply, and stepped nimbly across a series of beams until she reached the cornice. The flooring had been laid for three or four feet at the point where she was standing. Adjusting her kerchief more tightly about her head, she leaned on the tiling, and gazed across the river and far out to the Sound, touched here and there with the shadows of ships, the glint of sails, and lines of trailing smoke.

Several sharp whistles blew.

"Noon," she said to herself. "The men will be going down."

Antonio in the meantime had reached her side.

"Agnese, it's like a strong wine today. It is a hot flame in me. It isn't always so. I should let nothing stop me, otherwise. As you stood there, Agnese . . . your cheeks, your eyes, your neck! You will not let me suffer. I love you only."

She continued gazing, hardly hearing what he said.

"Only you, Agnese . . . not even my children. Won't you understand? Once the houses are up, as I have said already . . . we shall have money enough. We can go to the West, to South America. We're thirty . . . life has begun but now. Will you live with a corpse? Shall I live with a fountain of tears?"

He was standing close to her, so that she could feel his breath warming her cheek.

"See, Agnese," he continued. "The water runs out and out to the ocean, the ocean you and I have already crossed. There was to be happiness here. Remember how our hearts leaped at the thought. And what is there now?"

He was as unaware as Agnese of the men enfilading past them as they sought the ladder leading to the floors below. Neither could hear the sotto voce comments, or the louder frank expressions when the men reached the lower story.

"Don't blame them . . . they're a match!"

"She ought to be my wife. She'd walk the chalk line, I'm telling you."

"The little bitch . . . a man at her heels every time!"

The men at work on various parts of the buildings had gathered on the ground floor for their luncheon of sandwiches of hot peppers and huge slices of salami or sausages washed down with beer or wine. As usual, one of the younger men had finished sooner than the others and, having strung his mandolin across his shoulders, began to sing. The merry melancholy of the tune brought both smiles and silence. As it floated up and up, only an occasional word reached the ears of Agnese and Antonio, but the music mingled with the sun-warmed wind and played about their thoughts like the colors of an unformed dream.

"Nun scappa, ch'i' nun songo o' mammone
ti addimmanno 'na cosa e nient'ato. . . ."

"Agnese, Agnese. . . ," Antonio pleaded. "Say the word. A day after this business is settled, and off we'll go."

A pause intervened. The great silence of the rooftops seemed the more intense for the movement of the water that gathered in billows, ran toward the dock and broke noiselessly. Across the yards to their right, a red blanket bellied out into the wind, and as suddenly straightened as the breeze raised it; but it fell back without a sound. Everywhere there was motion, and nowhere sound.

"Nun scappa, ch'i' non songo o'mammone. . . ."

The mandolin, tinkling like beads of glass, and the voice like a clear flute came up to wake Agnese from her revery. She turned abruptly to Antonio.

"I have told you," she said. "There must be no more of this. You swore to it on that night. I vowed it to my own heart. We must finish these houses. I love only one man. I was wrong to leave him. Better have stayed and fetched for him than this . . . you and that other one, and he too, and I, miserable wretches. Besides, there is Giovanni. There are your children . . . and Catarina. You are mad, Antonio, to suggest it . . . run off. If it were just to have me! Well, yes I might say. Why not? They call me vile names. You, too, will be calling me one for talking this way. Yes, this is a free land. I am my own boss. Yes . . . I might say yes tonight, Antonio. Meet me tonight. Then you would come. What after? Would you be content? Would I? Antonio, at heart I am as bad a woman as they call me. I have wanted you, and Gelsomino, and Doctor Grace, and oh . . . him too at times. Like an animal, Antonio, my eyes flaming, my whole body tender for a touch of you. See how I talk. I am shameless. But you will understand. It was not love . . . it was savagery . . . only one man I have wanted and loved . . . but he and I won't meet again and I am going to say good-bye to all this. Work from now on, only. Work — that's the American cure. Work — and Giovanni — work, Antonio, and nothing more. Be good and understand. No more of this, Antonio, as you love me!"

"*Nun scappa, ch'i' non songo o' mammone.*"

Agnese's lips smiled but her eyes gleamed with sadness. "Hear," she cried with sad raillery. "Hear, Antonio, what he sings. 'Don't run. I'm neither gnome nor goblin.' . . . Don't hang your head. Look up at me. . . . Oh, then, I'll sing for you . . . I'll sing until your heart grows glad. I'll sing until the world hears how our hearts are cracking, yours and mine."

She placed her arms akimbo, shawl in her hands, and spread out across her arms. Her black eyes darted, the color mounting to the olive of her cheeks. She smiled as she sang, tossing her head now to one side, now to the other:

"*Nun voglio suffrì cchiu*"

"Quiet, for God's sake, Agnese, quiet," cried Antonio, smiling too, but awkwardly.

"*Fa chello che buoí tu!*"

"They will all be coming up. Agnese, *per l'amore di Dio* . . . quiet!"

She lowered her voice, and leaned forward to be closer to Antonio. Both her posture and the diminished volume of her voice gave a touch of mingled coquetry and malice to the song. The song was like a voice added to the wind, filling its pauses softly and swinging off with it into the spaces of the sky.

"Agnese," pleaded Antonio. "This is madness. Stop it!"

"*A me non penzà cchiu*"

"Agnese, will you break my heart indeed? The men will be here now. Listen to the whistles. Stop it!"

His smile had given way to the combined expression of his rising love and his great concern.

"I shall seize you in my arms, and break your madness in my madness! There will be an end of the comedy, Agnese. We shall have to flee then, or there will be blood. No more, Agnese, no more, *per l'amore di tutti i Santi.* . . . Here are the men!"

Agnese's hysteria terminated as suddenly as it had begun. Her cheeks paled, and her lips were compressed into a quivering line. Antonio looked with fear upon the disquiet in her eyes.

"What are you standing there for?" he shouted to the workman on the ladder. "Others are coming up. Get a move on you. It's past the hour. Is this a picnic?"

He leaned over and yelled into the shaft.

"Why the slow march? Is this a funeral?"

The men were unaccustomed to hearing Antonio break into such anger. They clambered up noisily and went to their work. The hammers began their rhythmic pounding into the smiling winter silence.

"That's my heart you hear, Antonio," Agnese said in low tones. "They're hammering it down. It jumped into life a minute ago, and now it must be nailed down for good. Don't look so sad, Antonio. You'll make the world laugh at you . . . your mustaches should stand up firm and bold. I have had a mad love too, but it stayed in my heart. Come, about our work. Work only from now on, remember. Work only. . . ."

"Well, well, well," one of the workmen shouted no sooner had Antonio and Agnese disappeared into the shaft. "This is where they take their ease!"

"A minute sooner, and we might have caught them body to body!"

The incident trickled good-humoredly into the homes and stores in the neighborhood.

The old push-cart woman, Filomena, held up her palms to her informant.

"She sang and danced on the roof! It would have been a sight for my old eyes. But what a foolish girl. After all, we're still Italians!"

"The things the men said," whispered the other woman, balancing on her head a huge loaf of bread shaped like a cartwheel. Evidently the numerous skirts and petticoats that made a circular plateau around her tight waist helped in the nice adjustment of the heavy loaf. "You ought to have heard!"

"There's not a word of truth in it," Filomena cried, as she filled a sheet of newspaper with spinach. "She sang for the happiness of the completed work. Who would not?"

But when it came to Michele's ears, he blanched, and his eyelids blinked painfully. Open-mouthed he listened, and though he tried to smile, he could say a word neither of pleasure nor surprise. As he went to the shelf with the razors and colorful bottles of perfume, he opened a drawer, drew out the rabbit-knife, and put it quickly into his pocket.

XVIII. THE LONG JOURNEY

– 1 –

The same afternoon, Gelsomino had written a letter to Giovanni, which he had left to the artist to deliver. This was the letter:

"*Dearest Giovanni:*

You will, of course, have forgiven me for not being able to come to the entertainment and exercises to be furnished by your school club this afternoon. Your grandfather will be there and the good woman who helps you at home. That will be a good representation, I know. You must believe, however, that I shall be thinking of you when you make your speech and when you take part in the little drama, and I am expecting you to do so well that you will win honor for yourself.

I was very happy, yesterday, to have had such a long talk with you. I was happy that we were both of us happy, you because you were so pleased with your new painting, and I because we were together and went over your future with such enthusiasm. It was the last time we could be in each other's company, and the hours we spent were very sweet to me. My heart will always carry the accents of your voice and the loveliness of your idealism. They will be the only memory that I shall have that will be both a joy and a regret to me.

Very soon, you must understand by this time, I shall be leaving New York and I shall be going on a long journey. You see, my years of wandering have become a habit. I must be always on the move. And I shall be so far away and in such places that it will be impossible for me to keep in communication with my friends here.

But if there is anyone from whom I shall be yearning for tidings, it will be you. It will seem a womanish confession to you that I should show such weakness as I am revealing in these remarks. Nevertheless, I am anxious to let you know that I shall have a prayer on my lips for you at all times, that I shall supplicate the blessed Jesus to keep you whole and sweet, your heart pure, and your innocence complete so that you will be capable of fulfilling the dear dreams of art that flood your soul.

My friend, I might almost say my son, you, too, store in your heart an image of me, and no matter what happens in your life, what you hear, or say, or do, let my memory be as precious to you as yours will be to me. You say that my chance word gave you the ambition to become a painter. 'A painter is like God,' I said. I can add no more to those words. To explain them will be the work ahead of you. . . .

You have been a dear friend, and so I shall feel justified in asking you to continue to be one, and especially to follow loyally a pledge I shall exact of you now. Do not ask why I do this. Your feelings are delicate enough to understand that if I ask it, it must be for a reason that is sufficient. Please, dear boy, make no inquiries of me and in particular say nothing of this letter, nor of me, to anyone. After all, this is a little thing to do. I have been just a passerby with whom you have on occasion talked. Keep my memory as something too personal to speak about.

May the dear God watch over you, the sweet mother of Christ who died for us intercede always for you, Christ our Savior be forever at your side, that your life may be fulfilled of its sweetness and its joy, and may the Spirit of the Holy Ghost be constantly in your heart and in your words, now and for everlasting.

Your affectionate friend,

GELSOMINO MERLINO."

– 2 –

Father Donato had been told by the younger priest what had taken place between Agnese and Gelsomino in the church, and to the curiosity excited in him by the constant attendance at the altar of the gaunt, emaciated man was added the desire to help. The older priest, a gray-haired and quiet man, performed his office with a sympathy and a tenderness that made him sought in confession and in personal sorrow by the great mass of his parishioners. To discover that one of them had consistently avoided him was a source of grief to him, and he had often included Gelsomino in his prayers and had moreover pleaded in them for an opportunity to be of assistance to one so evidently distressed.

"Thank you," he said to the stout little priest, as he stood reverently holding his chubby hands together. "Thank you for telling me this. I shall talk to him."

Dawn had barely transformed the twinkling darkness of the church into the serene gray of its daily appearance when Father Donato passed softly by the kneeling figure of Gelsomino, and as softly went to the altar and himself kneeled in prayer. A few minutes later he rose, intuitively realizing that Gelsomino had also stood up.

"*Pax vobiscum,*" he said quietly, making the sign of the cross in the direction of the other man, "in the name of the Father, the Son, and the Holy Ghost. . . ."

"Amen," whispered Gelsomino, lowering his head.

"My son," quickly continued Father Donato. "What is it that afflicts you? May I not help you? You may speak to me as in the confessional. I am not a man . . . I am the Spirit and the Word. I am the Lord God and the Son, and the Holy Ghost.

"You are in the grip of a great sadness. I have seen you many times but only today has it been clear to me that I must speak to you and if I can, offer you the peace of God and His mercy everlasting. Open your heart unto God through his Son, Jesus Christ, our Lord and our redeemer."

"Blessed be the Lord!" cried Gelsomino, falling to his knees, and seizing the hem of the priest's cassock in his hands. "*Benedio mihi, Pater!*"

"Amen," intoned the Father Donato.

"I am a miserable sinner, and for my sins have I come here to do penance nightly and daily. Be merciful to me, O my God. . . ."

"Be merciful, Sweet Lord. Help this afflicted man that his sins may be cleansed. . . ."

"For I have been one of Thine anointed, even a priest of Thy Holy Church, and I have been guilty of the sin of concupiscence, nay, of the sin of lust, for I have known the sin of the flesh, and I have been untrue to my vows, and to Thee, Holy and Omnipotent One. . . ."

Father Donato did not answer. Instead he raised Gelsomino to his feet, and said quietly:

"Come with me to my own room. Tell me all of your story there."

In the small bare room with its white-posted bed, its wooden floor, and the image of the Virgin at one end, and the Crucifix of the bleeding Christ hanging over the bed, Gelsomino finished his narration. At the conclusion of it, both men kneeled at the bedside, and prayed silently. When they rose, Father Donato said immediately:

"I am happy for having spoken to you. You must leave the place where you are living just as soon as practicable — within two or three days, if not at once — and take up your living here until the Bishop's letter arrives. You must immediately abandon your work. You must not see Agnese again, nor, if possible, your son. Go now, and set about your task of leaving."

– 3 –

"Gino," said Gelsomino as he and his friend sat down to their last meal together. "Your pupil certainly gets along . . . that picture of the ragged boy poking his finger into a hole in his coat! Well, now, that is very well done."

"For a boy excellent! He has talent . . . he has talent," assented Birrichino, throwing olive after olive into his mouth. "Strange how he picked it up! He works like a spider . . . never tires, never tires. 'Go home, now,' I say. 'Enough for this time.' 'No,' he answers. 'I want to finish this. Signor Merlino will be disappointed.' There's the explanation, Gelsomino. Oh, you have a hold on the boy, a magic transference from you to him of a power, a force, a charm! I am afraid, though. . . ."

Birrichino tossed another olive into his mouth, reached over for the bottle of wine, and listened intently to the babble and gurgle as he poured it with affectionate slowness into the glass.

"I am afraid, though. . . ," resumed the artist, quietly.

"Afraid? Afraid?" Gelsomino leaned over the table.

"Oh, it's this way. The boy's talent seems like a forced march. It'll keep going so long as the one in command exerts the pressure of his will. . . ."

Gino noted the rapid drooping of his friend's eyes, and a sudden sharp loss of color.

"I mean, should you ever leave or in some way lose his respect and love. . . ."

"You mean he will abandon his painting?"

"Oh, no, not that. . . . He might though, at that. . . . Yes, he might! But he certainly will lose something, industry, for instance, a bit of his skill, the dreams, the coloring . . . oh, I don't know what. . . ."

The silence that fell on Gelsomino was so genuinely the expression of a pain that could find no words, that the artist himself became quieted, lay down his work, and gently stroked the hand of his companion, where it lay an inert, pallid symbol on the table.

"Well, it seems so to me. I have watched him . . . there's a love between you two as deep and as tender as between boy and girl. Queer how such things happen! In some fashion the love gets into his brush, his paints, his themes. That's all I mean . . . should it end. . . ."

"Then you think," Gelsomino took up the sentence with a sort of feverish anxiety, "then you think his talent will end. Oh, I hope not, I hope not. . . . It's too fine. It's too deep and strong. . . ."

"Why, there are tears in your eyes, Gelsomino. . . ." Birrichino pressed the hand he was stroking. . . .

"No, it seems such a coincidence, Gino, for you to tell me this tonight."

"Why, you are not going?"

"Yes, immediately. Don't ask why, or where. . . ."

The artist accepted the explanations of Gelsomino without pressing too closely for details.

"Oh, the boy will be pained. . . ."

"I know, Gino, and I want you to help him. You will know how. Give him my letter . . . It will explain much. Let me go, Gino, with perfect trust in your kindness. . . ."

"Need you doubt it, need you doubt it?"

"Be as a father to him, as friend, *Gino bello . . . Gino bello. . . .*"

He fell over on the table, his head in his arms, and wept convulsively. But he ceased almost as quickly as he had begun and, accepting Gino's assistance, started putting together his few belongings.

"I had a letter, Gino, only today which calls me back to a place I left years ago. In less than a week I shall sail . . . I am glad to sail, Gino . . . glad as if my heart had filled with light and the light were a silence too. Don't you be sad!"

And then and there the men shook hands, looking into each other's eyes with a steadiness that kept down the tears.

"But I am sad, Gelsomino."

– 4 –

Gelsomino hurried into Doolan's and Crino's saloon on his way to the parish house. Crino, more corpulent than ever, sat at one of the round shining tables gazing liquidly at the tips of his shoes and thence on to the polished brass rail that ran the length of the counter. He had to do it over a protuberance of stomach that compelled him to throw his head slightly backward. The gaudy chandelier of a myriad crystals made a colorful havoc of the puffs and excrescences of muscle and mustaches on his florid countenance.

"Well, Gelsomino," he called out in English. "You stand there foolish-like. What's on your mind?"

Crino's original vigor still boomed in his voice, but it was insufficient to cause the slightest stir of his body. But though his voice boomed, it also expired in a veritable series of wheezes and whoofings as if he were destined to be perpetually out of breath.

"I came to tell you that I am leaving."

"Hell, no!"

The news was evidently too much even for the great masses of fat that were Crino's legs. He jerked them in and under his expansive abdomen.

"Going to leave!" he thundered to the white-coated bartender that had suspended his activities to look at his enraged proprietor. "Going to leave!" In fact, all the activity in the place stopped. The waiters stopped, the men playing cards stopped, the crowd at the steaming lunch-counter stopped, a new entrant stopped, holding the door ajar and permitting the cold wind to flicker the sawdust here and there.

"You can't, damn you," he bellowed, bringing down his creased hand with a violent bang. "You can't. Who'll I get in your place . . . ha . . . ha?"

But if the activity had become silenced in Crino's outburst, it was replaced immediately by the noise of a quarrel in the rear rooms of the saloon. A gagged voice, the sound of a fist striking a face, a suppressed wail of fear, a torrent of throaty curses, and then there was silence again. The customers jumped to their feet. Tables shuffled, a glass fell to the floor. . . .

"Damn them," Crino wheezed. "Damn the god-damn bums. Got to throw them out. Can't use this place no more . . . damn. . . ."

Violent as these words were, it was obvious that he dared say them only in whispers that denoted a fear of the very men he was denouncing. He jerked his head from bartender to Gelsomino and back to tire door in spasmodic contortions of his neck.

But just as if his denunciations had been a prayer, the rear doors opened violently, and there rushed out a typical rowdy of the neighborhood pursued by several others. His face was bleeding, his clothing torn and covered with globs of mingled sawdust and blood. He was out of reach of his pursuers, and might have made the door but that he stumbled over a chair, and fell in a heap at Gelsomino's feet.

"Oh God, oh God," he wailed, covering his head with upraised arms. "Oh God, oh God. . . ."

Gelsomino stooped over him while the other men made a rush for their fallen victim. They were pasty-faced young men of about twenty, tight-trousered, tight-waisted, with caps at a jaunty angle over their leering eyes.

"The bastard. . . ."

"The son of a bitch. . . ."

They attempted to kick at their victim as he lay shielded by Gelsomino.

Fearing trouble, many of the customers had left. Some stood at the door, held by curiosity but ready to bolt in case events required.

"What the hell?" shouted Crino, who had attained his feet with as much alacrity as he could employ. "What the hell . . . ha . . . ha . . . ha?"

"Been blabbing . . . the bastard!"

The bleeding boy, feeling himself unjustly accused, made a movement to get up and face the gang again. He rose partly to his knees and shouted:

"The cops seen the fire. . . . I didn't squeal . . . the cops seen it . . . see. . . ."

So encouraged he felt by the protection afforded him by both Gelsomino and Crino that he continued his screaming defense of himself.

"The cops seen it . . . the front bricks wasn't up yet . . . see . . . it's the truth, Stocks, honest, Stocks, honest . . . the cops could see right through the houses . . . easy! . . . Honest. . . ."

"Awright, damn you," shouted Stocks. "Shut your trap now."

At this point the immaculate Paul Variglia emerged from the rear door and sauntered up to the crowd. Placing his cane and hat in his left hand, he smiled with one corner of his mouth, and his presence had the instantaneous effect of producing a silence in which only Crino's puffing and the low wail of the beaten man could be heard. He inquired innocently of Crino, "What's happened?"

"God-damn lot of roughnecks fighting."

"Yes?" Variglia raised his soft voice ever so slightly. "What do you think of that, hey?"

And then he turned leisurely to the gangsters.

"You here with your crowd again, Stocks? Why don't you get out, hey?"

The question was more than its genial tone suggested, for it had no sooner been asked than there was a general exodus. The young men stuck their hands in their pockets and slunk away, shuffling the sawdust left and right.

"And you, there, get up. What do you want to kick up a row around here for, hey? Go on, get out."

If Variglia smiled wanly, the boy smiled as if fear in a grotesque exhibition of its power had taken his lips and forcefully contorted them.

"They'll get me outside. . . ," he whispered in an agony of fear.

"Well, you don't belong here," Variglia answered gently as ever. "Get out."

"That's the way, Crino," he winked, and then slightly swinging his cane proceeded himself to leave.

"Up to something," wheezed Crino. "Maybe going to set fire to Agnese's houses."

Gelsomino stared in horror.

"Better not warn her. They'll get us all . . . they got a good look at everybody here."

– 5 –

Father Donato was out when Gelsomino reached the parish-house with his bag and trunk. Like all workmen in the neighborhood, he had placed the small trunk on his shoulder and, with the green-canvas bag in the other hand, had walked to the church. He had walked as rapidly as he could, so rapidly indeed that he gave the impression of escaping a relentless pursuer always close at his heels but too demoniac in his cruelty to seize his victim at once. He dropped to his knees at the side of the bed he was to occupy, pressed his hands in prayer, and lowered his head.

But he could not pray.

Crino's words kept up a continual clatter in his mind like stones in a moving box. Every thought he had became crushed in the impact.

"Set fire to Agnese's houses!"

He rose to his feet.

"They'll get us all."

However, it was not that which kept Gelsomino back. He recalled all too vividly the scene in the church and he knew, as Agnese knew, that the impulses of many years back had not spent themselves completely only because he and she had suffered and worked apart from each other. For an intense moment they had seen in full clarity the recesses of their memories, and as she did, so did he perceive that stronger than their present aims, more compelling than her work or his entering the monastery, the days of their youthful love glowed and warmed their hearts, their minds, their bodies even.

"Set fire to Agnese's houses!"

It was only a guess of Crino's, possibly a chance surmise that might or might not be true. What could he really know of the movements of these men? He himself had waited many times upon them, had overheard their conversations, had been present at many of their quarrels. Never had he learned the slightest detail of their doings. What he had gathered was a general awareness of their vicious mode of life, but nothing more. What could Crino know?

"If only to see her again!"

The thought was flame, a flame that coursed through his body with the suddenness of wind, and left him cold, shivering, helpless.

"But it's to save her — her and Giovanni!"

He stood speechless.

"Father Donato!" he called quietly, timidly in his heart. "Father Donato, it will be just to warn her. . . . She will not be alone. I shall only say, 'Keep a watch . . . they will set fire to your houses!' . . . Just a word of warning . . . and I shall see her again. She will look at me . . . I will hear her voice . . . no . . . no . . . I will not lay my hands upon her . . . will not stroke her hair . . . only to warn her. . . ."

– 6 –

He ran from the room, and hurried to Agnese's home. The streets were dark. Most of the shops had closed. A quick wind, cold and persistent, drove before it sprays of paper-scraps that scudded and rattled on the sidewalk and against the sides of houses. Save for an occasional light in the window or store the street in which Agnese lived was in the deep shadow of a moonless winter night. The room at the top of the brownstone stoop was the only one lighted in the Dantone residence.

"Suppose she is alone . . . it is only to warn her. . . ."

He rang the bell softly. He had not looked around at all, had not noticed anything, not even the window of Michele's barbershop casting a yellow blanket of light upon the sidewalk. Otherwise, Gelsomino would have seen the figure of Michele standing behind the glass door of his shop, peering intently into the obscurity.

"Agnese, Agnese," cried Gelsomino as she opened the door.

"Gelsomino. . . ."

The hall was too dark for them to see the frightened pallor of their faces, their still intense eyes. But their voices were like sensitive fingers that felt the quickening rhythm of their pulses, and through it the music of the love that had never been silent and was now pouring its frantic crescendos through all their beings.

"*Agnese . . . Agnese mia,*" he sobbed.

"*Gelsomino . . . caro Gelsomino,*" she whispered.

She pressed her small lithe body full against his in an agony of surrender, a surrender that at the same time was a conquest of herself.

She wept convulsively, wept with abandon for the first time in the thirteen years of their separation. No matter how he stroked her hair, held her face between his hands, kissed her on her forehead, her lips, he could not still the pulsations of her body as the grief that had become gladness shook her heart.

"You suffered, too!" she said between her sobs. "And I . . . but you are . . . here now . . . here!"

"Always . . . always. . . . "

"And I too . . . always I called your name . . . so often!"

"And I . . . and I . . . Agnese!"

They were so completely lost in the ecstasy of their new wildness that they could not have heard the key turning in the door, and when at last the door flew open they still clung to each other as if nothing could part them now.

What happened was an instantaneous merging of a hundred separate gestures so rapid, so unpremeditated, that they seemed to have been like a quick cry without a sound. Agnese was conscious, however, of a piercing shriek of pain, a single, clear note rising and rising and getting thinner and thinner. Then she heard it no more as if she had become deaf at the very instant that it began. But she saw Michele's face in the dimness . . . a horror of red eyes, open mouth, in a frantic amalgam of fear, pleading, and the joy of conquest. With a childish gesture, he was holding out his hand to her. In it he held the curved rabbit knife shining with the wet gleam of blood.

She snatched it out of his grip, not feeling it gash the muscles of her palm. With indescribable swiftness she adjusted it in her grasp and plunged it quickly into Michele.

She knew it had struck something hard. It turned in her fingers, and as she grasped the handle again she was conscious of a clammy warmth.

She wanted to shout, but everything about her achieved a sudden illumination as if a light blazed and roared close at hand. She held her breath. The glare threw into vivid silhouette the body of Gelsomino with his head reclining on the stairs, the face of Michele, a mass of twitching muscles smeared with blood. There came a pounding at the door, and a black shadow, opaque and unmoving, stood between her and the red luster.

She heard a voice whispering from afar, "Agnese . . . Agnese."

"Where shall I put it?" she asked of the distant speaker, as she kept looking helplessly at the knife in her hand.

The blaze had become the scarlet rough tongue of an animal licking with a rasping noise, the translucent glass of the door.

"Where, where?" she kept asking.

The light was brighter and noisier, jumped and subsided, wagged to the left and right with grotesque solemnity. But a soft clang of bells came through the roar and the flame.

"Like on the feast day," she thought. "Gelsomino," she cried, "Gelsomino mio, *Gelsomino bello*. You remember the feast days . . . the sweet days. . . ."

The light was now so steady she could see the body of her lover, one arm parallel to the rails upholding the banister, and his head reclined on the stairs. His face caught the fleeting red shadows that came through the glass, the slightly open mouth with its suggestion of a smile, mocking the sinister expression of the eyes, one staring wide open, the other showing under the drooping lid. His chin, sunk low on his chest, shone, a red glob.

"Gelsomino . . . Gelsomino," she called.

And a voice at her feet answered in the accents of pain, "Agnese . . . Agnese. . . ."

Michele caught her skirt in his hands, clutched it feverishly, moaned in agony. . . .

"Gelsomino," she called again, and kneeled down despite the tugging at her skirt.

"Why do they bang on the door?" she thought. "Why are they ringing the bells so loudly?"

And as she leaned over to stroke the face of her lover, she felt the knife slip from her hand. She heard the soft thud as it struck Gelsomino's chest, and then her ears rang with the shouting of men, and her face became suffused with the heat of a flame that was too close at hand.

– 7 –

Antonio had finally forced the door open. The impulses that had brought him to Agnese were too driving to be arrested.

"The houses, Agnese," he cried desperately. "The houses. . . ."

Through the oblong of the open door were framed the new buildings enveloped in flames.

Agnese looked up.

"The houses, Gelsomino," she cried.

She rose unsteadily to her feet, the gashed hand in her mouth, biting it as she always did to keep down the volcano of her feelings. With quiet, steady eyes she gazed upon the houses burning in the night.

XIX. CHRISTMAS DAY

– 1 –

Christmas fell only a week after the grand jury had voted against holding Michele for trial. The home-coming had been arranged by Concetta and partook of all the qualities of a triumphal festival. Filippo, the accordion player and now chief barber, had bought a string of giant crackers and exploded them at the exact moment that Michele entered the house.

"This is foolishness, Concè," Agnese said.

"We're all so happy, Donn' Agnè, all so happy. Catarina and Antonio are inside. Everybody's waiting for you. Don Gaspar has brought chocolate, hot and rich, and *dolci,* and bottles of cordials. . . . Don't scold. . . . We are so happy."

And it was Concetta who insisted that the holy Christmas was to be observed in the Dantone family with all the elaborate ceremony of food and drink to which she was accustomed.

"It ain't like you lost your money, and it ain't like you lost a relative. Why, it's a blessing you got your husband back. He did what any man would've done — didn't he now? Besides you got Giovanni, Luigi, your father. . . ."

And so on Christmas Eve the mantelpiece, the tables, were covered with *struffoli, tarallini,* bottles of cognac and liqueurs. The odor of extensive cooking filled the house. In one corner of the dining room Concetta had had the carpenters on the construction job erect a holy crib. At the foot of a paper mountain opened a stable in which was a manger with the infant Christ, the Holy Virgin seated at its side. They were all wooden images, carved by peasants in Italy and imported by Concetta long before. Wooden images of the cow, the ass, and the sheep gazed into the face of the sacred child. A gilded star cast its brilliance over the scene, and coming down a mountain path were the figures of the three wise men of the East. A blue star-studded canopy hung over it, the curtains drawn until the stroke of midnight when *Il Bambino di Gesù* would be born.

In the huge leather chair, like a huddle of old clothes, sat Michele, a shrunken loose-jointed mass. His face, twisted into grimaces by the constant movement of the muscles, was a chalk-white save for the red scar and the restless eyes. In his lap his fingers, interlocked, traced a slow horizontal arc back and forth, back and forth unceasingly.

Luigi had spread a newspaper on the table and was reading silently. Concetta sang at her work in the kitchen. Once she came in to bend over Luigi's shoulders:

"We're going to have the *zambognari!*"

"Bag-pipers, Concetta?"

"Surprise for Donn' Agnese. Like in the old country. . . ."

"You'd dance at a funeral."

"And why not if he's going to heaven?" she exclaimed in great anger. "Are we going to be thinking of death on Christmas Day?"

"Look at that living death. . . ."

Concetta walked over to Michele and shook him by the shoulders. "Michè," she shouted at the top of her voice. "We're celebrating tonight. Christmas Eve. The bag-pipers and all!"

She paraded up and down in front of him, mimicking the swinging gait, the puffed faces, and the perpetually moving arms and fingers of the bag-pipe players. At the same time she hummed and wheezed in a lugubrious falsetto an old-world carol which, despite her crude mimicry, still retained its suggestion of simplicity and calm. Like a half-wit child Michele turned a simpering face to her and followed her movements with a delight that expressed itself in incoherent gurgles and staring eyes.

"Stop it, Concè," cried Luigi, getting up. "Stop it. What do you want to do, torture us all?"

However, not even the entrance of Agnese put an end to her insistent gayety.

"*Donn' Agnè, Donn' Agnè,*" she cried, "oh for a band of pipers now this merry Christmas time!"

She resumed her merry moaning and parading. But Michele fell back into his forlorn huddle. His eyes lost their sparkle, and his face the pathetic leer of a delighted idiot child.

"Why, yes, Concetta," answered Agnese, throwing off her shawl. "We shall have them. I stopped into Don Gaspare's café and told him to send the pipers here at midnight. We've always had it pleasant this holy night."

"It beats me," muttered Luigi.

"The barbershop's doing well, Michè," Agnese announced to her husband. "I say the barbershop's doing fine," she shouted. "Very fine. Just went over the accounts. My father makes a good boss."

She seated herself at his side, and parted his hands.

"Don't keep holding your fingers like that," she said. "What will Doctor Grace say? Tomorrow, if it's nice, you must sit out in the yard and get the sun. Don't make that funny face. I say yes. . . ."

One who heard only her tender quiet tones and observed the affectionate way in which she held her husband's hand would have concluded that Michele, stricken as he was with the total loss of coherent controls over speech and gesture, must feel the warmth of her love in his heart and rejoice that in his misery, sympathy and kindliness surrounded him. But one glance at his frightened eyes, at his shrinking body, and his head pressed into his chest like a sick bird's, and the horror of his reactions stamped itself with vivid sorrow into one's mind. It was obvious that the murder had left nothing but a physical breakdown in its wake. The mind had driven into the flesh the memory that would have eaten with fire into his days. His life would have become an inferno of shrieks and sight of blood steaming and puddling at his feet, but some merciful dispensation of nature had transformed the agony of the spirit into the impotence of the flesh. And by some subtle freak of compensation, it was this very impotence that kept Michele a helpless disordered bundle and made it impossible for the hatred in his heart to break through, stiffen his disjointed fingers, give his body the momentum of his savage desire to seize her, choke her with slow, sure force and leave her like a fowl kicking in the dust. At her every touch he drew himself further and further into his cringing looseness, and the more he tried to summon to his lips the words of his hatred, the more his mouth twisted into a grimace that seemed simpering gratitude and pleasure.

Luigi clenched his fists at his sides and shuddered.

"Almighty God," he thought, "why didn't you send him to the chair — for his sake — for her sake?"

He hurried out of the room into the kitchen.

"They're like animals in a trap, Concè," he all but wept, "like animals in a trap, gnawing at each other, and they can't move, can't get their teeth out. . . ."

"You big fool, shut up," Concetta seized the lapels of his coat and shook him. "Don't we all know it? Do you want to make things like real hell? Whistle, Luigi. Jig. Do a tarantella. Go out there with castanets-like in your hands and hop, hop, hop to the song of the merry pipers. . . ."

– 2 –

Agnese rose early Christmas morning and left the house before the others were up. She glanced up at the buildings opposite which, despite the fire, were now practically completed, and smiled.

"Ashes — ashes!" she said to herself, addressing them. "You're built up almost, and who knows there was a fire in you? Like me. Who knows the fire in my flesh — burnt up, all burnt up. *Madonna mia,* give me strength."

She hastened to catch the trolley car on the corner. The conductor had a friend standing at his side, a hunchback with paunchy eyes but thin shriveled cheeks. He stared at everybody that came in.

"Who's the dame?" He nudged the conductor.

"An Eyetalian — the one with the shawl, ha?"

"Good looker, ain't she?"

"You bet. Say, you know what?" The conductor leaned over to whisper. "They say she stuck a guy with a knife . . . he's pushing up the old sod now."

The hunchback's face lighted up. "That's what I thought. Gee, I been wanting to get a look at her. Got to tell the old lady I seen her."

"Got away with it too. Got lots of dough, they say, see — and got away with it."

"You don't say . . . got away with it. God!"

The extent of his surprise was too great to be comprehended in the phrase. So he kept repeating it in an awed whisper as he stared, seemingly fascinated either by the vivid shawl or the serene olive of Agnese's face with its inescapable touch of ardor. The conductor placed himself in front of him, and cried:

"Hell, stop eyeing her up like that. Want to start a row? Hell!"

– 3 –

Several hours later Agnese was standing at the side of Gelsomino's grave. It was in a new part of the cemetery and so in its immediate vicinity the earth showed brown and damp, filled with loose stones that caught the wet shine of the bright cold day.

"I thought I could have talked to you," she said slowly. "You knew I would come. It's not too late, darling, no, it's not too late. I am closer to you now, for I am all yours now, unashamed. And you, too, you are part of all of me, my words, my steps. . . .

"I could not come sooner. Your friend Birrichino — he hates me. He accuses me in his heart. He would not say where he buried you. Only yesterday Giovanni told me. I have come, see. I have come. My face is against your cheek. Don't you feel it? I feel yours and hear your laughter. For you are pleased, too . . . like me.

"You must have heard my prayers about Giovanni. I came to tell you about him, too. He is very sad. A fire burns in him too. He is always painting. Do you know why? Because he loves, and you are with him when he paints. . . .

"You ask about Michele. At night I see you standing by my bed and you say, 'What about Michele?' Michele — he hates me. There's a fire in him too, but it's all hate — all hate. He can't say a word with his mouth, can't walk, and he must be helped to eat. His body's like a baby's when the bones don't harden. But inside of him there's hate — an old man's hate. . . .

"You understand, *caro,* you understand. I had to save him. When I struck him with his knife, there was a flash came to my mind. 'Strike him,' I heard, 'Strike him and they will say Michele was struck first and then killed Gelsomino to save himself.' So I struck him, and I lied. I prayed to the Madonna before I lied. And I prayed to you, too. I thought it would be my penance — to be with him all my life. But poor man, it is a worse penance for him. I must learn to put my arms around him and kiss him just as if he was you. That shall be my cross, Gelsomino . . . but it will be you. You I shall kiss, you, my darling. His lips will squirm under mine . . . grow cold . . . they're like a living wound . . . but they will be yours — yours. . . ."

She kneeled, bent her head, and seemed to be praying. Gradually she smoothed over a portion of the grave. She removed several small stones and put them into a heap at her side.

"I never weep, Gelsomino. I just bite my lips, my hands. But not that anymore. I shall just think of you, and how much you suffered. Can I suffer half as much?

"How glad I am this is a beautiful place. There are trees. They will have leaves in the spring with the good weather. There's a lovely monument right near you. See, it's the Holy Virgin with the Child. . . .

"Oh, Gelsomino, what a thought came to me. This is consecrated ground. You must be in heaven, and the Holy Virgin must be talking to you and asking about me, and about Giovanni. Tell her we love her . . . and tell her I love, always loved you, that you belong to me, and I to you. . . ."

VIA Folios

A refereed book series dedicated to the culture of Italian Americans in North America.

Pino Aprile, *Terroni: All That Has Been Done to Ensure That the Italians of the South Become "Southerners,"* Vol. 72, Ethnic/Cultural Studies, $20

Emanuel Di Pasquale, *Harvest,* Vol. 71, Poetry, $10

Robert Zweig, *Return to Naples,* Vol. 70, Memoir, $16

Letizia Airos and Ottorino Capelli, eds., *Guido,* Vol. 69, Italian/American Studies, $12

Fred Garaphé, *Moustche Pete Is Dead! Evviva Baffo Pietro! The* Fra Noi *Columns 1985–19855,* Vol. 67, Literature/Oral History, $12

Paolo Ruffilli, *Dark Room,* Vol. 66, Poetry, $10

Helen Barolini, *Crossing the Alps,* Vol. 65, Fiction, $14

Cosmo Ferrara, *Profiles of Italian Americans,* Vol. 64, Italian/American Studies, $16

Gil Fagiani, *Chianti in Connecticut,* Vol. 63, Poetry, $10

Piero Bassetti, Niccoló D'Aquino, *Italic Lessons,* Vol. 62, Italian/American Studies $10

Grace Cavalieri and Sabine Pascarelli, eds., *The Poet's Cookbook,* Vol. 61, Poetry/Recipes, $12

Emanuel Di Pasquale, *Siciliana,* Vol. 60, Poetry, $8

Natalia Costa-Zalessow, ed., Joan E. Borrelli, translator, *Francesca Turini Bufalini: Autobiographical Poems,* Vol. 59, Poetry, $18

Richard Vetere, *Baroque,* Vol. 58, Fiction, $18

Lewis Putnam Turco, *La Famiglia / The Family,* Vol. 57, Memoir, $15

Nick James Mileti, *The Unscrupulous: Scams, Cons, Fakes, and Fraud That Poison the Fine Arts,* Vol. 56, Humanities, $20

Piero Bassetti, Paolino Accolla, Niccolo D'Aquino, *Italici: An Encounter with Bassetti,* Vol. 55, Italian Studies, $8

Giose Rimanelli, *The Three-Legged One,* Vol. 54, Fiction, $15

Charles Klopp, *Bele Antiche Storie,* Vol. 53, Critiscism, $25

Joseph Ricapito, *Second Wave,* Vol. 52, Poetry, $12

Gary R. Mormino, *Italians in Florida,* Vol. 51, Italiana Americana/History, $15

Gianfranco Angelucci, Giuseppe Natale, translator, *Federico F,* Vol. 50, Fiction, $16

Anthony Valerio, *The Little Sailor,* Vol. 49, Fiction, $8. **OUT OF PRINT**

Ross Talarico, *The Reptilian Interludes,* Vol. 48, Poetry, $15

Rachael Guido DeVries, *Teeny Tiny Tino's Fishing Story,* Vol. 47, Children's Literature, $6

Emanuel Di Pasquale, *Writing Anew: New and Selected Poems,* Vol. 46, Poetry, $15

Maria Fama, *Looking for Cover,* Vol. 45, Poetry, $15

Anthony Valerio, *Toni Cade Bambara's One Sicilian Night,* Vol. 44, Memoir, $44. **OUT OF PRINT**

VIA FOLIOS

A refereed book series dedicated to the culture of Italian Americans in North America.

EMANUEL CARNEVALI, DENNIS BARONE, ED., *Furnished Rooms,* Vol. 43, Poetry, $14

GEORGE GUIDA, *Low Italian,* Vol. 41, Poetry, $10

GARDAPHE, GIORDANO, TAMBURRI, *Introducing Italian Americana: Generalities on Literature and Film, a bilingual forum,* Vol. 40, Italian/American Studies, $10

DANIELA GIOSEFFI, *Blood Autumn/Autunno di sangue,* Vol. 39, Poetry, $15/$25

FRED MISURELLA, *Lies to Live by,* Vol. 38, Stories, $15

STEVEN BELLUSCIO, *Constructing a Bibliography,* Vol. 37, Italian Americana, $15

ANTHONY J. TAMBURRI, ed., *Italian Cultural Studies 2002,* Vol. 36, Essays, $18

BEA TUSIANI, *con amore,* Vol. 35, Memoir, $19

FLAVIA BRIZIO-SKOV, ed., *Reconstructing Societies in the Aftermath of War,* Vol. 34, History, $30

TAMBURRI, ET AL, eds., *Italian Cultural Studies 2001,* Vol. 33, Essays, $18

ELIZABETH G. MESSINA, ed., *In Our Own Voices,* Vol. 32, Italian American Studies, $25

STANISLAO G. PUGLIESE, *Desperate Inscriptions,* Vol. 31, History, $12

HOSTERT & TAMBURRI, eds., *Screening Ethnicity,* Vol. 30, Italian American Culture, $25

G. PARATI & B. LAWTON, eds., *Italian Cultural Studies,* Vol. 29, Essays, $18

HELEN BAROLINI, *More Italian Hours,* Vol. 28, Fiction, $16

FRANCO NASI, ed., *Intorno alla Via Emilia,* Vol. 27, Culture, $16

ARTHUR L. CLEMENTS, *The Book of Madness & Love,* Vol. 26, Poetry, $10

JOHN CASEY, ET AL., *Imagining Humanity,* Vol. 25, Interdisciplinary Studies, $18

ROBERT LIMA, *Sardinia/Sardegna,* Vol. 24, Poetry, $10

DANIELA GIOSEFFI, *Going On,* Vol. 23, Poetry, $10

ROSS TALARICO, *The Journey Home,* Vol. 22, Poetry, $12

EMANUEL DI PASQUALE, *The Silver Lake Love Poems,* Vol. 21, Poetry, $7

JOSEPH TUSIANI, *Ethnicity,* Vol. 20, Poetry, $12

JENNIFER LAGIER, *Second-Class Citizen,* Vol. 19, Poetry, $8

FELIX STEFANILE, *The Country of Absence,* Vol. 18, Poetry, $9

PHILIP CANNISTRARO, *Blackshirts,* Vol. 17, History, $12

LUIGI RUSTICHELLI, ed., *Seminario sul racconto,* Vol. 16, Narrative, $10

LEWIS TURCO, *Shaking the Family Tree,* Vol. 15, Memoirs, $9

LUIGI RUSTICHELLI, ed., *Seminario sulla drammaturgia,* Vol. 14, Theater/Essays, $10

FRED GARDAPHÈ, *Moustache Pete Is Dead! Long Live Moustache Pete!* Vol. 13, Oral Lit., $10

JONE GAILLARD CORSI, *Il libretto d'autore, 1860–1930,* Vol. 12, Criticism, $17

HELEN BAROLINI, *Chiaroscuro: Essays of Identity,* Vol. 11, Essays, $15

PICARAZZI & FEINSTEIN, eds., *An African Harlequin in Milan,* Vol. 10, Theater/Essays, $15

JOSEPH RICAPITO, *Florentine Streets & Other Poems,* Vol. 9, Poetry, $9

VIA FOLIOS

A refereed book series dedicated to the culture of Italian Americans in North America.

FRED MISURELLA, *Short Time,* Vol. 8, Novella, $7

NED CONDINI, *Quartettsatz,* Vol. 7, Poetry, $7

ANTHONY TAMBURRI, ed., *Fuori: Essays by Italian/American Lesbians and Gays,* Vol. 6, Essays, $10

ANTONIO GRAMSCI, P. Verdicchio, Trans. & Intro., *The Southern Question,* Vol. 5, SocCrit., $5

DANIELA GIOSEFFI, *Word Wounds & Water Flowers,* Vol. 4, Poetry, $8

WILEY FEINSTEIN, *Humility's Deceit: Calvino Reading Ariosto Reading Calvino,* Vol. 3, Criticism, $10

PAOLO A. GIORDANO, ed., *Joseph Tusiani: Poet, Translator, Humanist,* Vol. 2, Criticism, $25

ROBERT VISCUSI, *Oration Upon the Most Recent Death of Christopher Columbus,* Vol. 1, Poetry, $3

Published by Bordighera, Inc., an independently owned not-for-profit scholarly organization that has no legal affiliation to the University of Florida, the John D. Calandra Italian American Institute, or State University of New York at Stony Brook.

www.ingramcontent.com/pod-product-compliance
Lightning Source LLC
LaVergne TN
LVHW020539100826
845148LV00010B/1533
9781599540382